Second Opinion

Center Point
Large Print

Also by Hannah Alexander and available
from Center Point Large Print:

Collateral Damage
Keeping Faith

Hallowed Halls Series:
Hallowed Halls
Dandelion Moon

**This Large Print Book carries the
Seal of Approval of N.A.V.H.**

Book One of The Healing Touch Series

Second Opinion

HANNAH ALEXANDER

CENTER POINT LARGE PRINT
THORNDIKE, MAINE

The text of this Large Print edition is unabridged.
In other aspects, this book may vary
from the original edition.
Printed in the United States of America
on permanent paper.
Set in 16-point Times New Roman type.

ISBN: 978-1-68324-138-6

Library of Congress Cataloging-in-Publication Data

Names: Alexander, Hannah, author.
Title: Second opinion / Hannah Alexander.
Description: Center Point Large Print edition. | Thorndike, Maine :
Center Point Large Print, 2016.
Identifiers: LCCN 2016030042 | ISBN 9781683241386
    (hardcover : alk. paper)
Subjects: LCSH: Emergency physicians—Fiction. | Medical
personnel—Fiction. | Large type books. | GSAFD: Christian fiction. |
Romantic suspense fiction.
Classification: LCC PS3551.L35558 S43 2016 | DDC 813/.54—dc23
LC record available at https://lccn.loc.gov/2016030042

Second Opinion

CHAPTER 1

Gina Drake awakened from a storm of dark images and screams, an endless strobe of confusion. She cried out and tumbled from sofa to floor. But she didn't know which sofa or which floor, where she was or why.

It was happening again.

She winced at an onslaught of ragged light from a strange window. Past blobs of furniture she saw a door and pulled herself off the floor to stumble toward it. Had to get out of this place. Had to get to air. She was suffocating, couldn't get enough oxygen, couldn't fight her way past the attack of piercing light.

A garbled cry, soft and plaintive, reached her through the pounding of her heartbeat. That sound checked her escape for just a moment. But she couldn't see past the tearing in her eyes. The cry didn't repeat before the waking nightmare returned to envelop her in terror. She grabbed the doorknob and forced her way outside. Had to find her children, protect them!

She tripped and nearly fell. That strange cry reached her once more, this time from behind. She turned and saw nothing except blurred shapes and gray splotches. She had to escape. There was danger here. She ran into the haze.

• • •

Evan Webster stared at his father across the dinner table, thinking about the pills he'd taken. Shouldn't he be feeling better by now? He glanced at the large clock on the wall. Twenty minutes and nothing had changed. Kent had told him they would give him more energy, make him feel more alive, be more coordinated. Ha! Coordinated. That would be an improvement.

A sudden hard thump of his heart startled him.

"Evan, are you okay?"

He looked up into his dad's gentle eyes and nodded. Maybe the pills were working. He took a deep breath and once again felt the thumping pressure of his heartbeat pound through his system. He even felt the jolt of its force for a couple of seconds. This wasn't what he'd expected at all.

"How's the goulash?" Dad's voice sounded a little different. It came in spurts of sound.

Evan blinked. Weird. "Good, Dad." He straightened in his chair and forced himself to eat, trying hard to concentrate on what he was doing.

"You're not eating much," Dad said.

Evan took a bite and chewed automatically. He usually loved Dad's special family recipe, which was why Dad cooked it almost every visitation weekend. Tonight it tasted like dirt. So did the homemade rolls and the butter, even the milk.

Dad laid his fork at the side of his plate, picked up his napkin, and patted around his mouth in his precise way. He watched Evan for a moment, then swallowed and cleared his throat. Norville Webster, Evan's father, tried to be precise and thoughtful in his movements, his words, his whole life.

"So, how's life treating you these days?" Dad asked. "Is it good to be out of school for the summer?"

"Not really. I like school." He wouldn't admit that to a lot of people but Dad understood.

Evan already missed his friends. He looked forward to seeing some of them tonight. He glanced at the clock. Ten minutes before he had to leave for the theater and he hadn't broken the news yet. He reached for his milk glass. His arm jerked involuntarily. He nearly knocked over the glass and his hand continued to jerk. He placed it in his lap, hoping Dad wouldn't notice.

"Did you get a summer job at the mill?"

"They won't hire me until I'm sixteen." Five months before he could get a driver's license. Five whole months. Would he last that long? Every one of his friends had their licenses.

"The school grades were okay, then? Your mother didn't send me a copy of them this semester." Dad stared at the table. His voice had that casual tone he used when he wanted to disguise his disapproval of his ex-wife.

An alien rush of anger caught Evan unaware. "Why didn't you complain to *her* about it?" he snapped. "You could have called her. You don't have to use me as your messenger—" His voice skidded to a stop as Dad blinked at him in shock.

It surprised Evan too. He seldom got mad at his father and when he did he never said anything. *What is happening to me?*

Some of the color drained from Dad's face. "I'm sorry. You're right."

"Oh no, hey listen, I didn't mean—"

Dad held his hand up. "I know better, I just forget sometimes. I guess the grades were as good as always."

Evan slumped in his seat, feeling worse than ever. Dad was bitter because Mom had won custody. And Mom would rather be with her stupid boyfriend than with her own son. Why did she fight so hard for custody when she didn't want it? She was the one who'd wanted the divorce in the first place, not Dad.

It was getting easier and easier to hate life.

"Evan?"

"Yeah?" Evan looked up again to find those serious eyes studying him a little too closely.

"Is everything okay? The grades *were* as good as always?"

"Oh sorry. I meant to tell you I'm on the honor roll again. And I got an achievement award in English. My teacher says I should think about being a writer." His heart thumped loudly a couple more times and he flexed his neck muscles to push away some of the tension that made him want to squirm in his chair. "Ms. Bolton wants me to help on the school paper next year."

Some of the lines of terminal sadness lifted from Dad's expression for a few seconds. His pale lips flexed in the closest thing to a smile Evan had seen tonight. "That's great. I'm proud of you."

Evan hunched his shoulders forward then straightened and leaned closer to the table. At least he was good for something. He stared at his skinny arms and hands. He'd never been good in sports. Everything at school seemed to revolve around football or basketball or something else that demanded coordination. The jocks didn't need anything between their ears to be popular, they just needed the right moves. Evan didn't have those.

"Evan?" Dad's voice rose slightly. "Are you okay?"

"Huh? Yeah I'm fine."

"I said I'm proud of you. I always have been."

"Thanks, Dad." The good thing was that Dad meant what he said. He always did. Not like Mom, who'd promised to come to the debate last month then canceled at the last minute because her boyfriend showed up. Dad was there, though. He'd made it embarrassingly obvious to every-one in the audience who his son was and how proud he was of him. Dad had never been the silent type.

Too much pain hovered in this house. Evan loved his father but he took everything way too seriously. And Mom wasn't just impatient, she was spastic—always nagging him to pick up his things and do his laundry and put the toilet seat—

"Evan," Dad said.

Evan blinked and looked at him.

"You sure you're not coming down with something?"

"Oh sorry. Yeah." Actually, he didn't feel that good right now. His head was starting to hurt. "I'll be okay." He placed a final forkful of Dad's homemade goulash into his mouth and washed it down with the milk that tasted like dirt. He could feel Dad still watching him. It made him nervous. The pills. Yeah, that's what he was feeling and it wasn't good. Strange that he'd expected the mixture of caffeine and pain relievers to make him feel better. All he'd wanted was to stop feeling so bad all the time. So sad.

Dad cleared his throat again. "So is she still seeing Mr. Tygart?"

"Yeah." Swallow food. Get out of the chair. Make the excuses. Apologize. Get out of here. Meet Kent. Ask him exactly what was in those pills. Evan felt like a rock being skipped across a pond. He pushed back from the table. "I'm supposed to meet some of the guys at the theater for a movie. I'd better leave now if I'm going to get there in time." His voice caught, held, vibrated.

"Oh." Dad was obviously disappointed. He'd probably rented a movie for tonight. He was always doing stuff like that. His enjoyment came when Evan enjoyed a movie. Mom said that was one reason she divorced him, because he suffocated her.

"Do you need a ride downtown?"

Evan shrugged. "It's only four blocks."

Dad slumped in his chair. "Well then, I'll see you when you get home. Hurry back after the movie?"

"Sure will." As Evan grabbed his jacket and pushed his way out the front door he felt a tingle shoot down his back and into his legs. How much caffeine was in those pills he took?

Levi Drake watched out the front door for his mother. It was getting dark. She never left them alone after dark. He knew the shadows outside were just bushes but sometimes he thought they could be monsters. He hated the dark.

He turned on the porch light and then the living room light and then he walked over to the two lamps and turned them on. He walked through the rest of the house turning on all the lights he could reach and then sat down on the couch next to his little brother Cody. They couldn't turn on the television because the rules were no TV when Mom couldn't sit and watch it with them.

"Mommy's not home yet." Cody scooted closer and pressed his head against Levi's arm. "Go find her."

"She'll come back soon." Levi hoped Cody wouldn't start crying. Cody was only four and he threw tantrums when he didn't get his way, especially when Mom was gone.

"Does Mommy have fur now?"

Levi looked down at his silly brother. "Fur?"

Cody nodded. "Like the werewolf."

"Mom isn't a werewolf."

Cody nodded again. His eyes got big. "Uh-huh. Cartoon werewolf."

"Oh." That old cartoon Mom put into the television sometimes was Cody's favorite. Levi liked it too. He was a nice werewolf who ran away when he started to grow fur so nobody would see him. He bashed the bad guys and saved the children.

"I'm hungry." Cody patted Levi's side.

"We can eat when Mom gets back." Levi turned to look out the window. The cars driving along the street had their headlights on. What if she couldn't find her way home in the dark?

He'd tried to stop being afraid when Mom left them alone but he couldn't. He wasn't as grown up as she needed him to be. This time she'd looked scared and she was breathing funny and she didn't answer him when he asked if she was sick. Maybe she really was the werewolf. Maybe she was out there right now saving other little kids from the bad guys.

But if she was doing that, why did she always cry and tell them she was sorry when she came back home? She said she had bad dreams that scared her but that everything would be okay. Levi didn't feel okay now.

Cody patted Levi's leg. "Can I have soup?"

"I'll get you some crackers. When Mom comes we can have soup." Levi slid off the couch.

Cody climbed down and followed him. "You cook soup, Levi."

"Mom doesn't want us to turn on the stove when she's not here. I'll get some cheese. You like that, Cody. Cheese and crackers." Levi got some slices of American cheese out of the fridge and used a step stool to reach the crackers in the cupboard. But when he opened the cupboard door there were all the cans of soup stacked on top of each other next to the box of crackers.

Cody caught his breath. "Soup! I want soup, Levi! You cook soup!" His voice grew so loud Levi wanted to cover his cars with his hands.

"I can't. Mom said six-year-olds aren't supposed to play with fire."

"Soup soup soup! I want soup!"

"Stop it, Cody!" Levi turned around and almost fell off the step stool. "Shut up!" Mom would get mad if she heard him say those words.

Cody shouted louder. "I want soup! I'm hungry!" He banged his fist against the cabinet door below the sink and stomped his foot.

"Okay, I'll get you some soup. Just be quiet!"

Cody kept banging and stomping but he stopped shouting. Levi was hungry too. Where was Mom? Why didn't she come back?

Levi grabbed a can with the noodles on the front picture and set it carefully on the counter. Then he pulled the box of crackers out and set that beside the can. He had to do everything just right the way Mom showed him. He stepped down from the stool and opened the cabinet door for the pots. He pulled out the one she always used to cook the soup and closed the door.

Cody stopped the banging and stomping. "I can help!"

Levi jerked the pot away and said in his meanest voice, "If you touch anything I won't feed you."

Cody looked at him in surprise for a moment. His lower lip stuck out and big tears filled his eyes. A whine grew in his throat and burst into a loud cry that went through the kitchen like a car horn. Levi tried to ignore it as he pulled at the ring on the top of the can. It was hard to do anything with Cody screaming behind him. The ring wouldn't move.

Levi got a knife from a drawer and stuck it under the ring until the top came up. He got the lid off and poured the soup into the pot, only splashing a few drops out onto the floor. He reached up and turned the knob on the stove to the place where Mom always turned it. He heard a *click click click* sound but nothing else happened. He turned it off again, told Cody to be quiet, and then turned the knob back on.

Click click click but no fire.

Cody kept screaming. Levi climbed onto the first step of the stool and turned the knob a little farther . . . just a little bit and then once again . . . and a big whoosh of fire reached out for him. He jerked back and fell off the stool. He landed hard on the floor and for a little bit he couldn't breathe.

Cody stopped crying.

Click click click.

Levi tried to see the fire around the bottom of the pot but he couldn't. Mom said when it clicked he had to turn the knob some more to stop it because it might not be safe. But he wasn't sure if he could get up to turn that knob.

"Levi?"

Click click click.

He looked up to find Cody bending over him, eyes wide and scared. And the clicking kept on. Levi's head hurt where he'd bumped it.

Cody bent closer. "Levi?"

He had to try hard to be a big boy for his little brother. He raised his head and then pushed himself up and sat for a minute while Cody watched.

The clicking continued.

Levi shook his head and pushed himself to his feet. He had to get to that knob. He could hear the soup sizzling on the sides of the pot. He reached the knob and turned it. The clicking stopped. He pulled a spoon out of the drawer and stuck it into the soup. It looked easier when Mom did it. There were too many things to remember and he couldn't think very well with Cody patting his leg.

He turned to Cody. "It's okay, I'm getting soup. You go sit down in your chair."

"Are you hurt?"

"No. Go to your chair." Levi put his hands on his hips like Mom did when Cody was being bad. "I mean it, Cody. Sit down!"

Cody started to cry again but he went to his chair. Levi stepped up onto the stool. He reached for the spoon he'd put in the pot. The spoon was hot. His arm jerked backward, knocking against the handle of the pot and tipping the pot over to the side.

Hot soup splashed out onto Levi's shoulder. He screamed. Cody's cries mingled with his.

Evan's hands shook as he walked down the dark street. He felt like hurling. He couldn't go into the theater like this. His heart thundered in his ears.

"Hey!" A voice came from the street so suddenly it scared him. He jerked around to see his friend Kent in a pickup truck smiling at him through the open passenger window. "Get in. Dad let me use his truck. We'll go cruising. The movie's lame."

Evan rushed over and pulled the door open. "I thought you said those pills you gave me were supposed to make me feel better. Where'd you get them?"

"A friend. Don't worry, you'll be okay. Get in. Haven't you ever done speed before?"

"Speed!" Oh no. Oh no. Oh. No.

"Hey relax, it'll give you go power."

Evan jumped into the truck and slammed the door. He wanted to strangle the jerk. "It's making me sick! Why didn't you tell me what it was? Where'd you get it?"

"Peregrine gave me some last week." Kent sounded suddenly defensive.

"Who's that?"

"Don't you know anything? He's a guy who hangs out around town."

"Peregrine? You mean like a falcon? What a stupid name. Is he a pusher or something?"

"No way. He gave me the pills. He's okay. He's in his twenties and the guys like him 'cause he'll buy booze for them on weekends."

Evan buried his face in his hands. He was suddenly taking illegal drugs that came from some loser who thought he was a bird of prey. Why hang out with Kent anyway? It wasn't as if he had any brains.

"Evan? You okay?"

"No! How could you do this to me? I don't do drugs."

"You didn't have to take it. Don't blame me."

The tingling in Evan's arms and hands accelerated. It felt as if ants had burst into his veins and arteries and were crawling up his neck. "Do something! This feels awful."

"What am I supposed to do?"

Evan felt another spurt of rage. His heart beat louder, faster, like it might explode. He grabbed Kent by the arm. "Get me help!"

❧ CHAPTER 2 ❧

Dr. Grant Sheldon knew better than to believe in love at first sight. Forty years of living had taught him not to get carried away by surface attraction but he had lost his heart after one glimpse of Dogwood Springs in a morning blanket of late spring dew. Love for this place had claimed him when he first drove down to interview for this job.

The Ozark hillside village had a bustling homey five-block downtown with bricked streets and streetlights that looked like century-old gaslights. The town's modest population of seven thousand gave welcome relief from the teeming hordes of St. Louis.

Settled deep in the southern Missouri hills thirty minutes from Branson, Dogwood Springs offered Grant the convenience of taking off for a weekend with his kids without a long drive.

He'd also been wonderfully surprised when he walked into his prospective place of employment for the first time a month ago and saw the state-of-the-art facilities. Mr. William Butler, the sixty-year-old administrator of Dogwood Springs Hospital, had announced with pride that they'd completed the final touches to this ten-bed emergency department about six weeks before and would soon be considering the addition of mid-level providers to help the ER docs.

Except for the present lack of nurse practitioners or physician assistants, staffing at the hospital was great. This administration wasn't stingy with payroll. Tonight, only thirty minutes into his second shift, Grant already felt as if he'd come home for good. They hadn't seen a gunshot wound here in months according to Mr. Butler and that had been nothing more than a flesh wound from a hunting accident. No more knife and gun gang emergency work for Grant Sheldon. This was a great town for raising a family.

The ER secretary turned and waved to get his attention. "I have a call from a man who's on his way here with his son. He suspects a drug overdose."

Grant stopped. The elation slipped away. "Did he say what drug, Becky?"

"Speed."

His shoulders slumped. "Let me know when he comes in." He glanced at the chart holders on the far wall where files for six patients waited. An eleven-year-old boy was in radiology being x-rayed for a possible broken wrist from a bike wreck and he needed sutures. His mother had already fainted twice at the sight of his blood. Now she was a patient herself. Her husband had asked for their pastor to be called. RN Lauren McCaffrey had done so just a few minutes ago.

Three patients—all with similar intestinal flu symptoms—were stable. It was a little late in the year for an epidemic and that concerned him. He'd seen two patients last night with the same symptoms, so he couldn't rule out some kind of community-acquired virus. Tests didn't show influenza. Perhaps Mr. Butler would speed up the process of hiring mid-level practitioners if the department remained this busy.

Grant pulled out a chart and studied it. He stepped into the patient exam room and introduced himself to eighty-eight-year-old Mrs. Cecile Piedmont while Lauren jotted down vitals.

The sharp-eyed lady sat up in the bed and gave him an appraising glance. Her white hair was only slightly ruffled from the nasal cannula oxygen tubing hooked over her ears. Though she appeared pale to him, he had no way of knowing if that was her normal coloring.

After a few seconds of silent study, she nodded. "Hello, Dr. Sheldon. I'm not really having any pain right now." Her voice didn't waver. "I hope I'm not wasting your time. Sounds to me like you have other patients who need you."

He pulled the exam stool next to her bed and sat down. "Why don't you tell me how you feel?"

"I'm only here because my children ganged up on me. They're always doing that."

"When did the pain start?"

Again, that thoughtful pause. "I felt a couple of twinges this afternoon but I didn't think much about it." Her dark eyes studied him while she spoke. "You're new in town aren't you?"

He couldn't help smiling at the lady. "I worked my first shift here last night. Do you remember what you were doing when you first felt the pain?"

"I was out picking up some tree limbs in the front yard. When I stepped out the front door this morning I could have sworn half my trees had dropped their branches from last night's storm." She leaned forward and lowered her voice. "Don't tell my son. He's been after me for months to hire someone to do my yard work for me."

"Is he the one who brought you here?"

She nodded. "I shooed him out to the waiting room. He makes me nervous with all his fussing. Family is wonderful, Dr. Sheldon, but if I let all five of my kids smother me like an old woman I'd never get anything done. I hope the rest of the tribe doesn't come racing here before you release me." She frowned at him. "You *are* going to release me aren't you?"

"We'll see." Grant reached for his stethoscope.

A frantic voice reached the room from the central desk. "Someone help us! My son's been overdosed!"

Grant quickly excused himself and stepped out to see if there was a life threat. A balding man stood at the patient window with his arm around the shoulders of a skinny teenager.

The boy had his arms wrapped across his chest, as if he thought his body might fly apart. His frightened gaze darted about the room and bounced from Becky to the desk to Grant and back to Becky.

As Grant expected, tonight's second RN and a tech rushed out the door and came back in guiding father and son to an exam room. RN Muriel's voice carried well as she calmed them. Grant would check on the boy as soon as he made sure Mrs. Piedmont wasn't in immediate danger of cardiac arrest.

"Doctor, you go ahead and see about those people," the lady said when he returned to her bedside. "That's a real emergency."

"Trying to get rid of me?" He checked her chest with his stethoscope.

She watched Grant as he listened to her chest and studied the monitor. A wealth of warmth

24

suddenly glowed from the creases around her eyes. "Do you have a family, Dr. Sheldon?"

He suppressed a grin. She obviously wasn't as worried about her health as her children were. "I have sixteen-year-old twins, a boy and a girl. They're at home getting settled in." He wasn't sure he'd convinced them they were doing the right thing by moving out of the city. Especially Brooke.

The door opened and the EKG tech came in pushing her portable machine.

"Mrs. Piedmont, here's the person we were waiting for," Grant said. "We'll get more information with more plug-ins to your system. While she's doing her thing I'll give you some privacy but I'll come back and check the results." He squeezed her arm and left her in capable care.

The sound of beeps reached him from across the ER where Muriel had connected the overdosed teenager to the monitor. That rhythm was too fast. Grant stepped into exam room eight to find the fifteen-year-old boy lying in the bed, attached by electrodes to the machine that relayed his elevated heart rate with the beeping. Muriel, an experi-enced nurse in her late fifties, had already dressed him in a gown. His respirations were double what they should be, his eyes obviously dilated. The father's extra-high forehead was furrowed with concern.

Muriel prepped the patient's arm with iodine

swabs and picked up an IV needle. The boy watched her movements with strange intensity.

Grant cleared his throat and both father and son turned toward him. "Hello. I'm Dr. Sheldon. I understand we have a possible overdose problem."

"Thank goodness." The man rushed to Grant's side. "I'm Norville Webster and this is Evan."

"Ow! That hurts!" the boy cried out and jerked back as Muriel inserted the needle.

"Just relax. The pain won't last long." She braced her arm against his and continued her work as she gave Grant the boy's vitals.

"My head's killing me," Evan complained. He reached up and massaged his forehead, his long slender fingers shaking.

Grant stepped up to the bed. "Evan, what kind of drug did you take?"

"It's speed," the teenager said. His words were choppy, irritable, and his voice grew louder with each word. "That *jerk* gave me some pills but he didn't tell me they were speed. I thought they were legal, like maybe some caffeine. I feel like I'm going to crawl out of my skin." His movements became more agitated and he nearly pulled the IV from his arm before Muriel could secure the catheter. "Do something!"

"He came running into the house crying and shaking and rubbing his arms," his father said.

Grant gave Muriel orders then turned back to Evan. "Can you tell me how much you had?"

"All I had was two stupid pills! How could I have known the jerk would trick me into taking speed? I've never done drugs in my life and now I've ended up in the hospital? How could this happen? Can you stop this? I feel like my heart's going to bust through my ribs."

"We'll need a urine sample and then we'll be able to give you something to calm you down."

"Hurry. Please."

"How long ago did you take the pills?"

Evan glanced around the room in confusion. "About an hour or so. Maybe two. I don't even know what time it is."

"Probably a little over an hour," the father said. "It couldn't have been thirty minutes from the time he left the house to the time he came bursting back through the door. He was supposed to walk down and meet his friends at the theater." He glared at the floor. "Some friends."

Evan stared down at his own shaking hands. "I only took two pills."

"I wish I could tell you illegal pills were regulated," Grant said. "One never knows what to expect with them but you did the right thing by coming here." Two pills could easily pack enough punch to kill. Evan didn't need to know that yet. His heart was already under enough strain.

"Charcoal, Dr. Sheldon?" Muriel asked.

Evan's eyes, already wide with fear, got wider. "You're going to ram a tube up my nose?"

27

Grant grinned at him. "If we can convince you to drink it for us we'll forgo the tube. It should help neutralize anything that's left in your stomach. Muriel, I'll be in three."

He left the room. The respiratory tech should be finished with Mrs. Piedmont's EKG by now and the police needed to be notified about the illegal drug. He shook his head as he battled disappointment. An overdose of an illegal drug on his second shift in Dogwood Springs. What disturbed him the most was that Evan appeared to be the victim in this case, a clean-cut healthy teenager caught unaware.

It could have been Brooke or Beau. Grant realized that the only way to keep himself, his own children, and his patients safe was to remain a cynic even here in Hometown USA.

He stopped at the central desk. "Becky, I need you to call the police to report some illegal drug activity."

The forty-something secretary turned from her computer keyboard and peered up at him over the top of her reading glasses. "Dr. Sheldon, Evan Webster's mother and I belong to the library club. I called her and told her he was here and she's on her way in. If I call the police on her kid, she's going to bust my head."

"Blame me, then. Catching a dealer is more important right now. I'll be in three."

When Grant entered Mrs. Piedmont's room he

greeted her and read the EKG printout. It wasn't good.

Mrs. Piedmont's face reflected his frown. "Please don't tell me you're going to have to keep me here, Doctor."

"I don't think this is just a pulled muscle. Would you mind describing the pain you felt?"

"Oh, I had those twinges and then kind of a cramp in my chest that didn't want to let up for a while."

"Did you have cramping or pain anywhere else?"

Mrs. Piedmont's gaze remained steady on his face. "My left arm felt like somebody was squeezing it after I picked up that last big old dead branch and piled it up on the stack. It's fine now, though. I didn't hear anyone mention your wife. I'm on a greeting committee at church— we Baptists like to stick everybody on a committee—and I'd like to call on her with some of my home-made rolls."

Grant was touched. "Thank you for offering. I'd love some homemade rolls but I want to get you feeling better before you do any more work in the kitchen or in the yard." He paused. "And I'm a widower. Tell me, have you had these pains in your chest before today?"

Her smile dimmed. "I'm so sorry. I lost my husband when my children were young, too. How long has your wife been gone?"

"Two years. We were in an automobile accident." Her sincere interest didn't feel intrusive but again he needed to refocus the conversation. "Mrs. Piedmont, tell me more about your chest pains recently."

She considered that. "Haven't had any that I can recall. I was hoping it might be indigestion. You know, you'll want to get your children into a church youth group. Our own Lauren, here, helps keep those teenagers occupied. And she has a way with the young ones, too." Mrs. Piedmont beamed at Lauren, whose long blond hair was pulled back in a serviceable ponytail and whose delicate features held only the barest traces of makeup. "Soon as she joined our church this spring, she pitched right in and started volunteering to help. She's good with the kids and she teaches Sunday school." The lady hesitated for less than a second. "She's single you know."

Lauren looked up from her work again, her green eyes sparkling with laughter. The healthy color of her complexion deepened a shade. "Mrs. Piedmont! Would you please let Dr. Sheldon do his job? How do you think he's going to feel if you keel over before he gets a chance to treat you?" She shook her head and her smile widened. "That'd be a shame."

Grant placed a hand on his patient's arm. "I'm sorry, but I'm afraid I'm going to have to ask you to humor me and eat hospital food tonight."

Her face quieted with the seriousness of his expression. "I overdid it this time, didn't I?" She laid her head back against the pillow. "My kids are going to tie me to my rocking chair."

❧ CHAPTER 3 ❧

Gina Drake came to herself in the heaviness of evening, shivering as a gust of cool wind puckered gooseflesh down her legs. She raised shaking hands to her face. The sharp teeth of pain bit into her feet and she realized they were bare.

She blinked and stared around her at squares of illumination from nearby homes. In the deepening gray of late twilight, she recognized the outline of the elementary school and then looked down at the merry-go-round where she was sitting. She'd found herself here before. Some of the fog cleared from her brain. Tonight she'd run here in a panic, unable to control her terror or recognize her surroundings.

Her breath caught when the truth hit her. She'd left her children alone. "Levi. Cody."

She jumped up. Gravel dug into the flesh of her bare feet. She stumbled to the grass and braced herself, gasping with pain. She had to get to the boys. It was dark. They'd be scared wondering where she was. She tried to ignore the pain as she limped across the playground. She was still weak and shaky and she shivered as the dew-soaked grass stung the cuts and bruises of her broken flesh.

"Stupid, stupid," she muttered at herself as frustration and fear shadowed her. How much more afraid must her children be?

"Don't be scared," she whispered to them. They had to be okay. They were good boys and Levi always watched after his little brother. He was so mature for a six-year-old.

But her fear mounted as she reached the sidewalk and limped through the shadows beneath the overhang of the building. What was happening to her? The terror that had overcome her had also blocked out pieces of time. The terror was more than just a panic attack. Wasn't it?

She thought of Aunt Bridget's problems and black helplessness nearly overwhelmed her. Levi and Cody needed her. She was all they had.

Gina's head ached and her heart felt as if it were being squeezed into a tiny space. She couldn't keep leaving her own children frightened and alone. The last time she'd done this, Levi had been in tears when she returned.

Bad dreams. It had to be nightmares. Something was frightening her and whatever it was had been so horrible her mind refused to recall it. She remembered in vivid detail the horror all those years ago. . . .

Gina welcomed the pain in her feet and the ache in her head. She deserved the pain. What kind of mother ran out of the house and left her children alone?

Her throat swelled with tears of frustration and self-loathing. Trying to ignore her shaking legs, she broke into a stumbling run on the uneven sidewalk. Fresh pain sliced up her calves from her wounded feet. Had to get home, had to reach the boys, had to comfort them, make sure they were okay, try to explain one more time why she'd left. If only she knew.

As she caught sight of her house up ahead, with lights shining from every window, Gina felt another tug at her heart. Levi hated the dark. The abundance of lights reproached her. She reached the front sidewalk and saw a square of white against the solid oak darkness of the front door. A quickly scrawled note struck her with accusation: *Levi has been hurt. I'm taking both boys to the emergency room. Agnes.*

Lauren McCaffrey felt a slight wave of nausea as she pierced the paper-thin skin of Mrs. Piedmont's right arm with an IV needle. She ignored the distraction and took care not to cause her patient any more pain than necessary.

The lady didn't even flinch, didn't glance at Lauren but continued her conversation with Dr. Sheldon as if Lauren hadn't touched her. Success.

"I suppose I should have told you this before, Doctor," Mrs. Piedmont said, "but I had a brother who died suddenly of a heart attack when he was forty."

Lauren completed the IV and her nausea passed quickly. She didn't have time to wonder about it as Grant continued to question Mrs. Piedmont.

"You don't smoke?" he asked.

"Not since I was twelve. My brother and I tried to smoke one of those roll-your-own cigarettes out in the barn. My brother got sick and upchucked on my good shoes. I dropped the cigarette into a pile of hay. I nearly caught the barn on fire before we could put the silly thing out. We both got our butts paddled and that put an end to my cigarette smoking." She leaned toward Lauren. "How about you, Lauren, did you ever smoke?"

"No, ma'am, I never did. I chewed tobacco once, though."

Dr. Sheldon grinned at her. "What happened?"

"I didn't know I was supposed to spit. I got the same results as your brother, Mrs. Piedmont." Her stomach made it known that this topic was not good subject matter in its present condition.

She was once more checking the monitor for vitals when someone knocked at the exam room entrance. She glanced up to make sure Mrs. Piedmont was properly covered, then went to the door and pulled it open to find Pastor Archer Pierce standing in the hallway. He grinned and stepped forward, his kind eyes calm and reassuring as always.

"Hi, Lauren. I saw Calvin Piedmont out in the waiting room and he's practically chewing the vinyl cushions on the chairs. I promised I'd check on his mother." As he peered past Lauren his grin broadened. "Cecile, what are you doing in bed at this time of night?" Though Archer was a couple of years younger than Lauren, she envied his spiritual maturity.

He had short and slightly ruffled brown hair. Combined with his quick, friendly smile, those features gave him a boyish look that camouflaged his true maturity. He stepped into the room and crossed to the bed to give their patient a kiss on her cheek. "I guess you know your son's mad at you."

The lady took Archer's hand in both of her own. "Let him be mad. He didn't call you down here to see just me, did he? I told him not to."

"He didn't call me. I'm the chaplain on duty tonight. Lauren called me." He glanced around at Lauren and winked. Her face grew warm. No wonder the number of females in the church youth group was increasing weekly.

As soon as the thought occurred to her she chided herself. Even if he *was* single and good-looking, with the movements and physique of a star athlete and an incredible sense of humor, he was her pastor. He was also an old friend. Lauren realized she should know better but she'd never had a great deal of control over whom she found attractive.

Belatedly, she realized she had made no introductions and was staring at Archer like one of the love-struck teenagers in the youth group. The heat beneath her skin increased. Could she be coming down with a touch of the virus some of their patients had brought in with them tonight?

"Archer," Mrs. Piedmont said, "this is Dr. Sheldon. He's new in town and he has twins who are sixteen years old. Don't you think we should get them involved in some of the activities you and Lauren have going?"

"Of course." Archer reached out to shake Dr. Sheldon's hand. The two men assessed each other with the quick, respectful once-over that men used when sizing each other up for a game of one-on-one basketball. The smile remained in Archer's eyes and it was genuine. He had an easygoing grace about him that Lauren knew would help comfort the patients.

Dr. Sheldon returned Archer's greeting with equal warmth then turned back to his patient. "Mrs. Piedmont, we'll wait for the results of those blood tests—they shouldn't take long—and then I'll contact your family doctor. If you start feeling any more pain, please let us know immediately."

Mrs. Piedmont laid her head back against the pillow and smiled up at him. "I'll do that, Doctor. Would someone tell my son that I'm still alive? I know he's fretting."

Archer nodded and stepped out as the ER

secretary stepped in. "Excuse me, Dr. Sheldon, I just received a call from a woman who is bringing in a burned child."

"Did she say how bad?"

"She said some hot soup splashed onto his shoulder and he's blistering. I could barely hear her for the screaming in the background."

"What's the ETA?"

"She said it'll take her about ten minutes to get here. The neighbors are bringing him in. She says she doesn't know where the mother is. The boys were at home by themselves."

He frowned. "Boys? More than one?"

"Two little boys, six and four. It's the six-year-old who was burned. They want their mother but nobody knows where she is. It's a good thing the neighbor has watched the kids a couple of times. She has written permission for treatment with all the information."

"I'll go set up for it," Lauren said. She checked the monitor one more time, laid a reassuring hand on Mrs. Piedmont's arm, and excused herself.

Less than ten minutes later, the mingled sobbing shrieks of two frightened children burst through the ER and brought Lauren rushing to the front of the department. She saw Dr. Sheldon carrying a blond-haired little boy in his arms. A woman in her fifties entered behind him with a younger child.

"I saw her run out of her house about forty-five

minutes before I heard the boys' screams." The woman's voice rose in a crescendo of panic. "I didn't think anything about it. I mean, how was I supposed to know there wasn't a babysitter?"

The neighbor absently stroked the head of the child in her arms, carrying him as if she was accustomed to holding children. "When I heard the screams I didn't know what to think. These boys are never loud—their mother makes them mind. They're good boys, especially for children without a father." The little boy in her arms cried out again and reached for his brother. Tears dripped from his scrunched face.

"Did you bring the permission for care, Mrs. . . . ?" Dr. Sheldon asked over his shoulder.

"Walker. Agnes Walker. It's here in my purse. I baby-sat for Gina a couple of times when she got called in to work suddenly and couldn't get her regular babysitter. Please, can't you give Levi something for pain? He screamed all the way here."

"We'll get the cool saline applied as quickly as we can. Meanwhile I'll need the information. Does this little guy have any drug allergies?"

"None I know of." Mrs. Walker tried to put the younger child down but he shrieked again and grabbed her around the neck.

Dr. Sheldon carried six-year-old Levi into exam room two and settled him onto the bed where Lauren had already set up for the burn treatment.

He removed the little boy's shirt to reveal a softball-sized patch of blistered skin on the right shoulder. "Lauren, start the cool saline on this. Get Lester to help you." His calm deep voice carried over the cries of the children.

Levi caught his breath. "It hurts, it hurts. Where's Mama? I want my—"

"It's okay, sweetheart, we're going to take care of you." Lauren eased him down onto the bed and prepped for the saline soak.

Dr. Sheldon bent over the child and assessed the burn quickly. "It's going to be okay, Levi. Did the soup splash you anywhere but your—"

"Ow. That hurts!"

"We're going to take the burn away." Dr. Sheldon gave Lauren a nod to proceed with the soak. "You'll be feeling a lot better in a few seconds."

Lauren grabbed a handful of four-by-four-inch gauze pads and lowered them toward the burn. She quickly squeezed the saline bottle until it wept onto the thick layer of towels below.

"I burned myself once when I was a little older than you," she told him. "Mom put ice on it until it stopped hurting." She kept up a continual flow of soft talk, never a difficult thing for her. She had the gift of gab the way some people had a special touch with a paintbrush. Except for times like this, however, she seldom treasured this "gift."

Tears continued to well in Levi's eyes and drip down the sides of his face, dampening streaks of his hair to dark gold. "Where's my mom? I don't know where Mom is and Cody's still crying. He was just hungry. It isn't his fault."

"Of course not, sweetheart," Lauren assured him. "Mrs. Walker is with him while our secretary tries to find your mother. Did she say where she was going when she left?"

"No, she just ran out the door. She looked scared and she didn't have her shoes on. Mom always tells us we have to wear our shoes outside but she didn't wear hers."

"Levi," Dr. Sheldon's voice was gentle and soft. "Has your mom ever done anything like that before?"

"Yes, but she always wore her shoes before."

Dr. Sheldon's voice remained calm and casual. "So your mother always wore her shoes the other times she left you at home alone?"

"Yes," Levi replied, then his eyes widened and he shut his mouth tightly, as if he had picked up some strange tone in Dr. Sheldon's voice.

"Lauren, continue the saline soaks and I'll see if we need the Demerol." With a smile of assurance for Levi, Dr. Sheldon walked out of the room. Lauren heard him ask Becky about Levi's mother then give orders to call the child abuse hotline.

"Why did the doctor leave?" Levi asked between sniffles.

"He has another patient." Lauren brushed the strawberry blond tendrils of hair from his forehead and indicated for Lester, the tech, to take over the application of saline while she did her assessment. "Levi, did your mother tell you why she was leaving today?"

"No, but I think it was because she was scared."

"What scared her?"

Tears continued to stream down Levi's cheek in spite of his obvious efforts to be brave. "I think it was one of her bad dreams."

"Did I hear that your mother's name is Gina?"

"Uh-huh."

Becky's voice rose from the central desk. "Mrs. Walker, did you say the patient's name is Levi Drake?"

Lauren stiffened with surprise. "Levi, your last name is Drake?"

The child nodded, still tearful.

She laid a hand against his soft cheek. "Your mother works here."

Levi blinked at her and nodded again. "She helps people breathe better."

Oh no. Dr. Sheldon had just left orders for Becky to call the child abuse hotline on one of their best respiratory therapists.

❧ CHAPTER 4 ❧

Grant slipped into exam room eight to see how Evan Webster was doing. The EKG showed no more than an elevated heart rate. Two large empty Styrofoam cups sat at the bedside with the residue of charcoal clinging in droplets to the inner surfaces. Grant was impressed. Evan had managed to swallow all that gritty stuff in a short amount of time. He obviously wanted the drug out of his system.

The boy's father stood watch next to the bed as if he thought his son might come under physical attack. Grant knew the feeling. He had hovered just that way beside Beau's hospital bed during those horrible months after Annette's death. But no matter how close he hovered or how willing he was to place himself between his son and harm, he hadn't been able to prevent Beau's physical and emotional scars.

When the father saw Grant, he straightened and rushed toward him. "Dr. Sheldon, my son doesn't ordinarily do this kind of thing. He's an honor-roll student, a good boy. I don't want you to get the wrong impression of him."

"I'm not here to judge your son, Norville, I just want to work with you both to make sure this kind of thing doesn't happen again." He read the vitals displayed on the overhead monitor. Muriel had administered Ativan through Evan's IV. Though the heart rate was still elevated, it had slowed and his blood pressure was dropping.

"How did you like our house beverage tonight, Evan?"

"I kept it down." There was no change in the boy's expression.

"That's good. How are you feeling? Any better?"

"My heart's still beating too fast."

"It'll take a while to get back to normal. Does it still feel as if it's going to beat out of your chest?"

Evan considered the question solemnly. "I guess not."

Grant checked his vitals. "It looks as if we might have this under control but I still need to keep you here two or three more hours."

Evan laid his head back and groaned.

Grant noticed the faint evidence of the charcoal around Evan's mouth and traces of dried tears on his face. "I have to ask you some questions."

Evan nodded.

"I need to know why you took the drugs tonight. Were you—"

"I took the pills to feel better." He looked at his father then ducked his head. "I've been kind of down and my friend told me they would give me a lift. You know, he said they would give me some go power."

"Did you know "go" is another name for speed?"

Evan shook his head. "I'm not into that stuff at all. Nobody said anything about speed before I took it. He told me I'd feel better."

"Better than what?" his father asked. "There was nothing wrong with you before you took the stuff."

Evan sighed and gave the ceiling a long-suffering look. "I don't tell you everything, Dad."

"Obviously not." Norville had clearly been taken by surprise. Grant was increasingly convinced that this truly was Evan's first experience with illegal drugs. Still, he'd been fooled before.

The boy sighed again. "Dad, if I tell you about something that's bothering me, you automatically blame Mom. And if I tell her something, she blames you."

"Evan," Grant said, "speed does just what it says. It speeds up your system."

"Yeah, I can tell, but I didn't know those pills were illegal. I just thought maybe he'd gotten it from his parents."

"Who is *he?*" Norville demanded.

"Somebody I thought was a friend." The resentment in Evan's voice was clear.

"I need to advise you that the police will be here to talk to you in a few minutes," Grant said.

Evan jerked upright in the bed. "What! The police? You called the police on me?"

Norville groaned and leaned back against the exam room wall. "Evan, what have you gotten us into?"

"I'm sorry," Grant said. "I have no choice. The authorities have to be aware of any drug activity in the area. I would advise you to cooperate with them in every way possible."

"No problem. I'm in the mood to send some drug pushers to jail."

Norville stepped over to Grant. "Evan's so young. He's a good kid with great grades. If this gives him a police record, he'll—"

"The police will be looking for information from Evan, not retribution."

Norville bit his lip. Lines of despair settled around his forehead and eyes, aging him by at least ten years. "I suppose I understand the necessity of reporting this to the police but do you think it would be possible to keep his mother from finding out about this? We're divorced and she has custody. She'll raise the roof if—"

"I'm sorry, she's already on her way in," Grant said. "I know this is difficult for you, Mr. Webster." Grant couldn't help feeling empathy for this man. Parents of teenagers seldom had it easy these days. "Your son is only a year younger than my twins. I can imagine what I would be going through right now." He studied the man more closely. "Would you like to speak with a counselor?"

Norville reached up and rubbed his tired eyes. "Yes, I'd like that."

"Our minister on call tonight is Pastor Archer Pierce. He's already here."

Norville looked at his son.

"Mom'll freak," Evan said.

"Too bad. We need some help."

Grant recognized the light, clear sound of Lauren McCaffrey's voice several seconds before he stepped to the threshold of Levi Drake's exam room and saw her perched on the stool beside the bed. The child listened intently while the energetic nurse concluded an exciting story of a battle with great dramatic emphasis. At just the right time she put the saline bottle down and replayed the slinging of the stone, her hands moving gracefully in the air. As the giant finally fell in a mighty tumble to the earth, Grant could almost feel the earth shake at the impact.

Levi's lips were parted and his eyes shone. "More! Tell me more! What happened after that?" He was so engrossed that he didn't see Grant standing in the doorway. "What did David do after that?"

"Exactly what I was going to ask," Grant said.

Lauren looked over her shoulder at him and a hint of a flush spread across her cheeks. He'd already learned that she blushed easily. "Oops, I've been caught." She picked up the bottle of saline and re-wet the gauze on Levi's shoulder. "I still have the Bible storybook my mother used to read to us when we were kids, though I don't need it because I have all the stories memorized. Especially the ones about brave boys like Levi."

Grant couldn't decide if she was chattering so fast because she was embarrassed or because she was trying to keep Levi's mind off his pain. Probably a combination of both but for Levi the spell was broken. As soon as Grant stepped to the side of the bed the little boy's eyes lost their look of enchantment.

"Sounds like you and Nurse Lauren are having a good story time," Grant said softly. "How does that shoulder feel now?"

"It hurts sometimes. Are you going to give me a shot?" His voice held a tremble of fear.

"Let me check and see." Grant pulled the gauze back from the burn. The patch of angry red was covered with blisters. "What does the pain feel like when it hurts?"

"Like needles."

"Sounds like that really hurts, then," Grant said. "You probably wouldn't mind being stuck once if that would keep you from feeling like you're getting stuck over and over again."

"He's very brave, Dr. Sheldon," Lauren said. "As soon as I apply more cool saline, he says the burn goes away again. He never complains. He's worried about his little brother so we had Becky go check on him." She reached over and brushed a wisp of hair from Levi's forehead. "We decided if he could just go swimming at his friend's pool until he heals and if Cody could go with him, everybody would be happy."

"My friend doesn't live in Dogwood Springs, though," Levi said seriously. "He lives in Oregon, where we used to live. Where's my mom?"

Grant replaced the gauze and sat down beside the bed, eye level with the child. "Some people are looking for your mother, Levi. But while they do that, we've called someone to come in and make sure you and Cody will be okay. Mrs. Walker's in one of the little waiting rooms with Cody, helping him color some pictures. Lauren, would you please give us some Silvadene?"

She nodded but didn't stand up immediately. "Dr. Sheldon, Levi's mom works here at the hospital." She paused, holding his gaze. "Gina's a respiratory therapist."

For a moment the impact of her words didn't register. When they did, Grant suppressed a groan. Although calling the child abuse hotline was the required action for him to take to protect the children, it could be perceived as an accusation against Gina Drake. What concerned him more, though, was the fact that someone with her level of expertise and sense of responsibility wouldn't be likely to neglect her own children like this. Something else was going on.

"How many people are searching for her now?" he asked Lauren.

"I'm not sure. Becky's taking care of the calls."

"Tell Becky to call the police for an immediate neighborhood search around their house in case they haven't already done that."

"Yes Dr. Sheldon." She handed him the saline bottle. "His shoulder is probably going to start burning again before I get back."

He took it and urged Levi to lie back down.

Levi stared at him with open accusation. "You're calling the police on my mom."

Grant soaked the gauze with fluid and laid a hand on the child's unhurt shoulder. "Not to arrest her. We want to make sure she's safe. We want to take care of her."

Levi's lips parted in alarm. "You think she's sick?"

Grant hesitated. No reason to worry the child yet. "We just want to make sure she's okay."

"Why wouldn't she be okay?" Levi's voice rose with urgency. "She wasn't sick, she was scared."

"Okay, Levi." Grant used the soothing voice he once used with his own children when they were younger and something frightened them. "I'm trying to find out why she left you and Cody, because I don't think she does that a lot, does she?"

Levi studied Grant's face in silence for a moment and then shook his head.

Grant was relieved when Lauren stepped back into the room and resumed her place beside Levi, burn cream in hand.

"Becky is calling the police now, Dr. Sheldon. She said the hospital social worker, Rose, should be here any time."

"But what if Mom's home now?" Levi asked. "Can't I go home?"

Grant felt a familiar ache as he looked into the child's frightened eyes. "If your mother arrives at home, someone will find her and send her here, Levi. Meanwhile, I want to keep you here long enough to make your shoulder stop burning." He watched Lauren apply the cream. Levi barely flinched at her touch.

"There you go," she said with a note of soothing tenderness. "You're so brave and strong. This is special medicine that makes the burn go away fast but if it doesn't you need to let us know, okay?"

Levi nodded. The child was more worried about his mother than he was about his own pain.

"How long before Cody and I can go home?" The voice was more insistent this time.

For a moment Grant didn't answer. Then he sighed and sat down, once more eye to eye with Levi. "I'd love to be able to send you home, Levi, but you need a grown-up with—"

"Mom will be home soon." Levi's eyes spilled fresh tears down his cheeks. "She's never gone this long. She's probably looking all over for us."

There it was again, the admission that Gina had done this kind of thing before. What would cause a responsible mother to leave her young children at home alone? Grant looked at Lauren and saw her watching Levi with a troubled gaze.

"I know you've already answered a lot of questions for us, Levi, but would you answer some more for me?" Grant pulled some tissues from a box on the desk and handed them to Levi.

The little boy studied Grant's face carefully, took the tissues, and nodded.

"You said something about your mother having bad dreams. Can you tell me anything about those dreams? Does she ever describe them to you?"

Levi shook his head and reached up to dry the tears with his hands instead of the tissues. "She cries sometimes when she has them and she runs out of the house. Then later when she comes back she's always sorry."

"How many times has this happened?"

The child frowned. "It never happened before we came here to live."

"And you don't have any family in this town?"

Levi shook his head. "Mom and Cody are my family. Mom told us that's all we need to be a family."

Grant squeezed Levi's arm as his own heart squeezed inside his chest. Why did it have to be that way so many times? Divorce and death and illness were vicious enemies. He wondered how these children had lost their father.

He turned to speak to Lauren but her eyes were closed and her face was very pale with a sheen of moisture across her forehead. She opened her eyes, caught him looking at her, and looked away quickly. She dabbed at her forehead with the back of her hand.

She turned to the child. "Levi, would you like me to bring your brother in to see you?"

"Yes!" Levi straightened and tried to sit up. Something in the doorway caught his attention a his mouth rounded in a big O. "Mom!"

Lauren looked up and gasped. "Gina!"

❧ CHAPTER 5 ❧

Surprised and relieved, Lauren rushed toward Gina. The poor woman, disheveled and flushed, limped into the room wearing white cut-off shorts and a tee shirt. Smudges of mascara below her eyes looked like bruises. Her short auburn hair fell across her freckled forehead in tangles. Her anguished focus centered on Levi and on the gauze that covered the wound on his shoulder.

Levi sat up and reached his arms toward his mother. "You're back! We were looking for you. Were you scared?"

"Oh Levi," she whispered, taking him carefully

into her arms. "What happened? There was a note on the door at home telling me you were here. Are you okay?"

"Yes, but don't touch my burned place," he said.

"I won't. I see it. I'm so relieved you're—" She drew back and leaned down to look at his shoulder. "How did it happen? How did you get burned?"

"Soup. Nurse Lauren has been pouring water on it and putting this gunky stuff on it and telling me stories about a boy who killed a big mean giant with a slingshot. I could kill a big mean giant, too. Can I have a slingshot, Mom?"

Gina pulled his head against her chest and pressed her lips to his hair, her eyes squeezed shut. Tears streamed in a sudden flood down her cheeks.

"Dr. Sheldon was worried about you," Levi continued, his bright voice muffled against her shirt. "I didn't know where you were and people are looking for you. What happened?"

She sniffed and straightened her shoulders as she gave Lauren and Dr. Sheldon a look of appeal. "How bad?"

"He's going to be fine," Dr. Sheldon said. "He's got a second-degree flash burn but it's only on his shoulder, where you see the gauze. We've already cooled it down with saline and the burn dressing looks as if it will help a great deal."

She leaned back down to look her son in the eyes. "I'm sorry, Levi."

"Why are you crying? Did you get that dream again?"

She blinked and darted a glance toward Dr. Sheldon. "I-I don't remember a dream. I'm okay now. Where's Cody?"

"Cody's fine, Gina," Lauren assured her, noticing with dismay that the nausea she had experienced earlier was returning. What was wrong with her? "We were worried about you."

As Gina took a step backward she stumbled and cried out. Lauren looked down. At first it looked as if Gina had on canvas shoes that were tie-dyed a vivid red. A closer look revealed the splotchy brown-edged appearance of drying blood.

Dr. Sheldon leaned forward and laid a hand on Gina's shoulder. "Mrs. Drake, I'm Dr. Sheldon. I think I need to check you over and make sure—"

She raised a hand and shrank from his touch. "I'll be okay now that I have my boys." She avoided eye contact.

But Levi saw the shoes. "Mom, what did you get on your shoes?" He bent over the side of the bed and studied them closer.

"It's okay, don't worry about me. I guess I stumbled on some rocks. I must have stained my shoes when I pulled them on."

"You don't remember what happened?" Dr. Sheldon asked.

"You ran away without your shoes this time!"

Levi exclaimed. "You're not supposed to do that." He winced as if the burn had returned to his shoulder.

Lauren drew his squirming body back down on the bed. "Levi, try not to move very much. Your mom's safe now so you don't have to worry about her. We'll let the police know she's here so they can call off the search."

Gina caught her breath and looked up at Lauren, shock and fear streaking across her face. "The police?"

"We were worried. We didn't know what had happened to you."

"We needed to find you." Dr. Sheldon hesitated. His gaze skimmed Levi's face and then he looked once again into Gina's eyes. "I cannot stress enough how important it is for us to examine you as soon as possible."

She shook her head. "I need to see Cody."

"But Mom, you're bleeding," Levi said.

"I'll take care of it when we get home."

"Levi." Dr. Sheldon knelt again. "I need to take care of your mother's feet in another exam room. That'll be okay with you won't it?"

Levi's copper-colored eyes, so much like his mother's, studied Dr. Sheldon's face soberly. "You'll put medicine on them?"

"Yes, I'll take good care of her." He straightened and reached for Gina's shoulder to guide her out.

She stiffened and pulled back. "Please, I need to be with my children."

"Later," Dr. Sheldon said. "If not for you, then for the sake of Levi and Cody. Levi tells me you don't have family nearby that we can call."

"No family." Adamant. Firm.

"Friends then?" he asked.

She shook her head. "We've only been in Missouri a few months." Her attention switched from Dr. Sheldon to Lauren and she must have detected something in Lauren's expression that disturbed her. "Why? What's going on? Why do you want to bring—" Her eyes filled with sudden panic. "Cody. Where's Cody? Is there something—"

"Cody's safe in one of the other rooms with your neighbor." Lauren placed an arm around her shoulders.

Gina pulled away. "I want to see him. Please."

"You don't want him to see your feet like this," Lauren said gently. "It could scare him. Why don't we bring him in here with Levi so they can be together, then we'll bring you back in here as soon as you're treated, okay? Your feet don't look good right now." She raised her eyebrows in a question to Dr. Sheldon.

He nodded. "I'll have Mrs. Walker bring Cody in here and we'll let him know his mother's safe."

Lauren got a wheelchair from the front of the ER and pushed it into the room.

"I don't need that," Gina said. "I can walk—"

Lauren took Gina's arm in a firm grip. "You can ride more easily and prevent further damage."

Gina looked again at her son, then relented and allowed Lauren to wheel her out.

Gina was a couple of inches shorter than Lauren's 5'5", with muscular arms and legs that didn't appear to get a lot of sun. In spite of her obvious physical strength and her facade of self-sufficiency, she seemed frightened and vulnerable at the moment. It wasn't a side of Gina that Lauren had ever seen before.

Whenever Gina came into the emergency room to treat a patient, she was friendly, with a good bedside manner and a quick wit. According to the patients, she also had a tender touch.

"Something else is going on," Gina said as Lauren wheeled her close to the bed. "What?"

Before Lauren could answer, Dr. Sheldon joined them and closed the door behind him. "Gina, I'm sorry." He pulled a stool over and sat down, hesitated, then leaned forward, resting his elbows on his knees. "You know that as a physician, if I even suspect the possibility of child abuse I'm mandated to report it, just as you are in your position as a respiratory therapist."

Gina's mouth flew open. She caught her breath. Her face lost all color and she grasped the arms of the wheelchair. "Child abuse!" She looked from him to Lauren with open pain. "You reported me for—"

"We know better than that now," Lauren assured her.

Dr. Sheldon reached across to help Gina out of the wheelchair. "As soon as someone from the Division of Family Services arrives, I'll inform them of the change in circumstances."

"They can't take Levi and Cody." The panic in her voice chilled Lauren.

"No, Gina." Dr. Sheldon's voice was gentle and patient. "They're coming to make sure the children are okay. When we called them, no one knew where you were."

Gina covered her face with her hands and moaned. "This can't be happening."

Lauren knelt in front of the younger woman and grasped her by the shoulders. "That's why we need to give you a physical and neurological exam. We have to prove you're physically and mentally capable of caring for them yourself so that no questions arise. Look at it as a professional. It only makes sense."

Dr. Sheldon stood up and pushed the stool out of the way. "Let us help you onto the bed so we can examine and treat you." He reached for her elbow. She jerked away.

"Please, Gina." Lauren kept her voice soft and unthreatening.

Gina's full lips formed a straight line and she

narrowed her smudged eyes. "You said Agnes Walker brought them in. She has letters for permission to treat. Why couldn't you just leave it at that?"

"Because she saw you racing out of the house about forty-five minutes before she heard your sons screaming." Dr. Sheldon's voice was not accusatory. "They were alone in the house all that time and she didn't know it. Even though you obviously didn't leave them intentionally, Gina, they were still alone long enough to be injured. Now you've told me that you don't remember how you injured your feet. For your children's sake and your own we need to find out what's going on here. I'll treat your injuries, do a neurologic exam, and take blood and urine tests."

"But you're still going to turn me over to DFS?"

"We aren't going to 'turn you over' to anybody." He leaned closer and made eye contact. "What we'll do is ask them to back you up with support and advice while we try to find out what's wrong with you."

"Those people don't want to help me." The tension in her voice emphasized every word. "They want to take my kids away from me. I know what they'll do."

"No, Gina," Lauren said gently. "I know our staff social worker. Rose will do all she can to help your family through this crisis." She placed an arm around Gina's shoulders once more.

Gina's face puckered and she covered it with her hands. "Maybe this *is* all a nightmare. I should never have come to Missouri."

Finally, Gina allowed Lauren and Dr. Sheldon to help her onto the exam bed. Lauren removed the blood-soaked canvas shoes and placed them in a biohazard bag.

"Those people can claim I'm mentally incompetent," Gina said.

"They won't," Lauren said.

"But what if they do?" She had her eyes closed and she rested her head on the pillow, tears running unchecked down the sides of her face and into her hair, darkening it to deep burgundy. "And what if they're right?"

"What makes you think that?" Lauren asked.

Gina shook her head.

Lauren helped Gina turn over onto her stomach and set to work cleaning the blood from her feet as Dr. Sheldon pulled on some sterile gloves and checked for injuries. He found two deep cuts, one with a sliver of glass about the size of half a toothpick in the left instep. No wonder she'd been limping when she came in. Lauren was amazed she could even walk.

Dr. Sheldon requested a suture tray. "Gina, I'm going to try to remove this glass gently but if it hurts too much let me know and I'll numb you up first. You'll need sutures anyway."

Gina nodded wordlessly. He retrieved the fragment and gently explored both cuts for more glass. She didn't flinch. There was no active bleeding at this point but it looked as if Dr. Sheldon would be doing several sutures in both feet.

"I don't think there's any more glass but we need x-rays to make sure." He removed his gloves. "You're going to be sore for a few days. Lauren, irrigate the wounds while I'm gone. We'll get urine after I sew her up. I'll finish examining her later." He walked to the door and opened it. "I'll give Becky orders."

Dr. Sheldon was gone for several seconds before Gina gave a heavy sigh. "The social worker really might find me to be incompetent. I think I'm losing my mind."

Archer was talking quietly with Cecile Piedmont, one of his favorite church members, and calming her son Calvin, when Dr. Sheldon returned to the exam room. The man smiled at Cecile and stepped over to check her vital signs.

"I notice the family hasn't descended on you yet," Dr. Sheldon said.

"Only for lack of time," Cecile grumbled. "Most of them live out of state but Calvin and Archer assure me they're on their way." Her expression cleared. She leaned closer to Dr. Sheldon. "We couldn't help overhearing that poor woman and her little boy next door," she said quietly. "Is everything going to be okay?"

"I sure hope so." There was a firm quality in his gentle voice. He obviously honored patient confidentiality. He made a notation on the chart.

"So when do I get to go home?" Cecile asked. "I'm ready *now*."

Dr. Sheldon chuckled. "Why don't you take the rest while you can get it? From what I hear, when your family arrives you'll probably cook up a meal for the whole gang."

"I need to keep active." Cecile said it without a glance at her concerned son.

"Mom, the tests haven't even come back yet," Calvin said gently. There was a special tenderness in his gaze. Archer knew he was more worried than he allowed his mother to see.

"It won't be long now," Dr. Sheldon said. "You do remember what I said, don't you? I may want to keep you overnight, so don't get your hopes too high before we know for sure. Now, do you mind if I borrow your pastor for a few minutes? He's suddenly popular."

"That's fine," the lady assured him. "He's heard all my latest stories, anyway, and I think we're pretty much prayed out."

Dr. Sheldon motioned for Archer to follow him. "I've got another job for you if you're game."

Archer stood up from his bedside seat and followed the man out the door. "I didn't realize what busy people you ER docs are on Friday nights."

Grant chuckled and led the way out into the hall. "I wish you'd call me Grant. According to Lauren, you can tame a room full of crazy teenagers. Since I have two of those myself, I have no doubt you could handle an ER full of patients."

Archer easily kept pace with Grant's long-legged stride. "Cecile tells me you have twins."

"Yes, a girl and a boy, Brooke and Beau. And they are about as opposite as twins can be." There were faint lines around Grant's eyes and mouth. They were lines of kindness, which spoke of sleepless nights, long hours of work, and lots of smiles and laughter. Archer guessed him to be somewhere near forty.

"I've made a lot of trips to the hospital with church members over the years but somehow being a hospital chaplain seems different to me," Archer said.

"Why?" Grant stopped to pick up another chart at the circular central desk.

"I guess you could say the members of my church speak my language. They expect me to pray. They expect me to quote Scripture and give comfort."

"I'd be disappointed if you didn't do that. Wouldn't most people expect the same from you? It's why you're here."

"As long as I don't proselytize, right?"

"Giving comfort and praying isn't proselytizing,

63

it's being a chaplain. Give yourself time to get accustomed to the pace. It can be crazy sometimes."

"I've noticed. So fill me in, Grant," Archer said. "What's this next case about?"

Grant checked the chart and turned to lead the way across the room, keeping his voice low. "In exam room eight, we have a fifteen-year-old, Evan Webster, who suffered an overdose of speed. He appeared as shocked as his father to find out what the pills were he took."

Archer wondered if that was a hint of doubt in Grant's voice. "You think he's lying?"

Grant shrugged as he slowed his steps. "I'm from St. Louis. I've seen too many schoolchildren with track marks on their arms and too many virgins with child." He gave Archer a rueful grimace. "Sorry. Just call me Dr. Cynic. Anyway, the boy's father has asked for family counseling and that's a good sign. I think the shock hit him pretty hard, which is another good sign. It means he probably hasn't had this kind of experience before."

"Meaning it's possible the boy is telling the truth?"

"I want to believe that. To complicate things, the father and mother are divorced and the mother has custody, so she's been contacted and is on her way in. The police will be here soon to question Evan. You'll probably be just about in the epicenter when everyone arrives. I also have the impression she isn't keen on people in the ministerial field for some reason. Lauren tells me you teach a class on drug awareness."

"Yes."

"Good. I want my kids to attend."

Archer nodded, wondering about his next case. Ordinarily before a counseling session like this, he would have a prayer session alone. This time he wouldn't get a chance. Even so, he couldn't clear his mind of the young woman with the two little boys. Gina. That was her name. And Levi and Cody. No husband or father?

"What can you tell me about Gina Drake?" he asked.

Grant looked at him. "You know her?"

"Hey, Dogwood Springs is my hometown. I know everybody within a fifty-mile radius—at least it seems that way when I try to keep a secret. I've known Lauren since we met at church camp as kids. Her younger brother is my age."

"How do you know Gina? She's new in town and—"

"I don't," Archer admitted. "I was eaves-dropping. No way could I miss what was going on in that room, even if I'd tried, which I didn't. Mrs. Piedmont is right, these exam room walls are pretty thin and I learned years ago that eaves-dropping was a good way to stay ahead of the game and know what to pray for next. Would you at least ask Gina if I may pray with her? It sounds like she'll need some friends."

Grant slowed to a stop with a smile and a thoughtful shake of his head. "I'll ask. Have I said thanks for coming in tonight? I think the volunteer chaplain program is going to help the staff as much as it helps the patients."

Archer hadn't received encouragement like that in weeks. "This place sounds more like a hospital for wounded souls than wounded bodies."

"The two seem to go together." Grant gestured toward an exam room. "Norville Webster and his son, Evan, are in there."

Archer took a sustaining breath as he raised a silent prayer to heaven. "Let me at 'em."

Lauren pressed some tissues into Gina's hand. "As soon as I get your feet cleaned, I'll put some temporary bandages on them and wheel you over to get your x-rays. We can check on your children as we go past."

"Thank you." Gina's voice was muffled against the pillow. She sniffed and mopped her face with the tissues. "I'm sorry about this. I'm not usually such a baby."

"You're not acting like a baby, you're acting like a worried mother with two children and a medical condition she doesn't understand. I wish I knew what to tell you. I don't think I'd be as brave under the circumstances." Lauren quickly revised her words. "Not that the circumstances are hopeless, Gina. My impression is that Dr. Sheldon is knowledgeable and thorough. If anyone can figure out what's going on, he can." Lauren bit off her babbling as she finished cleaning the wounds and placed Telfa dressings over them. She wrapped both of Gina's feet with gauze. "You can turn over and sit up."

When Gina did as she was told, Lauren saw that the mascara had spread farther across her face. Time to try to lighten the mood, if possible. "Honey, you look like you've got a couple of shiners." She pulled her gloves off and reached for a paper towel. "Hold still for a minute." She dampened the towel and went to work on the makeup mess.

"Levi and Cody will think their mother suddenly turned into a raccoon." She grinned to assure Gina she was teasing.

Gina closed her eyes and held still while Lauren dabbed around her eyes. "Thank you."

"For what? You'd tell me if my makeup was smeared, wouldn't you?"

The copper-colored eyes opened again. "Thank you for taking such good care of Levi. He doesn't usually trust strangers so quickly."

"He's precious. I'd love five just like him but I need a husband first."

Gina grimaced and looked away. "Why? You can't depend on them. I tried."

"I can't imagine a daddy not wanting to stay around to watch those two angels grow up."

"Their father barely waited until Cody was born before he took off with somebody who didn't have any kids to tie her down." Gina's voice was layered with pain.

Lauren placed a hand on Gina's shoulder. "Then he's the one who will lose the most. Your children have a mother who obviously loves them very much."

"I left them alone tonight." Gina's voice wobbled. "I made a vow years ago that I would never allow my own children to feel the way—" She stopped and bit her lip then straightened her shoulders and sniffed. "I'm sorry. This isn't your problem. I'll figure it all out later. Do I still look like a raccoon?"

Lauren wiped the last smudge then stepped back to admire her handiwork. "Aha! Now I recognize you. You're Gina Drake from Respiratory, the one who's so good with children. No wonder your own kids are so sweet."

Something warmed in Gina's eyes and Lauren thought she caught a hint of a smile before the worry took root once more.

"Levi was so brave while we treated him, Gina."

"Do you think he'll be okay to come home tonight?"

"We'll be sure and ask Dr. Sheldon." Lauren continued to chatter about how cute both little boys were and how the neighbor had told the staff how obedient the children usually were. She allowed her chatterbox mode to continue instead of stifling it midstream.

At first, Gina watched Lauren's face closely, as if she might be trying to detect any false note. But soon her expression relaxed. Lauren realized she was probably seeing a side of Gina Drake that few of her co-workers ever saw. Ordinarily, the respiratory therapist was calm and kind but strictly professional. She kept to herself. She never showed any vulnerability. Some of the less inhibited male members of the hospital staff claimed that Gina was a snob because she turned down all invitations to lunch, dinner, breaks, or breakfast. Lauren always quickly informed them that was simply because Gina had good taste.

"Lauren," Gina said at last, interrupting the quick-paced monologue. She held Lauren's gaze with her own and worried her full lower lip with her front teeth.

"Yes?" Lauren sat down on the stool so they were eye to eye.

Gina's mouth worked silently for several seconds. Her face flushed and her eyes watered again. "I'm scared."

"Of course you are, honey. Who wouldn't be?"

"I don't know what's happening to me."

"That's what we're going to try to find out." Lauren leaned closer. "Meanwhile, I want you to know that you do have a friend in town. I haven't been in Dogwood Springs very long, either, and I know how lonely it can get."

"Where are you from?"

"A beautiful place called Knolls. It's about an hour's drive east of here and sometimes I think I must have been crazy to move. Do you ever feel that way?"

An invisible strain of tension seemed to fill the room. "No. Never. At least not until this happened."

"Good. I'll give you my home phone number before you leave tonight and you can call me any time."

"Am I going to be allowed to leave?" Gina asked. "With my children?"

"We're going to do everything in our power to see that you do. In the meantime it won't do you or your children any good to worry about it."

Gina studied Lauren's eyes for several seconds, then some of her tension dissipated, as if she had run out of energy to continue.

"How about lunch Monday?" Lauren asked.

There was a flash of surprise and then a nod that seemed to open the gates to a flood of gratitude. Lauren had never before noticed what an expressive face Gina had.

"Can I go see my boys now?" she asked.

"Of course; then we'll get your x-rays. Let me get you back into the wheelchair."

❧ CHAPTER 6 ❧

Archer stepped into exam room eight to face Evan Webster. The skinny fifteen-year-old sat upright in the bed, his longish brown hair tangling into brown eyes that darted back and forth. He was obviously stressed to the edge of his endurance.

A middle-aged, balding man with hands rubbing together fretfully occupied a chair against the wall. He stood as Archer crossed the room.

"Are you the minister?"

"Yes, hello, I'm Archer Pierce. I'm the volunteer chaplain tonight."

The man took Archer's hand with both of his own in a firm grip, as if Archer had suddenly announced he was their sure salvation. "Norville Webster. Thank you for coming to see us, Reverend Pierce."

"Please call me Archer."

"Thank you." A heavy frown fell back over Norville's patrician features as he returned his attention to the teenager in the bed. "Meet Evan, my son." He spoke the words as if his son had just developed a terminal illness.

A reflection of pain crossed the teenager's face but disappeared into a fresh composite of high tension.

"Hello, Evan," Archer said gently. "I understand you've had a rough night."

The boy nodded, arms crossed tightly against his chest. "It's going to become the worst night ever as soon as my mom gets here." He gave Archer a sympathetic look. "Tell her you're a doctor or a tech or something. Don't tell her you're a preacher. She hates them."

"That's enough," Norville snapped. He turned to Archer. "Sorry. I tried to raise my son with more manners but lately it seems like he's following in his mother's footsteps."

Archer winced inwardly when he saw the look of surprise and raw pain in Evan's face. So there was open animosity between the estranged parents and they used their son as a weapon.

"Lucy and I are divorced," Norville said. "She has custody, except for those rare occasions when she can't find an excuse to keep him from coming to my place on visitation weekends." The bitterness was evident in his voice as well as his words. "If he weren't so unhappy living with her—"

"Dad," Evan said quietly. "If you'd stop blaming Mom for everything and—"

"I'm not just blaming her, I'm—"

"Yes you are." The teenager leaned forward. "Why don't you give it up and get on with life? I mean, it's over." His voice gentled. "She isn't coming back."

"Just because your mother decided it was over—"

"Hold it." Archer held his hands in a T, calling time out. "Accusations won't do us any good at this point. We need to focus on how to improve this situation for the future."

"I don't think that's going to happen," Evan said.

This time it was Norville who took the hit. "See what I mean?" Norville asked Archer. "It's my weekend to keep him and no sooner does he get to my place than he gulps his dinner and darts out of the house like I'm contagious. Then he comes back later, zoned out of his brain on drugs looking to me for answers." He slumped back into his chair. "And I don't have any."

There was only one answer to all of the pain Archer saw and felt in this room. If these were members of his congregation he would know exactly what to say. But he'd been told repeatedly not to proselytize at the hospital. He felt like a tethered mule.

Still, he needed to say something, if for no other reason than to allow them time out from their own battle of words. "The first thing to realize," he said, "is that you're not alone. Drug use in all age groups has permeated the country— probably the world. Evan, I think the experience you had tonight might have given you a taste of the danger."

Evan nodded. "I know better than to take anything from anyone."

"You and your parents are welcome to attend the class I teach on Tuesday nights. We have some pretty open discussions about drug use and abuse."

"I'll go with you, Evan," Norville said. "I'll do anything it takes to keep this from happening again."

"Dad, I'm not doing this again, okay? I made a mistake. I didn't intentionally drop speed."

The exam room door swung open. A tall, slender woman with short brown hair and angry eyes stormed into the room.

Norville glared at her.

The woman gave Archer a quick look of curiosity then shut the door behind her.

"Mom, don't blow your top," Evan said. "The doctor says I need to stay calm."

"I know what the doctor says." Her voice was husky and slightly hoarse, her words clipped. "I just finished talking to him." She leveled a chilling glare at her ex-husband. "I should have known you weren't even capable of keeping a fifteen-year-old boy out of trouble for a single night."

Norville returned glare for glare. "I bet you'll love having a son with a criminal record."

"Dad, I'm not going to have a criminal—"

"So what happened?" Evan's mother crossed

her arms in front of her. Archer saw that her hands were shaking as she dug her nails a little too sharply into the flesh of her arms, as if she was using the sting of pain to keep her emotions under control.

He reached a hand toward her in concern. "Ma'am, let me get you a seat."

"What did you take?" She stepped to her son's bedside, ignoring Archer.

Evan rolled his eyes. "A couple of pills, okay? I thought they were probably analgesics laced with caffeine."

"The doctor said you tested positive for methamphetamine."

"I didn't know that when I took them."

"Why did you take them if you didn't even know what they were?"

Evan's jaw muscles clenched and unclenched as he stared hard at the wall. "I just wanted things to be different."

"Different from what? You're out of school so you don't have any stress. You don't even have a job for the summer. So what do you have to get away from?"

"It isn't easy being a rope in a tug-of-war."

"You've been listening to your father again."

"Stop it, Lucy," Norville said. "None of that's going to do any good right now."

Lucy pivoted toward her ex-husband and Archer saw from the play of light across her face that her eyes were filling with tears. A flush crept up her neck. "Maybe you should give it a try sometime. It's called discipline. All *you* ever do is try to undermine my authority and win some popularity contest with Evan."

"I don't try to undermine anyone's authority, I just try to give him a little attention when he's with me. That happens seldom enough these days."

Archer stepped forward. "Mr. and Mrs. Webster, Evan is still experiencing physical difficulties from the drug and—"

"My name is not Mrs. Webster." Lucy glared at him. "Who are you, anyway?"

"I'm sorry I didn't introduce myself sooner. My name is Archer Pierce. I'm a volunteer—"

"He's a counselor," Norville said quickly. "He's a volunteer counselor for the hospital. I requested the visit."

"A shrink?" she demanded.

"No ma'am," Archer said, "I'm acting chaplain tonight." He ignored the expression of distress that crossed Norville's face. He wasn't about to lie to this woman. "I know enough about Evan's case to realize he needs to calm—"

"You're a *preacher?*"

"I'm a pastor here in Dogwood Springs." Archer kept his voice gentle but firm and he watched the monitor with growing concern.

"My son doesn't need a preacher," Lucy said.

"He needs to calm down," Archer said.

"How old are you?" she asked.

"My age is none of your concern. Your son is."

"Do you have any children?"

Archer completely understood Norville's hostility toward this woman. Archer had been in her presence for what? Sixty seconds? He already had to force himself to remain calm. What must Evan be feeling?

"Are you even *married?*" Lucy placed her hands on her hips.

"Your son's heart rate is increasing."

Lucy spun on Norville. "Trust you to drag someone like him into the middle of this mess!"

Evan raised his hands to his ears. "Stop it."

Norville stepped between her and the bed. "You're making things worse."

"Stop it!" Evan snapped.

His mother ignored him. "Oh, that's right, it's always my fault. That's because you're not man enough—"

"Shut up!" Evan shouted the words. "Everybody get out of here and leave me alone!" His face had reddened and tears filled his eyes. His rhythm gyrated across the monitor. "I can't take any more of this. Doctor? Where's the doctor? I've got to get out of here." He reached for the IV site and grasped it as if he would pull it out.

Archer and Norville converged on him in tandem and Norville grabbed his arm. "No son. Don't."

"Leave me alone." Evan tried to jerk away.

Norville held steady. "Evan. Stop. I'm sorry. Calm down and lie back. I'll get the doctor. It's going to be okay. I need to control my temper. I promise I'll try harder."

Evan did not look convinced. "All I ever hear is fight, fight, fight. You can't even stop when my life might depend on it. You don't care about me at all. You're too busy hating each other. What if I *do* become a drug addict? What if I *do* go out and kill myself? You would love it. That would just give you more to fight about."

Evan looked at his shocked mother and the lines of his face drew down until they mimicked his father's sad expression. "Get out."

Archer was reaching for the door to call for assistance when it swung open and Grant stepped inside followed by Muriel. The doctor appeared calm and unhurried, his expression serene, even friendly, with no indication that he'd heard any-thing out of the ordinary through the walls of the exam room.

"Folks, we've had a slight change of plans. The police are here to take Evan's statement." His deep voice remained unperturbed as he indicated Norville and Lucy. "If you would like, feel free to continue your discussion in one of our hospital's private conference rooms." He gave Archer an understanding glance and stepped back to allow the parents to file out of the room.

Norville hesitated. The worry lines of his face continued a silent argument.

Lucy remained standing beside her son's bed. "I'll stay, if you don't mind."

"I mind." Evan turned his back to her and pulled his arm, at last, from his father's grasp. "I don't want either of you in here."

"If you'll forgive me," Grant said, "our ER has a one-visitor policy. I think it's best for our patient if we abide by it. Muriel will stay with him and make sure he's safe." His voice was sympathetic but firm. Archer felt a wash of relief as the embittered exes relented and grudgingly filed from the exam room. He also felt a heavy sadness for this broken family as he followed the parents out the door, listening to the low-voiced sniper fire continue between them.

Archer did not attempt to rejoin the conversation. His presence had already caused enough disruption here tonight.

Grant checked Evan's vitals and waited with his hand on Evan's shoulder, the bell of his stethoscope pressed against the bony chest, the heart rate stabilized. As he left Muriel with the boy, he reminded himself to never do anything like that to his own children. He would rather remain single for the rest of his life than see that expression of frustrated pain and anger cross Brooke's or Beau's face. Of course, Brooke had a very expressive face and she used it to great advantage.

He caught sight of Archer Pierce trudging along the hallway, hands in the pockets of his Dockers, head bowed—whether in deep thought, or prayer, or despondency Grant couldn't tell. He was exactly as Lauren had described him—a friendly, thoughtful young man with an air of maturity that belied his age. Lauren had said he was thirty-three. She had said a lot of things about him. All good. But even if he *was* mature and confident, that headlong attack from Evan's mother couldn't have been comfortable.

"Thanks for stepping in to help, Archer," Grant said as he caught up with the young minister.

"You're welcome."

"I trust you've had an interesting evening so far."

Archer walked with him toward the central station. "Very. Is Evan going to be okay?"

"He'll be fine unless he decides he still hates his life and takes permanent steps to make his parents pay for their behavior."

"I'd never before considered how much spiritual suffering joins forces with physical suffering to attack a patient when he's down."

Grant nodded. "That is why it was such a good idea for you to be here. Do you plan to talk to the Websters again?"

"I'll find Norville later and let him know I'm available if he needs to talk."

"Good. Are you ready to tackle another case?" Grant asked.

Archer looked at him hopefully. "Gina Drake?"

Grant couldn't prevent a wry smile. The man was either very brave or an incredible glutton for punishment. Or maybe he was doing exactly what God had called him to . . . did people actually do that anymore? "Lauren convinced her to talk to you."

"She did?"

"She seems to think all you have to do is snap your fingers to make all the evil and pain in the world disappear. Wish I had that talent."

Archer chuckled. It was a relaxing sound. "We're talking about Lauren McCaffrey? The Lauren who beats me in basketball and volleyball and earlier this spring had to cut a fishhook out of my arm in the middle of a fishing tournament?"

Grant leaned closer and lowered his voice. "The one who thinks you could almost walk on water." He stopped and cleared his throat. Grant had learned quickly that Lauren was a talker and that she often revealed more about herself than she realized. Archer probably had no idea she had a crush on him. Grant had heard other staff members discussing it, though, so Archer was probably the only one who hadn't caught the undercurrent.

"She knows better," Archer said with a fond

smile. "She saw me nearly drown at church camp twenty years ago. She and her brothers dragged me out and pumped the lake out of my lungs."

Grant was intrigued. "You've known Lauren for twenty years?"

"Actually, for twenty-five. Church camp, rival schools, that kind of thing. Lauren and her brothers and sisters were deacon's kids in a sister church in Knolls, so since my dad was our church pastor, we were thrown together a lot through the years. I was good friends with her younger brothers and she tolerated me back when I had a huge crush on her."

Grant grinned and shook his head. Small towns. "Anyway," he said, "I can't tell you how much it means for you to be here. These people need to know they count with someone and sometimes we docs get so busy we can't afford to take the time to give them as much reassurance as they need. That's where you come in. Think of it as an interactive sermon."

"Interactive, huh? I like that." Archer bent down for a quick drink at the water fountain. "I think this really was a first offense with Evan."

"I hope," Grant said. "Forgive my cynicism."

"You don't sound like a cynic to me. You sound like a man with common sense. Have the tests come back on Mrs. Piedmont?"

"Yes, and they don't show anything significant." Grant paused. "Still, I'm concerned that she does have underlying heart pain. I've spoken with her family doc and he says she can go home as long as she sees him Monday."

"That'll make her happy. I'd volunteer to take her but I'd have to wrestle her children for the privilege."

"I hear she goes to your church."

"Yes. I've known her all my life. Wonderful lady." Archer paused and glanced at Grant. "She's good at collecting information, too. She already knows a lot about you. While I was in her room earlier, she told me about your wife's passing. I hated to hear that."

Grant winced involuntarily. It still hurt after two years.

Archer's intense gaze flickered momentarily. "I'm sorry."

Grant nodded to Lester, the tech, who was escorting a patient toward the exit. When they were out of earshot, he continued. "You'd think a man would have recovered from his wife's death after two years."

"Actually, my father always told me to give someone at least three years to grieve the death of a spouse," Archer said. "How do your kids feel about the move to Dogwood Springs?"

"My son, Beau, doesn't seem to mind."

"It's a big change from St. Louis."

"According to my daughter, Brooke, we might as well have moved to Jupiter."

"We'd love to have your whole family visit our church, if that isn't proselytizing." He smiled at Grant.

Grant hesitated. "I'd like the kids to go."

"We have an active youth group, especially since Lauren arrived. She's great with the kids."

"I think they would like that," Grant said.

"And how about you?"

Grant didn't answer. He was glad when Archer didn't push the matter. They walked toward the central desk, where two police officers in black uniforms leaned against the waist-high counter exchanging casual, friendly banter with Becky. The secretary worked the computer keyboard and kept up with their conversation without missing a stroke. The men straightened when Grant and Archer approached.

"Tony, good to see you, bud." Archer stepped forward to shake hands and punch the shoulder of the senior officer. He turned to Grant. "I graduated from high school with this guy. He was valedictorian."

"Archer, don't you ever sleep?" Tony asked.

"I do that at my desk at work," Archer joked. "Sometimes it shows in my sermons. Not that you'd notice, since you're hardly ever at services. When are you going to earn enough seniority that you don't have to work every Sunday?"

Tony grinned and shrugged. "When your

sermons start sinking in and the crime rate goes down. So far, you're not making much headway. Is our patient ready for questioning?"

"Yes," Grant said, "but be gentle with the kid. He's suffered enough."

The two officers nodded and sauntered toward exam room eight. They'd obviously been here before and knew the layout.

"I do want to talk with Gina," Archer said. "When can I see her?"

"Don't get your hopes up," Grant warned. "She may not say much but I think she's particularly afraid of our social worker. She isn't willing to discuss anything at this point." He stepped over to the chart rack and pulled out a clipboard. "Rose Pascal went in to speak with her once already and didn't get a very good response. Unfortunately, you're not going to have time to prepare or talk to her before you're thrown into the fray."

"What fray?"

"There's an IIS therapist driving down from Branson. They want to have a wraparound meeting tonight, if—"

"Uh, wait, you've lost me. Sorry I'm so green. Apparently my daddy didn't teach me *everything* I needed to know about pastoring. What is an IIS therapist and what is a wraparound meeting?"

At that moment the door opened to exam room four and Lauren stepped out. "Good, you're both free. I've got Gina's feet bandaged and I'm ready to put her in the wheelchair for a trip to the conference room. Rose Pascal and Natalie Frasier are already in there with Agnes Walker, Gina's next-door neighbor. We have an aide watching the children for us during the meeting. Can you come now?"

"We'll be right in," Grant told her.

She retreated and closed the door.

"Wraparound meeting?" Archer asked.

"It's a term we use when dealing with child protection." Grant reached for a pad of paper and pulled an ink pen out of the pocket of his lab coat. "Ideally, when a family's in crisis the social workers assigned to their case like to have a meeting with everyone connected to that family so they can brainstorm the best ways to provide support when help is needed."

"That sounds like a good idea."

"Gina claims no family but her children. She's fairly new in town, so she hasn't had time to make friends. And except for the employment physical she had before she came to work here, I'm the only physician who's seen her since she arrived. Lauren has chosen to take an active role. Thanks for your offer to help."

"You're welcome. What is an IIS therapist?"

"IIS stands for Intensive in-Home Service. The therapist does exactly what her title suggests. She's an employee of the state who goes into the home of the family in crisis to research ways to improve the family relationship. She does exhaustive counseling to help the family learn to cope with their crisis so that they have a better chance of staying together."

Gina's exam room door opened once more and Lauren guided her out in a wheelchair. Gina's coppery eyes had darkened to aged bronze and were wide with fear. Her hands gripped the arms of the wheelchair so tightly that the veins stood out in stark relief against the whiteness of her skin.

"We're ready," Lauren said. "Are you guys coming?"

"We're right behind you," Grant said.

❦ CHAPTER 7 ❦

Lauren was wheeling Gina into the small conference room when nausea suddenly struck again, this time with stomach cramps. As she emitted a soft moan, she squeezed the handles of the wheelchair and gritted her teeth to keep from doubling over.

Gina turned to look up at her. "Lauren?"

All Lauren could do was nod, taking a deep breath in through her nose, out through her mouth, using the old trick she often suggested to patients.

She couldn't get sick now, had to get through this meeting. Gina needed her support.

Dr. Sheldon stepped up behind her and touched her elbow. "Is something wrong?"

Lauren shook her head, took another practiced breath and felt a flash of perspiration bead her face. She had to concentrate.

Archer joined them. "Lauren, you don't look so great."

She rolled her eyes and nodded. Talk about your sensitive men. She would never forgive herself if she created a spectacle by rushing from the room, leaving poor Gina feeling isolated. Of course, it probably wouldn't help things if she lost her dinner in the middle of the conference, either.

With a final deep breath, Lauren settled Gina at the table then turned to find Dr. Sheldon pulling a chair out for her. She thanked him and sank down.

He leaned closer until she caught a faint scent of aftershave that smelled like crushed citrus leaves. "Pardon me for being blunt but are you sure you'll be okay?"

"I need to help Gina through this meeting."

"Anything I can do?"

"Phenergan would be nice but there's no time."

He nodded. "I'll get you some as soon as this is over." He excused himself and stepped around to sit at Gina's other side.

Rose Pascal entered at her usual brisk pace, carrying an armload of cold sodas from the machine in the ER waiting room. Lauren accepted one gratefully and held it to her face for a moment, ignoring the curious glances she received. Its bracing coolness gave some relief. She popped the top and took several hesitant sips. It stayed down. She leaned back in her chair. Maybe this would just go away again.

Along with Dr. Sheldon and Archer Pierce, who both sat to Gina's right, the meeting participants consisted of Gina's neighbor, Agnes Walker; the hospital social worker, Rose Pascal; and the IIS therapist, whom Rose introduced as Natalie Frasier. The therapist was a tall young woman who was so slender she appeared to be all sharp angles. She was probably in her late twenties or early thirties, with a serious, earnest expression on her long face. Several times Lauren noticed her casting Gina curious, compassionate glances.

There was no evidence of the friendly chatter and jokes that often accompanied conferences in this room but Lauren had been to a wraparound meeting before; they were often tense.

Rose chatted quietly with Natalie, who was seated at the far end of the table with her note pad and ink pen. Gina stared at the table without acknowledging anybody.

As soon as everyone settled, Rose called the meeting to order, made introductions, and gave a brief overview of Gina's predicament. Rose had short gray-blond hair and gentle gray eyes with laugh lines radiating from them; her voice had a decided Ozark accent-heavy on the r's.

As the hospital social worker spoke, Gina's tension seemed to radiate across the room. She clasped her hands together on the table. Her fingertips whitened. Lauren stole a quick look at her face and saw her full lips drawn into a tight line.

"Gina, I'm not gonna bite," Rose said. "We're havin' this meeting to find out how we can help your family stay together while we keep your children safe."

Gina nodded without looking up.

At Rose's request, Dr. Sheldon quoted Gina's test results. They revealed nothing helpful. Neurologically she was normal. She tested negative for drugs and her chemical levels were comparable to the normal numbers she'd had on her employment physical.

"What about blood sugar?" Gina asked softly, still staring at her hands clasped at the table.

"Eighty," Grant replied.

Gina issued a soft sigh and shook her head. "Normal?"

Lauren empathized. If they'd discovered a blood sugar problem they would have something with which to work.

"I want to emphasize one thing." Dr. Sheldon closed the folder. "I observed Gina interacting with her children when she was reunited with them tonight. They were happy and talkative, with very trusting, loving dispositions. Both children appear well cared for and well behaved."

"They are very sweet children. I visited with them for a little bit." Rose leaned forward. "Gina, don't you remember anything about tonight's episode?"

"I already spoke with Dr. Sheldon about this." Gina's voice was unemotional, as if she was keeping herself under tight control. "I worked overtime today and Levi and Cody ate a late-afternoon snack at child care, so they didn't want dinner when we got home. I was tired and I rested on the sofa in the living room. That is the last clear recollection I have until I realized I was sitting on the merry-go-round at Levi's elementary school, several blocks from our house." Her voice wavered.

"It's okay, Gina," Rose said softly. "Take your time."

"My feet were already injured at that time and I don't know how. All I have is a vague memory of fear as I searched for my children."

"Panic attack, perhaps?" Rose suggested. "I know you're still kind of new here and perhaps your concern for your children's well-being—"

"I've moved before and never experienced panic attacks." There was a note of defensiveness in Gina's voice.

"But I got the impression from Dr. Sheldon and your boys that this kind of thing's happened before," Rose said.

Gina met her gaze, then looked at Dr. Sheldon. She swallowed hard and nodded.

"Do you remember ever having any kind of warning signs?" Dr. Sheldon asked.

Gina sighed and shook her head.

Rose picked up her pen and jotted something in her notes, then laid her pen down again. "Gina, how do you feel about an overnight guest?"

Gina looked up again, obviously startled. "Overnight? You mean—"

"I mean that in order to keep the same thing from happening again, we will need to either request that the court have Levi and Cody temporarily removed from the home on an emergency basis—"

Gina gasped and grabbed the table edge as she came part way out of her chair. "No! You can't—"

"We don't want that either," Rose said quickly. "Another option is for Natalie to stay with you and your children until we can set up somethin' else." She gestured to the IIS therapist, who had observed the interaction in silence from her end of the table.

The young woman watched Gina with an expression of gentle concern. "I'd be glad to stay with you tonight to make sure the children will be okay if you have another episode." She had a deep voice, husky but soft.

Lauren's stomach cramped suddenly. She picked up her soda and took another sip, trying once more to will the nausea away.

"This would also give you some time for your feet to heal," Rose continued. "Ordinarily, we'd try to bring another adult family member into the picture but you don't have family, right?"

"None." Gina's reply came a little too quickly.

Lauren's nausea grew worse. Her mouth started to water. She pressed the can against her temples and neck, taking several quick breaths. Not now.

"Later we'll try to set up an emergency plan with Mrs. Walker." Natalie gestured to Gina's next-door neighbor, Agnes Walker, who had brought the children in tonight. "She's willing to be on call in case you or the children need her. We'll set up appointments with your physician for a complete physical work-up. We will also require you to have a psychological screening."

"A psychological exam? You want me to go to a psychiatrist?"

None of Lauren's attempts to stave off the nausea worked this time. The cramps grew worse and her stomach heaved. Gina had just turned to her, eyes filling with tears, with one hand reaching out to her when Lauren had to push back from the table. She covered her mouth with her hand and ran from the room.

Grant looked up in alarm as Lauren rushed out. Why hadn't he ordered the nausea med before the meeting?

"Is Lauren going to be okay?" Rose asked.

"I'll check on her in a minute," he assured her. He turned his attention to their patient, whose facade of control had slipped away, leaving her teary-eyed and shaky, especially after Lauren's abrupt departure. "Gina, you need to understand that we are only trying to do what's best for you and your children. Rose and Natalie are attempting to create a support network for you so that—"

"You're the ones who don't understand." Gina's voice wobbled. She swallowed hard and took a breath. Before she spoke, she gave Rose a look of entreaty. "Before suggesting anything else you threatened to take my children away from me."

"What we're talking about is providing a safety net for your children should you have another episode like tonight's," Rose said.

Gina bit her lower lip and looked back down at the table. "By threatening to take my children, you're forcing me to do whatever you say. You're holding me hostage."

"I'm sorry if it sounded that way."

"I don't like the idea of some stranger coming into my house and telling me how to take care of my children."

"I understand that," Rose said. "I'm a single mother myself. Would it help you to know that four people have already volunteered to be on call over the next few weeks in case you run into a crisis?"

Gina's lips parted in surprise. She looked around at the others in the room.

"We will arrange a schedule so there will always be someone available," Natalie said. "Dr. Sheldon has given us his numbers for both office and home. The same with Archer Pierce." She gestured toward Agnes Walker. "Your neighbor will step in whenever you need her. Lauren McCaffrey was the first one tonight to ask if she could be a part of the team. I will be available for you twenty-four/seven and I'll be spending a lot of time with you in these next few weeks. You have some friends who want to be there for you, Gina. You're not nearly as alone as you think you are."

Slowly, Gina met Rose's gaze again and then she looked at Natalie. She blinked back tears and her chin trembled. "Okay," she said quietly. "Tell me what I need to do."

The ER was peaceful at last. Grant completed his last chart, placed it on top of the stack, and walked down the short, broad hallway to the exam room where Lauren rested. At her insistence, he had left the door ajar earlier so she could hear what was going on in case they got busy.

He knocked, then at her soft reply he pushed the door open and stuck his head inside. "How are you feeling?"

She started to sit up. "Better. The shot worked wonders. Do you need me?"

"Stay put. Muriel has everything under control."

She sighed in obvious relief. "Thanks. What-ever this virus is, it's nasty. I don't understand—I had my annual flu shot."

"And we know how few viruses those cover." He walked to the sink, dampened some paper towels, then folded them and placed them on her pale forehead.

Her clear green eyes closed and her face relaxed. "Thanks, Dr. Sheldon. You'd make a good nurse. Has Gina left yet?"

"Yes. Natalie took her and her boys home about thirty minutes ago. Gina said to tell you thanks."

Lauren gave him a sleepy grimace. "I aban-doned her."

"She understood. She was concerned about you. Mrs. Piedmont went home, too," he said softly.

Lauren's face relaxed further and her lips parted as her breathing deepened. Good. The medicine would help her sleep. Maybe she would feel better when she woke up.

Grant didn't leave immediately but stood watching her in silence for a few seconds. With her blond hair loose and splayed out across the pillow and her face relaxed, she could almost pass for a teenager. But she had the heart of a seasoned nurse. He had known last night, the first time he worked with her, that they would make a good team.

It still surprised him how many times she

anticipated his orders and how quickly she met the needs of the patients. She did not grow cranky or irritable even when the volume picked up. He appreciated her gift of gab, especially since she always seemed to say the right thing to put the patients at ease.

He shut the door behind him as he left to check on Evan Webster. Lauren had somehow convinced the teenager's parents to take their argument to a private conference room. Evan probably wished they'd disappear for good. Poor kid.

Grant slipped into exam room eight, managing not to wake its occupant. The monitor continued to beep, its reassuring screen showing a normal sinus rhythm. Wisps of brown hair lay across Evan's forehead in damp tendrils, eyelashes fanning above his cheeks. All the lines of anxiety had disappeared with slumber until only the appearance of childhood innocence remained.

There had been so many times when Grant wanted desperately to lift the cares of the world from the shoulders of these young ones. He wanted to bar the doors and protect them from the anger and bitterness of mismanaged parenting and divorce and the seduction of the dark side of life. But what made him think he could help? Without Annette's loving guidance he didn't even know how to help Brooke and Beau heal from their grief.

A slight sound from the bed drew his gaze back

to Evan's face. The boy's eyes were open and blinking sleepily. He yawned, stretched his arms, and caught sight of Grant.

"I'm sorry," Grant said. "I didn't mean to wake you."

Evan looked around the room cautiously. When he saw no one had accompanied Grant the tension eased from his face. "So, you going to spring me now?"

Grant stepped over to the bed. "Not yet. All your vitals look good but I don't want to take any chances with you."

Evan nodded and gave him a tentative smile. It transformed his face. The kid had dimples and a cleft chin and sparkling brown eyes.

"I hope you told them where you got the speed."

"I told them." The smile disappeared. "Peregrine. I think it's some stupid street name. He's this guy who cruises the streets with high-school kids on Friday and Saturday nights. He's got to be the pusher."

"He's a friend of yours?"

Evan shook his head. "No way."

"I thought you said your friend gave you the pills."

"Peregrine gave them to my friend in the first place. Passed them out free. Isn't that what a pusher does to get people hooked?"

Grant nodded. "It's a typical sales tactic all

across America, only this kind is deadly. Did you give the police your friend's name?"

"Yes." Evan sighed. "Now my friends won't have anything to do with me. They barely put up with me as it is."

"Why is that?"

"I'm a grade ahead of all my old classmates." He shrugged. "It gets lonely sometimes. A guy's got to have somebody to hang out with."

Grant refrained from saying that the wrong friends can be worse than having no friends.

"I guess my parents think I'm a drug addict."

"I doubt it. They got a scare tonight."

"They hate each other."

"You're not the object of their hatred."

"Tell *them* that."

"I think they know it. They need to realize you're taking the brunt of their antagonism."

Evan closed his eyes and his lids fluttered as if he was holding back tears. "What am I supposed to do about it? I'm not even old enough to drive, so it isn't like I can get out of the house. When I'm at Mom's all she can do is whine about my uptight dad. When I'm at Dad's he's always pumping me for information about the guy Mom's dating."

"I hope they realize why you took those pills tonight."

Evan blinked up at him. "Why is that?"

"You already told your father. You're struggling

with the divorce and your parents' hostility. I want to make sure you don't change your mind about taking more pills when the adults aren't around. That's what I did."

Evan's gaze focused. "You?"

"Illegal drugs existed when I was in high school, too," Grant said dryly.

Evan frowned and rose up on his elbows. "What happened? Did you get hooked?"

"I did."

Evan's eyes widened and he sat up. "Really?"

"Really. It was hard to break the hold drugs had on me. I wouldn't want you to go through that." While Evan was sitting up, Grant checked his vitals, listened to his heart and breathing. He was satisfied with the boy's progress. Soon he could go home—wherever that might be tonight.

When Grant walked out of the room he was surprised to find Archer standing there, arms crossed over his broad chest, leaning against the wall. They nodded to each other and Archer pushed away from the wall to walk beside Grant. The only sounds they heard were the muffled beeps of Evan's monitor and the click of computer keys down the hallway at the central desk—and Archer's squeaky rubber-soled shoes. For this moment it was peaceful.

"I heard what you told Evan," Archer said.

Grant looked at him. "There's not much privacy in a small-town ER."

"I was just going in to check on him myself. It took a lot of guts to tell him what you did. You accomplished more in there talking to that kid for a few minutes than I did with the whole family earlier. I'm sorry I didn't do better."

Grant slowed his steps. "Were your parents divorced?"

Archer blinked. "My parents? No. I can't imagine anyone with a happier marriage."

Grant lowered his voice. "Were you ever addicted to drugs?"

"No."

"I was on both counts."

"Then apparently that's what it took for you to reach Evan."

"Being a drug addict and the product of a broken home isn't anything to be proud of."

"Not until you bare your underbelly and risk your reputation just to help a hurting kid," Archer said. "That changes everything."

Grant shook his head, haunted by old frustrations as he thought about Evan. "Nothing ever really changes. Kids still get beaten up by their own parents and allow themselves to be tricked into believing lies."

"And then along comes someone like you, who opens his heart to all those people who've been caught by the lie."

Grant stopped walking and turned to take a closer look at Archer Pierce, at the direct, blue-eyed gaze filled with a gleam of . . . what? Admiration?

"I saw how patient you were with Cecile Piedmont and how gentle you were with Gina Drake," Archer said. "I saw the way you handled the Websters without further upsetting Evan."

"I'm the doctor in this ER. That sometimes gives me an aura of authority."

"I wish I knew how you did it. My father has always had a calming presence like that."

Grant frowned at the younger man. Didn't he realize the influence he had? "That's how it works. Heart to heart. One person at a time. You see their pain and you identify. And you listen. That's the big trick." Grant shrugged and looked away. He'd shared more than he had intended. "I worked in a busy ER in St. Louis. It felt like an assembly line. They expected a doctor to listen to his patients for sixty seconds and be able to diagnose. But I've found over the years that I like to give them more than a minute. It took some hard lessons before I learned."

A slow smile spread across Archer's face. "Ever thought about being a pastor?"

The question startled Grant. "Never." Enough sharing for one day. "Pastoring's your job."

"I checked on Lauren. She's fast asleep," Archer said.

Grant felt a twinge of something when he thought of Lauren McCaffrey. Her soft friendly voice, her gentleness with Levi, her admiration for Archer all touched him. That was unusual. He felt almost guilty, as if his admiration for a beautiful woman was something sinful.

"The drug I gave made her groggy," he told Archer. "Why don't you go home and rest while you can? If we need you we can call you back in. There's no predicting what could happen here between now and morning."

❧ CHAPTER 8 ❧

Archer stepped through the front door of the beautifully decorated but very lonely parsonage and sank into the first available chair. Enough light came through the window from the street to outline the living room without switching on a lamp. He wanted to rest in the silence for a moment.

Jessica had decorated this room only a few weeks before she left on tour with a musical group from Branson. Archer felt the impact of her joyful personality every time he entered his home. He still missed her.

"Oh Lord, where from here?" he whispered into the silence. It had been his heart's cry for the past month—ever since Jessica tearfully returned the engagement ring. That was the day all his plans for the future took a new twist. He was still trying to sort his life into some kind of logical order.

At thirty-three he was young to be the pastor of such a rapidly growing church, especially as a single man. He could take no credit for it. His father had been called to the ministry of Dogwood Springs Baptist Church thirty-four years ago, before Archer was born. This had always been home. When Dad retired last year, Archer was completing an interim position as a youth pastor in Branson and was falling in love with the most talented singer—and the most beautiful woman—in a town filled with talented musicians.

It had seemed a simple choice at the time to take the position as pastor of the church family he had known all his life and to ask Jessica to marry him and serve with him.

Now he wished he'd been more cautious before committing to either. What had made him think he could compete with the calling God had given Jessica? How could he have expected her to settle for the life of a small-town pastor's wife when the stage beckoned for the special message she'd been chosen to give?

The problem was that the breakup had not only devastated him but it had also put him in an uncomfortable position. His church—which had always been known for its somewhat legalistic sense of order—had called him as pastor with the implicit understanding that he would soon be a married man and that his wife would serve with him. Many of them wouldn't have agreed even to that arrangement if he hadn't been one of their own.

Archer also knew that some of the older, more traditional members would have preferred an older leader. Only a few days after his breakup with Jessica, word had spread and he'd begun to hear complaints. Or maybe he'd just begun to listen to them.

He was putting in more hours than ever before, trying to attend everything—committee meetings, youth events, ball games at the high school. He tried to be available for the members of his church every day of the week. If God had called him to Dogwood Springs Baptist, then God would show him how he would be used.

To the surprise of many of the older members, the church was growing. Sunday school classes were becoming overcrowded. During the last Wednesday night business meeting a heated discussion had erupted between the old-timers and the newcomers about whether or not they should begin holding two services on Sunday mornings. If they waited much longer, the decision would be taken out of their hands; the auditorium was often so packed they had to bring in extra chairs from the classrooms.

Sadly, some of the longtime members were even complaining about the growth. Wednesday night Bible study had become so popular they'd moved the meetings from the classroom downstairs to the main auditorium. Some worried about the extra money needed to heat the auditorium comfortably for another service.

Those worriers were the same people—thankfully, few in number—who complained because the personnel committee was presently searching for a part-time youth director to take some of the load from Archer's shoulders. He had to carry it all until they found someone. But as the deacons kept saying, he was getting paid for the effort. Couldn't let those devoted people down.

He was making his way through the darkness to bed when the telephone rang. He frowned and turned on the light, then glanced at the shadowed numbers of the clock on the fireplace mantel. Tonight had been so packed with action he couldn't believe it was only eleven. It wasn't until he caught sight of the calendar on the wall beside the phone that he remembered the significance of this day. Jessica should have arrived home from her tour.

His hopes flared. He grabbed the phone. "Hello?"

"Yes, is this Reverend Archer Pierce?" It was a man.

Of course it wouldn't be Jessica. He should have known. Still, the disappointment stung. It took Archer a few seconds to recover and place the voice. "Yes. Norville? Is Evan okay?"

"He was fine when I left the hospital." Norville blew a sigh over the telephone. "His mother decided I was a bad influence on him and she's taking him home with her. The poor kid decided to keep the peace and do what she says, even though this is my weekend to have him." There was a pause. "I . . . I just wanted to apologize again for all that mess tonight."

Archer sat down again. "You don't have to apologize. I wish I could have been more help to you."

"Maybe you can. I told Dr. Sheldon I would like counseling. That hasn't changed. Evan's mother would never take him." The sharpness of his words shot through the receiver. "But she doesn't control every single minute of his life. Not if I have anything to say about it. I have visitation rights every other weekend . . ."

The unhappy voice continued to float through the receiver in a wave. Archer leaned back and listened. The poor guy probably just needed to talk.

". . . can't see past the hood of your car . . . !"

". . . shouldn't have a license to drive more'n a tractor . . ."

Angry words thrust through the darkness until the velocity behind them pounded Lauren from her sleep. She opened her eyes, shook her head, and sat up. Her vision cleared. Light filtered through the crack between door and jamb from a brightly illuminated hallway outside. She was still in the ER.

And still on duty! With a gasp, she swung her legs over the side of the exam bed then paused to make sure the nausea didn't hit again.

"None of your family's ever been worth shootin' . . ."

". . . cows and pigs are smarter than . . ."

For a moment Lauren listened with dismay to the growling of two angry old coots somewhere beyond the door but then Dr. Sheldon spoke with calm authority. They fell silent.

Lauren flipped on the light and turned the water on in the sink. After a quick splash at her face, she grabbed a paper towel and dabbed at her mouth. She'd need a mask to protect the grumpy patients from influenza germs—if this was, indeed, the flu. She grabbed a mask from the supply room next door and tied it over her face as she stepped along the hallway toward the zone of conflict.

Muriel Stark stood with her hands on her hips in a pose of formidable threat at the entrance to exam room two. Lauren suppressed a giggle. The last time she'd seen her coworker bare her teeth like that was when some drunks had stumbled into the ER one Saturday night, one with an obviously broken nose and a glare in his eyes that told everyone within striking distance that he wasn't ready to shut up and go home. Muriel had called the police and told the drunk that if he caused any more trouble in her exam room he'd find his nose sewn to the wrong end of his body.

Muriel could be pretty convincing when she wanted to be—her bark was backed by an underbite and a substantial neck, which gave her a very slight bulldog appearance. But one look into the cozy warmth of her brown eyes had dispelled forever any doubts Lauren might have had about the woman's professional calling.

Lauren caught up with the athletic nurse at the central station. "Muriel? What's going on in there?"

The older woman turned and looked at Lauren's mask. Her eyes narrowed and her fists returned once more to her hips. "What are you doing up? You're sick. I can handle this."

"I'm feeling better. What's happening?"

Muriel rubbed her chin and shook her head. She pointed to exam room two, keeping her voice low. "Two neighboring farmers. From what I can make out, Old Brisco was following his neighbor, Scroggs"—she pointed to exam room three—"too closely from behind. Scroggs got blinded by the headlights in his rearview mirror and missed a sharp curve out in the hills east of town. Unfortunately, since Brisco was following too close, he joined Scroggs in his plunge off a hillside."

"Hurt badly?"

"Maybe some broken ribs on Brisco, a possible broken arm on Scroggs and he's got a lot of cuts and bruises. Obviously nothing got their vocal cords. They put two ambulances and two fire trucks out of commission for the hour it took to pull them out of the hollow."

Lauren went to the sink and washed her hands. "Which one do you want me to take?"

Muriel gave her a warning glare but Lauren grabbed one of the charts. "I'm feeling better and I'm still on duty." She glanced at the chart. "I'll take Brisco." Before Muriel could protest, Lauren strode into exam room two.

Lester, the tech, was busy picking glass out of Mr. Brisco's thinning gray hair, which was not an easy chore because Brisco wouldn't hold still. If he had broken ribs he didn't realize it.

"Man's a thief, to boot!" He grimaced and grabbed the right side of his chest. "He's been a thief all his life. His daddy was a thief—"

Lauren stepped forward. "Hello, Mr. Bris—"

A muttered expletive reached them from the next room, then, "You're the only thief in this county!"

Brisco grabbed the rail on the left side of his bed and raised a gowned leg, as if preparing to climb. Before Lauren could reach for him, he grunted and fell back. Lester grasped him by the shoulders and Lauren rushed to his side.

"Mr. Brisco, you could do further—"

"If he'd fix his fences every once in a while, instead of forcing his neighbors to put out all the time and money to keep them fixed, his harebrained bulls wouldn't keep knocking them down all the—"

"See?" came Scroggs's crackly bass from the next room. "I knew it! I knew it was you! Them sixteen new calves in your back pasture are half mine."

"Gentlemen." Dr. Sheldon's voice was deeper than Lauren had yet heard it. "The county courthouse can handle paternity suits. Our hospital is strictly for your physical problems. We need to attend to the injuries at hand and worry about old history when I know you're out of danger."

For the next few moments, while Dr. Sheldon directed treatment and Lauren limited her activities to noninvasive procedures due to continued fuzzy-headedness from the anti-nausea med, the men remained silent. Lauren knew it was too good to last.

"On top of all that," Brisco muttered a few moments later, while Lauren cleaned the cuts on his face, "his pigs stink up the whole countryside."

There came a grunt from the other room. "My pigs don't stink!"

Brisco gave Lauren a satisfied nod. "It's his pigs, all right. All the neighbors are noticing it. Smells like the stockyards."

"Smells like money, you mean," came the

retort. "Ever heard of that stuff? It's green. I guess you ain't got any, or you wouldn't be stealing my fertilizer at night."

Brisco's weathered face reddened in anger and he jerked away from Lauren's hand. "I'm not stealing your fertilizer, you foul-breathed, lazy bum."

"Gentlemen," Dr. Sheldon chided once more, "I don't want to have to get tough with you but the police station isn't far from here."

"I heard you, I heard you." Brisco rested his head against the pillow and allowed Lauren to complete her clean-up job.

It didn't take long for her to realize she wasn't feeling that great yet. After she completed her chore she went back to bed.

". . . has a right to choose. He's old enough to make his own decision about where he's going to live." Norville's voice wasn't filled with nearly as much anger now as it had been fifteen minutes ago. He was winding down.

"I'd be glad to speak with Evan if you feel it would help." Archer suppressed a yawn.

Norville allowed a short, airless silence. "Yes. I think that would be good if he can convince his mother to ease up on her stranglehold." There was another pause and then a sigh that sounded like relief. "I'm sorry for taking up so much of your time tonight, Archer. Maybe you're right. Maybe

I need to give it some more thought before I stir up any more trouble with that woman."

"How about a tentative appointment time for you to bring Evan in to see me?"

"I'd better wait on that. After tonight she might call for a new hearing to reduce my visitation time."

"If you have a chance to speak with Evan, why don't you ask him if he wants to meet with me? Meanwhile, I'll keep you in my prayers." Archer said a gentle good-night and disconnected. It was times like this that he wondered if it wasn't better to remain single and not risk the possible grief that came from a difficult marriage. But then he thought of his parents.

Good marriages were possible with the right foundation and proper nurturing. Dad had spent a lot of quality time with his family and had often included them in his ministry. Mom had been a stay-at-home mother who was the epitome of a pastor's wife. In spite of their busy schedules they reserved time to spend together every week, without children, without church. Their marriage had always been a priority for them.

Archer jotted a note to call Norville next week to see how he was doing. He hadn't realized, when he volunteered for the chaplain program, how much time he would be spending on follow-up care or how many more notes he would be accumulating.

He'd discovered years ago that if he wrote everything down in an organized notebook, life wouldn't be quite so hectic and he wouldn't be so likely to forget anything or anybody. Church members hated it when he forgot to visit. Unfortunately, he'd lost that organized notebook months ago and he'd regressed to an old sloppy habit of placing sticky notes wherever he happened to be standing or sitting at the time. Now he could never find the notes he needed—at least not when he needed them.

Periodically, he got his exercise running madly through the house grabbing up colored notes like a kid on an Easter egg hunt and then struggling to place them in proper order.

It was getting late, so Archer tore off the square of paper and stuck it on the coffee table then wrote a reminder to catch Lauren when she was feeling better and ask her if she would be interested in organizing a fishing trip specifically for Norville and Evan. They could also invite Grant and his twins. That should be an interesting combination.

Archer liked Grant. The man had a solid core of human decency and compassion. That compassionate nature extended past the patients to include staff. He'd been gentle, attentive, and reassuring with Lauren tonight when she was sick.

Archer's gaze swept over the room and again he thought of Jessica. Why not call her? He had a good reason. She was scheduled to sing in a

Fourth of July concert at the church; it wouldn't hurt to touch base and make sure she hadn't changed her mind.

He picked up the phone and dialed the number as he allowed his gaze to linger on the rich warmth of a floral border Jessica had painted over the threshold into the living room. He couldn't forget her excitement and passion as she planned the colors she would use in each part of the house. She'd helped him choose special pieces f furniture, joyfully planning for the future.

And then one day it was over, attended by many tears and sweet words of apology. She blamed herself. She wasn't ready to commit.

He had buried the ring in his top dresser drawer under some handkerchiefs his mother had given him for Christmas last year.

Voicemail picked up and he listened helplessly to the rich tones of Jessica's recorded voice.

"Hi, Jessica, this is Archer. I guess you're not home yet. I'll call later."

A click interrupted Archer's message and then, "Hello? Archer? Don't hang up, it's me." The soothing rhythm of Jessica's greeting floated over him like a tonic.

"You made it."

She hesitated briefly and then Archer thought he heard a soft intake of breath. "Hi." There was a smile in her voice and he could picture her face perfectly.

He closed his eyes and savored the hesitant-hopeful greeting. "I'm sorry, I didn't realize you might already be asleep."

"I wasn't. Not quite, anyway. We got in at about three this afternoon and I took a nap as soon as I walked in the door. How's life in Dogwood Springs?"

He wanted to tell her how lonely this town was without her. "Growing. I thought I'd better call and check on your schedule." His heart accused him of being a liar even as he said the words. He didn't need to hear about any schedule. "Are you still planning to give us a concert at the Independence Day celebration?"

"Of course." She gave a soft sigh. "Was that all you wanted?"

He hesitated. Was that disappointment he heard?

But she said nothing more. Jessica had always been more comfortable than Archer with the tension of a lull in a conversation. He'd found her ease with silence to be attractive—along with every other quality about her that made her uniquely Jessica Lane.

"I also wanted to know how you were doing," he said at last.

She sighed again with a soft groan that told of her weariness. "It was a long trip."

"Difficult tour?" He wanted to sound sympathetic. Instead that nasty little inner voice betrayed itself. Something in him hoped she'd been homesick and never wanted to go on tour again.

"As I said, it was long. Heather loved it." Jessica's younger sister, Heather, sang with her. "She didn't want to come home. I guess I'm just not into touring the way I used to be. Living out of a suitcase was never my life's dream."

Yes! Archer cleared his throat. "More of a home girl than you thought?"

He sensed a change in her silence. Better not push it. "I guess I could be happy in Branson the rest of my life."

How about Dogwood Springs? "Why travel out of town when you live in a music center?"

"Exactly." She sighed again and he knew she was probably stretching out on the floor, flexing her legs, arching her back to unkink the muscles.

He closed his eyes and pictured the delicate curves of her face, the hazel eyes, the light brown hair that fell to her shoulders and never behaved.

He held his breath and his heart took a couple of extra hard beats as he swallowed his pride. "Jessica, I've missed you." He barely contained the words that wanted to follow—and I love you and I haven't been able to get you out of my mind . . .

"I know." There was a breathless, waiting quality to her voice. "I've missed you, too. Why don't we keep in touch?"

He frowned. Keep in touch? What did she mean

by that? "Um, okay, you mean, like, we'll always be friends? That kind of thing?" He wasn't sure he was up to that yet.

"How could we ever have dreamed of anything else without a firm friendship first?"

First? That might not be too bad. In fact, it could be a good idea. "You mean as in a close relationship where we spend time together and share our thoughts and dreams for a future?"

"Archer." There was a warning in her voice. "When I say friendship I mean friendship. Buddies, you know? Friends who can be casual with each other, who can be themselves with each other, who don't have to pass the scrutiny of five hundred church members."

Archer felt a jolt of disappointment at the sharpness of her final words and it took him a moment to recover.

This time she was the one to break the silence. "I'm sorry, Archer. That came out a little rough."

He thought about Norville's depression earlier and identified with it. No wonder the poor guy could barely function right now. A woman could really pack a wallop when she wanted to.

"Still working thirty-six hours a day for the church?" she asked.

Archer frowned. He was working for God. Big difference. "Do I hear sarcasm?"

"Hyperbole, pal. Unfortunately, it's almost true. You try carrying on a relationship with someone who has dedicated himself to serving a church instead of a marriage."

"Ouch." Still, she hadn't said she hated him. She hadn't said she was tired of him.

"I've had a month to think about why I broke it off and that's still pretty much what I came up with. I've missed you like crazy and I wish so badly that we could see each other right now. But I also wish we could have a normal relation-ship without a bunch of voyeurs eavesdropping on our dates and spreading rumors about us."

"You sound so bitter."

"I know and I'm trying to work through that. I'm just not there yet." She sighed. "I'm sorry."

"It's okay." There was still hope, wasn't there? "I like the idea of the friendship thing. I'm not sure I can be around you for hours at a time without wanting to kiss you, but hey, I'm a preacher's kid. Well disciplined. I can do it. Probably. Okay, maybe a little kiss here and there, you know, a peck on the cheek and if you'll hold my hand I can probably get by for a while."

"Archer." The laughter returned to her voice.

"Yes?"

"Good night."

"I'll call you."

"Or I'll call you."

"I'd rather have the permission to call you. That way I won't have to sit and watch the telephone, waiting for it to ring."

"It'll do you good."

"I'm not that great at waiting."

"Good night, Archer."

"Goodnight."

There was a soft click and then a dial tone.

He sighed. Then he smiled. She'd missed him.

❧ CHAPTER 9 ❧

The savory fragrance of grilled onions and hamburgers mingled with the sounds of footsteps, talk, and laughter in the cafeteria on Monday. The comfortable familiarity blunted the edge of homesickness with which Lauren McCaffrey had struggled since moving to Dogwood Springs late in February. She stood waiting while Gina Drake paid for her own food—she should've known the independent young woman would not allow anyone to pay for her lunch—and then led the way toward a quiet corner of the dining area where they could talk in relative privacy.

Sliding her tray onto a two-person table, Lauren gazed out the window at the hillside town of Dogwood Springs. It was a pretty community, with winding streets and lush foliage. Sometimes the citizens complained about the inconvenience of those winding streets but they worked better than speed bumps to control traffic.

After a quiet prayer of thanks, Lauren looked

across at Gina, who was already biting into an onion ring, although she had her gaze lowered as if to respect Lauren's privacy as she prayed.

The golden-red highlights of Gina's hair glowed in the indirect sunlight from the window and the freckles across the bridge of her nose made her look about ten years old instead of twenty-eight. Her job had brought her into the ER countless times, helping with codes or treating patients with breathing problems. There had never been a patient complaint about her and as Lauren had mentioned the other night, she was especially good with children.

"Busy morning?" Lauren asked.

"Not bad so far. You?" Gina still didn't look up, almost as if she was still embarrassed about Friday night.

"Hectic. I haven't been this busy since I left Knolls. I'm amazed I could get away to meet you but I'm glad I did."

"I haven't thanked you for helping me Friday night." Still keeping her gaze to the table, Gina took a bite of her cheeseburger.

"I wish I could have done more. I was so sorry to run out on you like that. How did the over-nighter go with Natalie?"

Gina stopped chewing, swallowed, and caught Lauren's gaze. "What did you think of her when you met her Friday night?"

"I couldn't form an opinion based on the few

121

words I heard her say; my stomach was getting most of my attention." There were so many things Lauren wanted to ask but where to start? Gina wasn't exactly the most talkative person. "Are your feet healing?"

Gina nodded. "I'm a fast healer and I have a high pain tolerance. Are you over the flu?"

Lauren hesitated. She was still having bouts of nausea and weakness but not as bad. This didn't feel like any flu she'd ever had. "I'm better." She leaned forward. "Gina, I meant what I said the other night about wanting to be here if you need me. I know how it feels to be alone in a new place."

Gina took another bite of onion ring, chewed and swallowed, and sipped on her soda. There was a hesitance in her gaze. "Thanks. So how do you adjust from night shift to day shift?"

"I don't ordinarily work nights, I was just covering for someone else Thursday and Friday. Do you always answer a question with another question?"

A slight flush colored Gina's cheeks and then she returned Lauren's grin. "Sorry. It's an old habit."

Lauren resisted the urge to ask Gina why she felt the need to use such a defense mechanism.

"Natalie's pushy, huh?"

"She was nice enough," Gina admitted at last. "She helped me get the boys to bed Friday night and she slept on the sofa because I don't have a guest bedroom. That couldn't have been comfortable as tall as she is. She fixed us breakfast and lunch Saturday morning then made arrange-|ments for Mrs. Walker to check on us a couple of times a day."

"That was pushy?"

"No, but then she insisted on taking us back to the ER Sunday morning for Levi's wound recheck. And she wanted to take him herself so I wouldn't have to walk so much. I just don't feel comfortable with all that attention. I like to take care of things myself."

Lauren couldn't miss the undertone of suspicion in Gina's voice. "She wants to help you, just like I do and Archer and Dr. Sheldon."

"How can those people help me if they don't know what I need?"

"What do you mean when you say 'those people'?"

"Family Services." She gave Lauren an obviously forced smile as if she was trying to pass it all off as a joke. "Never trust anyone in the government."

Lauren put her hamburger down. "I don't work for the government and I want to help."

Gina smiled—this time the smile seemed genuine. "Okay, after work tonight I'll let you check my feet and change my bandages. Will that satisfy you?"

Before Lauren could answer, an overhead page

blared from the speakers in the center of the dining room ceiling. She was being called back to the ER. Stat.

At the same time, Gina's pager went off and she checked it. "Oh-oh, sounds like something's up. They need me too. Think it's a code?"

"Could be. Here, put all your stuff on my tray and I'll shove it into the ER breakroom on my way by. Maybe we'll get a chance to eat later."

"I wouldn't count on it."

Grant Sheldon stood watching the flashing lights reflect against the glass of the ambulance entrance while the EMT wrenched open the back doors of the van and reached in to pull out a stretcher. On that stretcher was eight-year-old Stacie Kimble, who had been one of Grant's flu patients Friday night. Stacie was unconscious; according to the last report, her breathing was markedly labored. Her blood sugar was off the scale. Her temperature was normal, as it had been Friday night. Had he missed something then?

Grant had already told Vivian to call an airlift helicopter for stand by for transit to a larger hospital in Springfield.

Stacie's mother had told the paramedic that Stacie had still been sick last night, so they had allowed her to sleep in this morning. When Mrs. Kimble tried to awaken Stacie for a late breakfast, the child wouldn't wake up.

Grant looked back to make sure everything was set. He'd had Lauren paged minutes ago so she should be back soon. The other nurse, Emma, was already setting up for a possible intubation.

Meanwhile, Grant worried. As he recalled, Stacie's brothers had also been ill with flu symptoms but no elevated temperatures. Most of their other flu patients had presented without fever. This was a strange one.

He had requested a copy of Stacie's chart from Medical Records as soon as he received the first call and would check it when it arrived.

The secretary, sixty-three-year-old Vivian, waved at him from her desk at the circular central station. "Dr. Sheldon, Archer Pierce is driving the parents in. They're members of his church."

"Good. Thanks." He hoped Archer was able to keep the parents calm. The less distraction the staff had from their work right now the better Stacie's chances.

Christy and Bill, the paramedic and EMT, came rushing through the open doors with Stacie lying on the gurney with a strap over her legs and chest. Emma waited in the designated exam room.

"Dr. Sheldon, respirations are dropping and she's just starting to have apneic periods," Christy said. "I was unable to get a line in—she's really dry."

As he issued orders on his way to the room Grant was glad he had two experienced RNs on duty.

The child was on a 100 percent non-rebreather mask. Folded two-by-two-inch gauze pads were taped in place on each arm, marking the failed IV attempts. He could barely hear her breath sounds above the swish of closing doors and the squeak of rushing footsteps. She was wearing down.

Grant motioned to Vivian. "Call for airlift."

Just in time, to Grant's relief, Lauren walked through the employee entrance followed by Gina Drake.

He gave orders for treating an unresponsive child as he prepared to do an emergency intubation.

Lauren and Gina went to work and he turned back and directed the EMT to put an ambu-bag on Stacie to help her breathe.

Stacie barely reacted when Gina stuck her for the blood gas.

The intubation was fast and smooth. When Grant aimed a light into the child's eyes, he noted the pupils were a little sluggish but equal and not dilated. Further checking showed no evidence of cerebral edema. Not yet.

Grant placed his stethoscope over the patient's chest, listened, nodded. Her heart rate was starting to drop. Good. "Vitals?"

Lauren gave them to him. Blood pressure was still low. He did more physical checks. Not as bad as it could be. Just as Gina walked back in with the results of the blood gas, Mr. and Mrs. Kimble entered the department with Archer. Grant stepped outside the exam room to speak with them.

Friday night Mrs. Kimble had been calm and unperturbed. Today her face and eyes were red from crying. "How is Stacie? What's happening? What's wrong with her?"

"We had to do an intubation to help her breathe better," Grant explained. "Right now they're taking an x-ray to make sure we have that tube in the right place. We're waiting on some blood tests to come back so I can make a better diagnosis."

"You mean you don't even know what's wrong with her yet?" Mr. Kimble demanded. Grant could hear the accusation in his voice. Part of him could identify with the father's fear. It was just panic. He'd felt the same way. He'd even asked thatsame angry question. More would probably follow.

He gently explained what the staff had done so far, the tests they had taken. "I have a probable diagnosis but I don't want to jump in prematurely. We've called an airlift helicopter to fly her to Springfield."

Mrs. Kimble grasped her husband's arm with both hands. "She's that bad?"

"I want to get her there as quickly as possible to a place with the ability to determine that," Grant explained. "I suspect diabetic coma."

Mrs. Kimble's face twisted in pain.

"She's very dehydrated," Grant continued gently, "so what we have to concentrate on now is getting her rehydrated so we can give her insulin and lower the sugar level."

Mrs. Kimble swallowed and dabbed at the tears in her eyes with her fingers. "You're telling us our daughter—whom you were supposed to treat Friday night—now has diabetes? And you thought it was the flu?"

A lab tech came walking through at that moment and handed Grant another printout. He checked it quickly. The blood sugar was 527. "We seem to have a city-wide epidemic right now and diabetes can often be brought on by an initial infection of some kind. What we need to concentrate on at the moment is her care from here on."

The x-ray tech came out, pushing her portable machine.

"I want to see her now." Mrs. Kimble pulled from her husband's grasp and moved as if to walk past Grant.

Archer stepped forward and took her by the arm. "Kelly, not yet." His voice was suddenly filled with deep authority. Grant could see how he must command the respect of his congregation. "Come on, my friends." Archer placed an arm around each parent. "We have some serious praying to do while we allow this capable staff to work."

CHAPTER 10

Archer watched as Kelly stalked across the consultation room, arms crossed over her chest. "Why won't he let us at least see our own daughter?" She stopped and turned back, eyes widening in alarm. "Archer, you don't think he's hiding something from us?"

"No." Archer kept his voice sympathetic but firm. "Dr. Sheldon will do what he says and he will be honest with you. Your daughter needs our prayers right now."

Kelly walked over to her husband and stepped into his open arms. "I'm so scared," she whispered.

Seconds later there was a knock at the door and Grant stepped inside.

"Mr. and Mrs. Kimble, the Lifeline helicopter has radioed us. It will be here in about five minutes. Would you like to see her?"

Kelly exhaled a great sweep of air and sprang to her feet before her husband could help her. "Is she awake?"

"No, I'm sorry."

"How is she doing, Doctor?" Steve asked quietly. "Have you started the insulin yet?"

"No." Grant walked with them as he explained the balancing act they had to do in Stacie's treatment.

Archer stopped in the doorway and let them go on without him for a moment.

Steve and Kelly were new to the congregation. Sometimes, they could be difficult. Some of the other parents with young children in the church had complained about Kelly's sharp tongue and Steve's impatience. They both had a lot of spiritual maturing to do. But wasn't that the case with every Christian?

Archer had often heard his father explain that prickly people in the church had their function, too—they were God's tools to hone the edges from all the other Christians, who also had their weak spots. Aside from their negative points, Kelly was a tireless nursery worker and Steve often had insights during Bible study on Sunday morning that no one else had considered.

Archer walked to the doorway of the exam room where Stacie still lay unconscious. Lauren stood beside Kelly with an arm around her shoulders, talking quietly with her while Steve stood gazing into his daughter's face. Grant jotted notes on a chart. He looked up and caught Archer's eye with a hesitant smile.

"Can we talk for a minute?" Archer asked.

Grant nodded and followed him out of the room.

They found a quiet corner out of the way of foot traffic. "Are you going to drive them to Springfield?" Grant asked.

"Yes, they'll need someone with them for a

while. I wish we could assure them she is going to be okay."

"I thought preachers had the innate ability to trust God in all things." Laced through Grant's deep voice was the questioning tone of a seeker. Archer knew he didn't mean to offend.

"This one still struggles," Archer said. "In fact, I don't know very many people who have the ability to trust completely in every situation."

Grant smiled. "It's nice to know that even you have doubts from time to time." He turned and gestured toward the room where the Kimbles waited. "I think she has a good chance. She seemed to rouse a few minutes ago, not to complete consciousness but enough to encourage us. Do the Kimbles have family in the area?"

"No. I'll contact some church members and see if I can find some folks to make the drive to Springfield and take turns sitting with them." Archer hesitated. "How dangerous is her condition?"

"The mortality rate in children for diabetic ketoacidosis ranges from 5 to 20 percent."

Archer felt an icy stab of fear while Grant used doctor-speak to describe the illness.

"I don't suppose you could put that in English, could you?"

Grant nodded. "Sorry. Let's just say her body's chemical balance isn't as dangerous as it could be."

"Good." Archer glanced again toward Stacie's exam room. "I realize the Kimbles aren't handling this thing very well."

"They care about their child. Excuse me, I need to check on a couple more things before the flight team arrives." He walked back to the exam room and spoke to the Kimbles as the *whomp-whomp-whomp* of rotary blades grew louder and echoed through the room.

As Grant entered the room, Lauren stepped out of it and strolled toward Archer. He saw a sheen of wetness against her cheeks and realized how this must be affecting her. Stacie was in her Sunday school class and Lauren had a soft spot for the children.

"Are you okay?" he asked.

"I'm fine." She turned to gaze back through the open door of Stacie's exam room. "I just hate to see that lively little girl having to struggle with diabetes for the rest of her life. Still, she's strong-willed like her parents."

"That's what Grant told me. I'm driving the Kimbles to Springfield," Archer said. "If you weren't on duty I'd ask you to go with us."

She looked up at him in surprise. "You would?"

"Of course." Didn't she know the soothing influence she had on patients? "You could interpret the medicalese."

She gave him a thoughtful half smile. "Thanks for the suggestion but I still have a lunch date with

Gina. When things slow down here a little bit, I'm going to see if we can slip away to the break-room and resume our talk."

"You're already touching base with Gina? I thought you were sick this weekend."

"I'm better."

He grinned. This woman amazed him. "Lauren McCaffrey, you're one of the most supportive, insightful, and compassionate people I know. I wish we had fifty more just like you in our con-gregation."

He should have known that would make her blush. Compliments always embarrassed her. "And since you're already making friends with Gina," he added, "could you find it in your heart to go with me to visit her when things slow down a little? Say, next week after she's had a chance to adjust and heal?"

A smile lit her green eyes. "I'd love to." She glanced toward the ambulance bay as the flight crew came in wheeling their gurney. "I need to give a report. If I don't get another chance to talk to the Kimbles will you tell them I'll be praying?"

"Of course." Archer watched her rush to meet the entering crew. Stacie would be on her way up in just a few moments. Time to prepare her parents for lift-off.

The hamburgers and onion rings were cold by the time Lauren and Gina made it to the staff breakroom but Lauren was thankful they could make it at all. Normally the noon rush hit them hard on Mondays and didn't let up the rest of the day.

Lauren shoved the food into the microwave and reached into the fridge for soda as Gina limped to the window and stared out across the valley below them.

"Looks like your feet are beginning to hurt," Lauren said.

Gina shrugged. "I'll be fine."

"You could have asked off for the next couple of days to give you time to heal."

Gina turned from the window and pulled a chair out to sit down. "I'm too new to take any sick days and I need the money."

The microwave beeped and Lauren pulled out the heated, soggy food and sat across from Gina. "Your supervisor probably doesn't even know about your injuries, does she?"

Gina grabbed an onion ring and held it up with a grimace. It drooped and some of the coating plopped off. "No. You're not going to tell her are you?" She didn't give Lauren time to answer. "So why did you move to Dogwood Springs?"

Lauren chuckled. "One thing about you, Gina Drake, you'll never bore anybody with stories about yourself."

Gina smiled and sipped her soda. Lauren decided not to fight it. "You want the real reason I moved or the one I gave my parents?"

"Both." Gina pulled a chair to her side of the table and put her feet up, as if settling in for a good story. Lauren couldn't keep from smiling at the childlike curiosity that suddenly filled those pretty eyes. Her expression reminded Lauren of the one on Levi's face during her story about David and Goliath.

"I'm thirty-five and have never been married. Does that tell you anything?" Lauren said.

"So? Why would you want to be?"

Lauren knew she was talking to the wrong person about marriage. "I have two older sisters and two younger brothers. All of them are happily married and have provided the doting grandparents with nine grandchildren. My mother keeps reminding me I need to start carrying my share of the load. She wants an even ten, at least. You know how parents are."

Gina's smile drifted away like a stray thought. "Not normal ones."

Lauren repressed her curiosity. "Mine have a tendency to meddle."

"That's why you left home? Really?"

Lauren grimaced. "Let's just say my prospects in Knolls, Missouri, were recently reduced."

"Why? Did all the men die?"

"No, but the one man worth marrying got engaged to someone else."

"That had to hurt."

"And it didn't happen until after I made a fool

of myself over him." Lauren still cringed when she remembered the way she had behaved with Lukas Bower, boldly asking him to go fishing with her, making a point to sit near him in church, going out of her way to engage him in conversation and spend time with him at work. And then he'd proposed to Mercy Richmond. "So now it seems as if my family's biggest project is to get poor lonely Lauren married off."

"You're kidding, right? You don't look lonely to me."

Lauren hadn't intended to spill her personal problems out to a person who had an over-abundance of her own problems. "We all get lonely sometimes."

"You have four brothers and sisters and they're all happily married?" Gina's voice took a cynical tone. "Nobody's divorced? Nobody's fighting?"

"Sure they fight. My baby brother had a lot of trouble settling down but his wife is mature enough to handle him."

"You told me the other night you'd love to have kids," Gina said.

"You bet I would. But for that I'd need a husband." Lauren leaned forward. "Enough whining about my problems. How are things going with you? Do you have an appointment for a physical exam?"

"Tomorrow afternoon." Gina grimaced. "I just

hope they find something. Maybe low blood sugar, even though it didn't show up the other night or during my employment physical." She studied Lauren for a moment. "Do you get many patients here in the ER with panic attacks?"

"A few. Do you think that's what you're having?"

"I don't think so." She frowned and leaned back in her chair. "I don't think you lose your memory during a panic attack. Friday night I didn't know where I was but I knew I was terrified."

"Of what?"

"All I remember is the fear. I was looking for my children but I didn't even know who they were. According to Levi, I was looking at him. He said I ran past him and out the door and when he called to me I didn't seem to hear him." Gina took the time to eat another droopy onion ring and swallow several gulps of her soda. "What if we'd lost Stacie?"

Lauren was becoming accustomed to Gina's sudden subject changes. "You mean how would I have felt if she would have died?"

"Yes. I've assisted with a lot of codes, so I've seen some patients die. It's always tough to take. But you *know* Stacie."

"I think being raised on a farm taught me a better understanding of death as a natural part of the life cycle," Lauren said. "I learned not to be so afraid of it. I'll never get used to it, though, especially when we lose a child. But heaven makes it easier."

"Heaven." Gina's deadpan voice gave Lauren a glimpse of her thoughts. "You wouldn't feel that way about your own death." It was a gentle challenge.

"If I suddenly find out that I have some deadly disease that's going to kill me in a few months, I'll probably do the normal thing and grieve. But it's a comfort to me to know God has all that under control."

Gina shook her head adamantly. "Nobody's ever going to control my life again."

Lauren admired Gina's independent spirit even as she felt sadness for the difficulties the younger woman faced. "Somebody else already is," she replied softly.

"If you're talking about the social workers, forget it."

"I'm not talking about humans." Lauren leaned forward. "My grandma used to say that if we weren't under God's control we could slip into dangerous waters in our lives."

Gina put her burger down. "Everybody in your family is a Christian?"

"Most of them."

Gina's expression held disbelief. "I wasn't raised that way."

"When I realized I couldn't do everything right in my life, I went to Someone who could. In a way, it's like getting a second opinion when I encounter physical problems that my doctor can't treat, only the second opinion of Jesus Christ is totally accurate."

Gina finished her soda and took her feet out of the chair. "So how do you like the new ER director?" Another abrupt change of subject.

"I like him."

"Did you notice anything interesting about him?"

Lauren shrugged. "What?"

"Like he's gorgeous and kind and single and good with patients and single."

Lauren laughed. "I thought you weren't interested in getting married again."

"I never said anything about me. You're the one whose mother wants you married. You're the one who wants to have kids before it's too late. I think he looks like Antonio Banderas—you know, that actor? Except, of course, he doesn't have a Spanish accent or a ponytail. And he's a whole lot younger."

"And?" Lauren prompted.

Gina leaned back in her chair and smiled. "He's not my type."

"What's your type?"

Gina shrugged. "I usually go for irresponsible guys who run as soon as the subject of commitment comes up. How about you?"

"A praying man," Lauren said. "In fact, he must be sold out enough that people who don't share his faith would call him a fanatic." Again, she thought of Lukas Bower. Some people had called him a fanatic. A few had laughed at him behind his back because he prayed for his patients.

"Must not be many of those around," Gina said.

"Why do you say that?"

"As pretty as you are, you should be married with six kids by now," Gina said. "I mean, you look younger than I am."

Lauren tried to force a smile but it probably gravitated to her face in the form of a grimace. Gina couldn't realize how insignificant that made her feel. A radical Christian would be able to look past the outside package to the spirit inside. So maybe that meant she was lacking in spiritual depth. She'd come to wonder that in the past few years, especially with the repeated questions from Mom and co-workers and well-meaning church members. She'd tried to tell herself that she was just selective or that the right person hadn't come into her life yet. But how long was she supposed to wait?

Gina's eyes widened. She leaned forward. "It's the reverend."

Lauren had never been able to suppress a blush. She took a bite of her burger.

"Would you even want to be a preacher's wife?" Gina made it sound like a horrible thing.

Lauren glanced toward the breakroom door. "Shh!"

Gina lowered her voice and giggled. "You would!"

For at least the millionth time in her life, Lauren wished she wasn't quite so readable. "Don't act so shocked. It isn't as if he's married but please don't tell anyone else." This was so embarrassing. There had never been a hint of any kind of romantic relationship between her and Archer. "I shouldn't even be thinking about him like that. I mean, he's my pastor. And he's younger than me."

"How much younger?"

"Two years."

"Don't forget the studies that advise that a husband should be seven years younger than his wife. Has he asked you out yet?"

Lauren lowered her voice. "Of course not."

"Why 'of course'?"

"He's only been officially unattached for a little over a month."

"Your biological clock is ticking," Gina teased.

Lauren grimaced. "Like a time bomb. Maybe I should just ignore it and let it wind down. Not everybody is meant to be married and have a family. There are a lot of things I'm free to do now that I wouldn't be able to do if I had other commitments."

"But you want children," Gina said. "You were good with Levi the other night."

"I'd love a child." Lately she hadn't been able to ignore the tugging ache in her heart when any patient under the age of ten came into the ER.

"Do you think Archer would be a good father?"

"Almost any man can father a child. Archer would be a good daddy."

There was a startled gasp from the other side of the partially open door. Lauren froze. Someone had heard them. There was a swish and a squeak of shoes. Lauren jumped up and ran to the hallway in time to see a familiar flowered smock covering the oversized end portion of Fiona Perkins.

Oh, this was just great.

"Who was it?" Gina asked.

"The one person in this hospital who's reputed to have a bigger mouth than mine. I think I'm going to be sick."

Gina laughed. It was a light, tinkling sound but it didn't make Lauren feel better.

❧ CHAPTER 11 ❧

By seven o'clock Wednesday evening the second week in June, traffic in the emergency room had steadily increased until eight of the ten exam beds were occupied. Grant was tempted to put in a pointed request for an immediate mid-level provider. They didn't have time to wait.

During the week and a half following the heart-stopping scare with eight-year-old Stacie, Grant

Sheldon had discovered many interesting things about Dogwood Springs. A sweet sense of community spirit ran deep in this town and it seemed to be one of curiosity mingled with compassion, especially when word spread about Stacie's fight with diabetes.

At least three people had stopped by the ER while Grant was on duty, not for medical care but just to meet him, welcome him to town, and find out more about him. He was invited to join the local Kiwanis Club, which met for lunch each Tuesday at the Copper Pot Café. He was given a free month's subscription to *The Dogwood*, the local newspaper. The current issue featured a picture and dramatically written article about Stacie's plight.

After the episode with Stacie, Grant had kept count of the patients with flu symptoms who presented to the ER. He didn't like what he found. The numbers approached epidemic proportions but when he tested for influenza the tests returned negative.

At the end of a busy Wednesday in the ER, Grant picked up a chart from the circular central desk and turned to give report to his night shift replacement, Dr. Mitchell Caine, a primary care doc who had his own practice in town and moonlighted in the ER.

"What's this I hear about shift reductions?" Dr. Caine was an impressive-looking man, maybe an inch shorter than Grant's 6′ 2″, with silver blond hair and steel blue eyes, which, at the moment, revealed an edge of displeasure.

"I want to shorten the shifts until we can hire mid-level providers. I might start by adding overlapping double coverage for the busier evening hours."

"And when will this take place?"

"I hope to put some of it into effect for next month's schedule. Business is picking up and we don't want our staff worn out by twelve-hour shifts."

"Perhaps it would be wise for you to learn a little more about Dogwood Springs before you start making decisions that could disrupt a lot of lives, Director," Dr. Caine said. "I need my twelve-hour shifts and tomorrow is my day off. I can sleep then." He reached up to straighten the crisply starched lab coat that he wore over dress clothes instead of donning the traditional ER scrubs.

"But you worked all day today, right?" Grant asked. "It appears you're going to be busy here tonight. Would you want to be a patient of a doctor on his twenty-third hour?"

Lines of irritability deepened around Caine's eyes and mouth. "We aren't that busy in this town yet. There are usually several hours during the night when we only have a trickle of patients."

"Even if there's only one in at a time the doctor can't sleep through it."

"Do you know how expensive it is to run a family practice these days?" Caine's voice grew deeper, the words more clipped. "The paperwork requires an extra employee just keeping up with government regulations."

"I can empathize with you, Dr. Caine. Just be glad we have hospitalists or you'd have to take call."

Caine raised a hand as if to ward off Grant's words. He gave a grimace of a smile, as if he was trying to pass off his irritation with humor. "I'm sure you're right but you'd be more sympathetic if you had a wife with a Ferrari."

The buzzer sounded at the front window and he heard a slightly familiar, crusty voice rise above the normal chatter of the bustling ER.

"Would you stand up? I'm not going to carry you. Hey! Listen to me, I've got some cracked ribs, you know."

There was a grunt and a moan. Grant stepped around the partition that separated the ER proper from the reception area and waiting room. There stood the two feuding farmers, Brisco and Scroggs, whom he'd last seen after their hillside crash.

Mr. Brisco braced himself against the reception counter and grimaced as he held his previously loudmouthed neighbor by the right arm. Mr. Scroggs was swaying like a drunk and he had a small blood-encrusted cut over his left eye. The

145

cast on his left arm was stained with dirt and blood.

Grant turned and signaled for a nurse then walked around to the entry door and into the waiting room. He gently eased Brisco away and took Scroggs. "You shouldn't be lifting any weight yet, Mr. Brisco. Let's get him to the back and lay him down. Did you two get into another tangle?"

"Nope, somebody else walloped him on the head," Brisco muttered as he tagged along behind them. "Right there in his own barn in broad daylight. What's this world coming to?" His voice shook with indignation.

Grant ushered Scroggs into one of the two exam rooms that remained empty and gently sat him on the edge of the bed. Brisco hovered by the door. The nurse murmured comforting words to the old farmer as she took his shirt off and replaced it with a gown. Grant pressed his stethoscope against the patient's back. The breathing sounded fine.

"I found him lying on his face in the middle of his barn floor," Brisco said as the nurse checked Scroggs's blood pressure.

"Unconscious?" Grant asked.

"I think he was just coming out of it. I'd driven over to complain about the fence being down again." He looked down at his ailing neighbor. "It's your turn to fix it this time. Look what you're doing to get out of it." His voice carried through the ER with nearly as much volume as last time, as if Scroggs was hard of hearing.

"Mr. Scroggs," Grant said, checking the cut, "can you talk to me?"

The farmer's eyes opened slightly. He winced. "What do you want?"

"Can you tell me what happened? How long ago?" Grant pressed his stethoscope to the older man's bony chest. Heart sounded okay, too.

"I heard something out in the barn when I came in from the field this afternoon." He reached up and felt for the cut on his temple but Grant intercepted his hand and guided it away. "Thought it was a possum."

"That's not what you told me when I found you," Brisco interrupted. "You told me you thought I was in there stealing your fertilizer."

"I decided to get a jump on him," Scroggs said with a grimace. He laid his head back on the pillow. "Either the possums in these parts are getting bigger, or that rat-faced weirdo who hit me wasn't no possum. I should've laid this here cast to his skull. He was bending over the spigot of my fertilizer tank. I shouted and he jumped at me with some metal container in his hand. Knocked me out cold till I heard Brisco snooping around."

"He was already acting all loopy and odd when I found him," Brisco said. "Not that it was too noticeable. He's always loopy and odd."

"Wait a minute, Mr. Scroggs." The farmer's previous statement had registered with Grant at last. "Could you describe him to the police?"

"Guess I could. I saw him but not for long."

Grant excused himself and stepped out of the exam room. He walked over to the secretary. "Barbara, call the police," he said softly. "We have a crime victim who needs to make a statement."

Lauren joined him at the central desk. "The police? Again? What is it with you, Dr. Sheldon? Maybe you should start parking your car someplace else so they won't know you're here."

Grant looked up at Lauren and smiled. "Maybe I should." He took a closer look at her then frowned. She looked pale with dark circles beneath her eyes. "I thought your shift was over. What are you still doing here?"

"Probably the same thing you are—trying to help our replacements get caught up. But two more patients just checked in and we've had three calls. Care to guess the most common complaint?"

"Nausea, vomiting, dizziness, headache."

"You got it. I'll hang around a little longer or they'll have to call in reinforcements."

"You don't look like you're feeling much better than the patients."

"How kind of you to notice." Lauren's voice

held just the right inflection of amused offense. Grant chuckled at her. Over the past two weeks they had grown comfortable enough with each other to tease. He liked her sense of humor. He had learned to trust her judgment. The last time Grant had felt this comfortable with someone he had eventually married her.

The thought disturbed him. He glanced again at her as she stepped to the automated drug dispenser and punched in her code number on a keypad.

He continued to watch her. He would show this much concern for any member of his staff. Right?

A motor whined and a drawer popped open. She reached for an ampule of the antiemetic he'd prescribed. "It comes and goes."

"You need to go home and get some rest. You're back on duty in the morning."

"So are you." Lauren gave him a tired smile. "I don't see you checking out yet."

"Don't push yourself too hard. You know how many return patients we've had with this stuff."

On his way back to the room Grant realized Lauren was right about the police. He'd been calling them a lot since he arrived. It wasn't a good thought but maybe things would settle down. Even the quietest of towns had their share of trouble. At least he didn't know all the officers by their first names yet.

To Grant's surprise, he found Dr. Caine at Scroggs's bedside asking questions, listening to his heart and breathing, issuing orders to the night shift nurse and asking questions about the attack. Brisco was gone.

"Dr. Caine, I can finish up here," Grant said.

"I've already taken over." Caine held up his own chart. "You're off duty, you can go on home."

But how long would it take one physician to get to the remainder of the patients with the waiting room filling up so quickly? Perhaps tonight would be a good one to test the double-coverage waters, at least for a little while. He'd been on duty for twelve hours but he could hang around for a little while and leave before he got too tired. As Lauren had said, he was also scheduled to be back on duty in the morning.

At the desk Grant picked up the chart on the next patient to be seen and walked to exam room three, thinking about Caine's Ferrari-driving wife. He could almost hear Annette saying, "Why, honey, we couldn't fit the whole family in a car like that." When he closed his eyes, all he could see was a hazy outline of her face.

Maybe it really was time to go home and get some rest.

But when he saw his next patient, an older lady who was miserable with the same flu symptoms that it seemed half the town was enduring, he knew it wasn't time to leave yet. Mrs. Henson looked at Grant with obvious relief when he introduced himself. She'd been waiting more than an hour and a half. She was gracious but her two younger sisters complained about the long wait.

Grant apologized in spite of the fact that it would have been impossible for him to get to her more quickly. He'd had two patients with chest pain come in by ambulance only a few moments before she arrived. Two auto accident victims had followed. This was most often the time of night when everything hit at once.

Mrs. Henson's fast heart rate and dizziness, with the absence of a fever, combined with several bouts of vomiting, indicated that she was dehydrated; Grant ordered further tests. After his experience with little Stacie Kimble, he didn't want to take any flu-like complaint lightly.

Two hours after he was scheduled to be off work, when he was fighting fatigue and Mrs. Henson was feeling better, he discharged her with orders to return if she got worse. He must have treated twenty other patients with the same symptoms and same test results in the last week.

He wrote his final discharge sheet and was retrieving his medical bag from the call room when he heard the sound of male laughter from one of the exam rooms in back. And then he heard something he'd never heard before— Lauren McCaffrey's voice, suddenly deep and strong with authority.

"Keep your hands off me!"

• • •

The fingers of Lauren's right hand tensed into a fist and she felt a tingle race up her arm. She hadn't wanted to punch anybody this badly since she was in fifth grade and Kevin Pulaski made her youngest brother cry. After she'd finished with Kevin that day, he'd apologized to her brother and never bothered him again. It didn't matter that the patient to whom she now spoke was twice as big as she was with the body of an all-star wrestler and the brains, at this moment, of an inebriated microorganism.

She shouldn't have stayed this long, should have gone home when her shift was over. But even if she felt a hundred percent she would not have been gracious about being manhandled, pinched, or groped. Within the space of five minutes this bozo had managed to do all three under the guise of drunken awkwardness and then faked a look of wide-eyed innocence. To make matters worse, she had turned just in time to catch his friend reaching out to her with obscene intent. When she caught him he chuckled and lowered his arm, sitting back in his chair with a leer that promised that, given the opportunity, he would try again.

"The two of you can keep your hands to yourself, or I can call the police and charge you with assault."

"Sorry."

"No you're not."

Her patient's face darkened to deep red and he finally looked into her eyes—a surprise, since up until now he'd barely lifted his stare above her rib cage. "Can't blame a guy for trying."

His inebriated buddy snickered again from his seat in the only chair in the room.

Lauren wanted to walk out of the room and out of the hospital and leave this guy to wait until one of the male nurses got a chance to come in. But the new female grad would probably get stuck with him and something similar would happen to her. Any other time, Lauren would have been more alert. No matter how modestly she dressed, sometimes this kind of thing happened.

She took a deep breath and reattached the blood pressure cuff, taking care to keep every vulnerable area of her anatomy away from his wandering touch. She hated dealing with the obnoxious drunks but it was part of the job in the emergency room. She had to remind herself that they, too, needed medical care.

All the automatic blood pressure machines were in use, so she pumped the manual cuff by hand and placed her stethoscope on the man's muscle-bound arm. She'd pumped it to maximum and was just getting ready to release the valve for a reading when Dr. Sheldon stepped into the room.

"Lauren? Is everything okay in here?" His presence had never been more welcome.

"Uh, nurse," the patient grunted, "are you trying to squeeze my arm off?"

Lauren released the valve and checked the numbers. She turned gratefully to Dr. Sheldon. "Mr. Beneker fell off his backhoe today. He has lower back pain. A couple of hours ago he began to experience blurred vision." The reek of alcohol suggested a good explanation for the blurred vision.

Dr. Sheldon picked up the chart and stepped to the patient's side. "So Mr. Beneker, you're a heavy-equipment operator?"

"Yeah."

"You're from Springfield? What are you doing all the way out here in our neck of the woods?" Dr. Sheldon was a big man with a commanding presence. His voice of authority seemed to sober the men a little. He was professional in every way, yet he seemed to establish control with every word. Lauren noticed his characteristic smile was missing.

While Grant gathered more information, she moved to the end of the bed as far away from Beneker and his buddy as she could get.

"Got a job clearin' a dump site a few miles out of town on Highway Z," Beneker said. "They're getting it all cleaned up for this big inspection some company is doing before they buy. Wantin' to put in some kind of water-bottling plant at Honey Spring."

Lauren stifled her curiosity. Honey Spring was her favorite fishing spot. She hoped a new bottling plant wouldn't disrupt the creek.

Dr. Sheldon took out his penlight and did a neurological test on Beneker, checked his reflexes and asked a few more questions. "I'll request an x-ray of your lower back just to be safe. We're going to run a few tests, including blood alcohol and drug screen. Did you lose consciousness?"

The patient frowned. "What's this about a blood screen?"

"It's policy for workers' comp claims. Were you unconscious at any time?"

"No. Hold it. That's not fair. I've been off work for a while. I've had a couple of beers since quitting time and the test'll show that."

"We'll take that into consideration and allow for it."

"I'll run the orders." Lauren turned to leave.

"No need," Dr. Sheldon took the man's chart and turned to her. "Eugene's on duty tonight. He'll take care of this one. Why don't you go home and get some rest."

She didn't argue. She also took her time leaving the room, intrigued by the sudden grim set of his jawline.

"Mr. Beneker," she heard him say as she reached the hallway, "this hospital doesn't allow its staff to be mistreated."

"What?" Beneker exclaimed.

"We don't tolerate sexual harassment. What we do is call the police and file charges." The doctor's voice was steady and calm.

Lauren squeezed the tip of her tongue between her teeth to keep from smiling but she couldn't bring herself to walk away.

"What d'you mean sexual harassment?" Beneker's voice had gotten mean. "She was touching me all over the place."

Lauren walked away then but she overheard Beneker threaten to file a complaint. Once again, Dr. Sheldon's voice was calm when he replied. Lauren could have hugged him.

CHAPTER 12

At six-forty-five Thursday morning, Grant Sheldon couldn't help noticing the magnificent beauty of summer as he maneuvered his car along the curving street toward the hospital at the crest of the steep hill. Flower boxes burgeoned with color. The gingerbread trim on brightly colored Victorian houses sparkled after the rain from last night's storm. Sodden limbs littered the picket-fenced yards.

He hoped Mrs. Piedmont wouldn't try to clear her yard this morning. He'd received word from her family physician that she would be fine as long as she took her medication and didn't overstress her heart.

He pulled into the employee parking lot just as an ambulance eased out of the bay. Here came the familiar tightening in his gut.

Inside he found two tearful middle-aged women with familiar faces, clinging to each other beside the reception window. When one of them spoke, he remembered his flu patient from last night, Mrs. Henson. These were her younger sisters who'd complained about the wait.

Mitchell Caine came through the doorway that connected the waiting room with the emergency department. His broad shoulders drooped beneath the stained lab coat. His bloodshot eyes held that familiar, dull look of frustration that every physician experienced when a patient case had not gone well. It was obvious that he had gotten no sleep last night. He looked past Grant as if he didn't see him and turned his attention to the two women.

"I'm sorry. We did all we could." His voice was rough with fatigue. "She went into cardiac arrest and we tried to resuscitate her." He shook his head. "She died five minutes ago."

The impact of the words hit Grant with an almost physical force, just as it did the sisters. He had been working in emergency medicine too long to be surprised by this kind of occurrence but it shouldn't have happened. Last night there were no signs that their sister was experiencing anything more than a simple case of the same virus attacking the rest of the town.

Instead of attempting to comfort the women through the onslaught of grief that followed the announcement, Dr. Caine turned his stiletto glare on Grant. "I'm not the one who needs his hours cut. The patient you saw last night just died of heart failure."

Grant bit back a flare of temper and remained calm. "I don't think this is the time or the place for a discussion about work schedules. Let's limit our attention to those who are grieving."

Lauren watched in shocked silence from the waiting room door while Dr. Sheldon pushed past Dr. Caine and approached the weeping women. He spoke a few soft words and ushered them into a private alcove. As they went, Lauren heard him offer assistance with calls and arrangements.

Dr. Caine passed Lauren on his way through the door into the emergency department. When the telephone rang for him a few moments later, she overheard the secretary, Vivian, explain that he had already left for the day. Thank goodness.

The man had issues.

After the hearse had left with the body of Mrs. Henson, and her sisters had left with other family members, Lauren caught sight of Dr. Sheldon walking toward the work desk at the rear of the department. She picked up the file she'd pulled and carried it to him as he sat down.

"I thought you would want this." She laid Mrs. Henson's chart in front of him. "I didn't find a thing out of place. None of her tests last night showed a heart problem." Without waiting for an invitation, she pulled another chair over and sat down. "Of course, you're the doctor and you might find a lot of things I wouldn't know to look for."

Grant studied the pages for a few moments then shook his head and leaned back in his chair. "I would make the same call again. That's what scares me. She was feeling much better before I sent her home. And she had no history of heart problems, no chest pain, nothing on the monitor when I saw her. I could have done an EKG but I saw no reason for it last night."

"Dr. Sheldon, you—"

"Would you mind calling me Grant?" He asked. "I like to be a little more casual around the office if it isn't against some kind of company policy I haven't yet read."

"Of course I wouldn't mind." She felt a pang of compassion for this man who always seemed to have everything under control. "Stop second-guessing yourself just because of a doctor who never bothered to read this chart last night."

"How do you know?"

"I had to search all over the department for it. He doesn't know what went on between you and this patient." Dr. Caine was using this poor woman's death to further his own agenda but it wouldn't be professional to mention that aloud.

"Thank you." Grant picked up the chart and sorted through the pages once again. Lauren had made copies of everything she could find. "Lauren, how long have you been an ER nurse?"

"Ten years."

"Have you ever seen a viral epidemic in early June such as the one we seem to have here now?"

"Nothing like we've seen here. Especially not in June."

"And you've experienced it yourself, even though you had a flu shot."

"Yes, and we've had several patients return with reoccurring bouts, though it only began around the end of May when you started working here. The severity is what concerns me."

His face relaxed with the first smile she had seen today. "Are you saying I make people sick?"

With some other doctors she would begin to tread lightly about now. She grinned at him. "We'll just have to wait and see, won't we? Do you mind if I offer a suggestion?"

"I'd appreciate it."

"I could call some friends of mine in Knolls and see if they're having the same problem. Dr. Lukas Bower would have picked up on something like this quickly. He would definitely see it in the ER if it was anywhere in town. Dr. Mercy Bower, his wife, has her own clinic. This is her day off but I could try to catch her at home. Maybe some of the other hospitals in surrounding towns have experienced the same thing."

"Excellent idea. I'll ask our secretaries if they'll keep track of our viral patients for the next few days and make some calls to the local physicians. Meanwhile, I'll have Medical Records pull some old files and I'll make some phone calls myself. The patients might be able to tell me something." He paused and thumped his fingers on Mrs. Henson's chart. "Her sisters are requesting an autopsy."

"Because of what Dr. Caine said this morning?"

"That could have something to do with it," he said dryly. "The coroner doesn't have to agree to it. If he doesn't, they'll have to pay for it themselves. I'm going to call and urge him to abide by their wishes."

Lauren really did like this man. "It could be risky for your career if they find something."

"It could be more risky for the citizens of Dogwood Springs if we don't."

"I hope your attitude spreads out a little in this town. We could use it." Unfortunately, if the pathologist found blocked arteries or other signs of previous heart problems in Mrs. Henson's body, the family could decide to sue for malpractice, even though the records for last night showed nothing amiss. It didn't mean they would win. Still, this was America, where people sued in search of hidden treasure.

"I find it comforting that there's a doctor willing to dig deeper," she said, "to find out if there really is a problem or if all these cases are coincidental."

Grant smiled again and Lauren realized Gina was right, he did look a bit like a more cerebral Antonio Banderas in his prime. Without the ponytail.

"Have you ever considered changing careers?" he asked.

"Changing?"

"You could be a counselor. You're good with people. You listen."

"You think so?" The man was serious? "I've been told I talk faster than a runaway freight train."

"I never noticed. Much." Grant's smile widened. "What I do notice is how people open up with you. Mrs. Piedmont dotes on you like you're another grandchild. Archer obviously thinks you're great."

Archer? Really? "He does?"

"He's mentioned it."

Lauren wanted to ask about other things Archer might have mentioned but this conversation wasn't about her love life—or lack of it. "Has he mentioned the fact that you are invited to attend our church and bring your kids any time you feel like it?"

"He's mentioned it."

She sensed she'd hit a nerve with that one. "Of course, you may already attend church somewhere."

"No." His tone couldn't have said more clearly, though gently, "Don't go there."

She nodded. She'd seen that look often enough. "It must be hard raising teenagers alone. Your wife has been gone two years now?" She knew she was getting more and more personal but he didn't seem to mind. Much.

"It will be two years next month."

"I'm so sorry, Grant. Lately I've been whining because I'm homesick and here you are grieving over something that has changed your life permanently. I've never even been married. Now I'm babbling like—"

"You're not babbling." He leaned back in his chair and stretched his long legs out in front of him.

"Someone once told me that the period of mourning after a death actually serves to honor the memory of the one who passed on."

Grant nodded as if thinking about her words for a moment. "I like that. It fits. Annette deserves to be honored."

"It sounds as if you had a good marriage."

"We did. We were best friends before we even dated." He looked over at her. "I think it's vital to like someone before you love them. Thanks to her deeply ingrained belief system we took the time for that."

"Annette was a Christian?"

"Yes." Grant fell silent and his movements stilled. The chatter of the tech and the secretary, punctuated by hints of laughter, filled the space where words, for a few moments, refused to enter. Then the telephone rang and the chatter stopped.

"For the record I, too, once called myself a Christian," Grant said softly.

She concealed her surprise. "Once?"

"Once. Annette carried the weight of spiritual leadership in our family since the children were little. She was their teacher. She tucked them in at night and prayed with them. Sometimes it seemed she tucked half the world in at night. She reached out to so many people and all I did was my job."

"You're a doctor and from what I've seen you always go beyond the call of duty. How much more caring could you get? It sounds like you two were a good match."

The warmth that deepened in his dark gray eyes revealed more to Lauren about Grant's love for his wife than any words could have.

The triage bell rang. Lauren got up to check on their first patient of the day and as she walked away she thought she heard Grant sigh.

• • •

"Hello, Archer."

The rich, melodious voice startled Archer so much he nearly dropped the receiver. Then he smiled and leaned forward in his chair, resting his elbows on his desk. "Jessica? Is this possible? Are you actually *calling* me at last?"

There was a soft chuckle at the other end. "I know I deserved that."

"You sure did. If you only knew how many times I've sat at home alone by the telephone, watching it, waiting for it to ring."

"And it never did."

"It always did. But it was never you."

Another chuckle. "I'm booked at the theater most nights, remember?"

"You're not only booked, you're booked up. Congratulations. Every time I've tried to reserve a ticket for your performance, they've been sold out."

"Why didn't you tell me? I could have gotten you a ticket."

"You told me not to call you."

She didn't answer for a few seconds. "I'm sorry. I was wrong. You can call me."

Thank you, Lord. "So what finally made you break down?" He had so many things he wanted to talk to her about. Archer was suddenly in the best mood he'd been in for weeks.

"Well get this, I missed you."

Oh, yeah. It felt good to hear her say that. "It took you long enough."

"No it didn't. I just couldn't bring myself to pick up the telephone and dial the church number. I didn't want to take a chance on disturbing you on your cell if you happened to be counseling someone or visiting members. When I dialed your home number I never got an answer." There was an unspoken question in her voice.

"When you block caller ID I don't know it's you or I'd call you back."

"Business as usual."

"Sounds like it."

"Why didn't you leave a message for me?"

"Because sometimes a recording just doesn't get the job done. So how've you been doing?"

"I've . . . um . . . taken on another little job."

"Oh Archer, you didn't."

"It didn't seem like much at first."

"That's what you always say. What is it this time? Are you the music director now, too? Let me guess, graded choirs as well as adult choir practice on Wednesday nights."

"Not music."

"Then what? Did your janitor quit?"

"Nope. I had a lot of time on my hands without you so I volunteered to be an on-call chaplain at Dogwood Springs Hospital."

This time the silence was longer, more thoughtful. Jessica was the one person in the world with whom he could read the silences as well as the spoken words. He had come to know her that well. "Do you enjoy that kind of work?" she asked.

"Enjoy isn't exactly the word I would use. It only started out to be one night of call a week."

"And now?"

"And since that first night I discovered that I can't just let those patients go without a follow-up. I'm getting more personally involved."

"Of course you are." Her voice held affectionate warmth. "It's your nature to care about people."

He loved it when she talked like that. "To put your mind at ease, the church is searching for a youth minister to take some of my duties and Lauren McCaffrey is helping out a lot with the kids until we get someone in officially. She's also helping me keep in contact with some of the patients since she's an ER nurse."

"Lauren. Didn't she just join the church a few months ago?"

Jessica's voice was still soft, thoughtful, but for some reason Archer felt a touch of tension. "The last part of February. She came from Knolls. Remember? I told you about her. I've known her forever."

"She's a very pretty woman. Single, isn't she?"

"Yes. That's why she has free time to help me."

"If memory serves, the kids at the church stuck to her like Velcro."

"That's the one. She's great."

"Was the chaplain position Lauren's idea?"

"Only my participation in it. Our new ER director requested that the program be put into motion while he was still negotiating with the hospital on his contract. Lauren called me as soon as she heard about it. When can we get together?" he asked, changing the subject abruptly.

There was a quiet hesitation. "Friday is still your day off, isn't it?"

"Yes." Oh no, hold it. That wasn't exactly true. He had a couple of appointments tomorrow but maybe he could fit everything in. "How about lunch?"

"How about making a day of it? I can get you a ticket to our afternoon show at two."

He bit his lip, thinking. Yes, it could be done. "I'd love it. I have a counseling session in the morning and then Lauren and I are making a visit late tomorrow afternoon to follow up on a patient. I should be back in time for that."

"Oh. Well, I guess I'll see you tomorrow about noon?"

"I'll pick you up. Thanks for calling, Jessica."

There was a long silence. "Sure. Goodbye."

Somehow, when Archer hung up, he didn't feel quite as elated as he would have expected to. It might have had something to do with Jessica's sudden apparent lack of enthusiasm. Maybe she wasn't feeling well. Archer hoped she hadn't caught the bug that was going around.

❧ CHAPTER 13 ❧

Sergeant Tony Dalton gripped his gun and crept with soundless steps across the concrete front porch of the only unoccupied house on Sycamore Street. With a quick nod he signaled for his younger partner, Henry, to come in closer. The station had received a call ten minutes ago about suspicious activity here. The caller described an intruder he saw slip into the building just after dawn.

His description sounded uncomfortably familiar. For the past six weeks Tony had been after a man who used the street name "Peregrine." The man befriended the teenagers who cruised on Friday and Saturday nights.

The problem with Peregrine was that he always seemed to be a step ahead of them, as if he had inside information. He knew whom to approach and he knew how to avoid arrest. Tony had no doubt that the man was a drug kingpin but until two weeks ago no one had been willing to talk.

Thanks to frightened but brave Evan Webster they now had a little more information to go on. And thanks to old Mr. Scroggs, who had a good memory for detail, they might even have a good case with which to nail this guy. If Peregrine thought he could hide out in this empty house, he'd underestimated the neighborhood watch.

Avoiding the windows, Tony inched toward the front door. The two officers going around to the back of the house would be in place by now. He made no noise, cast no shadow, but before he could reach the knob and test it he heard a soft thud of footsteps inside the house.

"He's moving," he whispered to Henry. "Get into place."

From the back of the house came a cry of alarm and a report of gunfire.

Tony signaled for Henry to stay by the door and quickstepped to the side of the porch. He turned the corner just in time to see a dark figure retreating into the trees with two officers in pursuit.

"Door's unlocked," Henry called from behind him. "I'm going in."

Tony swung around. "No!"

His partner pushed the door open as Tony rushed toward him and shoved him aside. The telltale hiss of a popped cork preceded the blaze of spewed ammonia that caught Tony full in the face like knives of fire stabbing his eyes.

On instinct, he did not inhale as he stumbled off the porch into ankle-deep grass. Only then did he allow himself to breathe. He gasped and screamed with agony.

"All's fine in Knolls, Lauren."

"Let me guess—the only repeat customer you've had lately has been Cowboy."

Lukas Bower's deep baritone laughter gave Lauren a feeling of peace she hadn't expected—and for reasons she wouldn't have imagined a few weeks ago. "He's adding camels to his ranch. When he got his first shipment the bison didn't take too kindly to the newcomers. He had to do some herding and fix a few fences."

"Nothing new, then."

"Nope. Are you really concerned about an epidemic?"

"I think it's a definite possibility at this point," she said. "We lost a patient this morning who presented to the ER last night with simple viral symptoms. A little girl had the same symptoms a couple of weeks ago and she developed diabetes. Dr. Sheldon has been reviewing the case and can't find anything unusual."

She explained more about the problem and found herself relaxing further. Lukas was still the brilliant doctor she had worked with. Now that she was removed from the situation in Knolls, however, she realized it was his kindness and dedication she had responded to. He was an attractive man in every way. She simply liked him. Maybe she hadn't made quite the fool of herself she'd always believed she had.

Then again maybe she had. "Thank you for your help, Lukas. I'm sure Mercy would have mentioned any unusual problems at the clinic."

"Yes. I wish there was more I could do."

"If you hear of anything would you let me know?"

"Of course."

After she thanked him and hung up, Lauren leaned back in her chair and tried to study the notes she had been taking for the past thirty minutes. Instead, she considered what she'd told Gina last week about the reason she came to Dogwood Springs.

From her teen years into her twenties, Lauren hadn't been terribly interested in dating. Her passion was her career. At one time she'd planned to become a doctor. Her large farming family, however, didn't have the money for medical school and Lauren came from a long line of McCaffreys who hated debt. She took to nursing as if she'd been made for it and she put her whole heart into it.

Now all of a sudden, in the space of a year, she had reacted to two attractive men like some o the hormone-driven teenagers she used to run around with in high school. Her biological clock truly was ticking and her mother's constant reminders about grandchildren didn't help.

But something else was at work here. She was lonely. Everywhere she looked she saw married couples, engaged couples, families all spending time together. Sure, a lot of those families had problems but at least they had someone to come home to. Maybe the married couples who complained about their spouses wouldn't be so critical if they knew how it felt to live alone, if they could imagine not having a confidante to share their thoughts with or a companion who cared more for them than anyone else in the world. Everybody she knew had someone else.

Until recently, despite her wish for children, Lauren had been able to deal with the single life. But in the past year she'd come to realize that this sense of being alone in the world in spite of loving parents and brothers and sisters might be her experience for the rest of her life.

She didn't want to live that way.

And yet, how many more times did she want to express her attraction to a man only to discover he had no interest in her whatsoever?

Grant came back and sat down beside her.

She gave him her report. "Nothing out of the ordinary in Knolls, Branson, West Plains, or Harrison. Whatever this is, it's selective."

"So it's all local." He completed his first stack of files and shoved it aside. "It could be an epidemic but it doesn't seem to be spreading yet. I'll do some more checking and then talk to our administrator. Right now I doubt if anyone will pay much attention and I could be jumping to conclusions that are all based on suppositions. I'd like to interview some patients before we take this further. Maybe they're all eating at the same restaurant or something. We might have a new version of Typhoid Mary on our hands. Except this isn't typhoid."

Lauren watched him for a moment as he jotted a few notes. "Grant, do you mind if I ask you one more personal question?"

He laid the pen down and slid the writing pad aside before he turned to make eye contact with her. "Let me guess, you want to know the time and date I became a believer."

She smiled. "How did you know?"

"Because it's something Annette would have asked." He looked away briefly.

"Oh? Was she as nosy as I am? You don't have to tell me anything. It's none of my business."

"I was seventeen."

She smiled her thanks and he returned the smile. "You'd have liked her."

"I'm sure I would have loved her. How did you two meet?"

"I was doing speed. I was getting drunk when I couldn't get high and I was staying away from home on weekends; my parents were going through a nasty divorce. I didn't want anything to do with them."

For once she didn't know what to say. She had discovered after working only a few shifts with this man that he was very forthright about himself, both with patients and the staff. If he didn't know something about a patient's case he admitted it. Rather than causing confusion, his honesty inspired confidence. He was willing to share facts about his personal experiences if he thought it would make an impact on one of his patients. But he had never shared this much before.

"Annette was a newcomer to my high school in eleventh grade," he said. "She was an innocent. A teetotaling Christian. She didn't want anything to do with me except get me 'saved.' She had these magnificent eyes that seemed to look right through me. She talked with her whole body, with her hands constantly in motion."

"Yep, I'd have definitely been her best friend in school."

"For some reason I couldn't stay away from her," he said. "So when she invited me to a youth rally, I went." He shrugged. "Apparently, she thought she saw something worthwhile in me. It was only a matter of time before I was confessing my sins and praying for Christ to take control of my life." There was an edge of sarcasm in Grant's voice but it sounded more directed toward himself than God.

"Then what?" Lauren asked.

"I kicked the speed and the alcohol, started going to church, and stopped skipping school so often. My grades improved so dramatically I earned a scholarship the next year. I married Annette three years later."

Lauren leaned forward until Grant was forced to look at her. "After all this time, why haven't you forgiven yourself if you know God forgave you?"

"Don't you Baptists still believe there's such a thing as backsliding?"

"It depends on what you mean. Did you really expect to become a perfect person after you became a believer?"

"No, but I didn't expect to doubt my faith years later either."

"God is more than an emotional experience. Doubts are normal, Grant. There's nothing wrong with examining your faith."

"I didn't just examine it, I think I lost it."

"I've felt that way before but God's faithfulness isn't dependent on you."

Grant shook his head. "After the auto accident that killed Annette, my addiction found me again. I sustained a back injury in the crash and I had to have pain medication. I continued to need it after the damage healed. I was hooked again after all those years of thinking God had healed me for good."

"You know that happens a lot. It's the nature of the narcotic beast. It hits you before you know it and increases the pain between doses until you're convinced you can't endure without it."

"I should have realized it."

"Developing a physical dependency isn't anything like backsliding."

"Brooke and Beau were struggling to come to

terms with the loss of their mother. Beau was injured and enduring repeated surgeries and I couldn't be the father they needed because I was taking far too many narcotics."

"Legal drugs."

"They were narcotics. Don't tempt me to make excuses for myself."

"Are you still taking them?"

"No. I weaned myself down to two pills a day, then kicked it cold turkey. Not something I'd recommend but I did discover that it was, indeed, the narcotic that was enhancing the pain receptors. It can be a vicious cycle."

"So you're not addicted now."

"No."

"Not to drugs anyway, huh? Sounds like you're addicted to an old enemy."

He looked up at her.

"Guilt," she said.

Grant pushed away from the desk and stood, a strong signal to Lauren that she was attacking a wall he didn't want breached. He reached for the folders, stacked them, turned back to her. "Archer has invited my family to go fishing with your church's youth group a week from tomorrow."

She didn't react to the sudden change of subject. "That's great. We'll have fun."

He raised a hand. "Before you meet Beau, there's something you need to know about him. A piece of metal from the doorframe took a couple of slices out of his face during the accident. He suffered considerable nerve damage."

Lauren caught her breath. How much pain was one family expected to endure?

"He's had extensive plastic surgery since the accident. The best surgeons in the state weren't able to repair the damaged nerve," Grant said. "He cannot smile or laugh with his facial muscles. It's important to me that he isn't made to feel uncomfortable about it."

"Of course it would be. I'm glad you told me. I'd rather see you hover over your children than block them out after your loss. I've seen too much of the other."

"I don't think they appreciate the hovering very much."

"I think it's a loving trait," she said softly, feeling her eyes sting with compassion for this man and his wounded family. "Isn't that what parental love is all about? My parents hover too much. I may feel smothered sometimes but I always feel loved. Was Brooke injured?"

"She wasn't with us."

The secretary turned and waved from across the room. "Dr. Sheldon, we just got a call from the police. The ambulance is on its way here with an officer who caught ammonia in his face. The paramedic is requesting medical control."

Grant nodded to Lauren and they rushed toward the front.

. . .

Thirty-three-year-old Tony Dalton was guided feet first through the automatic double doors of the ER. His gurney was being pulled by an EMT and pushed by one of the police officers as a paramedic irrigated Tony's gauze-covered eyes with saline from a plastic bottle. His moans of pain were a definite improvement from the loud cries Grant had heard over the ambulance radio a few moments ago.

"Is that morphine easing any of the pain?" Grant asked.

"A lot," the paramedic said. "It's okay Tony, we're here now."

Two officers in black uniforms surged into the department before the entrance doors closed. They stayed out of the way but announced their presence to their sergeant.

"My wife? Where's Caryn?" Tony asked.

"Henry said he'd call her as soon as we drove off," one of the officers replied.

"I heard. I don't believe him." Tony's voice disintegrated into another moan. "He promised to wait for my order. He didn't."

"Our secretary will call your wife, Sergeant Dalton." Grant directed the attendants to the trauma room. "Is there anyone else you need us to contact?"

"Archer. Get Archer. My eyes burn so bad. Did they get the perp?"

"No Sergeant, he escaped out the back."

Tony moaned again. "I heard a shot."

"He fired at us when he ran out the back door but didn't hit us. We couldn't return fire. Too many homes nearby."

"Get back out there and help the others look. That slime is going to end up killing our kids if we don't stop him."

Grant helped the attendants transfer his patient to a bed. "Officers, no more questions until we start treatment on his eyes. Lauren, are the Morgan lenses ready? And have the litmus paper ready."

"I've got it. Here's the tetracaine."

He removed the gauze from Tony's right eye and winced at the damage from the caustic burns. The cornea and sclera were distorted.

Grant took the litmus paper and touched it to the eye then took the small vial of tetracaine from Lauren, snapped the top off and squeezed in four drops. Meanwhile the paper turned dark green. Very caustic. This man was going to lose his sight.

The tetracaine worked quickly. Grant placed a Morgan lens beneath the upper and lower lids of the right eye while Lauren hung the IV fluid from the bedside pole and connected the tubing to the lens to give continuous irrigation. They quickly repeated the process with the left eye.

"Do you have any throat irritation?" Grant asked Tony. "Shortness of breath?"

"Not much." He grimaced. "I didn't breathe it."

In spite of Tony's protests, Grant gave orders to administer additional morphine through the IV the paramedic had established. It was obvious the pain was returning.

Tony's face, neck, and arms were red with blisters.

Grant turned to the other RN on duty. "Emma, have Vivian call Lifeline and make sure that air-lift is on its way. Get me the ophthalmologist on call with Mercy Hospital in Springfield and notify the burn team. Call Archer and send him to intercept at the hospital. He'll want to be there for his friend."

Twenty minutes later, when the helicopter made its noisy arrival outside, a repeat litmus test still proved markedly alkaline. They continued irrigation. The prognosis for Tony's eyes, though better than when he first came in, was still discouraging.

At ten-thirty Thursday night Archer drove down a familiar street in Branson and parked in front of a residential complex. In the daytime, Jessica had an incredible view of a valley of trees and uninhabited wilderness. Despite a central theme of lights and shows and traffic and congestion, this center of entertainment still held a powerful charm just past the flicker of neon.

A glow outlined the front window of Jessica's townhouse. Maybe she was home from her show.

Archer could have called from the hospital in Springfield but since he had to pass through Branson to get to Dogwood Springs, he couldn't resist stopping. It had been too long since he'd seen her face and tomorrow he wouldn't have a chance.

When he rang the doorbell the front porch light came on almost immediately and he posed for the peephole with a smile and a wave. He heard soft laughter as the door opened.

Jessica had already removed her stage makeup. The strong smiling lines of her expressive face had a translucent glow. She wore faded baggy jeans and a purple T-shirt. Her wavy brown hair the shade of autumn oak leaves fell across her neck and shoulders as she reached for him and drew him into an enthusiastic embrace. He melted against her and held her close. And heaven was better than this? Amazing.

"Oh Archer how did you know? I was just thinking about how much I wanted to see you again, how much I've missed you." She drew back to look into his face.

Archer stood in the doorway watching the sparkle in her eyes and he knew he probably looked like the biggest dope in a town full of some pretty dopey people. He suddenly remembered every single reason he loved her so much.

Jessica took his arm and led him inside as he closed the door behind him. Then she sat on the sofa and patted the spot beside her. "Why did you come tonight instead of tomorrow? And what are you doing out so late on a weeknight?"

"A friend of mine was wounded in the line of duty today," he said as he sank to her side. He told her about Tony and about haunting the hallways at the hospital in Springfield for most of the day as he waited to hear from the doctors about whether or not Tony's eyes could be saved. They still didn't know when he left the hospital.

"I'm so sorry." Jessica's voice was a little softer than usual, as it always was after several long nights of singing. "You look tired."

"He was wounded protecting people like me."

She leaned closer to him and took his arm. "I know why you came here tonight."

"Why is that?"

"Because you're breaking our date for tomorrow and coming by to tell me in person was the gentlest way to do it."

"I came by for entirely selfish motives. I wanted to see you."

"But you did come to break our date because you're not going to be available tomorrow. You're taking your day off to go back to Tony's bedside because that's where you know you need to be and that's your chosen profession."

Archer watched her face, surprised by the fact that he saw no resentment there. Maybe some disappointment but in a way that was a good thing.

"You will slowly give your whole self to your profession the way Tony has. You're taking risks that may not be as dangerous physically but they take their toll emotionally. In the long run they will take just as much out of you."

"That used to upset you. What's changed?"

She gave him a gentle smile. "I've been thinking about this a lot lately. How can I find fault in what you do when I do the same? I work long hours and I don't always get enough sleep. I risk damaging my vocal cords when I don't take the time to practice and stretch my range before I tackle a demanding piece of music." She reached up and touched her throat. "And yet I keep pushing. When someone asks me to sing, I accept even to the point of overuse. Because I love it."

"Does this mean—"

She touched his lips with her fingers. "What it means, Archer Pierce, is that because I care so very much about you, I am going to send you home now so you can get some rest. And so can I."

"But maybe we could—"

"I'm waiting to hear from God about us. I have a tendency to be impulsive but you mean too much to me to leap into another commitment we might not be able to work out for ourselves. What we do affects too many people. And too much of my heart. I want to make the right decision for you and for me." With a charming display of that impulsive nature Jessica tried so hard to discipline, she gave him a sweet intoxicating kiss then stood and held out her hand.

She saw him to the door and out into the night. He drove home with the memory of her kiss enveloping his whole heart.

❧ Chapter 14 ❧

On Friday morning Archer pulled into the church parking lot ten minutes later than his typical time. That rarely happened even on a day off. Several members of the church family had called last night to ask about Tony. This was a church emergency.

Archer was tired but there would be no time to rest today.

"Good morning Archer." Mrs. Boucher, the church secretary, looked up from a stack of mail on her desk when he entered. "The Websters are already in your office waiting for you."

"Thank you." He took a deep breath and rubbed his neck in an attempt to restore some function to his tired brain.

Today Evan's eyes were clear and his gaze more alert. When Archer greeted him, he stood respectfully and shook hands. He had a firm grip much like his father's.

"I'm glad you could make it today," Archer said. He took a chair across from them instead of sitting behind his desk. "Evan, before I forget it, some of us are planning a little fishing trip next Friday. Would you like to join us?"

Evan's eyes widened with surprise. "Sure. If I can. I mean, I'd have to ask my mom first but she hasn't grounded me or anything." A fresh smile of eager excitement transformed him. "I'd really like that."

"Good. I'll try to pick you up around one-forty-five." Archer looked at Norville, whose expression mirrored his son's. "How about you? You're welcome to join us."

"I'll be at work but by all means take Evan with you. He's never been fishing before."

"We're planning to invite some other teen-agers from church. Since Dr. Sheldon just moved to the area with his son and daughter, we want to make them all feel welcome in the community, show them around a little."

Evan's expression brightened further. "Dr. Sheldon's going to be there? All right!"

Norville's smile faded into concern. "Does he know Evan might be there?"

The brightness left Evan's face. "Dad."

"No, I didn't . . . I mean . . . that isn't what—"

"If I know Grant, he'll be happy to see Evan," Archer said quickly. "I think they established a good rapport, don't you Evan?"

The boy slumped in his chair. "Yeah." He cupped his hands together in his lap.

Before Archer could say anything more, the

telephone rang at his desk. He glanced at it, surprised. Mrs. Boucher never sent him calls during counseling sessions.

Except for emergencies.

He reached across the front of the desk and picked up. "Yes?"

"I wouldn't have disturbed you," Mrs. Boucher told him, "but you need to take this call from a very upset Caryn Dalton."

"About Tony?"

The lady nodded. "You need to talk to her."

Archer would have to brace himself. "Of course." He cast Norville and Evan an apologetic look.

There was a click and Archer heard the soft sound of crying. "Caryn? What's going on? What's happening with Tony?"

For a moment she didn't respond. While he waited, he saw Evan lean toward his father. "You make me sound like I'm some kind of contagious sicko. I blew it, okay? Do you have to remind me about it for the rest of my life?"

"I didn't mean for it to come out like—"

"Archer?" Caryn's voice came shaky and faint across the line. Archer turned his back to the arguing family and switched gears again.

"What's happening with Tony? Are you okay?"

"The doctors just told us he's going to be blind. There's too much damage . . ." Her voice faded in and out with tears, mingling with the quiet discussion that continued behind him.

". . . what people tend to think when something like this happens. You'll have to rebuild your reputation one act at a time. It won't be easy."

"Archer," Caryn said at last, "can you come to Springfield? He needs somebody to talk to."

Archer checked his watch. It was eight-thirty. He couldn't just dismiss Evan and Norville. "I'll try to make it by ten-thirty. Meanwhile, I'll be praying." It was times like this he wished he could still call Jessica. When they were engaged there were a couple of times he'd called her to ride with him from Branson to Springfield when he needed to make a hospital visit. But now wasn't the time.

He disconnected and turned to find father and son still in discussion about the trouble Evan was having with his old friends and his difficulties making new ones and the ongoing battle with his mother.

Evan sat up straighter in his chair and made eye contact with his father. "You and Mom need to find some common ground where we can all practice behaving like intelligent human beings. I can't do this alone, Dad. It isn't just my problem, it's our problem."

Norville held his gaze for a moment and then nodded. "It shouldn't be your problem. I'm sorry."

Evan held his father's gaze for several seconds before his face reddened and his shoulders slumped. "Dr. Sheldon talked to me about it the night I was there. He understands."

"You're right," Archer said. "That's why I think you'd enjoy an outing with him and his family. But what your family's going through is a societal problem. Most important, it's God's problem, because He doesn't want you to struggle with it alone. Why don't we pray and bring Him into the equation?"

Norville looked relieved. Evan looked hopeful. Archer was excited. *Lord, wait until they see what you can do.*

Grant had never noticed how friendly folks could be in a small town but as he drove downhill toward City Hall, he counted seven people waving at him. And they weren't the angry waves of overstressed big-city drivers. Four of them were elderly pedestrians in jogging outfits and running shoes. One was a policeman in his cruiser, one was an older lady who was barely tall enough to peer over her steering wheel, and the last one was a gardener pruning blooms in one of a multitude of side gardens dotting the town.

Grant had never been an art expert but he'd always admired paintings of quaint village shops surrounded by flowers set deep into craggy hillsides with streams trickling somewhere nearby. In Dogwood Springs he felt as if he was living in the center of one of those pictures complete with streets constructed of brick. Virginia creeper vines climbed the concrete block walls of City Hall and a stream half-circled the building like a castle moat. Unfortunately, Grant had begun to realize that a snake could be lurking beneath the bed of cheerful flowers. Maybe more than one. Try as he might, he couldn't stop thinking about the nasty attack on Sergeant Tony Dalton yesterday. That trap had been set to cause serious injury. Someone in Dogwood Springs had a rotten heart.

At City Hall he pulled open the glass door and stepped into another picturesque scene—this time a Norman Rockwell. A huge high-ceilinged area the size of an old-fashioned ballroom reverberated with the chatter and laughter of at least fifteen conversations. Clusters of well-dressed people sat at tables around the great hall eating and drinking, laughing, and calling to one another. The smell of food reminded Grant that he hadn't even eaten breakfast and these people were already taking their morning break.

Two elderly men, two suit-clad women, and two children leaned over a table covered with pieces of a puzzle. In the top left corner, a square of blue and green had already been put together. One of the women at the table turned her head to the side and coughed. A child across from her sneezed into his hand then picked up a puzzle piece with that same hand.

Grant cringed at the thought of the germs they must be spreading. Annette used to tease him about what she called his obsession with infection.

He ambled over to the table. "Nice picture." He actually couldn't tell what the setting was supposed to be yet. "Is this a community project?"

One of the men appeared to be in his eighties. He placed a piece and chuckled with satisfaction. "Sure is." He didn't look up but selected another piece and continued to study the board. "This table's always busy." He gestured toward the wall to their west. His thick gray eyebrows formed a straight line across his face, lending gravity to the expressive good humor in his eyes.

Three framed scenes adorned the wall. Grant recognized two of them from his forays through Dogwood Springs and they all had a common theme—streams coursing across a meadow or garden or trickling down a hillside.

"It's the springs." The man straightened and squinted at Grant.

"Springs?"

"Not from around here, huh?"

Grant smiled and shook his head.

The man stood up, turned from the table, and held out his hand with a slight bow. "Ernest Mourglia. And you might be . . . ?"

"Grant Sheldon. I moved down from St. Louis recently with my family. This is obviously a popular place."

Ernest glanced toward the puzzle as if afraid

someone else might take his spot while he was otherwise occupied. "Jade got the bright idea a few months ago to have puzzles made out of pictures of our springs then sell 'em to the tourists."

"Jade?"

"You really are new here. Jade Myers is the mayor. Bright girl still wet behind the ears, not even thirty-five yet." A smile pressed itself across his craggy sun-worn face. "My niece. After they started selling the puzzles, Jade decided that wasn't good enough. She decided to make a city-wide effort to put 'em together and display 'em on the walls, kind of make it a showcase to draw some of that Branson traffic our way."

"She sounds like an industrious lady." And one he would speak with as soon as possible about the risk of the community puzzle.

"I didn't like it at first," Ernest continued. "Didn't want the crowds. This used to be a nice peaceful place to come and sit for a few hours and talk to a couple of friends who might wander| over for lunch. But now you wouldn't believe how many old friends I get to see every day." He shook his head. "Always need something to get you out of yourself when you live alone and can't find a fishin' partner."

"How many springs does the city have?"

Mr. Mourglia stepped closer, obviously glad to find a listening ear. "We've got fifteen of 'em inside the city limits and quite a few more outside, so we've got our work cut out for us. Just you wait, though. As soon as they get that bottling plant up and runnin' we'll be famous. And that'll be good for the puzzle business. Stores are already carryin' 'em all over town. Sellin' too."

"Bottling plant?" Grant had heard nothing more about that project since the big-equipment operator with the wandering hands mentioned it at the hospital.

Mr. Mourglia nodded. "That was another one of Jade's wild ideas. But I guess she convinced somebody to listen. They say it won't take too much of our water."

"Hey!" another man called from across the room.

Ernest turned and squinted, then brightened and turned back to Grant. "I might've found me a fishin' buddy after all. And he's my barber too. Maybe he'll give me a haircut if the fish aren't bitin'. Pleased to meet you, Mr. Sheldon." He reached out to shake hands again and said good-bye.

Grant felt a weight settle on him as he watched others wander up to the table and pick up where Ernest had left off. A community-wide jigsaw puzzle could feasibly be spreading the pervasive virus, which had already taken one life and threatened another and seemed to be infecting more people every day. What was he supposed to do, march into the mayor's office and demand she stop all the fun? Or maybe he should insist they sterilize the puzzle pieces every time someone new came to the table. But even that wouldn't stop it all.

He'd run some blood tests for Giardia and E. coli and a few other infectious diseases and found nothing. Not influenza, not some weird community-acquired pneumonia. He had a stack of files on his desk at least two feet high. His comparisons so far had turned up no related numbers that he considered significant and several times he'd almost convinced himself he was being paranoid. Almost.

Lives were definitely at stake. When Grant asked directions to the mayor's office, the receptionist told him Jade was out running errands. He decided to wait.

By ten-fifteen Archer was walking down a wide hallway of one of the major hospitals in Springfield. He'd spent a lot of time here over the years making visits with his father when he was still in high school and afterward on his own.

Some pastors dreaded this part of the job. He'd never found hospitals to be the most comforting of places to pass the day, either, but they were certainly one of the best places for a guy to go when he wanted to tell somebody about God. Stuck in hospital beds, people had to listen and most often they were eager to do so. Nothing could open the human heart to important matters of the spirit like a threat to life or health.

Today he wouldn't have to do any proselytizing. Tony Dalton had walked the aisle of the Dogwood Springs Baptist Church two months before Archer. Both of them were ten at the time. Both had been raised in church, attended the same Sunday school classes, and sang in the youth choir. And Tony had always done it better.

Tony got high grades. Tony got the solo tenor parts in choir. Tony excelled in math and sports and was valedictorian. Probably the only thing that had kept Archer and Tony from being the best of friends was Dad's open admiration for Tony. Archer had repented of his jealousy years ago.

Today Tony was in bed with white bandages covering his eyes. Caryn sat at his side with her forehead resting on his pillow, her sparrow brown hair falling across the tanned flesh of his arm.

"Hello you two." Archer swallowed in an effort to keep his voice steady.

Caryn straightened. Her pale face and blood-less lips showed how grief had drained her. "Hi Archer." She got up and walked around the bed to hug him. She felt frail in his arms. "Talk to him," she whispered.

Tony turned his head. "Arch?" He held his hand out, fingers spread in an unconscious gesture of vulnerability.

Archer stepped forward and took it. "You look

like you're doing a little better than you were last night."

The hand tightened on Archer's then relaxed. Tony laid his head back. He licked his lips, pressed them together, sighed. "Caryn said she told you."

"Yes."

As if he had to review the facts for himself in order to make sense of them, Tony repeated what Archer had already heard. "The eyes are too badly damaged." Tony's hand squeezed into a fist and he pressed it against his chest. "The insurance guys were here already. I'm a great candidate for full disability."

"They don't know you," Archer said.

Tony's voice grew ragged. "They want me to sit on my butt and draw checks for doing nothing the rest of my life."

"But we know better."

"I might as well be—"

"Tony." Caryn stepped to the end of the bed and gripped the rail with both hands. "Please don't talk like that, sweetheart." She gave Archer a beseeching look.

"Give yourself time," Archer said.

Tony shook his head. "My job is over. I'll never be a policeman again. I'll never be able to drive again. My wife will have to drive me around and watch after me like an invalid."

Archer saw the lance of pain race across Caryn's face.

"Anthony Dalton, I can't believe you would even use that word," Archer said.

Tony didn't reply.

"Did that chemical reach your brain as well as your eyes?"

Caryn's mouth flew open but Archer raised a hand. "Don't you remember that beautiful speech you gave graduation night? Come on, it wasn't *that* long ago."

After a few seconds of silence, Tony gave a barely perceptible nod. "I didn't know any better then. I do now. I was a stupid kid."

"You were obviously smarter then than you are now."

"Archer," Caryn warned.

"I bet he never told you about his valedictory speech, did he?"

She shook her head.

"He received a standing ovation after talking about the role of the physically challenged in the scheme of life, that they can be the strongest of us all because they're forced to fight harder and build extra muscle. Then he dissected the word *invalid,* explaining that everyone has validity. His inspiration had come from working with disabled children at the elementary school during his free hour."

Caryn blinked and looked back at her husband who had not moved.

"I remember the speech really well," Archer

added, "because Tony spoke the same passionate words to our congregation that next Sunday at Dad's request. And Dad reminded me of that speech for the next six months until I was sick to death of Tony Dalton's name."

At that, a bare hint of a smile touched Tony's lips and then it was gone. Caryn stood at the end of the bed still grasping the rail, her eyes suddenly focused on her husband's mouth.

"This accident has done nothing to invalidate who you are," Archer said. "It doesn't invalidate you in God's eyes."

"What good is a blind policeman?"

"As good as you're willing to be," Archer said. "What do you want to do? That's usually what you've done."

Tony's jaw muscles flexed. He shook his head.

Caryn stepped from the foot of the bed to her husband's side. "Sweetheart, you've always told me you want to teach." She looked up at Archer. "His chief told me two weeks ago that Tony knows more about meth production in our county than anyone else on the force."

"I'm also supposed to know more about the traps they set," Tony muttered. "Look where that got me."

"It isn't as if you can crawl into the minds of these people," Archer protested.

"I'm supposed to try. Otherwise I won't be much good to myself or anyone else."

"But that's crazy," Caryn said.

"No, it's essential." Tony sat forward and the keenly contained energy that had always been a part of Tony Dalton once more filled the air around him. "It's vital because the rules are always changing. All a guy has to do is let down his guard one time and it's over." Tony spread his hands. "You've got to think like a monster. We can't wait around until they change something on us; we've got to beat them at their own game." The energy increased.

Archer and Caryn looked at each other. Caryn nodded.

"I don't think it's over for you," Archer said to his old friend.

"It's dangerous out there. I told you the other night that crime is on the rise. I keep trying to warn people that our little town is in for trouble. Nobody wants to listen."

"I'm listening," Archer said. "Why don't you start by talking to my drug awareness class as soon as they spring you from here?"

Tony nodded. "They need to know. It's just so hard to keep up with all of it. I've been too busy fighting it."

"For the moment, I think that's changed." Archer looked across the bed at Caryn. She nodded. Tony's job would never end.

❧ CHAPTER 15 ❧

Lauren appreciated the changing seasons in the Ozarks and every season had its own special mood. Summer was her favorite in this town for the moment. These people did things a little differently—with more style, more extravagance, more flowers—than in her hometown.

On Friday afternoon, as she rode in the passenger's seat of Archer's two-year-old Kia, she drank in the effusive beauty of the hillside community while she allowed herself to enjoy the fact that Archer had sought her company for this visit.

"Grant Sheldon impresses me." Archer touched the brake and turned onto a road that wound between widely spaced homes, most of them painted in pretty pastel colors, with broad porches that invited visitors to make themselves comfortable on a porch swing or a wicker chair. The late afternoon sun highlighted Archer's handsome silhouette against a backdrop of blue sky.

"The staff likes him," Lauren said. "He knows how to handle people." She thought about the drunken jerk Grant had shut down Wednesday night. "He's making some good changes in the ER like shortening shift hours and overlapping schedules so we have double physician coverage at peak times. We needed that."

"Shortening hours?" He gave her a quick look. "And that makes him popular?"

"So far he's managing to do it without ruffling too many feathers." She thought of Dr. Caine. "Some feathers need to be ruffled and he doesn't mind doing that. You have to respect that kind of leadership."

Archer gave her his customary sideways teasing grin that she always thought made him look like a very young Paul Newman. "You wouldn't happen to be slightly biased would you? He's a good-looking eligible bachelor."

Without thinking, Lauren returned the grin in full measure and winked at him. "He isn't the only good-looking single guy in town." As soon as the words were out of her mouth she felt the warmth of embarrassment spread across her face. Perhaps she should have asked to ride in the trunk.

At thirty-five, she had long ago despaired of ever learning to control her tongue, whether it be talking too much or saying the wrong thing at the wrong time.

Until recently she'd never been uncomfortable in Archer's presence. Never before had she thought of him as anything other than a very likeable friend of her younger brothers. She'd arm wrestled and played one-on-one basketball with them and given them Dutch rubs when they got out of line and no grown-ups were around.

Only lately had she become increasingly aware of him as a very attractive man who had an inner light that filled his eyes with passion and excitement whenever he spoke about his love for Jesus Christ. That was one of the most appealing things about him. The better she understood him as a man and not just "one of the boys" the more powerful grew that appeal. She thought about her discussion with Gina last week. It had been difficult enough to get accustomed to the idea of Archer Pierce as her pastor when she joined the church. But it felt really weird to be attracted to him as a man, especially one who had been very happily engaged until a few weeks ago.

A stray dog ambled out onto the road and Archer stomped on the brakes. He didn't honk, didn't complain, didn't even shake his head, he just watched to make sure the animal was off the road completely before moving on.

"Lauren, did you hear about Tony?" He glanced across at her while she was still staring at him in admiration.

She looked away. "Yes. I called this afternoon to check on him. How's he handling it?"

"He's already making plans for a career change."

"I'll give Caryn a call."

"I thought you might." He signaled and turned onto Cascade Circle Drive.

The road wound through an older neighborhood that had recently received a facelift. The address they sought was in a cul-de-sac set slightly apart from the other more stately homes. Gina's house was an attractive dove gray color with burgundy gingerbread trim and Victorian lace curtains in the windows. It appeared enshrouded by an evergreen hedge that threatened to overtake the sidewalk and yard.

When Gina answered the doorbell she was barefoot except for bandages. She wore a pair of denim cutoffs frayed above the knees. Curls of golden copper hair tumbled across her wide freckled forehead. She could have passed for a carefree teenager except for the tight lines around her mouth and the flash of anger in her eyes.

"I don't know how much more of this I can take." Instead of inviting them inside, she stepped out onto the porch and allowed the door to shut behind her. She and Lauren had been to lunch a few times and the comfort of deepening friendship continued to grow between them. "That woman doesn't give me any breaks."

"What woman?" Lauren asked.

"Natalie. Who else? She's always here, always following me around the house asking me personal questions and grilling my kids. She's like a long-legged, long-necked goose who thinks my house is her own private lake."

"I'm sorry," Archer said. "Did we come at a bad time?"

"No." There was defensiveness in Gina's tone. "I have a right to receive company in my own home."

"Of course you do. You have a beautiful home." He stepped over and examined the sculpted gingerbread trim around a window.

Gina shoved her hands into the back pockets of her shorts.

Lauren didn't comment. She knew from several talks with Gina these past two weeks that her reluctance to accept help from Family Services went a lot deeper than just an independent nature. Something else was going on here and Gina showed no willingness to share.

The young respiratory therapist didn't smile much at work lately and several people on the emergency staff had noticed. Last week when Gina had her physical exam, none of her tests had shown a problem. She had placed her hope on some evidence of low blood sugar and that hope had been dashed when her tests showed normal. Her psychological tests had also revealed no problem.

"She's in the dining room with the kids right now," Gina continued, her voice softer but no less resentful. "She's probably trying to find out if I've been abusing them."

"Finding blame isn't what this is about," Lauren said.

Gina shrugged and sighed. "We'll see."

"Want to sit down and talk about it?" Archer asked.

Gina hesitated. The steady directness of her gaze shifted from him to Lauren.

He corrected quickly. "Better yet why don't you point me to your hedge trimmers and I'll have a go at the jungle that's threatening to take over your yard while the two of you talk."

The tightness relaxed from around Gina's mouth and a hesitant smile spread to her eyes. She told Archer where to find what he needed in her garage and he leapt from the porch. As he jogged away from them, Lauren couldn't resist an appreciative glance at the way the late afternoon sunlight teased flashes of flame from his short brown hair. The broad shoulders were also nice.

"I see what you mean."

Lauren blinked and looked at Gina to find an amused grin on her face. "What do I mean?"

"No wonder you like him so much. He's good-looking, sensitive, and he does yard work. Obviously athletic too. He has muscles where most men have flab."

Since there was no porch furniture, Lauren led the way to the front steps and sat down. "What's going on between you and Natalie? You're obviously still striking sparks."

Gina sighed and sank down, ruffling her hair with frustration. "I can't get used to her barging into my home and trying to take over my life.

205

She hardly knows me and yet she bombards me with all these questions, from my eating habits to the medicines we take to the kinds of cookware I use. She even checked out my vitamins. And she snooped into my family background. Called it a genogram. This woman wanted a family tree on me! Wanted to know what my childhood was like, how my parents raised me." She shivered. "It's creepy."

"Did you give her the info she needed?"

There was an expressive silence. "Only what she needed to know." Gina pressed her lips together as Archer returned from the garage, hedge clippers in hand. She lowered her voice. "My past is nobody's business."

Lauren suppressed a sigh. "An unbiased stranger might be able to find some clue about what's going on with you."

"Oh sure, and she might also find enough evidence against me to go flying into court and convince them to take my kids away from me. Last night she brought up the subject of foster care again. 'Just as a worst-case scenario,' she says." Gina glared at the sidewalk in front of them. "I told her if she didn't change the subject, I'd show *her* a worst-case scenario."

Lauren closed her eyes. Apparently the red hair really did come with a temper.

"Sorry," Gina said. "I'm venting. Honest, I'm not usually this cranky but it's been so long since

I've had anybody try to tell me how to live my life. She just barges in and plants herself in my home. And that other social worker, the one from the hospital?"

"Rose Pascal?"

"You heard what she said at that wraparound meeting. They can request that the court take my children away if I don't cooperate."

It would do no good to argue right now. All Rose wanted to do was ensure the safety of Levi and Cody while they helped Gina work out her problems. What continued to disturb Lauren was Gina's resistance to answering any questions about her past.

This young woman desperately needed a friend but there were places in her life that seemed untouchable.

"What upset me most," Gina continued, "was that last night Levi overheard when she was talking to me about foster care. After she left it took me nearly an hour to calm him down."

"Poor Levi." Perhaps Rose needed to find a more mature person for Natalie's assignment. "I'm sure he was pretty frightened."

"Wouldn't you have been scared when you were six if someone threatened to take you away from your parents?"

"Terrified."

"Anybody would be." Gina's voice spiked in agitation. She pressed her lips together, took a deep breath, glanced at Archer. "I'm embarrassed about my yard. I was going to trim those hedges but then all this happened." She let her hands drop to her lap. "It seems as if I always have something else to do and I'm not that great with yard work."

Archer finished one section and started stacking branches. For a few moments both Gina and Lauren watched him in silence.

"You remember what we talked about during our first lunch together?" Gina said at last. "About getting that second opinion?"

Lauren looked at her. "From the Great Physician." Had her words actually made an impact?

Gina continued to watch Archer though her expression told Lauren she wasn't really seeing him.

"The way you described it made it sound as if I would have to turn my whole life over to Him."

"He works best when we keep our own hands out of the way," Lauren said.

"It sounds to me as if I'd just be taking on a whole new set of rules and I'd still be in the same mess I'm in now. It wouldn't change anything for me physically. This Great Physician stuff is really just about spiritual stuff, right?"

Lauren gave Archer a wishful glance. She could use his support in this conversation. But then Gina might feel as if they were ganging up on her. "It's hard to explain because everything about your life would be so different."

"In what way?"

"Your whole mind-set changes. There's a feeling of peace when you realize this life isn't all there is. God loves you more perfectly than any parent could love a child."

Gina shook her head. "I can't imagine that."

"It's impossible for a human being to imagine God because He's so far out of our realm. When you turn to Him you become aware of His power in your life. The more you turn your life over to Him the more complete it becomes. You learn that living for Him isn't a chore or a burden, it's a privilege."

"Kind of hard for me to see it right now."

"The very things God calls us to do are the most fulfilling elements of our lives. We are all created with different gifts, different talents. I believe God gave me the gift of healing and so I use my healing touch with my nursing skills. I also have a gift for teaching and so I use that gift teaching children in Sunday school and working with the older church youth."

"But Lauren," Gina said, her voice suddenly going soft as she gave Archer a cautious glance, "what about children of your own? I know you want that more than just about anything else. Why won't He give you that?"

The question caught her off guard. Trust Gina to

find the chink in her armor. "He never said He wouldn't give me children. It isn't as if I'm in my seventies yet."

"If He's going to do it He'd better get going."

In spite of Lauren's desire to reach out to Gina, those words cut deeply and Lauren fell silent.

Gina caught her breath and looked at Lauren. "I'm sorry. That sounded mean and I didn't intend for it to be." She sighed and shook her head. "Go ahead and tell me about God."

Lauren detected a note of resignation in Gina's voice. Why even bother? Gina wasn't listening. All she wanted to do was argue and God was just a good subject to debate.

Gina touched Lauren's arm. "I'm sorry. I didn't mean for it to come out that way. But I do have a lot of questions and I don't know anyone else to ask. It isn't as if I can go straight to God like you can."

"You could."

Gina shook her head. "Not me."

"He would walk beside you and help you. He wouldn't just slap a bunch of heavy rules on you, He would gently guide you like a loving father."

"My father died when I was ten."

"Oh Gina, I'm sorry."

She didn't respond for a moment but continued to watch Archer. Lauren didn't know what to say. *Lord, please touch her heart. Let me know how to reach her.*

"He was a good dad," Gina said at last. "He cared enough to teach me important things even when I was young. I remember he used to give me an allowance and he always made me save half of it. By the time I was nine I'd saved enough to buy my own bicycle. Because I learned how to manage my money I was able to buy this house with very small monthly payments."

"I love my father very much," Lauren told her. "I can't imagine what it would have been like to grow up without him, grumpy and cantankerous as he gets sometimes. But God doesn't get cantankerous and He's always patient with me." Even when she made a mess of things like right now.

Gina slumped and looked down at her hands. "Sorry Lauren. It's kind of hard to compare God to my father." She sighed and spread her hands in the air. "I've got too much to think about right now."

"Of course. You can talk to me about it any-time."

The younger woman pulled herself up. "I think I'll go chcck on Natalie and see if the kids are finished. If they are, would you mind keeping them occupied for a while out here? That way maybe Levi won't overhear another argument."

"I'd be glad to."

Gina nodded and murmured her thanks as she rushed in the front door.

Lauren sighed and listened to the rustle of falling evergreen branches. The scent made her think of Christmas.

"You handled that well." Archer continued clipping.

Lauren stood up and walked over to gather some of the branches he'd scattered behind him. "You were eavesdropping again."

"I have ears like an eagle."

"Eagles are famous for their vision, not their sense of hearing."

"This eagle was born with 20/20 hearing."

"You never were medically inclined."

He chuckled. "Did I ever tell you that I have always admired your ability to overanalyze my jokes?"

"No."

"Didn't think so." He clipped a couple more big branches then stood back and admired his uneven handiwork. "Don't tell Gina I've never trimmed a hedge before in my life."

"I won't say a word." She studied the shrubs with dismay. "I won't have to."

"Your mother would have loved Dogwood Springs." Grant tapped the brake and slowed to wait for a pedestrian to jaywalk across the red-brick street. Under protest from Brooke he had rolled down the windows. Now he drove slowly so that the wind wouldn't ruffle her hair as she rode in rare silence in the middle of the back-seat.

"I wish we'd moved here sooner," Grant said.

There was a snort from the back, then more silence.

"Mom loved St. Louis too, Dad," Beau said.

Grant stopped at a traffic signal and watched that same pedestrian rush in front of them in the crosswalk. "I know." He turned his attention to his son.

Beau rested his arm in the passenger seat window and studied the quiet bustle of the downtown area with interest. His square jaw came from the Sheldon side of the family but the dreamy tenderness of his eyes behind those wire-framed glasses came from Annette's side. The dark gray color was pure Grant but the kindness and caring evident in them, in Grant's opinion, came from Annette.

"Maybe if we had come here a few years ago she could have learned to relax a little more, to take some time for herself every once in a while," Grant said.

Bcau gave his dad a pointed look. "You're dreaming again. She would have volunteered at the hospital and joined the neediest church and cruised the town in search of someone who didn't have a home or food."

"Light's green, Dad," Brooke said. "Come on. I've got things to do and people to see."

Grant waited until another jaywalking pedestrian cleared their path and then pressed his foot on the accelerator. "I guess you're right, Beau. She was a natural encourager." He glanced into the rearview mirror at his daughter. "It's a good habit to get into."

Brooke met his gaze in the mirror. "You'd be surprised what an encourager I would be if I had a car. You know that Meals-on-Wheels thing Mom used to do? I could do that."

Beau snorted. "How long would that last? You'd have to get up before noon."

"I made it to school on time every morning all year, didn't I? It can be done. For a car I'd do it."

"Tell you what," Grant said. "If you two get part-time jobs and earn enough this summer to pay half the price of a car, I'll sign for you to get a loan so you can pay off the other half."

There was a gasp from the backseat. "What? You're serious? You'd let us get a car?"

"Yes, but the two of you would have to share it and you'd have to make payments and share the cost of insur—"

A high-pitched squeal assaulted Grant's ears and earned him a dirty look from his son when Brooke unsnapped her seat belt and grabbed her brother around the neck in a stranglehold of excitement.

Beau fought her off. "Would you stop it? Put your seat belt back on."

"Why? We can't be going more than five miles an hour."

"Brooke," Grant warned.

She did as she was told.

"He's tricking us, Brooke," Beau informed her. "There's no way we'd be able to earn enough money for the kind of car you'd want."

"Oh shut up." Brooke giggled. "You could use a little of Mom's gift of encouragement yourself, you know. Let's start looking for jobs today."

While his children continued bantering, Grant once again allowed his thoughts to rest on Annette. It was true that she had been an encourager. Sometimes the job pressures that went with that particular role in life got her into situations she hadn't been able to handle alone. Her caring spirit had seemed to radiate from her eyes and hurting souls had read that compassion clearly.

Annette had given of herself when too many people only wanted to take. Too many abused and injured hearts were starved for the compassion Annette was eager to share. Grant had seen her in tears because she couldn't always meet the pressing emotional, physical, or financial needs of others.

Her natural tendency to encourage attracted people to her like wedding guests to the cake.

Grant had loved her completely. Throughout their romance and marriage, no other woman had drawn him. How could they? Annette was the standard by which he viewed all other women. When she gained weight with her pregnancy and later failed to lose much of it, the height-weight tables might just as well have been adjusted upward for the whole world.

Compared to Annette, every other woman had lacked that divine ingredient that had always attracted him to her.

Now it frightened him that someone else had begun to set a few of her own standards. Now if a woman didn't have a green-eyed smile that illuminated the room with sudden sunshine and didn't answer to the name of Lauren McCaffrey, she was relegated to the ranks of "Thank you but not interested."

Grant was aware that some poor nearsighted women occasionally seemed to find him attractive. Sometimes he even picked up on gestures of flirtation—Annette had taught him to watch for the signs.

But Lauren had never implied in any way that she thought him attractive or that she even noticed he was a male member of her species.

"Dad! Where are you going?" Brooke's sudden cry of alarm jerked Grant's attention back to his driving just in time. He had signaled to turn the wrong way onto the only one-way street in Dogwood Springs.

"Oops. Sorry." He switched off the signal,

waved into the rearview mirror in apology to the confused driver behind them, and drove another two blocks.

"Maybe we don't need another car," Brooke said. "You need a chauffeur."

❧ Chapter 16 ❧

When Archer was nine years old he had attempted to help his mom out one day by cutting his younger brother's hair. By the time he finished his brother was nearly bald, with stray tufts of blond hair sticking up from strange places on his scalp.

Apparently Archer hadn't learned his lesson because now, as he stood gazing at his latest effort, he realized that poor Gina would be left with privacy stubs instead of privacy shrubs if he continued.

In frustration, he laid the clippers on the sidewalk and started stacking branches and he continued to practice one of the things he did well—eavesdropping.

"Mama says I'm smart enough to read numbers and call for help on the telephone if she starts acting weird again." Six-year-old Levi sat tightly against Lauren's side as his little brother tried to squeeze in between them.

"Your mother's right." Lauren's voice was soft

and gentle. "One of those telephone numbers is for me."

"Yes and she wrote down some numbers and put them by the telephone so we can call for help because she says I'm a big boy and I'm so smart she knows I can do the job right." Levi paused and looked up at Lauren. "Do you have any more stories?"

"Werewolf stories?" Cody asked. "Like Mama!"

"Your mother tells werewolf stories?" Lauren asked.

"No, but Cody likes the werewolf cartoons. It's a good werewolf, though, like Mom. He acts weird and starts to make scary sounds in his throat like Mom."

"Your mom makes scary sounds in her throat." There was no note of surprise in Lauren's voice.

"Yes, like the nice werewolf who runs away so nobody will see him grow hair and claws. Mom doesn't want us to see her grow hair and claws so that's why she runs away. What happened to David the shepherd boy? Will you tell us a story?"

"Tell us a story!" Cody echoed his brother.

"I don't like that lady," Levi said. "She doesn't tell good stories."

"What lady?"

Archer looked over his shoulder and saw Levi point toward the door.

"You mean Natalie?" Lauren asked. "Why don't you like her?"

"She told Mama she's going to take us away and it made Mama cry. Is she going to take us away? I don't want to go live with somebody else."

"Of course you don't. Your mom will do everything she can to make sure that doesn't happen." Bless Lauren for her soothing voice.

"Mama said if Natalie took us away she was going with us," Levi said. "Mama says some people hit their kids and hurt them and the police have to take the kids away. Mama never does that."

"I'll tell you what, honey. Before anybody tries to take you away you tell your mama to call me and I'll bring my sleeping bag and come here and stay with you. Okay?"

"Okay!"

"Okay!" Cody echoed.

"Dad, where are we going?" Brooke leaned forward until she was nearly in the front seat with him and Beau.

"Do you have your seat belt on?"

"It's just a little loose." In spite of her attempts to behave like the typically bored teenager, Brooke couldn't conceal her interest in the quaint fixtures of the downtown shops. And she didn't try to hide her interest when they passed a group of young men working in shirtless glory beside a backhoe on a side street. She straightened and smiled and automatically combed her fingers through her super-short dark hair.

"Your radar's out again," Beau said.

"In full working order," she murmured.

Grant chuckled and glanced at his daughter in the mirror. Her dark gray eyes, peering out from beneath extra-long dark bangs, were, as always, overly coated with dark makeup. Her skin was flawless. Ever since Brooke was twelve, well-meaning people had commented on her beauty. Like her brother, she had inherited the firm Sheldon chin. Though few people knew it, she also had her mother's tender heart—something she attempted to disguise at every opportunity.

"You still haven't told us what we're doing here, Dad," she complained.

"I want you guys to see a little more of Dogwood Springs. Starting with City Hall."

Accompanied by his daughter's groans, Grant burst into a soliloquy of the popularity of the community puzzle and the possibility that the illness they were seeing in the emergency room could have been spread from City Hall.

That got Beau's attention. "Shouldn't somebody do something about it? If it's a dangerous virus and you've already lost a patient—"

"And if people are coughing and sneezing all over each other and spreading it everywhere, who knows where it could spread to next?" Brooke finished for him.

"Good question. I just hope the mayor listened to me. We'll soon see."

"Who've you called?" Beau asked.

"The staff called every town within an hour's drive and if there isn't an ER in the town they're calling the clinics."

"Branson?" Beau asked.

"Lauren called Branson for me. She called several area hospitals as well as some doctor friends from her hometown of Knolls. All of the towns have had a few cases of flu but nothing unexplainable like our situation."

"Good thing," Beau said. "You know Branson gets visitors from all over the world. If this is some horrible plague it could spread everywhere. It could make this town notorious. The Dogwood Springs Killer."

"Oh thanks, Dr. Beau, for that encouraging word," Brooke chided.

He turned in his seat to look at his sister while Grant parked in the City Hall parking lot. "You're going to have to be nice to me if you want me to help you get that car."

There was a long startled silence as Grant turned off the engine. He had just pulled the key from the ignition when there was a sudden rush from behind and Brooke tackled her brother from the backseat with a smothering hug, raining kisses all over his face.

"Oh, Beau, I love you so much! You really are

planning to help me earn the money for our car aren't you?"

Beau tried to pull away. Brooke giggled and held him closer. Beau's mouth spread into a grimace—the closest to a smile he could manage —and he gave an amused chuckle. "Not if you leave slimy lip gloss on my face."

She gave him a final kiss on his cheek and wiped at his face with her fingers. "You're fine."

"And you have to promise not to embarrass Dad or me in City Hall."

"Don't push it," she warned. "This will be your car too. Do you know kids still go cruising around here on Friday and Saturday nights and after school?"

The three of them got out of the car and strolled toward the picturesque building with Virginia creeper etched in green across its block walls.

"Just think," she said. "Cruising. Like they did in that old movie Mom showed us once. Remember *American Graffiti*? They drive around town with their windows down and yell at each other and play Chinese fire drills and honk when they see somebody they know."

"They do that instead of dating?" Grant asked her.

"How would I know? Who would ask me out on a date? Nobody knows me here."

"That'll change soon enough," he assured her. "Remember we've been invited to that fishing thing next week. We'll probably meet some kids from Lauren's church."

Brooke groaned again and the delicate but firm tilt of her chin grew a little firmer. "Fishing. What a thrill. I don't want to ruin your fun but really—"

"Try it. You want to meet guys. Besides, you'll really like Lauren."

In the middle of another groan, Brooke's footsteps faltered and her lips parted. Two young men probably in the upper range of their teens rode bicycles past them on the street. They were tan. They wore muscle shirts. They noticed her. One nearly collided with a car.

While Grant and his son enjoyed the show, Beau ambled over to walk closer to Grant. "So Dad," he said quietly, "Lauren's a nurse you work with?"

"That's right. She helps out with the youth group at the Baptist church, among other things. That's where I'd like to see you and Brooke attend. You'll like the pastor too. He's a good guy."

Brooke lost interest in the clumsy muscle-bound hunks and rejoined her brother and father. "They probably don't have cars if they're riding bikes," she said.

"Don't be so shallow," Beau said. "We don't have cars."

"I'm being practical. If somebody does ask me out, I'm not riding to the movies with his mother."

"I'll drive you, then." Grant reached for the door and opened it and they stepped into the bustling noisy city hall. "Or you and Beau could hurry up and buy that car so you could drive him."

"I'm not driving a guy around on our first date."

They mingled with the crowd. Grant had wanted to talk to his kids about something for a few days. Now the subject had arisen. With Brooke he had learned to take his opportunities when they presented themselves.

"Since we're on the subject of dating, how would you feel if I decided to test the waters again?" Grant felt as if he'd chosen his timing wisely. Brooke was less likely to become upset if her attention was diverted by a busy—

She stopped abruptly. "If you *what?*" The shock in her overly-darkened eyes and the crystal clarity of horror that threaded through her voice gave him a frisson of fear. "You'd go out on Mom?" Her voice grew louder. It seemed as if the hall grew quieter. Several people glanced their way.

"I never would have gone out on your mother. You know that." Grant kept his voice low in hopes that his irrepressible daughter would do the same. "It isn't as if I have someone specifi-cally in mind."

"I don't know how you could even think about it. Beau and I aren't testing the waters for a new mother are we? Why should you want a new wife?" If she had grabbed a microphone and called for the attention of the crowd, she would not have done a better job of attracting it. Silence surrounded them like a hovering presence.

"Brooke." Beau stepped to her side and leaned close to her ear. "Shut up, okay? Let's just check on this puzzle table and get off the stage if you don't mind." Without waiting for a reaction he took her by the arm and guided her forward.

Grant led the way through their curious audience toward the spot where he had last seen the puzzle table. And that was where he saw the only people in the building who had their attention diverted elsewhere. Their focus was on a puzzle—on the table.

There was one change. A small sign stood beside the table. It read, "At the request of medical personnel, please wash your hands before joining the table."

A snort sounded directly beside Grant. If he was lucky that sound had come from an angry bull. He looked. No, it had come from his daughter and it meant trouble. He reached out to take her arm before she could do further damage to his reputation and his career. She lunged out of his reach.

"I don't believe this day! I don't believe this town!" She stomped to the sign and pointed to it. "This is the way our illustrious mayor intends to wipe out the disease that's threatening our citizens? It's a joke, right?"

Grant and Beau looked at each other. Grant had learned to read the humor in his son's eyes. He saw it now. "Beau, don't you dare make light of this. Do you know what these small towns are like? I'll never live this down if we don't get her out of here."

"Head for the door, Dad. I'll grab her as soon as I get a chance."

"No, we're in this together."

Grant could talk to the mayor over the telephone tonight. Maybe she would listen better than his daughter did. He and Beau took Brooke by the arms and guided her out of City Hall. Just before they reached the doors, she caught sight of a map of the city and grabbed a free copy from the stand, still complaining loudly about the lack of civic responsibility she had witnessed today.

Grant knew much of what she did was for dramatic effect. She had these little embarrassing spurts of outspokenness lately—not embarrassing for her, of course, because she did not embarrass easily. Her theatrics were only embarrassing for innocent family members who happened to be nearby.

If Annette were here she would know how to react appropriately. It was a woman thing.

"You know, Dad," Beau said softly, as Brooke jerked away and marched ahead of them toward the car, "you might want to wait a couple of days before you broach the subject of dating again."

• • •

The sun had dropped behind the cloudy horizon in a blaze of fire opal by the time Archer and Lauren left Gina's house. Lauren couldn't stop watching the constantly changing beauty. But a nagging concern had begun to haunt her thoughts. It was stupid but she couldn't get it out of her mind.

"Archer, do you ever wonder if you'd make a better pastor if you'd been a rebel in your formative years?"

He gave her a quick look. "Why do you ask?"

"Because I've been wondering lately if I couldn't identify better with people if I'd experienced more of the things other people do. I mean people who weren't raised in a happy home. It's obvious Gina's had a painful past but I've never even been married, much less divorced, so why would she bother confiding in me? I don't have children. How can I understand her pain?"

"What you have is a caring heart. I think that reaches people faster than anything. You don't have anything to worry about. Actually, though, it's funny you should mention it."

"Funny?"

"That same thought occurred to me the first night I took chaplain call at the hospital. I've wondered about it a few other times."

"Did you draw any conclusions?"

"Only that sin never helped a thing. Maybe I could identify with people better but then maybe

I couldn't identify with God as well. I'm not saying I'm this pure and obedient Christian who never sins. I just don't think we should be ashamed of our obedience."

"I'm not ashamed," she said, "but sometimes I wonder if I might be a spiritual lightweight. I've never suffered a horrible loss. I don't come from a dysfunctional family . . . well, not too dysfunctional." They both knew Lauren's youngest brother had been a handful for her parents for a few years.

"But you're not afraid to get your hands dirty or immerse yourself in someone else's problems," Archer said. "Look how you're helping Gina. You don't have to be a single mother with a mysterious medical problem in order to be there for her. You just have to let her know you care and I think she knows that."

Archer tapped the brake and waved at a pedestrian in jogging clothes alongside the road. It was one of the older church deacons, Mr. Netz. He slowed his steps when he saw them and gave a halfhearted salute.

"I admire Gina's independent spirit," Lauren said.

He smiled. "Takes one to know one. You're pretty independent yourself."

"But she frustrates me. She won't let down her guard long enough for anyone to help her."

"It sounds like she's willing to let her guard

down with you. Be her friend. I think you're doing a great job."

"Thanks." She wasn't so sure.

"Oh, and Lauren?"

"Yeah?"

"You are definitely *not* a spiritual lightweight." He looked at her and she couldn't look away, even when he turned back to concentrate on his driving. It didn't take much attention from Archer Pierce to make her act like one of those giggling teenagers at church.

His expression grew sober as he turned onto her street. "I know the drug tests on Gina have all showed negative results."

"That's right. The printout we got on her the first night we saw her didn't show anything except caffeine and benzodiazepine, which is in a sleeping pill she's been taking for insomnia lately."

"Did the test show how much of the drug she had taken?"

She looked at him. "No, the test was just qualitative but the sample was sent off for further testing. The lab found nothing outstanding. You can't think her problem comes from drugs."

"I'm open to all suggestions right now."

"I think we can trust Gina."

"I'm glad. I feel she and her kids need protection from whatever is happening to her. But I know enough about drugs to realize that the tests can't rule out everything. Do you understand what I'm saying?"

Lauren hesitated. She understood but she didn't want to. She liked Gina. But it was true that as a health professional who worked with children, she was a mandated reporter. So were Archer and Grant. Their first priority was to protect those children no matter what. She just hated to feel like a traitor to Gina.

"Yes, Archer, I understand. I hope you're wrong."

"So do I."

❧ CHAPTER 17 ❧

"She's here," came the intentionally bored tones of Brooke's voice as she peered out the front window. "Oh, pu-*leeze* Dad, you didn't tell me she was a hillbilly redneck. Would you look at that? She's driving a truck. Oh hello, look at what she's wearing. Overalls. And no makeup. No wonder she's middle-aged and still not married. She doesn't even try."

Grant grimaced as he spread chicken liver pâté on a split croissant. They'd lived in Dogwood Springs a little more than three weeks and Brooke was still complaining. "She isn't even close to middle-aged and don't you dare say anything to her about what she's wearing. We're going to do fishing not fashion."

He wrapped the sandwich and wiped his hands on a paper towel, then rushed from the kitchen toward the front door to make a quick interception. The last thing he wanted was for his occasionally overbearing kid to frighten off the nicest nurse he'd worked with in a long while.

"A truck. I don't believe it." Brooke's favorite class in high school so far had been drama and she excelled in it. As far as Grant could see, that flair for the dramatic was the only thing Brooke and Lauren were going to have in common—that and the fact that they were both females. Pretty females.

The feminine lines of Brooke's face turned down in a good imitation of agony as her thick dark bangs fell into her overly made-up eyes. "Please tell me we won't have to all squeeze into that thing. If we do I'm not going. I don't care how many cute guys—"

"Nobody's forcing you to go," Grant said, "and the only cute guy even close to your age other than Beau is only fifteen." He resisted a smile. That would go over like a lead bubble. He peered out the curtained window of the front door. "Besides, it looks like her truck has a backseat. It's one of them-there city-girl trucks." His affected hillbilly accent failed to evoke a response from Brooke and he gave it up. His daughter was not his biggest fan since this move.

Too late he saw Brooke's eyes narrow with

sudden threat. "What do you mean only one other teenager?" she demanded. "I thought we were supposed to be going with a group from some-body's church."

"I guess all the kids your age have summer jobs. The pastor, Archer Pierce, is bringing Evan."

"What kind of a name is Archer?"

"Don't start. Lauren has gone out of her way to try to make us feel welcome."

"Want to know what I think?" Brooke's dark gray eyes tightened into slits of suspicion.

"Probably not."

"I think she's setting you up. She's going to haul us all out to the middle of the woods and murder Beau and me to get us out of the way and then she's going to cage you like an animal so you can be her—"

"Brooke that's enough."

"I was just going to say she wants you for her—"

"I don't want to hear it." And he certainly didn't want Lauren to hear it. He hovered over his daughter with his most authoritarian glare. "Think of someone else's feelings for once, Brooke. And don't you dare accuse Lauren of manipu-lating a date with me. She isn't interested. Believe me, I know."

She squared off with him shoulder-to-shoulder, undaunted by his size or his authority. "How do you know? What ditzy single desperate blonde wouldn't be interested in snagging a rich doctor with two adorable kids?"

Grant stifled a laugh. "She isn't ditzy, we're not rich, and—"

"Fine, have it your way. But when you wake up tomorrow morning with Beau and me hanging lifeless on hooks outside some hillbilly shack with bars on the windows and she's—"

Grant grasped her chin and forced her to look into his eyes. "I happen to know who she's interested in and it isn't me, so don't you dare embarrass me. How would you like it if I teased you about a guy you liked and—"

Her eyes widened. He took a sharp breath. He'd made a fatal slip.

She disengaged her chin from his grasp. "You like this female John Boy?"

He ignored the question. "If this woman were trying to snag me, don't you think she'd at least have dressed up a little and put on a little makeup?"

As the first touch of doubt entered Brooke's eyes, the doorbell rang.

Grant raised a hand for silence. "Shh! Zip your lips."

Brooke lowered her voice less than half a decibel. "So that's what you were talking about when you said you were lonely! I thought you said you didn't have anybody in mind to—"

"Brooke!"

"I'm just glad you cooked the food. Don't accept anything—"

He placed his hands on her shoulders and shushed her again. She grimaced. He opened the door.

Sure enough, Lauren did not look like her usual professional self, although her smile was still in place. It didn't even waver when Brooke issued a long heartfelt groan and slumped out of the room calling to her brother, "Hey Beau, it's time to hunt some fish!"

Lauren's long blond hair was pulled back from her face as usual and she wore baggy, comfortable looking bib overalls with a long-sleeved over-sized T-shirt. Oh yeah, everything about her shouted siren. Where was Brooke's brain?

The annoyed voice of his daughter continued its harangue from halfway down the hall.

Grant cringed. "Sorry."

Lauren's grin widened. "I take it they're still not happy about the move."

"Beau's doing fine. Brooke's willingness to go on this fishing trip is a testament to the fact that she is bored silly. They've both been looking for jobs the past week and there's nothing available, which could mean they won't get the car Brooke wants, which would mean the end of life as we know it—not necessarily for Brooke but for everyone who lives with her."

"They might find something if they keep trying.

I think the hospital cafeteria was hiring a couple of weeks ago."

"I'll have them fill out applications on Monday. Speaking of the cafeteria, I've packed food as promised. Are you ready for me to carry the cooler out?"

"Sure, let's get everything loaded and head to the woods. Archer will meet us there with Evan at about two." She glanced at her watch. "It'll take us about fifteen minutes to get there and then we'll have fifteen minutes to set up before they arrive. Isn't it great to be off on Friday? We should have the spot all to ourselves for at least a couple of hours, maybe longer."

Ten minutes later Grant found himself sitting behind the driver's side in the back seat of a gray Chevy Crew Cab pickup with a few years on it.

Grant had hunted down the fishing poles he and Annette had used years ago and after introducing his teenage twins to Lauren, he'd manipulated the seating so that Beau rode in front with Lauren. Grant was confident his son wouldn't cause any trouble; he would just sit with his nose buried in today's reading of choice, *The Merck Manual of Medical Information*. With a stranger in their midst, he had retreated into his customary shell. Judging by the way Brooke was behaving she was not to be trusted and Grant felt a need to hover.

"Hicktown, population seven thousand three hundred and seventeen." Brooke's deadpan voice broke the peaceful silence as they drove west out of town. "Does that count the cows?" She grinned at her twin brother in the front seat as she poked him on the shoulder. Her eyes darkened with disappointment when she didn't get a reaction. She pursed her highly glossed lips together and fell silent as Lauren picked up speed along Highway Z.

The city of Dogwood Springs, like many small towns of southern Missouri, sat in a patchwork square between checkerboard properties of the Mark Twain National Forest. Grant had visited this area years ago when he and Annette took one of their rare vacations. They'd dared to dream that someday, maybe when he retired, they would move here.

"What's Branson like now, Lauren?" he asked. "I haven't been there since before the kids were born."

"It's fun. It can get crowded," Lauren said. "Traffic's moving better than it used to since they built all those bypasses but I think they still sell souvenir T-shirts that say, 'I survived Highway 76 traffic.' I go about every month to a show or just to shop."

Brooke sat forward, eyes alert. "Do you ever go with . . . you know . . . a date or anything?"

Grant tensed and glared.

Lauren rounded a curve then glanced at Brooke in her rearview mirror, her expression casual. "I usually just go with friends or a church group. Branson has a lot of good shows. And they're not just country anymore. I think you might like Silver Dollar City. We take a group of high schoolers a couple times a year."

"Silver Dollar City?" Brooke's voice mimicked Lauren's slight Ozark accent. "Isn't that some glorified theme park? St. Louis has Six Flags."

Grant tapped her on the arm. "Be nice."

She rolled her eyes and gave a long-suffering sigh.

He glared at her. The stubborn set of her chin and the tension in her neck told him that his little girl was still resisting the move, resisting Dogwood Springs, and resisting any possibility that he might be able to enjoy the company of another woman.

It was times like this he missed Annette the most. Brooke needed a woman to talk to and to gripe at. He didn't feel up to the challenge of fielding pointed sarcasm the rest of the day. He seldom felt ill at ease with people but when Brooke was feeling irritable he never knew what to expect.

She was just like he had been when he was younger. Nowadays he tempered his words with some of the wisdom he'd learned the hard way. But Brooke was still learning. She occasionally behaved like a brat. What hurt him the most was that when she acted that way it gave people the wrong impression of who she truly was.

He must have gotten through to her, because for the next few minutes she was silent and peace reigned in the cab of the truck.

"Pastor, don't take this personal."

Archer braced himself. When someone said that, it was going to be personal.

"We've been praying about this."

Archer stared at sixty-eight-year-old Dwight Hahnfeld, swallowed hard, and gritted his teeth.

"Under the circumstances, we feel it would be best if you stepped down from your position." The deacon, who served this year as chairman of the personnel committee, did not sit down on the sofa as Archer had casually directed him but instead perched on one of the chairs in front of Archer's desk.

Dwight looked everywhere but at the object of his declaration. His two buddies rustled up their own chairs and pulled them forward to sit beside him. None of them looked Archer in the face.

As Archer sank into his desk chair and stared at the committee of three he felt the numbness of shock travel down his spine—almost the same kind of shock he'd felt when Jessica broke their engagement seven weeks ago.

"What are you talking about?" he finally asked when he could manage to speak without betraying his shock.

"I know this might come as a bit of a surprise," Dwight said, "but our best interests need to be with the corporate integrity of the church."

Archer felt as if he was listening to this man trying to speak a foreign language. Had the church taken a vote behind his back? "Let me make sure I have this straight. Am I being fired?"

"No no, nothing like that." Mr. John Netz, the most outspoken and active deacon in the church, waved his hand irritably. "We just think you might want to check out other jobs. Maybe other positions. Now that you're not getting married we don't think it looks proper for you . . ." He cleared his throat.

"A single man should not be leading a congregation," Hahnfeld declared. "According to Scripture, a pastor is supposed to be the husband of one wife. And he's supposed to be able to keep his children under control. How can you do that if you don't even have a wife? And as for children . . ." He shifted uncomfortably. "Well, you'd obviously need a wife."

Archer said a quick, desperate prayer for God to control his thoughts, his temper, his tongue. He waited, allowing the silence to lengthen enough that he could see the tension grow in the men facing him.

"You might consider a certain apostle named Paul."

Netz cleared his throat. No one replied.

"Not only was he a single man," Archer said, "but he was audacious enough to advise some people against marriage. He warned that having a spouse would draw a person's loyalties from God." He heard the force of his own words clipped into tight little knots of anger. He hated the sound of it. Archer seldom gave in to anger these days. Still, the words were true.

"That advice was directed toward those who could keep their bodies under control," Hahnfeld snapped. "Something you don't seem to be—"

"Dwight!" John Netz gave his buddy a quick, hard look.

Hahnfeld grunted and looked at his folded hands.

Archer studied them for a moment, wondering at some unspoken secret that blazed through the room. "What piece of gossip is it this time?"

The three men avoided looking at each other. They particularly avoided meeting Archer's gaze.

He didn't need this today. He shouldn't have even come into the office. This was his day off.

Besides that, Evan was waiting for a ride and Lauren and the Sheldons were probably already at the fishing spot.

But something was going on here. The community grapevine had obviously struck Dogwood Springs Baptist once again. Archer knew the signs; gossip was a nasty little sin that nobody wanted to admit to but was so hard to resist. Like a bag of chocolate chips—what would it hurt to eat just one little chip? And then another? As the three men continued to avert their eyes, the guilt stained their faces.

Archer sat back in his chair and sighed. "At least have the decency to tell me what the busybodies are saying I've done this time."

Silence screamed through the office.

"Maybe I can help prompt your memory." Archer tried to keep his voice gentle. "Let me see . . . I shouted too loudly at the softball game the other night."

The continued silence and averted eyes said no.

"Okay then, I forgot to visit someone in the hospital."

Gene Thomas cleared his throat and looked at Hahnfeld and Netz. He was the youngest and newest member of the committee. Judging by his obvious discomfort, Archer guessed he'd been coerced into this.

"He needs to know what's being said," Gene told them.

Netz stared out the window. Hahnfeld shifted in his seat and favored Archer with a brief look of sadness before shaking his head and averting his eyes once more.

"I'm not saying this is true, Brother Archer," Gene blurted, "but we feel that a pastor should be living such a pure life that ideas like this wouldn't take root in the first place."

"Ideas like what?"

More silence. Shifting in the chairs.

Netz finally straightened and looked Archer in the face, though he still couldn't quite make eye contact. "Brother Archer, I know you probably didn't do what they're saying."

"What are *they* saying?"

He dropped his gaze. "Well, when some pretty woman comes to town and joins the church and then you start spending all that time with her and then your engagement gets broken and then that pretty woman turns up pregnant, people—"

"What?" Archer nearly came out of his chair.

Netz looked back out the window.

"The only single young woman who has joined our church in the past few months is Lauren McCaffrey," Archer said.

Netz nodded. "That's right."

"Lauren McCaffrey is not pregnant. Where did you hear such a lie?"

Gene shrunk farther down in his seat. "They're talking about it over at the hospital."

"Don't you work at the hospital?" Archer asked.

"Yeah, I'm in Medical Records. One of the techs said she overheard Lauren telling somebody about it and then Lauren was sick the other night."

"Somebody lied." Archer would not listen to this any longer. He pushed back from his desk and stood. "If you'll excuse me." He nodded to them, too afraid of his growing anger to say more. He walked out of his office, leaving the committee sitting there like three stone statues.

When Lauren turned from the highway onto a rough potholed gravel road, Brooke seemed unable to keep her mouth shut any longer. "Hello? Where are we going? I thought we were going to a lake or something, you know, where there are, like, people and boats and swimming?" She turned her insistent gaze on Grant, her eyes widening in a very expressive unspoken plea for him to protest.

Grant laid his arm across the back of the seat and held his hand up for silence. "I guess you also expected a yacht with a pool and a waiter and maybe a movie screen with the latest releases? It wouldn't hurt you to be flexible for once."

He caught Lauren's quick glance of concern in the rearview mirror and was suddenly chagrined by the sharpness she must have heard in his voice. This outing was probably a bad idea but the kids couldn't just sit at home the whole summer.

"It's a neat place, Brooke," Lauren said. "Give it a chance, okay? The creek is fed by Honey Spring. The water is pure and sweet. This spot has the best fishing in the county. It's where all the old fishermen come to catch their limit."

"Limit of what?"

"Rainbow trout." Lauren seemed unoffended by Brooke's continued bratty attitude. "They stock it from the fish hatchery in Knolls County."

"There wouldn't happen to be any cabins out here would there?" Brooke cast Grant a wide-eyed stare. "You know, with, like, bars on the windows or something?"

Lauren gave her a quick glance in the mirror and shrugged. "None I know about. But sometimes I find empty beer cans and cigarette butts along the road leading to the creek, so it's obviously a weekend party spot. I avoid it then. Beau, have you ever gone fishing before?"

Beau glanced at Lauren then quickly turned away. "Yeah." His baritone voice barely reached the backseat. "Mom and Dad used to take us to the Mississippi River on Dad's days off when we were out of school." There was no missing the melancholy in his voice.

"Lauren," Grant said, "Archer tells me you're an excellent fisherman."

A wide grin lit her face. "He said that?"

"Just a couple of days ago." He glanced sideways at his daughter and was not convinced by her expression of disinterest. In matters of the heart Brooke was uncomfortably astute. "He told me you're quite an athlete."

"Fishing's been my favorite pastime for a long time." Her voice filled the cab with a lilt of pleasure. "As soon as I arrived here in February I started going down to the barbershop where the old fishermen hang out. They always know where the fishing's the best. The barber got tired of me after a couple of days and finally divulged the location of his favorite spot so I'd leave him alone. I've been coming here since trout season opened the first of March."

"So this is, like, what you do for fun?" Brooke caught Grant's attention and rolled her eyes.

Grant reached across the seat to catch his daughter's hand in a firm grip. "Lauren, it's hard to believe you've only been in Dogwood Springs a few months. You seem like such a part of the community."

"It's a lot like my hometown."

"Why did you decide to come here?"

Lauren's typically open expression suddenly closed. Intriguing. "It's a pretty town. Since the emergency department was expanding they made me an offer I couldn't refuse."

"And that would mean, then, that you weren't happy with your former job." Grant couldn't curb his own curiosity.

Yes, there was definitely some resistance in Lauren's attitude. "Knolls is a great town. I grew up there and I know everybody."

"So you moved here to get away from them?" Brooke asked. "Or maybe to meet more people."

"The hospital was the best. Last fall we had an explosion that leveled the ER. While that department of the hospital was out of commission I covered a few shifts here. Something clicked for me. When I decided to leave Knolls this was the first hospital that offered me a contract."

"That still doesn't explain why you decided to leave Knolls in the first place." Brooke said.

"I guess I felt like I was missing something."

"You mean like a man?" Brooke asked. "And you came here?" She lowered her voice to a bare whisper and leaned toward Grant. "Not exactly a rational decision."

Grant knew there were laws against passengers riding in the bed of a pickup truck but he wondered if the police might make an exception in certain cases.

"So why do you come way out here in the middle of nowhere to go fishing?" Brooke asked. "We're not doing anything illegal are we?" She gave her dad a teasing wink.

Lauren laughed. "Last time I checked my fishing license it was up to date." She looked at the book Beau held open in his lap. "Medicine? You planning to follow in your father's footsteps and become a doctor?"

Beau didn't look up. He just shrugged and nodded, his typical escape when in the presence of strangers—especially attractive ones of the female persuasion.

"Emergency medicine?" Lauren continued to prompt.

Beau looked at her then. Unlike Brooke, there was no mischief in his expression, just a self-conscious awkwardness. "I'd love to be a doctor."

Grant's heart squeezed at the sincerity in his son's voice. Beau was truly the child who most took after his mother, quiet and thoughtful, sensitive to the needs of everyone around him.

All of Grant's protective instincts had come out with his son since the accident and Grant knew his behavior sometimes rankled Beau's masculine pride. Brooke's attitude toward her twin brother had always been one of adoration. Though she teased him mercilessly at times, she made no secret of her love for him. The one thing the accident had not damaged was their relationship.

"Looks like you're getting a good start," Lauren told Beau. "Since you just moved here you might not be aware of the great health services program we have at the high school."

Beau shifted in his seat and gave her more of his attention. "Health services? Here?"

Lauren had a smile that seemed to encompass everything about her. "I know Dogwood Springs is the Missouri outback to you. No problem. I don't blame you since you're from the big city. Still, our school system is ranked with the best in the country, not just the state. If you take a health services course you'll be able to do some on-site training at the hospital."

Beau's eyes came alive and his self-consciousness fell away. "How old do I have to be?"

"Sixteen."

Even Brooke lost her bored expression for a moment and leaned forward. "You mean he'd get to give shots and everything? He'd love that. Mom and Dad got him this doctor set for Christmas one year and he wanted to put real needles in the syringe. Guess who was always the patient."

"He wouldn't give shots but he could take vitals," Lauren said. "Most important, he would be in on patient cases and be a part of the medical world." Lauren slowed the truck and turned onto an even rougher dirt track. "Of course, I'm sure it won't be as exciting in our ER as it would be in some big St. Louis trauma center."

"Not as dangerous either," Grant said. "Inside the hospital or outside. And the variety here is better. It seemed all I ever saw at the trauma center were life-and-death situations. The stress level was always high. Here I get everything from nosebleeds and sore throats to industrial accidents and heart attacks. I'll take this any day."

Brooke gave an ostentatious yawn and reached out to nudge Grant's arm with her fingers. "You're a born hick, Dad."

"That isn't a bad thing," Lauren said. "There's a lot to be said for small towns. We do have a lot of variety in our emergency room, and in a small town everybody knows everybody else. The patients are better than the local paper for keeping us up with the latest news." Lauren pulled beneath a stand of sycamore trees and parked the truck. "We're here."

Archer was just stepping out of the house in his fishing clothes twenty minutes late to pick up Evan when his home phone rang. He looked at the clock. It was probably Evan wondering where he was. Lauren wouldn't be calling from the creek because her cell phone didn't get reception there. If he didn't answer, Evan should know he was on his way. He should share his cell phone number with more people but then the interfering deacons could sink their teeth into him no matter where he was.

Still, someone could be calling with an emergency.

Before the phone could stop ringing, Archer fumbled with the door, rushed back inside, and grabbed the receiver. Couldn't let those devoted people down even if they did plan to fire him because of some rumor straight from the evil—

"Hello?"

"Yes . . . hello? Is this Archer? Archer P-pierce?" The words tumbled through the phone in waves of broken tension. Definitely female.

"That's me." He frowned when he recognized the voice. "Gina?"

"I think . . . is Lauren . . . do you know where she is?"

"Yes, but she's out of phone service. I'm here, though. Are you feeling sick? Do you need help?"

"Please . . . help me. They're all around me. They won't shut up. They won't leave me alone. I can't concentrate." There was a soft gush of air and then a sob.

"Who are you talking about? Who's there? Are you at home?"

"I'm at work. I didn't . . . don't want to tell . . . I've got to get away."

"No Gina, wait! Get to the emergency—"

The line disconnected.

Archer dialed the hospital. By the time he was transferred to Gina's department she'd left her desk. He gave a quick account of the problem to the woman on the phone then hung up and ran out the door.

Three weeks ago Gina had cut her bare feet. What would happen to her this time?

❧ CHAPTER 18 ❧

"My pole's jerking!" Brooke exclaimed less than three minutes after Lauren cast the line and handed her the fishing rod. "What should I do now?"

Lauren looked up from the fishhook she was baiting. Sure enough, Brooke's line was taut. "Tug hard to set the hook then reel it in like I showed you."

Brooke jerked on the pole hard enough to decapitate a trout and stumbled backward over a rock. She caught herself and turned to see if anyone was watching. Everyone was.

Lauren retained her sober expression with difficulty. How were the kids of Dogwood Springs Baptist Church going to handle Brooke Sheldon?

"Okay I got it. I think."

"Keep reeling," Lauren said. "Bring it on in to the bank."

"But it's so wiggly, and it—*aack!* What is that?" Brooke screeched. *"That's* a *fish?* Lauren, you take this thing! This is not—" With another screech she threw the rod toward the water and scrambled across the rocky shoreline away from the creek. "I can't do this!"

"No Brooke, wait!" Lauren shoved her own fishing rod into Grant's hands and leaped forward to rescue Brooke's catch. It hadn't escaped and she reeled it in. It wasn't until the taut line pulled the wriggling body up above the water's surface that she discovered Brooke was right.

It wasn't a fish.

"Snake!" Brooke's scream split the peace of the little fishing hollow and echoed from the cliffside across the creek as she did a skittering dance across the rocks. "I told you! I can't believe this!"

Lauren couldn't stifle her laughter. "Relax Brooke, it's a plain brown water snake. It isn't going to hurt us."

"Isn't going to hurt us!" Brooke shrieked in outrage. "Dad, I'm going back to St. Louis. I'm calling Grandma tonight and she'll come and get me. If she doesn't I'll catch a bus or hitch-hike. I mean it, Dad! This place is crawling with snakes! And don't forget the spider I saw when we parked. You know I hate those things!"

Lauren laid down her fishing rod and grabbed the line, still entertained by the sound of Brooke's outraged chatter. "Hey Brooke, watch this." She grasped the head of the poor struggling snake just behind the spot where the hook had caught it.

Brooke screamed again and Lauren winced. Okay, that was a bad idea but she'd truly wanted to prove the little thing wasn't dangerous.

"He's just scared. See? Even if he bit me he couldn't hurt me. Have you ever had a puppy?"

Brooke crossed her arms and nodded. "This is not a puppy."

"But a puppy can bite harder than this fellow."

"Puppies do not slither through the water and sneak up on people."

"Still, this guy's harmless. He didn't even swallow the hook. See? It just pierced his side. As soon as I release him he'll slip back to the creek and head downstream with the current. Grant, would you give me my tackle box?"

"You can't be serious." Brooke backed away, eyes and mouth wide open.

Without a word Grant put down Lauren's pole,

carried the box over to Lauren, set it down, opened the lid, and reached for a set of wire cutters.

"Are you crazy?" Brooke cried. "Just cut the line!"

"We can't," Grant said. "We've got to get the hook out or the snake could get snagged and suffer a miserable death."

Lauren looked up at Grant with fresh respect and saw from his calm expression that, unlike his daughter, he wasn't the least bit intimidated by the snake.

"Then kill it now so it won't suffer." Brooke's voice lost its edge of panic and instead was filled with a thick thread of frustration.

"No." This soft reply came from farther down the creek and they all glanced up to see Beau coming toward them with his first catch. "First do no harm."

"Oh no, don't you start too, Doctor Beau. And what is that thing you're carrying, a minnow? I've seen bigger fish than that in Grandma's aquarium."

To Lauren's surprise and relief, Brooke was sidetracked. Though her theatrically disgusted voice continued, it was now focused on Beau's measly catch. Lauren and Grant snipped the hook in two and gently removed it from the snake. Then while Brooke had her back turned, Lauren took the snake to the creek and released it. Beau kept his sister occupied throughout the operation.

"Good job," Grant said under cover of Brooke's harangue.

Lauren looked up at him. "Thanks Doc. You didn't do so badly yourself."

He nodded graciously with a slow appreciative smile. Grant Sheldon had dark gray eyes the color of a lake on a cloudy day, with firm straight brows that often belied a keen appreciation for humor. As Gina had remarked recently, he was an attractive man and Lauren felt comfortable with him. It didn't seem to matter to him that her face was scrubbed free of makeup and that her baggy old clothes probably stunk of bait by now and that he'd been witness to even worse in the past weeks when she'd been sick.

"Thanks for putting up with Brooke," he said softly as his twins—mostly Brooke—continued their friendly insults several yards away. "I should have warned you about her. Down deep she has a tender heart but her irritability hormones have kicked into overdrive the past year or so."

"I work with teenagers at church, remember? I just hope you don't expect me to patronize her."

"I'd be horrified if you did. She's bad enough already." Grant chuckled and glanced at his arguing children before his attention once more focused on Lauren. "I'm glad you invited us to come with you today. I'm having a good time." The way he said it made Lauren wonder if having a good time was a rare experience for him. "Even more important, believe it or not, I think my kids are enjoying themselves. They love to argue."

"I heard that, Dad," Brooke said suddenly from close behind Lauren. She looked at their blood-stained hands suspiciously. "What happened to the snake?"

Lauren made an obvious show of looking at her watch then she glanced toward the road. "I wonder where Archer is. He should have arrived with Evan by now. I hope everything's okay."

"You let it go, didn't you?" Brooke accused, though to Lauren's surprise, gentleness laced the girl's voice this time. A hint of a smile hovered in her eyes as she caught and held Lauren's gaze.

"Yes. I don't like to take a life unnecessarily."

Brooke made a face. "Tell that to the poor worms you sacrificed to the hook god. So where did you put him? He probably crawled into the tackle box to hide and then he'll slither out while we're cruising down the highway at a gazillion miles an hour and you'll panic and lose control of that hillbilly machine you call transportation and—"

She caught herself and her eyes widened. She shot her brother a quick apologetic look and immediately changed the subject. "Oh well, whatever. Lauren, who's this Archie guy? Is he your boyfriend?" She reached down and cautiously opened the lid.

"Archer's my pastor." Lauren bent to help

before Brooke could scatter her carefully organized gear onto the rocky bank.

"Is he married?"

"No."

"Is he old? I mean, older than . . . well, you know what I mean. Is he too old for you?"

Lauren gave Grant a look of confusion and found it mirrored on his face. "He's thirty-three."

"So if he hasn't taken a vow of celibacy or something why aren't you dating him?"

"Have you decided to become my personal matchmaker?"

The teenager continued to select and then discard sinker after sinker. "Never hurts to look to the future."

"Brooke." Lauren waited until the girl looked up at her. "I'm not dating anyone, okay? Get used to it. Amazingly, life goes on even for us senior citizens."

Brooke's dark eyes sparkled with humor before she directed her attention once more to the contents of the tackle box. "Don't you have any bait in here that doesn't writhe in pain when you try to attach it to the hook?"

"I did bring a little bag of Limburger cheese and some chicken livers but I don't think you—"

"That's good. Where is it?"

"Brooke," Grant said, "Limburger cheese doesn't smell too—"

"I don't care about the smell, I just don't feel

like killing any more innocent animals today." She reached into the box and pulled out a sinker that would anchor a small rowboat.

"Let me help you with that," Lauren said. "Bring your gear and we'll hike upstream a bit. You've probably scared all the fish away from this spot anyway."

To Lauren's surprise Brooke followed her without protest. "So what's this teen group like at your church?" she asked when they were out of earshot of her family. "Are there any hot guys?"

Lauren shrugged. "I'm too ancient to notice." She sank down on a boulder beside a quiet pool of water and scooted over so Brooke could join her.

"What about this Evan kid who's supposed to be here?" Brooke didn't sit down but walked over to the water's edge and started tossing pebbles into the water. "I know he's only fifteen but is he anywhere close to having a birthday?"

Lauren heard the despair in the girl's voice and allowed a brief moment of empathy. She knew what it felt like to be lonely for the company of members of the opposite sex, despite what she'd said. "I think you'll just have to meet him, Brooke. Give it some time."

"Sure, I can do that." Brooke's tone made it clear that sixteen-year-old girls did not find fifteen-year-old boys appealing or "hot."

"Were you active in your church in St. Louis?" Lauren asked.

Brooke nodded, picked up a pebble, and tossed it into the water. Her expression grew pensive. "Mom and Dad dragged us to church all the time."

"My parents did the same thing."

"I bet they didn't drag you away from all your friends and move you to the sticks two years before you graduated."

Lauren studied the girl's features for a moment. Brooke Sheldon was one of the most beautiful young women Lauren had ever seen. She had widely spaced eyes the same color as her father's, with thick lashes and perfectly arched eyebrows. Her chin came to a delicate yet very firm point that characterized her disposition perfectly. To Lauren's surprise, she felt another twinge of sym-pathy for Brooke that went far past compassion for this initial phase of homesickness.

Physical beauty could be a curse.

Lauren had known from a young age that people referred to her as the "pretty one" of the McCaffrey sisters, though she'd never been able to see it herself. She'd been the tomboy of the family, usually with dirt under her fingernails and on her face. She helped Dad on the farm along with her two younger brothers while her sisters helped Mom in the house.

To Mom's disappointment, Lauren had never dated much in high school. She'd had lots of invitations but for some reason the guys she went out with couldn't seem to understand why she didn't want to get physical.

That was when she discovered that most men didn't look past her face or her body. They weren't interested in what lay in her heart.

Brooke tossed a final pebble and turned to slump onto the boulder beside Lauren.

"I know you miss your friends," Lauren said. "I miss mine."

"So why did you move?"

"I'm the only one of my siblings not married yet. Too much pressure, not enough decent guys."

"At least you weren't forced to leave them. I was. Mom wouldn't have made me leave. Does Dad care? No." She picked up another pebble and tossed it.

"Good dads always care; they just don't always know how to communicate it. My dad's like that." Lauren re-baited her hook. "I don't remember him actually saying the words *I love you* but he didn't have to. He showed his love by the way he talked to me—or actually by the way he listened while I talked and talked and talked."

Brooke sighed. She got up from the boulder and picked up her rod. "So are you going to teach me how to cast this thing?"

Lauren shook her head and stood up with her own rod. This kid could wear a person out in a hurry. After five minutes of instruction and awkward casting that landed the hook in the water less than half a dozen times, Brooke gave a frustrated groan and slumped once more against the boulder.

"I thought you knew how to fish," Lauren said. "Beau said your family went to the river."

Brooke shrugged. "It didn't take. You didn't answer my question. If you were going to leave home, why didn't you actually go someplace?"

Lauren continued to cast. "Dogwood Springs is a place."

"No, it's a non-place. It's cut off from the whole world. These people practically speak a different language."

"It doesn't take too long to learn the dialect," Lauren said. "I like small towns. I've never lived in the city except when I went to nursing school and I was glad to get back home afterward." She reeled the line in and turned.

Brooke had her arms crossed over her chest, teeth biting into her lower lip as she stared into the water. The child was hurting. Anyone could see that.

"Brooke, it'll probably take you a while to get used to the slower pace but couldn't you at least wait until school starts before you pass judgment? You might surprise yourself and like it here, crazy as that may sound."

There was a long silence and then Brooke sighed. "I don't have a choice, do I?"

Lauren took her by the arms, stood her up, and

placed the fishing rod in her hands. "Maybe you could start by learning how to fish."

Archer reached the hospital in five minutes and parked in the spot marked for clergy. He leapt out without locking and ran toward the emergency entrance.

He raced through the nearly empty waiting room to the receptionist's desk. He recognized the young woman sitting there. "Gayle, I'm looking for Gina Drake. Did she come in here?"

The receptionist looked up at him with a frown. "Gina? She was in this morning to treat an asthma patient. I guess she's either on the floor or in her own department. What's up?"

She obviously hadn't taken his advice to come to the ER. "She might be . . . just have her call me if you see her, okay?" He gave her a wave and ran down the wide tiled hallway toward Gina's department, dreading what he might find. She'd wanted to talk to Lauren; maybe she was still trying to find her but she wouldn't be able to reach her.

He rounded a corner and nearly collided with Sarah Davis, the director of Respiratory. Her curly salt-and-pepper hair stuck out from her head at awkward angles and her glasses rested halfway down her nose as if she'd been too rushed to straighten them.

"What's wrong with Gina?" she asked. "I can't

find her anywhere and now you've got me scared half to death. What happened? Did she get sick?"

"I'm not sure. She called me from her desk and she sounded confused. I'm afraid she might be having another bad episode."

"What do you mean?"

"Don't you remember when she hurt her feet?"

Sarah stared at him blankly. "What are you talking about?"

Gina obviously hadn't told her boss about the problem. "I'll explain later. Right now would you please help me look for her? I think she's ill and she sounded confused. You check the restrooms. I'll go outside and see if she's on the hospital grounds."

Sarah's eyes widened in alarm. "Confused? You're talking as if she's lost her mind. What's wrong with her, Archer?"

"I'm not sure yet. Can I explain this later? Right now we just need to find her and make sure she's safe. Would you have someone call Rose Pascal?"

"The social worker?" Sarah exclaimed.

Archer controlled his impatience and laid a hand on her arm. "Please. Right now she needs help."

"Okay, I'll help you look for her," Sarah said. "But when we find her she's going to have some explaining to do."

On his way out the door Archer stopped by the emergency room and asked them to contact

Grant on his pager. Honey Spring had lousy cell reception, but maybe a pager would work since it had a different frequency.

The smell of Limburger cheese wafted through the air and mingled with the scent of raw chicken liver as Lauren surreptitiously watched Brooke brave the cheese with her bare hands. Her reasoning was acceptable—she did not want to gore a living worm on the hook.

The girl showed determination to adapt to something that must seem so foreign to her. Impressive. She also had a tender heart beneath the double layer of prickles.

They had moved upstream about another hundred feet to where the water was deep and clear above a set of rapids that sparkled in the dappled sunlight. Grant and Beau had joined them after Lauren caught three trout within five minutes. Brooke managed to frighten away the remainder of the fish—and probably the turtles, crayfish, birds, and any other living creature in the vicinity—by a loud screech of outrage after each of Lauren's successful catches.

The tender-hearted, prickly, determined kid needed a gag.

"This stream feeds a reservoir that supplies drinking water for about a third of Dogwood Springs," Lauren explained to them. "The people complain a lot about the minerals in the water messing up their pipes but I envy them. When I come fishing down here I usually bring some water jugs and fill them and use that for drinking water at home. It's the best I've ever tasted."

"Ewww." Brooke looked up from her intense concentration as she tried to fit cheese on a hook and get it to stick. "You drink this water? Animals poop in it you know."

"The spring isn't too far from here." Lauren gestured toward the shallows that tumbled over rocks and pebbles with a series of whispered splashes. "That's where I collect it."

"But what about the people downstream? That is so disgusting."

Beau turned and gave his sister a long-suffering look. "It's water, Brooke. All water comes from somewhere. The city tests it and if they find a problem they treat it. We're not that deep in the backwoods."

She made a face at him and returned to her baiting efforts.

Beau cleared his throat and stepped closer to Lauren. "Um, do you think you could get me the information about that health occupations course at school?"

"I'd love to." She looked over at Grant. "What do you say? You think he'll make a good ER doc someday?"

"The best." The pride in Grant's eyes touched Lauren. "I just hope he decides to work in a small town like Dogwood Springs instead of a big city hospital. Burnout doesn't happen quite so quickly."

"Dad," Brooke said, "Beau's been sneaking into your medical magazine stash when you're at work."

"I'm not sneaking," Beau protested. "Dad said I could read them."

Beau had a nice baritone voice with a gentle quality much like his father's. Lauren decided he needed to use it more often—if Brooke would ever give him the opportunity.

Brooke straightened and lifted the tackle box down from the boulder where she had placed it. "Okay, I've got the stupid bait stuck on the stupid hook. Now would you show me how to do this again, Lauren?" She stepped over to the water's edge.

Lauren picked up her own rod and demonstrated once again how to cast and actually place the baited hook in the water instead of around an overhanging branch or on the opposite bank. Lauren reeled the line in and Brooke got ready to execute her own cast.

Grant jerked his line and reeled it in. "Lost my bait again." He walked over to the boulder Brooke had just vacated. "I think I'm going to need some lessons next." He sat down and reached for the box.

Brooke drew her pole back. "Like this, Lauren?" She held the line with her thumb then whipped the rod forward.

"Ow!" Grant jumped up from the boulder and swung around in alarm, hands on his posterior. "Something bit me."

Brooke tried to reel in her line but it snagged. She jerked hard.

"Ow!" Grant said again. "What's going—"

The deep sound of rich laughter reached them and all three of them turned in surprise to find Beau with his hand over his mouth pointing at his father. Although the laughter was obviously genuine, there was no sign of humor in his expression. That was what Grant meant about the damaged nerves.

"Don't look now, Dad, but you're the catch of the day."

The fishhook, complete with bait, was embedded in the lightweight khaki of Grant's pants, in a very delicate rear section of his anatomy.

Lauren could not resist a burst of laughter at his look of amazement.

"Oh, Dad, you sat on my hook," Brooke said. "No wonder I couldn't cast it. You ruined my bait. Do you know how much trouble this is?"

Grant reached back toward the seat of his pants.

Lauren rushed forward. "No, don't touch it or you'll—"

"Ow!"

"Grant, you'll just set the hook that way. Here, let me—"

"Stay away from my pants." Grant turned and

266

backed away from her. "I can fix this myself." The natural tan of his face deepened a shade. "I'll just take a little stroll into the woods and come back with my dignity intact if you don't mind."

"Forget it, Dad," Brooke said. "You just helped Lauren perform surgery on a snake. What kind of dignity could you possibly have left?"

"Grant, really." Lauren took the line in a firm grip to keep the hook from stabbing him. "I can get that out in just a few seconds if you'll just—"

He swung away too fast and too hard. The line drew taut and tangled in Lauren's fingers. There was a quick rip and a gasp. A flap of khaki folded away from the slacks to reveal a flash of white underneath.

The four of them stared at each other for a moment of shocked silence.

"Oh Grant, I'm sorry," Lauren said.

A small titter reached them over the sound of the creek. Lauren turned to see Brooke red-faced and giggling uncontrollably.

Above it all came the sound of Grant's pager.

He gave Lauren a look of horror, pulled the tiny receiver from the waistband of his damaged pants, and checked the number. He groaned.

"Who is it?" Beau asked.

"Only the hospital has my pager number. Lauren, you told me cell reception is bad here so I didn't bring mine."

"No need, and I didn't bring mine, either, but we

can get to the hospital quickly. Let's get this stuff packed up."

"Dad," Brooke protested. "You can't go to the hospital with the seat ripped out of your pants."

Grant shoved the pager into his pocket and reached for the tackle box. "I don't have a choice, honey. It could be an emergency."

❧ CHAPTER 19 ❧

Grant's humiliation had died a slow death on the way to town and was gone by the time they reached city limits. Brooke was right; his dignity had never been terribly important to him, anyway, and Lauren seemed to take it all in stride. He imagined she was as distracted as he was wondering what kind of catastrophe might have caused someone to page him. It had never happened to him in Dogwood Springs before. Of course, he'd never been out of cell reception in St. Louis. The only time he'd been paged was during residency many years ago.

As soon as the four of them pulled into the employee parking lot of the hospital, Archer Pierce came running from the ER entrance to intercept them. There were no police cars, no ambulances, and no city warning alarms going off. Obviously it wasn't a city-wide emergency.

The young minister waved and motioned for

them to stop. While Lauren parked, Archer came toward them at a jog. He looked grim.

Brooke scooted forward, a tiny gasp of appreciation escaping her lips. "Who's that?"

"My pastor." Lauren shoved the gearshift into park, turned off the engine, and opened the door to get out. "The one who was supposed to go fishing with us." She shut the door behind her and hurried to meet Archer.

"Whoa Dad," Brooke said in the sudden silence of the cab. "You've got some hefty competition. He's hot."

"I wouldn't know." Grant opened the door.

"Dad!" She scrambled across the seat and grabbed him by his shirt sleeve. "Your underwear. You can't go in there like that."

"Something's up, Brooke, can't you see that? I don't have time to worry about my fashion sense right now." He tried to pull free but she held firm.

"This isn't fashion sense, it's social suicide!" She turned to her brother. "Beau, do something."

"Beau, stay out of this," Grant said.

Beau nodded. "Sure Dad, but it wouldn't hurt you to untuck your shirttail. That'll cover everything unless you bend over or raise your arms. If you're going to commit social suicide, you might as well be cool about it."

"Okay, I'll untuck. Keep your sister occupied for a few minutes, okay?"

"I charge for baby-sitting."

269

"Hey!" Brooke released her dad and reached for Beau's head.

He ducked. "Let's go check out the hospital. There'll be all kinds of guys doing summer work around here. We might even fill out a job application."

Brooke hesitated, obviously torn between the obligation she had to protect her father's social reputation and the opportunity to flirt with future dating material and take possible steps toward acquiring a car.

It didn't take long. "Just don't tell them who our father is. I'll beat you to the building. Bye, Dad. Keep your hiney covered."

Before Grant reached Lauren and Archer, the kids were racing across the parking lot toward the hospital building. Grant wondered briefly if Brooke remembered she still smelled like Limburger cheese. Now that he thought about it, he caught a whiff of it and realized he'd been smeared with it, too. And in a very unfortunate location.

"She said someone was after her and that they wouldn't leave her alone." Archer's words made Grant forget everything else. "She was terrified and she was looking for you, Lauren."

Grant rushed forward, tugging the tail of his shirt from the waistband of his khakis. "Who are you talking about?"

"Gina's having trouble again and they can't

find her," Lauren said. "Has anyone checked the elementary school grounds? That's where she went last time. In her confused state she must be looking for her children."

"But the school is near her house," Archer said, "not the hospital."

"What direction is the school from her house?" Grant asked. "If she's disoriented she might instinctively go that way again."

Archer pointed west.

"How long has she been gone?" Lauren asked.

"Only about twenty to thirty minutes. We can't rule out a psychological problem," Archer said, "especially after what she told me. She said 'they' were all around her and that 'they' wouldn't shut up. If she's hearing voices—"

"Some physical problems could cause that," Grant said. "Have you called her IIS therapist?"

"It's being done."

Grant checked his watch. "I hate to call the police on her again but I don't want to take any chances."

"I'll call Evan Webster," Archer said. "Poor kid's still waiting for me."

"IIS will see to the kids," Lauren said.

Grant nodded. "I'll have them take care of it. Check your watches and meet me in the ER in thirty minutes if you haven't found Gina. I sure picked a bad time to leave my cell phone at home."

They parted and began the search.

• • •

Fifteen minutes later Lauren found Gina rounding a corner on the sidewalk in a residential part of town not far from the hospital. Her head was bowed, her arms crossed tightly over her chest.

"Gina?" Lauren ran to meet her.

Gina looked up. Her face was wet and her eyes were red, but immediate relief eased the tightly drawn tension so obvious in her posture.

Lauren instinctively held out her arms and Gina walked into them and grabbed her in a tight, desperate grip.

"Are you okay? What happened? We've been looking for you."

Gina buried her face against Lauren's shoulder and shook her head.

"It's okay," Lauren soothed. "You're going to be—" But she couldn't promise Gina she would be fine.

"Help me Lauren," Gina whispered. "I think I'm losing my mind. I'm messing up everything. I thought I could control this thing if I could just concentrate hard enough to keep it from happening again. I'm so sorry."

"You don't have to apologize for being sick. Tell me what happened."

"I don't know. Maybe Rose was right. Maybe I'm having panic attacks. Or worse."

"Don't jump to conclusions. Just describe what happened."

Gina straightened and drew away. "I panicked at my desk and there were these . . ." She blinked and shook her head. "I tried to call you but I didn't get an answer and . . . I tried calling someone else . . . can't remember . . . then I found myself out here walking. I was terrified. How did you know where to look? What did I—did I do something?" She gripped Lauren's arms, eyes widening. "Did I hurt—?"

"No, it's okay, you didn't do anything wrong. You don't remember calling Archer?"

Gina frowned and looked around them, as if trying to pinpoint their location. "Maybe he was the one I tried next. It's so hazy."

"He's on your list, Gina. The plan worked. He located Dr. Sheldon and me. Dr. Sheldon organized an informal search party. Archer doesn't think anyone in your department even knew you were having a problem until he told them."

"Dr. Sheldon didn't call the police again, did he?"

"He didn't want to but I didn't have time to stay at the hospital. I needed to find you. I do know he's very concerned."

Gina grabbed Lauren's shoulders as if she suddenly had no strength to stand. "They'll take my boys. Oh, Lauren."

Lauren eased her down onto a three-foot retaining wall. "Slow down, honey. You don't want to go there. Remember you're not alone."

She sank down beside Gina, wishing she'd brought her cell phone or at least taken the time to borrow someone else's. The others needed to know Gina was safe. "Archer said you told him some voices bothered you." She hoped the younger woman didn't pick up on her uncertainty. "You told Archer they wouldn't shut up."

Gina's hands tightened on Lauren's arms. "Voices." She nodded. "That's so not good, you know. It means—"

"We don't know what it means yet."

"Hearing voices is a symptom of psychosis. Am I—"

"Dr. Sheldon said there can be physical causes."

Gina closed her eyes and took a deep breath. "I guess I'm in big trouble. Sarah didn't know anything about my first trip to the ER."

"She might have been able to help today."

"Or she might have suspended me for fear I'd have another episode while treating a patient. I'm so new here and I don't know who to trust. I could have lost my job. Now I probably won't have one when I get back."

"Dr. Sheldon will talk to Sarah. Are you feeling well enough to walk? I want to get you back to the ER. If we can run some tests on you right away maybe there's a chance we can find the culprit."

Gina nodded and stood up. She closed her eyes for a moment, opened them and joined

Lauren on the sidewalk. "The fear I felt was real."

"We need to find out where that fear is coming from."

"Maybe we don't want to."

"Of course we do."

Gina stared resolutely at the sidewalk in front of her. "I'm fine now."

"This fear you're talking about . . . any idea at all what it is or where the voices came from? Who they belonged to?"

Gina didn't respond. She seemed so closed in on herself, obviously battling something she didn't want to share.

"Gina?"

"Talking will just make it worse."

"Why do you say that?"

"I'm not sure I even can bring myself to talk about it."

"It?" So there was something to talk about. Maybe they were getting somewhere after all. "You need to try." Lauren tugged on Gina's arm but Gina pulled away.

They walked about half a block in silence.

"If I tell you something will you promise not to say anything to anyone?" Gina asked at least.

"Don't put me on the spot. Your safety comes first."

Gina touched Lauren's arm. "Please just listen. I've been doing a lot of research since I first started having these spells."

"Since you first started? When was that?"

Gina looked away. "They've been worse since I moved here in February. I felt periods of confusion before but I never lost time and I never left my kids alone at home. The fear wasn't . . . so bad before."

"So you're saying the problem's escalating?" That was not a comforting thought. "You should tell Dr. Sheldon about this as soon as possible."

"The stress of moving has obviously aggravated a problem I already had." Gina slowed her steps and her gaze darted up and down the street. "I've been researching fugue states," she said quietly. "That could be what's happening to me. Please, please don't tell anyone this or it could cause me to lose Levi and Cody."

"What would make you think fugue state?" Lauren asked.

Again, that darting gaze around them, behind them. "I haven't told this to anybody." She swallowed and searched Lauren's face.

"It's okay, Gina. You're not going to shock me."

"I had an aunt who was hospitalized with a mental disorder in Oregon." The words came in a rush as if she'd suppressed them for a long time.

"What was the disorder?"

"Please promise you won't tell anyone."

"But why? If there truly is a mental disorder then we can find it and treat for it."

"There's more to it."

"Hey! There you are!" They looked up to find Archer running toward them across the corner of a yard to their left. He crossed the street while Lauren's nerves screamed with sudden frustration. Five minutes ago she'd been praying for him to join them. Now she wished she'd had just a few more moments alone with Gina. She could feel Gina closing in on herself as Archer drew near, cell phone to his ear to tell the other searchers that Gina was safe.

Who knew when she would open up again?

❧ CHAPTER 20 ❧

Grant completed a disappointingly unremarkable neurological exam on Gina Drake. He put down the chart and hesitated, hating to dash her hopes. "Any other time I'd be happy to say you're fine, Gina."

She closed her eyes as tears slipped from them. Lauren put an arm around her. The social worker, Rose Pascal, sighed and shook her head, leaning into herself at the far corner of the exam room.

Rose was a pretty woman in her forties with the sad gaze of someone who spent too many hours worrying about other people. She had short gray-blond hair that she constantly fingered away from her eyes in a subconscious gesture of excess nervous tension. At this moment her hair was tufted, her face pale. If only Gina could see Rose's obvious concern as she stood quietly waiting.

The physician on duty had been more than willing to allow Grant to treat this patient. Emma, the RN on duty, had drawn blood and taken vitals, and Gina was on a cardiac monitor. Nothing seemed irregular.

Grant stepped back from the bed, tugging at the sleeves of his borrowed lab coat, which stretched too tightly across his shoulders. "We can only wait and hope something else turns up on the blood tests."

Gina brushed the tears away and looked up at him from the exam bed. "You've ordered another psychological exam?"

"You have an appointment for Monday morning in Springfield."

Rose stepped to the bed and laid a hand on Gina's arm. "You'll need someone to drive you."

Gina tensed. "I'll drive myself."

"If you'd only let us help you."

Gina gave Rose a look so filled with suspicion that Rose retreated to her corner.

When Gina turned to Lauren, her expression was that of a frightened child. "What am I going to do?"

"We've talked about this, remember?" Lauren's voice was brisk and filled with confidence, nothing less than Grant would have expected.

"You're here and you're safe. That's what counts for now. Maybe the tests will show something and Dr. Sheldon will be able to figure this whole thing out."

"And if he doesn't?" Gina rose up on her elbows. "What then? I feel like the vultures are waiting to pounce." She jerked her head toward Rose. "Tell her what Natalie said last week. It took me an hour to calm Levi down after he heard her talking about foster care."

Rose frowned. "What? In front of the children?"

"Natalie and Gina were discussing child care options in case Gina became incapable of caring for Levi and Cody," Lauren said. "Levi overheard her mention foster care and it frightened him."

The news obviously surprised Rose. She shook her head and groaned softly. "Of course it would, but Gina, did she actually threaten to take your children from you?"

"No, but what she said frightened my son. Ever since that wraparound meeting I've felt as if there's a shadow looming over everything I do. The minute I make a move out of line, my kids are going to be snatched away from me." Her bitterness held a familiar edge. Lauren had heard it several times in the past three weeks.

Rose sighed and spread her hands in front of her. "Oh Gina, no. I never meant that as a threat. I was simply voicing one of my own fears. Every day I do everything in my power to help keep families together—it's one of the main reasons I do this job."

Silence stole into the room as Gina stared at the bed railing.

"I'll do all I can to help you, Gina," Rose said softly.

Gina shifted on the bed and reached irritably for one of the monitor lines, as if the silence and the subject matter made her uncomfortable. "Dr. Sheldon, my readings are normal, right?"

"That's right," Grant said. "Everything appears good so far." Which wasn't really good. There was nothing to fix.

"Then can we take this thing off?"

"Let's wait a few more minutes before Lauren removes the electrodes. I don't want to give up too soon. We're still waiting on test results."

Gina slumped back down onto the mattress and looked at Rose again. Her gaze slid away. "Natalie didn't really threaten me," she said with apparent reluctance. "I'm not . . . I don't want to get her in trouble or anything. I just want some peace and quiet at home. I wish Archer hadn't called the whole city over a silly little phone call, because now she'll be all over me again."

"It wasn't a silly little phone call," Grant said. "I needed to be here as soon as possible to test you. I might have caught something if I'd been able to get to you in time."

Rose raked her fingers through her hair. "Gina,

I'll talk to Natalie. She's a young counselor—she's only been at the job for a year—and she's trying to do everything by the book. But she really wants to help. She's come to me about your case several times."

"I'll just bet she has," Gina grumbled. "She's come to me a few times, too."

"She's frustrated because the two of you can't seem to communicate."

"She doesn't realize how dangerous a little knowledge can be."

"What knowledge, Gina?" There was a thread of exasperation in Rose's voice. She turned and paced across the small exam room. "Is something else going on here? Is that why you won't cooperate?"

"I'm protecting my family."

"Natalie's on her way here now," Rose said. "Will you at least talk to her? Please?"

"I always talk to her."

Lines of frustration deepened around Rose's eyes. She took a step toward the bed, hesitant. "Gina," she said softly, "I know it's hard to trust strangers, especially whcn your children are involved, but the only reason I continue with this job is because I have a passion for seeing families kept together, especially a loving one like yours."

Something in Gina's face softened. She did not smile, and she did not relent, but the hard set of her jaw wasn't quite as defined as it had been a few moments ago. She nodded and closed her eyes.

Rose shook her head, shrugged at Grant and Lauren, and left the room.

As soon as the door closed, Gina's eyes opened. "Dr. Sheldon, do you mind if I talk to Lauren alone for a few minutes?"

"Of course not. I'll be in my office."

Archer found Evan Webster in the emergency waiting room. The fifteen-year-old sat in a deserted corner scribbling furiously in a notebook. He looked up when Archer sat down next to him but the expression on his face was one of intense concentration, as if he was still focused on his flow of ideas. A small red and purple bruise smudged his left eye.

"Did you take a tumble?" Archer indicated the bruise.

Evan's eyes darkened before he ducked his head and flushed. "I fell against my *friend's* clenched fist."

"A friend did that?"

Evan looked down at his notebook. "He's the one who gave me the pills. He got mad because I told the police about him. When his parents found out they freaked. He's being shipped off to spend the summer with his uncle, who's a retired marine. Kent wanted me to have some-thing to remember him by."

Good, the kid would be gone until school started. "I'm proud of you, Evan. You took a courageous stand and I know that couldn't have been easy. Sometimes friends are hard to find."

"Yeah." Evan slumped back in his chair.

"Hey, I'm sorry I kept you waiting for so long this afternoon."

Evan perked up. "That's okay. Unfortunately, I know how time flies when you're in the middle of an emergency."

Archer placed his hand on Evan's shoulder. "That's true. But I still wish I'd called you right away."

"Forget about it. I knew it had to be something important. I don't think you're the kind of guy who makes promises he doesn't keep."

Archer gestured to the notebook with a page full of scribbles. "Your father told me you're a fledgling reporter for the school paper."

"Not just the school paper." Evan straightened. "The editor at *The Dogwood* promised to read an article about my experience the night I came here with the overdose."

"Is he thinking about publishing it?"

"If it's good enough. I'm going to make sure it is."

"And you don't mind the fact that many people might read the story and judge you unkindly?"

Evan shook his head. "Writing is what I do. Most people know about what happened, anyway.

Word gets around. Besides, it shouldn't have happened at all and maybe my article will keep somebody else from swallowing pills just because some so-called friend tells him to."

"How do your parents feel about it?"

"Dad thinks I should do it." Evan shrugged. "I didn't ask Mom. She's planning a wedding and she's not going to be around much longer."

"She isn't? Are you moving?"

"*She's* moving."

"But you aren't?"

Evan shook his head. "She's getting married in a month and they'll live in Springfield. I told her I wasn't living up there and she said okay." He placed his pen in the center of the notebook on his lap and leaned back. "Just like that."

Archer grimaced. That had to hurt, even if the boy didn't want to live with his mother anymore. "You're moving in with your father?"

"Yep. She told Dad it's just for the summer but Dad thinks we can convince her to let me stay with him for good if we don't make waves about it for a while, especially since her fiancé probably isn't too crazy about me right now."

"Your father must be happy that you're staying with him."

A slow grin spread across Evan's face. "Yeah, he is. He says we'll start attending your church on Sundays and I can take those drug awareness classes you lead on Tuesdays."

Archer grinned. "Things are looking up."

"If you'll let me take notes for my article in class."

"Absolutely. We're going to have a special guest teacher next Tuesday. Do you remember reading about Sergeant Tony Dalton in *The Dogwood*?"

"The police guy who got blinded by that booby trap?" Evan looked impressed.

"That's the one. He's teaching the class."

"Yes!" Evan raised a hand of victory in the air and the excitement transformed his face.

Archer grinned. Some of his prayers for this boy were being answered. "We might still be able to go fishing for a couple of hours this afternoon. Are you interested?"

"Okay, that sounds like—" Evan's attention suddenly shifted and Archer heard approaching voices.

The teenager swallowed. His eyes widened. Archer turned and saw Grant's twins strolling side by side into the waiting room from the central hallway. Brooke and Beau. There had been no time for introductions earlier but Archer had noticed them in Lauren's truck when she pulled up in the parking lot.

"I don't care where they put me as long as I get a paycheck," the girl chattered confidently to her brother. "If I can jam raw liver onto a fishhook, I can empty a bedpan. Maybe they'll let you work in the kitchen."

"Maybe they'll let me do data entry. I can—"
Beau looked up and caught sight of Archer and
Evan. He fell silent and seemed to close within
himself.

Brooke saw Archer and stepped forward with a
sudden smile. She was a beautiful girl, obviously
without an ounce of shyness. She held her hand
out to Archer as he stood up. "Hi. You're Archer
Pierce, the pastor of Lauren's church."

"And you're Brooke, Grant's daughter." Archer
caught the smell as he released her hand. The
scent of Limburger cheese and apparently raw
liver wafted through the air. "Catch any fish?"

"I caught a snake." She rolled her eyes and
shuddered dramatically. She had expressive,
constantly moving features and eyes that, like
her father's, didn't seem to miss details. She
glanced at Evan and held her hand toward him.
"Hi, I'm Brooke Sheldon. Are you the guy who
got stood up this afternoon?"

Evan's ink pen fell to the floor as he took her
hand. He didn't seem to notice. "Yes, um, I am.
But Archer says we might be able to go back
out."

Brooke's smile most likely dazzled the recipient
of her favor into forgetting the unfortunate
fragrance accosting him. Her charm reflected
her father's easy grace. Her brother, on the other
hand, continued to hover a few feet away, hands
in his pockets, eyes downcast.

Archer completed the introductions. It looked as if the kids would have some time to get acquainted while they waited on tests for Gina.

After Grant left the exam room, Gina looked up at Lauren. "Will you take care of my kids if something happens to me?"

The impact of the question alarmed her. She and Gina both knew that despite Rose's assurances, if Gina became incapable of caring for her children, foster care might be a necessity.

"Please? In case something does happen, you're the only person I know I can trust."

The sounds and smells of the busy ER faded into the background as Lauren pulled a chair close to Gina's bed. She didn't sit down immediately. This was serious. "In the first place, Natalie and Rose and a lot of other people are doing all they can to make sure your children don't have to leave you."

"They'd place my babies with strangers. Please don't let that happen." Gina touched Lauren's shoulder. "I need to know they'll be safe. I need to know they'll be with you. I won't go back."

"Go back to where? Oregon?"

A chasm of fear and frustration filled Gina's eyes. The full lines of her face grew taut. "My children already adore you."

"But all your safety nets are in place and everything worked today. You called Archer and he took action. It was what we hoped for."

"I'm talking long term. We don't know what I'm going to do next. I can't take any chances with my children and their future."

Lauren reached for Gina's hand. "Remember I told you that you're not alone. I'll be here for you." She waited until Gina's grip relaxed a little. "What did you leave behind in Oregon? What are you so afraid of?"

Gina pressed her lips together and looked away.

"It's okay if you can't talk about it yet."

"M-my mother," she whispered.

"What about your mother?"

"She hates me. She's a wicked jealous shrew. If she knew about all this and had a chance she'd try to get the kids from me. Not because she wants them but because it would hurt me. And then she would hurt *them*."

Lauren swallowed, stunned. "And she's in Oregon."

Gina nodded. "Please don't tell anyone."

"I won't. I just have trouble understanding how a mother could hate her own daughter."

"I never understood it either and I've always been afraid I'd turn out just like her."

"You shouldn't worry. It's obvious to everyone around you how much you love your children. You said your father died when you were ten."

"That's when I lost my only friend in the house. My mother said he played favorites between me and my sister."

"You have a sister? But you said you didn't have any family."

"I don't." Gina's voice and eyes hardened. "Levi and Cody are my only family now."

"What about your sister?"

"She's five years older than me. She's the one who turned out like my mother. She hates me just as much. After my father died I learned the meaning of pain. Few days went by that I didn't receive at least a slap in the face from my sister for some imagined slight. It made my mother laugh."

"Your mother allowed your sister to abuse you like that?"

"Allowed? She encouraged it. My mother didn't hit me that often. She just let her anger build. I could see it coming for days and then when she went into a rage even my sister wasn't safe. I learned early to run away when Mother began to yell. It was like a shriek of warning."

"Oh, Gina."

"Two years after my father died, my mother remarried. I was excited, because I thought a stepfather would be a friend." She closed her eyes. "He wasn't."

"Did he hurt you too?"

"He made passes at me. He never forced it but he kept trying. One day my mother was in the laundry room that connected to the kitchen pantry while I was cooking supper. He didn't know she was there. He came up behind me and . . . he said something disgusting. She heard him. She came storming out of that laundry room like she was going to kill me."

"She blamed you?"

Gina nodded. "She punched me in the face and shoved me into the stove. My blouse caught fire and it burned my stomach. Three weeks ago when I found out Levi had been burned, I felt as if history was repeating itself no matter how hard I've tried to keep it from happening. It's like some evil cosmic game."

"No, Gina. It doesn't work that way. You're a logical human being and you know—"

"Just listen to me." Taking care not to dislodge the electrodes on her chest, Gina swung her feet over the side of the bed and leaned closer to Lauren. "Tell me if you don't think there's some kind of pattern. I was twelve when that happened. I went to school with a black eye from my mother's fists and when I was undressing for gym some of the other girls saw my burned stomach. They reported it to a teacher and Social Services stuck its nose into the mess."

Tears of sympathy stung Lauren's eyes. She swallowed them back.

"They took me out of my home and placed me in foster care," Gina said. "They seemed to think that would make everything better. It didn't."

"You must have been frightened."

"I was terrified. I didn't want to stay with my mother and sister but I didn't want to live with strangers either. When my father's Aunt Bridget found out about it and asked for custody, they didn't allow it because she had a history of wild bipolar swings. My mother got a real kick out of the fact that only a crazy lady would want me. Every time she saw me afterward she reminded me of it. She told me I was going to turn out just like Aunt Bridget."

"What were the foster homes like?"

"Confusing. Frightening. Awkward for them and horrible for me. Any time someone raised a voice in anger, I ran. I couldn't help it. I was too scared. I went through four foster homes in two years. They finally gave up on me and allowed me to stay with Aunt Bridget in spite of her history. They didn't have a choice."

"Have you been in touch with your aunt?"

"She died two months before I graduated from high school." Gina's voice caught and she fought a visible battle with tears. "Those years with her were the best years I can remember in my life and I owe her everything. When she left her estate to me, my mother and sister were livid. They protested in court but Aunt Bridget's attorney was prepared for them. It wasn't a fortune but it got me through college and gave me a good down payment on my home."

"Okay I'll do it."

Gina's eyes widened. "You'll take care of Levi and Cody?"

"If something happens to you. Which it won't."

Some of the strain disappeared from around Gina's eyes and mouth. The relief in the room was palpable.

"I still feel as if I'm paying for my family's evil."

"No wonder you have trouble trusting."

"I trust you, Lauren."

"That's a start."

"I heard voices," Gina whispered. "If I have inherited a mental illness, who's going to know how to treat that?"

"Could you be hearing your mother's voice? Maybe your sister's. What you're experiencing could be leftover fear from your childhood."

"You mean repressed memories?"

"Not repressed. You obviously remember them too well, you just haven't been able to deal with them. That was apparent to me immediately, because you've been so unwilling to talk about it before now."

There was a soft knock at the door and Grant stepped inside. He held a two-page printout, obviously the report on Gina's blood tests. He looked discouraged. "Lauren, you can disconnect Gina from the monitor now. She's in excellent physical condition."

❧ CHAPTER 21 ❧

Grant sat at his desk with stacks of reports in front of him. It took all his will not to toss one particular stack in the trash. Or across the room.

He rubbed his eyes, fatigued beyond reason.

When was the last time he'd experienced this many conflicting emotions within the space of a few hours? He had never considered himself a particularly emotional man. Annette, of course, had insisted differently.

Today he'd gone from frustration with Brooke's attitude to elation with Lauren's company, from humiliation when the fishhook ripped his pants to exhilaration when he thought they might finally discover what was wrong with Gina. That hadn't worked out. And now this.

He should have known what was coming when he saw the sheriff standing in the doorway to his office.

Grant shoved the pages to the side of the desk. The autopsy report on poor Mrs. Henson had cleared him of any blame but that gave him no comfort. She'd died from sudden cardiac death secondary to lethal arrhythmia. There was no stroke. There was no blockage of arteries. Case closed. It did not tell him why she had been so sick the night before she died and therefore it couldn't give him any clues as to why so many more people were developing symptoms of the illness.

He glared at the sheaf of stapled pages of interrogatories from a St. Louis law firm that specialized in personal injury claims. He'd seen their name on billboards and television ads in St. Louis.

"Knock-knock," came a friendly male voice from the open doorway.

Grant turned and motioned for Archer to come in.

"Any findings?"

"None."

Archer sighed and slumped into a chair beside the desk. "Frustrating. Where is she now?"

Grant pointed toward the flower garden outside the window where Lauren and Gina strolled shoulder to shoulder between brightly colored rows of varied blooms. At least Gina seemed to be opening up to someone.

"If it's frustrating to us, imagine how much worse it must be for her," Archer said. "I'm glad Lauren's working her usual miracle."

Grant shrugged away his depression and concentrated on what Archer was saying. "Miracle?"

"Don't get me wrong, I know it's God who works the actual miracles but sometimes it seems to me as if Lauren serves as a sort of vessel for them to flow through."

Grant knew what he meant. Annette had been that way.

"She's got this kind of radar that picks up on hurting people," Archer continued. "Where most people might avoid someone like Gina and her problems, Lauren dives in up to her neck, the way she did the first time Gina came in here. I've seen her do it a lot of times over the years." There was no way to miss the note of admiration in his voice or the affectionate smile on Archer's face as he, too, watched Lauren through the window.

Grant turned his back to the depressing burden on his desk and studied Archer closely. "All that and she's single."

"Maybe there's a reason she is."

"You mean because she's too busy for a relationship?"

Archer considered that for a moment. "Maybe this is a time in her life when God has chosen her to pour herself out for others. Someone who is married will naturally spend more time with a spouse."

"Is that why you're still single?" The words were out of Grant's mouth before he could stop them.

Archer's eyes flickered with a note of discomfort. "Good question."

"I'm sorry. I know you had a broken engagement, I just didn't think—"

"It's okay. I've wondered about that a few times.

When Jessica broke our engagement it seemed as if God was trying to tell me something about the necessity for singleness of purpose. Now I'm thinking maybe I just tried to move things along a little too quickly, going by my own timetable instead of God's."

"You mean you might consider marriage with the right person?"

"I already know the right person. My church thinks that the pastorate needs a husband and a wife to do the job. I can't keep up with all the responsibilities by myself."

"Maybe your church expects too much from a pastor."

A hint of a smile touched Archer's eyes. "I've thought of that too."

"I've noticed Lauren helps you a lot," Grant said.

"She does and I need to stop taking advantage of her generous nature."

"But she seems to enjoy it. She was having fun today. I know she was looking forward to your arrival." It had been obvious.

"Really?" A hint of a frown touched Archer's eyes. "I can't imagine why. I usually scare all the fish off."

"You couldn't possibly be as bad as Brooke."

The frown disappeared. "I wouldn't bet on that. Did you have a good time?"

"If snakes, limburger cheese, torn pants, and

screaming teenagers are your idea of fun I highly recommend it."

"I think Jessica might have enjoyed it immensely."

"Jessica?"

"My ex-fiancée." A thoughtful smile touched the pastor's eyes. "Maybe she won't be an ex for long, though."

"Oh?"

"I believe she might be coming around. We're friends. That's the best way to build a stronger future, right?"

"Absolutely." Grant was happy for Archer but for Lauren's sake he couldn't help feeling a twist of sympathy. She obviously felt more for the man than simple friendship. Could Archer be so clueless? Maybe he chose to ignore an uncomfortable situation.

Or maybe Grant was being overly analytical because he was struggling with that invasive little attraction bug himself right now.

"A wife would probably keep the normal small-town gossip to a minimum," Archer said.

"That isn't a good reason to get married."

"Of course not." Archer stared out the window and into the distance. "But this town needs something to kill out the nasty rumor mill."

Grant didn't ask what ugly lie had placed that sudden chill in Archer's expression. "Friendship is the most important thing for a solid, lasting marriage. I'm glad you're wise enough to know it." Though Grant couldn't always close his eyes and picture Annette's face, he could still feel the overwhelming emptiness in his heart. "That's what I miss the most about my wife. She was my best friend on earth." He missed her now especially. If she were still alive he would have immediately picked up the telephone and told her about the letter from the attorneys. She would have reassured him and been on his side. She would have contacted the best attorney she could find.

"I think your wife must have been a wonderful person," Archer said quietly.

"She was." Grant looked out across the broad hospital lawn again and watched as Lauren and Gina took a seat on a concrete bench in the center of the flower garden beneath the shade of a weeping willow.

Far to the right of them near the parking lot, Brooke's bright red T-shirt and shorts flashed in the sunshine, practically iridescent with the movements of her body. Brooke was never still. It was as if she had twice the energy of her quiet brother, who sat in silence beside Evan Webster on another concrete bench. Both boys watched Brooke, listening to whatever wild tale she was telling them.

Grant felt a familiar tug at his heart. He wanted so much for his children. But just as Archer felt

he needed a wife to help with church responsibilities, Grant needed his wife here to be the
mother of his children, to guide them in ways he
couldn't.

"I'll be free the rest of the afternoon to go
fishing if you still want to try it," Archer said.
"That is if Gina's going to be okay."

Grant nodded. "She's eager to get back to work
but Lauren forestalled her for a while. I'm not
sure we can stick another fishing pole in
Brooke's hand but I'm willing to give it a run."
Once again, Grant's eyes strayed to the offending
papers. He couldn't work up any enthusiasm for
the idea of fishing but he knew the diversion
would do him good. It would be good for the kids
too.

Archer studied Grant's face more closely.
"Something else is going on here. What is it?"

Grant sighed and reached for the interrogatories. "I'm being sued for malpractice."

While Archer waited for Grant and Lauren to
wrap up a meeting with Gina's supervisor and
unruffle some feathers with the IIS therapist, who
was trying so hard to convince Gina to trust her,
he strolled down the familiar main hallway of
Dogwood Springs Hospital, praying as he went.

Grant needed direction. Gina appeared to need
divine intervention immediately. Archer tried not
to brood about the painful meeting with his

personal referees. It was difficult considering that this very hospital was reportedly the origin of the mean-spirited gossip. Still, he had to tell himself that those three servants of the personnel committee meant well as far as their understanding went.

But he still hotly resented their willingness to attack an innocent women merely on hospital gossip. He also resented their intrusion and their willingness to listen to outright lies about him. Though he tried to shake off that resentment he wasn't having a lot of success.

It disappointed him to realize that even though Mr. Netz and Mr. Hahnfeld had watched him grow up in "their" church since he was an infant, they were willing to believe he would father a child out of wedlock and then deny all responsibility for it.

Even if they hadn't known Lauren as long as he had, couldn't they trust his judgment about her? What would make them even consider such a possibility?

A stray question occurred to him but he quickly dashed it away.

They should be able to trust his word. They should also know him well enough to give his friends the benefit of the doubt.

What if they were listening not only to this one hospital rumor but also to suggestions whispered by others in the congregation?

But he couldn't even think like that. Lauren had always behaved with the utmost propriety, so even though she did, at times, seem to seek his company a little more often than she had in the past, and even though he had caught hints from some of the elderly ladies in the church family . . . and even just now from Grant. . . .

No. It wasn't possible. Archer and Lauren had always been close. She was like a big sister. He was the one who'd had the crush when they were kids, not Lauren. She was obviously homesick right now. And since he was the only old familiar face around, it was understandable that she would gravitate to him for friendship.

How could such influential members of his church be totally lacking in spiritual discernment? Did he really want to be the pastor of a church so worldly minded?

And yet weren't all churches like this? It was what this world was all about.

Still, Lauren McCaffrey did not deserve this kind of treatment.

Archer rounded a corner and strolled into the small gift shop that was run by volunteers from the community. He saw Mrs. Piedmont in her pink smock talking to a prospective customer about a bouquet of flowers. When she caught sight of him her smile broadened in warm welcome and she waved at him. That smile soothed something inside him. At least she wasn't paying any attention to unfounded rumors. Mrs. Piedmont walked closer to heaven every day. Archer knew he was being selfish to hope she lived well past a hundred.

When he returned to the hallway and saw Fiona Perkins waddling toward him, Archer resisted the temptation to do an about-face and race away in the opposite direction.

"Hi Archer." She said it in a sly singsong voice that grated.

He braced himself. "Fiona."

Chunky and awkward, Fiona unfortunately had a personality to match. She had curly black hair and wide-set pretty blue eyes but as Archer and others had learned the hard way, her attitude could curdle water. He reminded himself that she needed to experience the love of Christ as much as the rest of the world.

She chugged up to stop at his side, peered into the gift shop as if to see what held his attention then looked back at him as a knowing grin creased her face. "Looking for someone?"

"No, I just—"

"She doesn't work Fridays." The grin broadened. "It's her day off, same as you. But you already know that don't you?"

While Archer was biting back a caustic reply, Fiona waddled away. He headed in the opposite direction. Typical of Fiona to leave her little innuendoes wherever she went.

One of the benefits of being born and raised for thirty-three years in one small Missouri town was familiarity with all the other natives, particularly with wonderful souls like Mrs. Piedmont.

Ironically, with other souls who were not so benign, familiarity was one of the drawbacks. Many natives had a tendency to know too much about a person's business.

Fiona had moved to Dogwood Springs with her family when Archer was a senior in high school and she was a freshman. She hadn't been overweight then but she had quickly become unpopular because of her spiteful spirit. When Archer went out of his way to be kind to her she developed a huge crush on him. Things went downhill from there.

"I give up!"

Archer stopped walking when the feminine voice reached him past a door that stood slightly ajar ahead of him.

IIS therapist Natalie Frasier burst through that door and nearly tripped over his feet. "I don't know what more I can do for her."

Lauren stepped out behind her. When she saw Archer she gave him an apologetic grimace.

"Gina?" he asked.

Natalie put her hands on her hips. "Lucky guess." Her voice dripped sarcasm. Her intense dark eyes shimmered with tears and she folded her long arms into a protective bony shield.

"She has her reasons," Lauren said gently. "I understand that now."

"I don't. I'm tired of fighting this. I give up. I'll file my report and it won't be a very good one."

"You're already giving up on her?" Archer asked. This girl didn't have much staying power.

Natalie gave an angry swipe at the tears on her face. "What am I supposed to do? I can't get any cooperation from her."

"I'll talk to her again," Lauren assured her.

"I will too," Archer said.

Natalie spread her fingers in front of her. "It won't do any good. She won't listen and you both know it. I'm finished. But just tell me one thing—why do a preacher and a doctor know so much more about my client than I do? I'm the one who's spent the past three weeks trying to get her to trust me."

"How many times have you threatened to take her children during those three weeks?" Archer asked before he could stop himself.

Natalie's eyes widened, and her face flushed brighter. "It was simply an alternative if we couldn't get everything straightened out."

"But it terrifies her and the children," Lauren said gently. "That's not the way to earn someone's trust."

"I'm just doing my job. Doesn't she see I'm trying to help her?"

"How would any frightened mother react to the threat of losing her children?" Lauren laid a hand on Natalie's shoulder. "That's her biggest fear. Natalie, if you file your report and give up on her today, what's going to happen to her?"

"I don't know. The decision isn't up to me."

"But you must have some idea."

The young woman gave an exasperated sigh. She took several long-legged paces along the quiet hallway, arms falling at her sides in a curiously helpless gesture. When she turned back the sheen of tears was still there.

"Is there another therapist in the area?" Archer asked. "Maybe another angle on this—"

"Now you're threatening my job?"

He paused and gave her a cool look. Why had Rose placed this inexperienced and self-absorbed young woman on Gina's case? "You think your job is more important than a young mother keeping her children?" He knew he shouldn't be talking like this but she brought out his hostility for some reason. Fiona hadn't helped, neither had the deacons. Maybe he should keep his mouth shut.

"Natalie," Lauren's voice remained gentle. "You're doing all you know to do, and you obviously care about your clients or you wouldn't be so frustrated. Gina still has time to realize that if you will just give her time to work with you."

"Do you know how much longer I have to

complete this assignment? Two weeks at best. Maybe three if I convince the right people I need more time but I'm not making any headway with this woman. She's like an armored tank. I don't have enough evidence to convince anyone to even read my report!" She waved a hand in the air. "Report? That's a laugh."

"The safeguards worked today," Archer said. "That's progress. Why don't you put that in your report?"

"If it will help you with the decision," Lauren said, "why don't I move in with Gina for the next week?"

"No." Natalie's angular face took on extra definition. "I can choose the hours I feel are necessary to work each case and I have at least a couple of weeks left. If she needs someone to stay overnight with her, I'll do it."

Doubt clouded Lauren's eyes but she said no more. Archer could identify. Two stubborn women could make a recipe for disaster.

With arms jutting at an awkward angle from her straight slender body, Natalie marched down the hallway and out the door.

Archer watched Lauren watch Natalie and he knew from past experience what she was thinking. "You handled that better than I did."

She turned back to him, still frowning. "I don't know about this, Archer."

"You can't carry the load of the whole world on

your back." Out of habit, he put a companionable arm across her shoulders. Realizing how the gesture might appear to onlookers, he abruptly withdrew it.

She looked up at him. "Archer? Is something wrong?"

Obviously, she knew him as well as he knew her. The words of warning were ready to spring from his lips but he stopped them just in time. "I just realized that your meeting is over with Natalie and if we wanted to we could round up the gang and go fishing."

The diversionary tactic worked just as he had known it would. Lauren smiled and the light of eager anticipation entered her eyes. "Let me check on Gina one more time then I'll find Grant. Oh and Archer, would you see if you can round up a spare set of large scrub pants? I think Grant could use some extra coverage. I'll meet you in the parking lot."

He watched her rush away. How on earth could he tell her that people in this hospital—and even worse, in the church she served so faithfully— had accused her behind her back of carrying his child? The operative phrase was *behind her back*. Surely no one would be so crass as to confront her with the rumor. Not even Fiona. The only reason he had been confronted was because those three deluded men actually thought they were acting in the best interest of the church.

It was a distinct possibility that Lauren would never hear a whisper of it because those people who loved to spread rumors so diligently wouldn't want to be caught in their lies. Dad had explained that to him years ago and he'd been proven right many times. So why cause Lauren unnecessary pain? What good would it do? She would only suffer humiliation for nothing.

No, he wasn't going to tell her.

Grant stepped out the back door at the east wing of the hospital, chafing at the sudden heat of the lush June day. He saw Brooke sitting on a bench by the smokers' area, still chattering to her brother and Evan Webster. The words *snake* and *stinks* drifted across the air to him.

Evan couldn't seem to close his mouth as he gazed at Brooke in youthful awe, laughing at every silly thing she said, automatically mimicking every nod of her head, every grimace, every smile. The poor kid was besotted already.

Grant smiled. In spite of his daughter's brazen audacity she was not a snob in the traditional sense of the word. Brooke wouldn't encourage Evan's adoration but she would be surprisingly gentle with it. Eventually they would be friends. She was always kind to hurting things, whether they were wiggling worms or unpopular people. In school she refused to play by the rules of the caste system that established the teenage pecking order. Consequently she had more friends than she could handle. She was very much like her mother in that way.

Today it looked as if she was being true to form. Maybe she would be okay in Dogwood Springs after all. If only Grant could convince her of that.

As he watched his kids interact with Evan he heard the door open behind him.

"You didn't warn me about her," came a sweetly teasing voice.

Grant turned to see Lauren smiling up at him from the open door. "I thought I'd let her catch you by surprise. You handled the shock well."

She crossed her arms and ambled outside. "It takes a lot to shock me."

Grant chuckled. "Did I tell you she's already hitting me up for a car?"

"I'd worry if she weren't."

They watched the kids in silence for a moment. "She's trying to grow up too fast."

Lauren looked up at Grant. "What about Beau?"

Grant shifted his attention to his son, to the serious face that held too much knowledge and pain for one so young. "Unfortunately, I think he already has and it wasn't his idea."

"There's something special about him," Lauren said. "He has one of the sweetest spirits of any young man I've ever met."

If she was trying to win Grant's undying affection she was going about it the right way.

"He has his mother's heart."

"He'll be a good doctor someday."

Grant allowed the assurance of her words to warm him. "He will if he can overcome his self-consciousness about his face when he's around strangers."

"He's very attractive." Lauren said it as a simple observation. "Much like his father."

The smile of pleasure spread across his face before he could do a thing about it. "Thank you Lauren. I didn't mean to imply that I thought he was ugly."

"I know what you're talking about but don't underestimate his ability to adjust. Look at him now. He and Brooke are obviously making a new friend."

"I think Evan needs some new friends."

"They'll be good for him." She paused a moment and an uncharacteristic frown marred her clear features. "You said something a while back that suggested you hovered over him too much." She spoke slowly and paused to glance up at him as if afraid she might offend him. "Is it possible he picks up on your concern? My parents are far too worried about my singleness at thirty-five. That hurts me because I know I'm disappointing them. I think families—especially loving ones—tend to be a little overprotective."

Grant was far from offended. "That's the word my kids use on me, especially Brooke."

Lauren's frown scattered with laughter. "Leave it to Brooke to point out exactly what she's thinking at any moment. I do wish you would bring them to church Sunday."

"I'll talk to them about it."

"They might be more willing to come if you joined them."

He paused. "I know. I'm not sure I'm ready for that."

"Have you been back to church since the accident?"

"A few times."

Lauren took a step closer to Grant. "My friend, it's no wonder you show such compassion for your patients. With everything that's happened in your life, you've experienced a taste of torture right here on earth."

"Are you talking about Brooke?" As soon as the words were out of Grant's mouth, he knew how inappropriate they sounded.

Lauren laughed so loudly the kids turned and looked at her. She placed her hand over her mouth. "If you ever want to talk about it, let me know."

Gratitude overwhelmed Grant. He swallowed. "I'll do that."

❧ CHAPTER 22 ❧

The next Wednesday morning Archer was sitting at his desk with the doors closed. Music drifted through the room loudly enough to drown out the clatter of computer keys and the quiet ring of the telephone at Mrs. Boucher's desk out in the church office. He was preparing a sermon, reveling in the heartfelt angst of Solomon in the book of Ecclesiastes and half expecting the three wise men to come tromping through the door again to update him on the latest atrocities circulating about his steamy philanderings.

He'd just begun to imagine what gracious words of compassionate wisdom might spring from his lips in such a situation when his telephone rang and crashed into his fantasy.

He picked up the receiver. "Dogwood Springs Bap—"

"Archer Pierce, I want to know what's going on at that church." The female voice was so filled with outrage that he didn't recognize it for a moment.

When he did he caught his breath. "Jessica?"

"I also want to know who gave grumpy old Mr. Netz my unlisted telephone number." The anger seemed to build with each word.

"He called you?"

"You'd better believe he called me. And get this: he thought he had a right to know why I broke our engagement. Of all the—"

"You're kidding."

"Do I sound like I'm kidding?"

Archer leaned back in his chair. *Lord help me.*

"So let's hear it."

He'd had every intention of telling her before this but he hadn't spoken with her since last Saturday. At the time they'd only had a chance for a quick meal in a busy restaurant between shows. The timing hadn't seemed right. Of course, Archer had known he was only delaying the inevitable. Well, here it was. "There is apparently a rumor making the rounds about an illicit relationship I've been conducting."

There was a short silence. "How silly. Those people should know you better than that. Are you supposedly having an affair with a married woman or something?" The dry, tired tone of her voice gave him comfort. She had dismissed the possibility without even giving it a moment's serious consideration.

"Not with a married woman. It's bad enough though. There is apparently a young woman carrying my child."

There was a gasp. "How could they even think such a thing, Archer? How dare they?"

Had he ever forgotten how much he loved

Jessica, this moment would have served as an excellent reminder. "Thank you," he said quietly. "You can't know how much that means to me right now."

"Why? Anyone in his right mind—any logical person without an axe to grind—would never listen to such garbage. Don't worry, it'll all blow over. I can't believe that man had the audacity to bring up the subject."

"It wasn't just Mr. Netz and it hasn't blown over. Some people want me to resign."

This time the silence was long and screaming with increased outrage. And then the tone of it changed. Though Jessica didn't say a word he could almost hear her mind working, could see her face growing still and her eyes darkening.

"Then resign," she said at last. "That church doesn't deserve you." She didn't wait for a reply. "In fact, maybe this is God's doing. You know what I heard yesterday? Your replacement at your old church in Branson didn't work out. They're looking for another youth minister and all you would have to do—"

"Wait, Jessica. Hold it. You're saying I should give in? Just like that?"

"Isn't that what they want?"

"I'm not interested in what they want, I only care about what God wants."

"What if God does want this? Besides, are they going to give you a choice? If those people want you to resign and you stay and fight, you could split that church right down the middle. Do you think that's what God wants?"

"If I resigned it would almost be like I was admitting to something I didn't do. How is that God's will? If I allow a group of petty gossips to control the future of the whole church, I'm playing right into the hands of evil. Are you saying that's what I should do? Leave the church to the devil?"

There was a soft sigh at the other end. "I don't know." It was almost a whisper. "I just don't know how things could have deteriorated to this point."

"Which things are you talking about, Jess?"

There followed another one of those tightly strung silences as Jessica gathered her thoughts in logical order. This time he couldn't read those thoughts so easily. Would she be this upset if she didn't love him?

"What I think I'm saying is that I can't marry that church."

He closed his eyes and bowed his head. *No Lord, please. Not this.* "I never asked you to marry the church, Jessica." He couldn't keep the sharpness from his voice. "And who said anything about marriage lately? We're not even engaged."

"I know, but I've been thinking about that a lot. Before Netz called me I had almost convinced myself to ask you for my ring back."

He felt the return of longing all the way to his feet. "Before he called?"

"Yes, but this brought everything back to me in a rush. Archer, I've been asking myself if I would have married you if you were still a youth minister. My answer was yes. I love you. That's the simple truth. If you weren't the pastor of Dogwood Springs Baptist we'd still be engaged. I know that's wrong. It's my natural instincts outshouting my spiritual maturity but that's how I feel at this moment. It scares me to death to consider putting myself at the mercy of a bunch of people who don't even have the discernment to tell the difference between fact and fiction."

Archer bit his lower lip and controlled his breathing with difficulty. "And what if I were to take my old job back in Branson, then five years after our wedding I once again became the pastor of Dogwood Springs Baptist? What would you do then? Would our marriage contract have to carry the stipulation that I never answer God's call in my life to pastor a church?"

The silence was telling.

"I thought you didn't believe in divorce," he said.

"I don't."

"I'm sorry, Jess. Nobody but God tells me how I'm going to serve Him." Archer couldn't believe he was doing this. How could he allow the love of his life to slip from his grasp?

"But if we were married it wouldn't be just you," she said quietly. "It would be us. Isn't that right?"

The truth of her words jolted him. He couldn't answer. He wasn't sure of the answer right now.

"I'm sorry," she said. "I know this must sound like I'm trying to manipulate you but I'm not. I'm just being honest."

Why couldn't he stop this? They belonged together. Hadn't God placed this special love in his heart for her? Or was that all just a part of his fantasy?

"Do you mind if I ask you something?" Her voice came across the line with sudden uncharacteristic timidity.

"You know you can ask me anything."

"Who is the young woman?"

"Does it matter? It's a lie. You just told me you didn't want anything to do with people who listened to such—"

"It will matter if someone else calls me and tells me about it. I would feel a lot better if it came from you."

"But why should it matter if it isn't true?"

"Archer."

"Lauren McCaffrey."

There was a long silence, and then she sucked in her breath. "Oh."

"But what difference does it—"

"Maybe you should consider something." Her

317

voice grew stronger. "If you're spending enough time with Lauren that people are beginning to notice, it's because you want to spend that time with her. You haven't asked me to come down there and accompany you on visits or go on retreats with the youth lately."

"How could I? You broke our engagement."

"You aren't engaged to Lauren."

"She's an active member of this church and she's an old friend. You know that. Be reasonable."

"I'm being as reasonable as I know how to be. I'm trying to be practical. Would you please do one thing for me?"

"What's that?"

"Would you please let me know what you decide about this church business?"

"Of course I will. We're still friends aren't we?"

"Friends?" Her tone was sharp and edged with pain. "You mean like you and Lauren?"

"That isn't what I mean. We'll still see each other, talk to each other."

"I thought I was strong enough to do that but I'm discovering some things about myself lately that I don't like. I'm confused right now and being with you adds to the confusion."

Archer closed his eyes.

"I'm sorry," she said.

"About what?"

"About being so . . . I don't know . . .

unpredictable. I guess I'm sorry about my own confusion."

"I'm confused about this too but there are a few things I have no doubts about."

"What are those?"

"I don't doubt God is ultimately in control and knows our hearts better than we do. I don't doubt I was called to this church when I came. And I don't doubt that I love you. Whatever happens from here on out, those are absolutes."

"Oh, Archer," she whispered. "I love you too." She fell silent for a moment and then she sniffed. "How does life get so complicated?"

His heart echoed her pain and frustration. "We make it that way."

As soon as Grant entered his front door Wednesday night he was struck by such a wave of nostalgia that he nearly staggered across the threshold. The effect was so powerful that for a moment he couldn't pinpoint the source. When he closed the door behind him the mingling aromas of jalapeños and onions fried in abundant amounts of real butter made him ravenous. It also confused him. That recipe had been Annette's. She was the only one who had ever made the Sheldon family's special white-hot chili.

Beau came out of Grant's home office at the far side of the living room with a notebook under his arm and an ink pen behind his ear.

"Hi Dad. Your professional liability insurance company called about the lawsuit today. The hospital faxed them the medical records they needed and they want to set a date with you for a preliminary meeting. They're hoping to settle out of court."

The euphoria died a sudden death. "Settle? Just like that? I remember that case. I reviewed the records they faxed to me. There shouldn't be a case."

"Works for me. Still, if you do have a case I want to go to court with you. I need the practice so I'll be ready for the day I get sued. Brooke and I start our new jobs at the hospital next week. Did you find any more clues about the Dogwood Springs Virus?"

"A few." Grant sniffed the air again. "What are you cooking?"

"Nothing. What did you find?"

Grant took a list out of his pocket and handed it to Beau, who took it eagerly. "Where's that smell coming from if you're not cooking? I don't think I'm having olfactory hallucinations."

"Smell? Hey," Beau said, reading the list, "is this true? Out of sixty-five flu symptom patients in the past three weeks only five of them were Medicaid recipients? That's way off the percentages you usually get, isn't it?"

"Yes. The rest were insurance or Medicare. I noticed that too." Grant tried to step around his son to peer into the kitchen but Beau was too busy studying the patient notes to realize the case studies didn't have his father's full attention.

Grant was beginning to feel particularly uneasy. By popular demand, he and Beau were the only ones in the household who cooked. Unless Beau and Brooke had gone behind his back and hired a housekeeper while he was at work—and they had threatened to do that a couple of times in the past year—the only other person who could possibly be cooking up those smells was his daughter. That was not something he wanted to contemplate after a busy day of treating fretful patients whom he could not diagnose satisfactorily.

"So this means we've got some kind of weird middle-to-upper-class virus at work, huh?" Beau asked. "Interesting. If you could get me a copy of the charts—"

"Are you sure you aren't cooking something in there? Did you order out?"

"No. I've got your copies of the hospital lab reports filed in your office. Along with the charts, if you could get copies of any x-rays—"

"I can't give you confidential patient information. You know that."

"You could if you hired me as your home office administrator. Really Dad. I have a lot more time than you do right now and I could use one of your access codes for a medical search." He leaned closer and lowered his voice. "I need the experience and Brooke's getting on my nerves."

Her voice reached them from the direction of the kitchen. "I heard that!"

If Grant's offspring-tracking radar was still working correctly, that voice came from somewhere in the vicinity of the stove. There was no way this could be a good thing.

Grant moved his mouth closer to Beau's ear. "She's cooking?"

Beau nodded, his face solemn.

"What is it?"

"She wants it to be a surprise."

Grant frowned. "She's still bothered by this Lauren thing, isn't she?"

Lauren barely made it to the breakroom bathroom before her carefully chosen dinner of nonirritating foods abandoned her. She'd had to call in sick twice this month, so she'd been making up the time by working extra shifts for two other nurses who didn't seem to have the same nasty little bug. Her legs lost their strength and she leaned against the side of the sink for several seconds to keep from sliding to the floor. Although she had only had minor bouts with this mystery illness during the first half of June, she hadn't been able to keep much food down the last few days. The sick taste in her mouth would require more than mouthwash or salt water to alleviate. And besides that she had a pounding headache.

Frustrated, battling fear, she patted her face with cold water. From experience she knew the weakness would probably go away. It had every time so far. For a moment she thought about calling Grant at home but what could she tell him that he didn't already know? The symptoms were the same as before, the same as most of the other patients.

She stepped out of the bathroom, pausing to lean against the doorframe, wondering if she should try to call another nurse to take her place. If this illness was contagious wouldn't she just make things worse for everyone if she stayed around here?

But she could wear a mask.

Fiona Perkins came waddling past her from the breakroom. She stopped when she saw Lauren's face. With a knowing grin she crossed her arms. "Morning sickness at night?"

Lauren didn't have the inclination or the energy to reply. She shook her head and waited for Fiona to leave. Maybe a soda would help ease the nausea. The ER was getting busier and she didn't want to let the others down.

She would be okay.

The last time Brooke had attempted to prepare a meal for the family, the three of them had nearly starved before lunch. She'd used hot water to defrost a can of frozen orange juice, had over-salted the oatmeal, and had cooked the eggs until they were hard enough to break teeth. That was sixteen months and two weeks ago. Grant remembered because Brooke had vowed never to cook for the family again. Beau had promised to hold her to that vow. He'd let Grant down.

Grant and Beau stared at each other across the dining room table while Brooke carried in huge bowls of steaming white-hot chili.

"I was looking through some of Mom's old recipes and I found this one." She placed cheddar and Monterey Jack cheese in the center of the table, along with some sour cream and a bowl of inexpertly torn lettuce. The drink of choice was milk. This family knew how to eat taste-bud-killing food with excellent natural tongue soothers.

Once again, for a moment, Grant was so steeped in bittersweet memories that he forgot to be afraid of the chili. He skeptically watched his daughter sit down and nudge her brother to put his research aside. She had the natural gift of gab but now she fell silent and waited for Beau to say grace. Prayer before meals was a family tradition Beau insisted on continuing and with which Grant whole-heartedly agreed—particularly for this meal.

After the blessing—which sounded most passionate in its sincerity—Grant took a sip of his milk and watched as his children did the same. He picked up his spoon. Then he hesitated.

Brooke picked up a leaf of lettuce. "Dad, did Beau tell you we've got jobs? I get to help in the laundry and Beau's in the kitchen. Evan's volunteering his time at *The Dogwood* for summer vacation." She rolled her eyes as if the very idea of working for no pay didn't register with her. "He's going to interview that Sergeant Dalton who got blinded by the ammonia trap."

"For *The Dogwood*?"

"That's what he said. I told him if they print the interview he should at least get paid for that. And I bet they print it because he's good. Have you read any of his writing?"

"Sure, Brooke," Beau said, "Dad has time to go rummaging through all those scribbles. The first thing Evan needs is an iPad. His handwriting's worse than Dad's."

Grant studied the chili more closely. It looked like Annette's. "So Brooke, where did you say you found this recipe?"

"I was looking through some of those file drawers in the back bedroom. I thought I might dig out some of those scrapbooks Mom put together every year. I found some old love notes she used to put in your lunch bag. Remember them?"

Oops. He should have put those in a more private place. "Yes I do." He had always looked forward to those notes, some of them homemade greeting cards with her creative stitching around the edges and her loving words of encouragement inside.

Brooke filled her spoon with chili and blew on it then took a bite, apparently unaware that Grant and Beau watched her with sudden deep interest. She didn't grimace. She didn't choke or stop breathing.

"Were you looking for something in particular in Mom's things?" Grant asked.

She took a swallow of milk. "Did you know you can smell Mom's perfume in those files? You know that honeysuckle stuff she wore? You can smell it. I just wanted to sit there and feel close to her. And I read some of the notes." Her somber expression lightened for a moment with a teasing glint. "Pretty intense stuff, Dad."

Grant willed away the flush that threatened to heat his face. Many of the love letters Annette had written to him were not intended for eyes other than his. Maybe he should have discarded them but he just couldn't bring himself to do it.

"Did it help you feel closer to her?" he asked.

Brooke put her spoon into the bowl and looked down at the table for a moment. "At first it did. Then I just got depressed."

"I know. I've done the same thing late at night when you two were in bed. Brooke, if it upsets you this much to think about my dating again I won't—"

"But that's just it," Brooke said. "I realized this

afternoon that I couldn't bring Mom back. We've been saving all her stuff, even her favorite recipes, like they were some kind of a shrine to her memory. But she wouldn't want us to. She would want us to go forward with our lives, not sit around whining. Reading her notes to you helped me realize that she wouldn't want you to be lonely."

Grant wanted to enfold Brooke in a big bear hug and tell her how much he loved her. But instead he did something even more loving than that. He put a huge spoonful of the chili in his mouth. He was encouraged when Beau followed his example. The mingling of flavors and the feel of the heat—just the right amount of heat on his tongue—snapped him into the past with such force he could almost feel Annette's presence.

When they were first married and struggling to exist on school loans and Annette's small salary as a bank bookkeeper, she had developed this recipe made with cheap ground turkey and white beans, which they ate at least once a week. Until the twins were old enough to speak for themselves, Annette continued the tradition at least once every month, even when it was no longer necessary to stretch money so far.

When the kids were eleven, Brooke gave notice that the chili gave her gas and if her parents really loved her they wouldn't make her suffer so horribly. The tradition was modified from then on to include spaghetti for the kids.

"Hey, this is good." Beau took another spoonful.

"Surprise," Brooke said dryly. "You thought I couldn't cook."

"We all thought you couldn't cook," Grant said. "This is delicious. But I thought you didn't like this chili."

"I knew you loved it though. And all I had to do was follow Mom's recipe. I started thinking about some things this afternoon while I was cooking."

"You?" Beau said. "Wow Brooke, you really have been busy today."

"Shut up, Beau. Dad, you like Lauren don't you?"

"She's a great nurse and she's proving to be a good friend."

"Especially if she's willing to put up with Brooke for an afternoon of fishing," Beau said.

Brooke dipped another ladleful of chili into her brother's bowl. "Keep eating, Beau. I hope you blow up like a blimp. Dad, Lauren kind of grows on you, doesn't she?"

"You mean like a wart or a boil?"

Brooke gave him a "get serious" look.

"She's easy to be around." What was he saying? She was a joy to be around.

"I was thinking I wouldn't mind seeing her again. I mean, if you wanted to take her out on a date or something. Every couple weeks or so."

Grant suppressed a smile. "You mean you *like* that female John Boy?"

Beau choked on his chili.

"Shut up, Beau. Dad, he's been making me feel guilty all week. He keeps telling me that I'm being selfish and hardhearted."

"You are," Beau said.

Grant placed his spoon back in the bowl. "No she isn't. She's going through the grief process in her own way. We've all been doing that. The death of someone you love changes your way of dealing with things. I know I've dealt with things poorly at times. I apologize. I'm trying to improve but it just takes time."

"You mean you're going to try to stop nagging us so much?"

"Brooke, Dad isn't a nag."

Brooke rolled her eyes. "He's even worse with you than he is me and he never lets up. 'Brooke, you're going to school to get an education, not to meet guys and form social relationships. Brooke, someday you're going to be sorry you didn't do your homework. Brooke, you're so much prettier without all that glop on your face.' "

"Okay, okay, I hear you," Grant said with a chuckle. It was a good female rendition of his voice and accent. "I'm not that bad, am I?"

"You're even worse with Beau, except to him you say, 'Beau, you're getting a great education but you need friends too. Beau, there's more to life than reading.' "

"Stop it, Brooke." All the humor had left Beau's voice.

"It's okay," Grant said. "It's good for me to take a strong dose of Brooke's reality sometimes. I know I probably smother you both a little too much."

"Because you care," Beau said.

"I think subconsciously I'm trying to be a father and a mother to you guys."

"You're getting the job done," Brooke said. "Having you for a dad is like having a couple sets of parents." She took a sip of milk and dabbed at her lips with a napkin. "So Dad, when are you going to ask Lauren out on a real date?"

"I'm not. It isn't that kind of a friendship. I already told you there's someone else she cares about."

"Oh yeah. Archer. But he isn't interested in Lauren. Doesn't she know that? I watched him the other day at the hospital and then later when we went back to the fishing spot. He treated her the same way he did the rest of us. Dad, you need to learn how to read people better."

For a moment Brooke's voice sounded so much like Annette's that it made Grant's eyes smart with tears. "Do you two know how much I love you?"

"Yes Dad, we do," Beau said. "We love you too."

Brooke put her spoon down. "If you're going to get mushy on us I'm going to bed."

CHAPTER 23

On Thursday morning multiple birdsongs greeted Archer from the lush foliage of the Netz's hedge-enclosed yard. He shut the car door behind him quietly. In case he decided to bolt he did not want to disturb the peace and alert Mr. Netz too quickly that he had company.

Archer wasn't sure he was ready for this yet. He'd called and made an appointment, though, to keep from backing out at the last moment.

When Archer was five years old he'd had a slight disagreement with his mother when she took him to kindergarten for the first time. He'd kicked and screamed and hung on to Mom's thumb until he thought he might pull it off. After that publicly humiliating episode, Mom and Dad decided their priority project from that day on was to teach Archer how to discipline his temper and his tongue.

Twenty-eight years later, as he walked up the neatly trimmed sidewalk to the Nctz home, Archer felt a distinct need to fall back on his early training and guard his tongue with utmost diligence.

There would be no "time out" if this conversation became too heated. He would get no spankings but he could hurt his personal witness of the God of his life. That would be so much more painful and lasting. He could recall his mother's gentle voice as he struggled through kindergarten and first grade: "Sweetheart, as soon as you have an angry thought you give it to God. He's the only one big enough to handle it."

As he pressed the button for the doorbell, Archer picked up on the trail of prayer he had carried with him all the way from the church. He resisted the urge to demand from God an explanation of what good could possibly come of this situation. He simply asked God for guidance. Divine guidance. Gentle guidance.

Archer heard the sound of creaking-wood footsteps inside the house. When the knob turned, Archer begged a final few words of prayer for self-control but he refused to fake a smile.

Mr. Netz pulled the door open then stepped back and held it for Archer. "Come on in, Pastor."

Archer followed him into a cozy sitting room that Mrs. Netz kept decorated for company. He sank into the straight-backed chair across from the old deacon. He wasn't in the mood to get tangled in the cushy folds of a comfortable sofa.

"Say your piece, Pastor, then I'll say mine."

Mr. Netz only called him Pastor when he was his most serious but there always seemed to be something serious going on around this deacon. Some people said he stirred up trouble just for entertainment when he got bored. Dad had disagreed with them but Dad tried to believe the best about people at all times. What would he say about this?

Archer leaned forward, elbows on knees, and waited until Netz met his gaze. "Why did you call Jessica?"

"I needed to know the truth."

"You're saying I didn't tell you the truth last Friday?"

Netz looked away. "It would've been hard to sit right there in front of three self-righteous trouble-makers and admit you'd done what they said."

At least the deacon had a good grasp of the situation. "In the years that you've known my family, have you ever known any of us to lie?"

"Nope."

"Then you could have come to me privately if you thought I was too much of a coward to say anything in front of the others." Archer could feel the sharpness biting at his words and he had to remind himself again to be gentle. "My private life is not subject to public display but if you were going to call someone it should have been me."

The gray brows lowered. "When your private life affects my church it is my business."

"What you've heard is vicious gossip. That isn't something to base a decision—"

"Why do you think I called Jessica? I wanted to make sure that what I had heard wasn't true." He looked away and cleared his throat. "I won't have my church—"

"*Your* church, Mr. Netz?" Archer asked quietly. "I thought we were God's church."

The older man leaned forward, his wrinkled gaze sober as he pinned Archer with a stern stare. "Dogwood Springs Baptist has been my church home for fifty years and we've always had our problems. I saw a scandal back in sixty-five that like to have split us in two. I don't aim for anything like that to happen to us again, not if I have anything to say about it."

Archer had heard about the scandal that occurred a few years before Archer's father was called as pastor. Memories were long in Dogwood Springs and more than one of the natives had told him about the church music director—a single man—who had supposedly been caught in a somewhat compromising situation with a girl who was a senior in high school.

The compromise? He'd been holding her in his arms in the hallway after church one Sunday. When the girl's parents heard about it they demanded and received his resignation. Half the congregation was furious about it since the music director insisted he had only been comforting the girl who had come to him in tears about a personal problem.

Archer should have heeded the warning as soon as he heard the story the first time. The people here were too quick to jump to unfounded conclusions. It obviously didn't matter if the person they were hurting had been one of their own since birth.

"Nowadays we make sure our staff leaders realize they are ministers, not just directors," Mr. Netz said.

"But aren't all believers called to be ministers of Christ? And as ministers, shouldn't we all avoid the specter of gossip in our midst? It hurts everyone it touches."

"That's exactly right. True or not, those kinds of things cause trouble. Why do you think I wanted to get to the bottom of it? Lots of our old members quit coming over the years and they didn't ever join anywhere else. It's like they got sick and tired of anything to do with church." He shook his head and sat back. "We can't take any chances."

Archer felt a pang of empathy as the painful memories etched themselves across the old deacon's face. Hadn't Dad grieved over the ones who seemed unable to find a comfortable place of service within their membership? Even though church attendance was up, Archer felt the loss when he looked out over the sea of unfamiliar faces in the congregation and realized the changes that had taken place since Dad was pastor. It was disheartening.

"Mr. Netz, even if your telephone call to Jessica was made with the best of intentions it upset her a lot. It might even have destroyed any future relationship there might have been between us."

The lines of sadness deepened. "I'm sorry." The deacon twined his fingers together between his knees and studied them for a moment then he looked back at Archer. "May not be worth much to you now but I guess I've had a hard time believing any kid of Pastor Aaron Pierce could do the thing they claimed you did."

"Thank you."

"You haven't forgotten my first name all of a sudden have you?" Netz chided gently.

Archer hesitated. He wasn't ready to forgive. He studied the deacon's face and silently recited a prayer his mother had taught him as a child. *Dearest Lord Jesus, keep me from sin, protect me from evil, and bring peace within.* It wasn't a mindless mantra but a heartfelt plea. He knew he needed to forgive Mr. Netz and restore their fellowship. The man had been sincere in his actions even though the basis for that action was a lie. But he'd gone about things the wrong way and he'd hurt Jessica and Archer and no telling who else. Even though he'd been sincere . . . "Please tell me you haven't spoken to Lauren about the rumor."

Mr. Netz blinked at Archer in surprise. "That wouldn't have been proper."

"You called Jessica. That wasn't proper. What's the difference?"

"Tell you what I'll do, Pastor. I'll go pick up that telephone right now and call Jessica back—"

Archer immediately leaned forward, hands upraised. "Please. No threats."

The man's surprise deepened. "I'm not threatening. She needs to know the truth and I don't think I explained things too well when—"

"She knows the truth, Mr. Ne—John." Archer saw relief ease some of the creases on the deacon's face. And that showed more than anything how deeply he cared. "The problem is that she doesn't want to be a part of a church that would carry that kind of gossip or even listen to it. The problem is . . ." Archer had to admit itto himself and the admission hurt. "She doesn't want to be a pastor's wife."

He could understand how she felt. In fact, right now he wasn't even sure he wanted to be a pastor. But it wasn't his decision, it was ultimately God's.

Archer stood up and offered his hand. "Thank you for seeing me, John. I trust you'll be able to manage the others."

The deacon shook hands with him, his large calloused fingers firm and strong. "I'll talk to them."

As Archer turned to leave he wondered if he should warn Lauren after all—just in case some other "well-meaning" busybody decided to get to the bottom of things.

"Tell me something," Archer said before he stepped out the door. "How did you get Jessica's unlisted telephone number?"

"I just asked Ruth Wecker. She's the choir secretary and she has the addresses and telephone numbers of anyone who is active in the music ministry." He walked Archer out onto the sidewalk. "That Jessica sure can sing. I hope this thing works out between you two."

"So do I." But he could do no more to help it along. The rest was up to Jessica . . . and God.

Lauren pulled into the hospital employee parking lot Thursday evening twenty minutes before she was due to start work. These night shifts were getting tedious. She would be glad when the hospital hired more nurses to work as needed so the full-time staff wouldn't have so much overtime when someone got sick. At least Mitchell Caine wasn't on duty tonight. That made a big difference.

She'd reached the edge of the parking lot when she heard a familiar female voice call to her. She turned to find Brooke Sheldon jogging toward her from the end of the block. Her short midnight brown hair formed a dark halo around her exotic woman-child features as she ran.

"I caught you! Dad told me you were scheduled to work tonight and he let me drive the car alone. Can you believe he trusted me? Aren't you early?"

She came to a breathless stop in front of Lauren.

"A little. Are you going to the movies or something?"

"No, I just wanted a chance to drive without Dad sitting three inches from my right shoulder gripping the seat every time I put the brakes on too hard or hissing through his teeth when I take a curve too sharp. You know how dads are."

"Yes, but I had a lot of practice before I took the wheel of a car. I drove tractors and trucks out on the farm. You learn quickly not to make a sharp turn or stop suddenly when you're pulling a wagon stacked high with hay bales and smart-mouthed guys."

Brooke's grin widened. "Can I walk you in? You have time to talk, don't you, since you're early?"

"Sure." Lauren turned and strolled beside Brooke. "What's on your mind?"

"Well, we were talking about dads. What's yours like?"

Lauren knew a fake pass when she saw one but she decided to play along. Brooke was up to something. It showed in the tender dimples in her cheeks. Her dark eyes filled with mischief.

"He's an old farmer and he makes a profit at it. He's the best daddy in the world."

"Does he ever get cranky?"

"Who doesn't? Supporting five kids on the wages of a farmer and a cake decorator might tend to make a guy cranky sometimes."

Brooke snorted. "No way! Your dad decorates cakes?"

Lauren rolled her eyes at the girl. "My mother does the cakes and helps with the farming but my father does most of the worrying for the family."

"What's it like to grow up on a farm?"

"I wouldn't know how to compare it to anything else. I had some interesting experiences. I remember one day an old farm rooster got after me and hit me in the leg with his spur."

"His what?"

"It's this hard appendage on the rooster's leg, shaped like a nail. They use them for fighting. It really hurts when you're a little kid and you get flogged with one. When that old rooster hit me I screamed so loud you could've heard me clear into town. When Daddy heard me crying he went out and wrung that old bird's neck. We had pressure-cooked rooster for dinner the next night."

"Eeeeww."

"It's just chicken. Nothing gross about it."

"It would be for me if I had to kill it myself." Brooke glanced sideways at Lauren. "You still call him Daddy?"

"Sure. It takes a special man to earn the title. He isn't just a father, he's a daddy, someone who continues to love and support me in that special way only daddies have." She saw that Brooke was still watching her with curiosity. "So why are we talking about cranky fathers? Yours couldn't possibly be cranky."

"Nope." Brooke looked away.

"Not ever?"

"Well . . . sometimes. Not too much. He used to laugh a lot but he doesn't do that so much lately. He's overprotective but Beau says that's a good thing. Maybe he'll outgrow it when we get older."

"Don't count on it. Mine is still that way and I'm thirty-five. He's always checking the oil and tires on my truck when I go home for a visit, and he asks me if I lock my doors at night."

"Do you?"

"Usually."

Brooke grimaced as if she couldn't imagine not locking the doors at night. "My dad wasn't so bad until after Mom died but then he got carried away. I think he just needs more distraction in his life—you know, someone else to take some of his attention."

"He could volunteer to help out at the church."

Brooke shook her head. "He's got enough stress in his life, he needs something . . . or someone . . . to take the stress away." She looked at her watch then indicated a concrete bench beneath the willow tree where she'd entertained Evan and Beau while Gina was being treated in the emergency room. "You don't have to go in yet, do you? Tell me more about yourself."

Lauren passed the bench and kept walking.

"You didn't hijack your father's car just to get to know me better. What do you really have in mind?"

"I didn't hijack the car," Brooke protested. "I asked him if I could drive out for some Chinese."

"And he said yes if you would drive straight there and back."

A sudden change of direction in Brooke's gaze worked like a lie detector. "I'm on my way there. One little stop doesn't mean—"

"The Chinese restaurant is on the other side of town."

"I took the scenic route. Dad should understand because he's always doing that. When we moved here he took the scenic route instead of I-44. It took us a whole day to get here."

Lauren glanced toward the ER parking lot. "It sounds like a nice drive. I need to get inside. It appears we're busy and we could be short a nurse tonight. Is everything okay? Is something bothering you? If there is I'd be glad to get together with you later and talk about it. I know the move has been hard on—"

"No, it's nothing like that. Dad's the one who's having trouble adjusting. He's lonely."

Oh, boy. How obvious could this girl get? "He is?"

"I think it would mean a lot to him to have someone to talk to."

"He and Archer seem to get along well together.

I've seen them holding some quiet conversations."

"Not that kind of lonely." Brooke's patience was stretching like an overextended bungee cord.

Lauren didn't allow herself to smile. "I know he still misses your mother. That kind of grief doesn't go away just because you move to a new town. It takes time." Grant would never have put his daughter up to this but what had given Brooke the idea that her father would be interested?

Brooke was silent for a moment and Lauren thought longingly of the cup of coffee she needed before she started work.

"So you're really not after my dad's body," Brooke said at last.

Lauren pressed her tongue to her teeth and kept a straight face. "Um, no."

"Don't you even think he's hot? I mean, would it hurt to go out to dinner with him?"

"You're asking me to go out with your father? The day we went fishing, I got the distinct impression you were encouraging me to go out with anyone *but* him."

"I didn't know you then. I do now. You're not the hillbilly I thought you were."

Laughter bubbled up in Lauren's throat and escaped before she could stop it. "I grew up in the hills, so that makes me a hillbilly. I enjoy working with your father and I've come to think of him as a friend but he'll need to procure his own dates,

343

Brooke." One of Grandma's favorite little idioms was "Never say never," but Lauren could not imagine herself involved in a relationship that would connect her to this outspoken handful.

Brooke rolled her eyes. "I get it. You aren't attracted to Dad in that way."

"It wouldn't matter if I thought he was the hunkiest man on earth, if I wanted to go out with someone he would have to share my faith."

"We're Baptists aren't we? What do you want from the guy?"

"I'm not talking denominations, I'm talking faith. There's a big difference."

"Dad knows God." Brooke's pretty eyes sparkled with the sudden gleam of indignation. "He used to go to church with us when Mom was alive but afterward he just kind of gave up. He made us keep going but he didn't go very much. We still pray before dinner." She stopped walking. "He really is a great guy, Lauren," she said softly, all the brashness suddenly gone from her voice.

"I can see that and I understand that your father is a Christian." Even if he didn't believe it himself right now.

"He can cook."

"I know."

"And he even does dishes and vacuums the carpet and scrubs toilets."

"Does he do windows?"

Brooke frowned. "Huh?"

"Never mind."

"What would one little date hurt? Dinner. A trip to Branson. Fishing."

"I know your father is a very special person and I know I'll come to cherish his friendship. He's lonely right now and it wouldn't be a good idea for me to encourage a kind of relationship that might be misleading."

"How do you know it would be misleading if you won't even go out with him one time?"

"Has anyone ever advised you to get into sales?"

"Does that mean you'll do it?"

"No." Lauren grinned. This was the most single-minded kid she had ever met. "I've got to get to work. You've got to get dinner for your family. Maybe you and I can go fishing again next week."

Brooke communicated her distaste for the idea without the slightest change of expression. "Can Dad go with us?"

"Sure. I'll call Archer. We can set up a date."

"It won't do you any good, you know."

"What?"

Brooke gave her a look of sympathy. "Dragging poor Archer along. Don't you think he would have asked you out already if he was going to?"

Lauren caught her breath. "Brooke—"

"Fine, don't take my advice." Brooke raised her hands in defeat. "At least I tried."

"See you later, Brooke." Lauren said it a little more sharply than she'd intended.

CHAPTER 24

On Friday afternoon Lauren walked down the central aisle of the circular auditorium of Dogwood Springs Baptist Church carrying a beautiful arrangement of peace roses and ferns in a cut-crystal vase. The roses would still be fresh for services Sunday morning, which was good because she was scheduled to work tomorrow and would have no time to check on them. She planned to rest as much as possible when she wasn't working.

The janitor was stirring up dust in the choir loft above the stage, vacuum cleaner wheezing loudly enough to drown out the chatter and laughter and occasional lyrics of a musical quartet beside the piano practicing a new song for Sunday service. Several of them waved at Lauren when they saw her. Five children between the ages of six and ten ran up and down the aisles of the church in a game of tag while their parents practiced.

Lauren loved the fact that this church family had put her to work right away in several different positions as soon as she joined. She especially enjoyed the trust they placed in her with their children. In her old church back in Knolls they would have watched and waited for at least five years before allowing a new member to serve on any of their committees to make sure they hadn't accidentally voted an axe murderer into their midst.

She arranged the blushing ivory roses on the Lord's Supper table, placed an old worn Bible on a stand beside them, draped a throw of ivory lace behind them, and stood back to see what else it needed. The table could use a good polishing. A pair of wire-framed reading glasses might help produce the effect she hoped for.

"Do you moonlight as an interior decorator?" came a friendly familiar male voice from behind her, raised loudly enough to carry over all the other sounds.

She turned with a smile to see Archer coming to a stop beside the central front pew with a dust rag in his hand. "Do you moonlight as a janitor?"

"Not if I can get out of it. Our part-time custodian is out with knee surgery, so I told ames I'd help out." He nodded toward the janitor in the choir loft, who smiled and waved with his free hand.

"You know I'm not artistic. I got drafted to take Mabel Long's place on the flower committee when she moved to live with her sister in Arkansas last month. I brought these flowers from Mom's garden."

"You went to Knolls today?"

"Yes, Mom was getting worried about me and

Dad wanted to check out the truck to make sure I'm keeping the oil changed. You know how they are."

"I sure do. So you're already on a committee? I thought they'd at least wait until the end of the summer to drag you onto their list."

"I didn't have to be dragged, I wanted to do it."

He held his hands up. "Don't let anyone hear you say that. You'll never have another moment's peace."

"Did you know our church has nineteen different committees? I found a booklet in the library that listed the names, addresses, and telephone numbers of every person on every committee and I couldn't believe it—I'm on three. I haven't figured out how I got so popular so fast."

"You and your big mouth."

"Don't start with me. You were probably the one who slipped them my name in the first place. Anyway, I'm happy to do it," she said. "I like to keep active and the extra involvement is helping me get to know more of the people in a short period of time."

"It shows they're tired of all the work they've created for themselves." There was a dry cynicism in his voice Lauren had never heard before. Now that she'd caught that strain of tension she noticed that even his teasing held a somber note today.

He stepped over to sniff the roses. "These smell

good. Your mom has a way with flowers." He sounded a little depressed.

Lauren studied him more closely. "You've been making yourself scarce lately. You're not coming down with the crud are you?"

"Not sick yet." He looked tired, though, and his face lacked its expression of lighthearted optimism that was his trademark.

"You sure?"

"Positive."

Good. That made one of them. Even today she continued to battle fluctuating bouts of nausea, weakness, and a nasty taste in her mouth, though she'd made sure her parents didn't pick up on it when she was home. She'd also kept her distance in case this stuff was contagious.

Archer lifted the Bible from the stand to thumb through its yellowed pages. He paused from time to time apparently to read different verses he found, then sighed and replaced it on its stand.

"Working on a sermon?" Lauren asked. What was wrong with him?

"I'm always working on a sermon." He sank down onto the cushioned comfort of the first pew. "I think the one I need to preach right now would be aimed mostly at myself." The janitor chose that moment to switch off the vacuum cleaner and Archer lowered his voice. "I've allowed myself to get upset by an unfounded piece of malicious gossip." He gave Lauren a quick glance then looked away.

"Malicious gossip is always upsetting." Lauren wondered briefly what it might be but then dismissed it as none of her business. She didn't really want to be reminded just how mean some people were. Still, Archer was obviously concerned about it. "Especially if it attacks us personally or someone we care about."

He looked at her, caught her gaze, sighed. If she didn't know better she would have thought that a blush was spreading across his face.

Two little girls came careening around from the side aisle and nearly toppled Lauren before she could catch them. Their mother stopped the music and called out to them to be careful. The vacuum cleaner started up again.

"You know about the rumor?" Archer asked under cover of the noise.

"Me? I haven't heard anything."

Something in his expression disturbed her. He didn't quite meet her gaze. Lauren stepped over to him and reached for the dust rag. "Mind if I borrow this for a moment? The table needs polishing."

He didn't reply, just stared toward the flower arrangement as if deep in thought and let her take the rag from his hand without comment.

She hesitated. "Archer? This sounds serious. The rumor isn't about Gina is it? Because if someone—"

"It isn't Gina." He smiled at that and it broke the tension. He reached up to massage his neck and shoulder muscles. "As I said, I shouldn't have allowed it to upset me."

Lauren watched him for a moment then returned to the table and gave it a good polishing. She climbed the steps to the pulpit.

Before she could begin polishing around the microphone, Archer came up the steps and took the rag away from her. "I didn't come in here to give you my job. I think you have enough to do already."

She shrugged and went back down to straighten the lace.

"Lauren," he said under cover of the noise. "We've known each other forever. I feel as if I can talk to you openly. Do you mind if I ask you a question?"

"Have I ever?"

"You're an independent lady with your own career. Would someone like you ever consider the possibility of being a pastor's wife?"

All thoughts of glasses and Bibles and flowers scattered from her mind and for a few seconds Lauren froze where she stood. She could not have heard that right.

"Lauren?"

"Uh . . . yeah?" She could barely hear his voice and by now the pounding of her own heart had joined the din. He could not know how that question affected her. And he couldn't know how much she would love to give the idea more serious consideration. So why was he asking her? And right here in the middle of a busy church auditorium of all places.

"Would you?"

She swallowed. "Honestly?" She braced herself and took the plunge, not allowing herself time to think. "I think the office of a pastor's wife would be one of utmost honor and joy. To share in a partnership like that with someone you love and who loves God and wants to serve Him would be close to my idea of heaven."

"But the people can be so hurtful at times." His focus still wasn't on her and it seemed as if he was barely listening to her words.

"The people?" she asked.

"The church." He glanced toward the singers who were busy collecting their music and purses and calling out to their children over the wheeze of the vacuum.

Lauren frowned up at him. Was he referring to this church?

"I know a lot of pastors who've left the ministry because they've been hurt deeply by members of their congregations," he said. "Their wives suffer along with them. We're always conscious of the fact that we are employees and not really part of a church family. We can be fired at any time if the church votes on it. And sometimes it seems as if half the members are constantly searching for some reason to do just that."

Lauren realized as Archer spoke that this conversation had nothing to do with her. The automatic disappointment she felt was first tempered then replaced by concern for his obvious struggle. "That doesn't happen in every church," she said gently. "It never happened at my home church in Knolls. Does this have anything to do with the rumor?"

He looked up at her at last and she could see the anguish in his eyes. "I guess I'm pretty easy to read."

"Do you want to talk about it?"

"I thought that's what I was doing."

"Well then, carry on." Once again she dug deep and found the willpower to keep her mouth shut. Sometimes she amazed herself.

"I never had an older sister but I can't help envying your brothers. They didn't appreciate you enough when we were kids."

"They pick their moments." Older sister. She took the unintentional slam in stride.

He laid the rag down and rubbed his face. "So in spite of everything you think it would be rewarding to be a pastor's wife?"

Again that little skip of a heartbeat. "I think the right person would feel it was an honor."

"Half of me wants to try to convince Jessica of that. The other half wants to warn her to keep running the other way."

This time the disappointment went all the way to Lauren's toes. Specters of Lukas Bower came back to haunt her. She'd known better. This time she'd known but she had allowed herself a small piece of hope in spite of the fact that Archer had been in love with another woman when she came to Dogwood Springs. This friendship was merely an old one that had grown comfortable for Archer over the years of church camp and school games and visits to the farm. Had she betrayed her silly little crush in some way?

Suddenly overwhelmed by feelings of foolishness, Lauren stepped down to the roses, inhaled their delicate fragrance, and allowed the silence to wash over her. She shouldn't be surprised. Maybe she could blame Grant because it was his suggestion a few weeks ago that made her wonder if she really might be a good pastor's wife. Grant was the one who had told her she was such a source of encouragement, such help to Archer and to others. He was the one who treated her as if she was someone special.

"You know," she said softly, "I've always loved the silence of a church auditorium when everyone's gone. I guess you have that experience every day. It probably grows old to you but somehow I feel a reverence here when I'm alone, kind of like I feel when I'm out on the creek talking to God. All I can do is remind you how much He cares." She was chattering again. "His will is going to take place no matter what we do here on earth. If it's His will for you and Jessica to be together it'll be in His time. Is Jessica afraid of being married to a pastor or is it this church that frightens her?"

"I'm not sure."

"Was it the rumor that caused her to break the engagement?"

Again that slight flush and then the shuttered look in his eyes as he avoided Lauren's gaze. The rumor. Did it involve her in some way? It couldn't.

"No," he said, "but it's messed things up since then. I think the aftermath of it is the reason we aren't back together."

Lauren tried not to judge Jessica for allowing something like a rumor to affect her commitment to Archer. "Please tell me it didn't originate here in our own church." She was fishing and she knew it was obvious. Even though she hated gossip, she wished she knew what this rumor was so she could help staunch it.

He stood up and shoved his hands into his pockets. "It originated at the hospital."

"Our hospital?"

"I shouldn't be talking about this to you. I'm your pastor."

"You're my friend and I'm yours." Lauren wanted to tell him that a woman who wouldn't accept everything about him didn't deserve his love but she had no right to advise Archer about anything, even if he did think of her as the older sister he never had.

Older sister.

All she knew about romance was that it always happened for other people, never her. And here she was worrying more about herself than about Archer. How selfish.

"She doesn't believe the rumor," Archer said.

"Of course she wouldn't. I've only met Jessica a couple of times but she struck me as someone with a lot of common sense." She was also beautiful and effervescent and larger than life without an ounce of fat. She was almost as tall as Archer, with riotous brown hair and eyes filled with warmth. She had the voice of an angel with an amazing range that held the listener breathless. Lauren had liked her immediately.

The auditorium door closed in the foyer, leaving Archer and Lauren alone.

Archer looked at his watch. "Time to get back to work. I have a meeting with a man about a computer. Ours is getting old and crotchety and since I'm the only one on staff who knows anything about them I get to choose the new system. Thanks for the counseling session, Lauren." He quickstepped to the aisle and out of the auditorium. She sighed as she watched him leave. Why should she even be surprised?

• • •

Lauren parked in the visitor section in front of the hospital and took the front entrance. She wasn't scheduled to work tonight but something about Archer's response to her questions continued to haunt her—particularly the part about a rumor. She found Gina straightening her workstation in preparation of leaving for the day.

Gina smiled when she saw Lauren. "Can't stay away from this place, can you?"

Lauren sat down in the extra chair and leaned close. "Have you heard any good hospital gossip lately?"

"Good gossip? No. There isn't any such thing."

"Any gossip at all?"

Gina's smile faded. "You don't listen to stuff like that."

So there was something. "What did you hear?"

Gina stood up and pulled off her lab coat then took great pains to fold it and drape it over her arm. She still didn't look at Lauren. "I'm always hearing things."

Lauren's stomach tightened. "You might as well tell me or I'll pester you until you do. Does it have something to do with me? And maybe Archer?"

Gina sat back down. "Why ask me since you already know?"

Lauren nearly retched. "How did it get started?"

"Remember when we caught Fiona Perkins eavesdropping on us?"

Lauren tried to recall what she'd said that day. "We were talking about Archer."

"It's just stupid stuff that'll blow over when everybody realizes it isn't true."

"When what isn't true? I told you I had a thing for Archer. It's true."

Gina blinked at Lauren then looked pointedly at her stomach. "Remember what else you said? That you thought he'd be a great father? People will realize you're not pregnant when you retain your figure."

If Lauren hadn't been sitting down she'd have crashed to the floor. She breathed deeply and sat back. The wash of shock and pain left her breathless. "People think I'm pregnant?"

"Oh no. You really haven't heard."

"Fiona is telling people I'm pregnant?" Lauren thought she might pass out. She suddenly wished she was a kid again and could get away with socking the big-mouthed class bully in the gut.

"It's stupid. I heard people talking about it upstairs today and told them to shut up. It didn't exactly endear me to my co-workers."

"It endears you to *me*." Lauren tried to force herself to gloss over this blade in the back for Gina's sake but it was too difficult. "So that's what Fiona meant Wednesday night."

"What did she say?"

"I lost my dinner in the bathroom—you know with this stupid bug that keeps hanging on—and she must've heard me. She made some remark about morning sickness. I had no idea what she was talking about."

"So you ignored her as you should have," Gina said. "Fiona Perkins is an interfering, mean, troublemaking—"

"Unhappy, hurting human being."

"Who needs to lose about a hundred pounds. I could help. I'd be glad to kick her—"

"The problem is that her rumors haven't hurt me as badly as they have Archer," Lauren said. Still, her pain was excruciating. Not only did her coworkers believe this of her but her church, too? "People are listening to her."

Gina leaned forward, her pale skin almost blue-white in the fluorescent glow of the overhead lights. "I'm not listening."

"I know. Thanks. Gina, are you feeling okay?"

"Other than starving to death, I'm fine. We had a busy day and I didn't get lunch. Want to come to my house for some macaroni and cheese from a box?"

Lauren shook her head and stood up. "Sounds tempting but I've lost my appetite. I need to do some thinking." A part of her still wanted to hunt Fiona down and punch her in the stomach. "Is your car still in the shop? I could give you a lift home on my way out of town."

"You're going out of town? I thought you worked tomorrow."

"I'll be back. I just need some open air. It's oppressive around here. Need a ride?" Lauren felt a crying jag sneaking up on her. She needed to leave soon.

"Thanks, but I'm going to walk home. I've got to do something to get some of this weight off. I don't want to end up fat and bitter and mean like Fiona."

"You won't." Lauren hesitated. She felt betrayed, deeply hurt, but it helped to think about some-one besides herself. "How are things going with Natalie? Or should I ask?"

Gina paused, thoughtful. "She's checking into Aunt Bridget's hospital records for me."

"You told her?" This was good news.

"I took your advice. I just hope you know what you're talking about. She said if I have any more problems she's going to start spending the nights with me. Just what I need, a constant slumber party."

The words were said with a grumble but Lauren thought she picked up on a touch of warmth.

"Are you going to be okay?" Gina asked.

"I'll be fine. You?"

"Yeah. Me too."

Something gave Lauren the feeling that they were both bluffing.

❧ CHAPTER 25 ❧

The tech salesman spent an hour and seventeen minutes showing Archer computer systems in various price ranges with varying gigabytes of RAM and processing systems. By the time the guy left, Archer was seeing the malignant negative of backlit screens on his lids when he closed his eyes. He realized he knew as much about computers as a Missouri mule knew about sermon notes; the present church system started looking much more attractive.

The next church member who complained about the appearance of the bulletin would find himself —or herself—the first appointed chairman of the computer search committee of Dogwood Springs Baptist Church. Archer would not feel the least bit guilty about it.

As the man carried his laptop out he left the door partially open. Through that opening, Archer saw John Netz sitting at quiet attention across from Mrs. Boucher's desk. Beside him sat Dwight Hahnfeld and next to him Gene Thomas. Computers suddenly became the least of Archer's concerns.

Why was he constantly agreeing to come to the church on his day off?

Mrs. Boucher said the dreaded words, "You

can go in now," and they stood in unison as if connected by manacles. Mr. Netz led the way to Archer's open door and paused at the threshold. The other two men nearly stumbled into him from behind.

In spite of giving in to sudden heart palpitations, Archer had to smile. Sometimes he had an ornery sense of humor. Here were three bumbling Christians taking their positions in the church very seriously, wanting to do the right thing. The problem was they sometimes tended to rely on their own judgment instead of taking their questions to God.

But at least they held positions of service. So few people were willing to do that these days. Some who did were power hungry but most were sincerely trying to serve God and their church.

Maybe they knew something about computers.

"Pastor, do you mind if we talk to you for a minute?" John Netz asked.

Archer pushed back from his desk and stood, then gestured toward the chairs they had occupied the last time they visited. "Come in and have a seat." He joined them, determined not to take an adversarial position behind his big desk no matter what they might have in mind for this visit.

In tense silence punctuated by muffled footsteps and creaking knees, the men settled themselves. The youngest member, Gene, as usual, perched so close to the edge of his chair that

Archer feared he would slide out of it. Dwight crossed his legs and cupped his hands around his knee, studying his knuckles. John cleared his throat. He was obviously the designated spokesman for this visit.

"Pastor, we—"

"John, have you forgotten my first name?" Archer asked gently.

The grooves deepened in Mr. Netz's wrinkled face and his gaze filled with uncharacteristic amusement for a few seconds. "Archer, we're here to apologize."

Archer waited, allowing those precious words to flow over him while he struggled not to allow his emotions to get messy.

"You were right the other day," Gene Thomas said. His youthful face, lacking the lines traced by experience and hard years of service, looked eager. "We shouldn't have listened to the gossip about you and it's my fault. I kept hearing things at work, and some of the people at church were . . . you know . . . grumbling about having a single pastor and I got worried that . . . anyway, I shouldn't have said anything about you."

Archer swallowed. "Thank you." This was the way it should be—imperfect Christians confessing their sins and struggles to one another. "I have to admit I was hurt and I couldn't help wondering how many others felt the same way you did."

"I've talked to some of them," John said. "Most

people see reason when you hit them in the head with it enough times. What counts is that they realize they're wrong."

"At least about you," Dwight Hahnfeld said quietly.

The other two men looked at him then at the floor. It was the first time he'd spoken since they had arrived and the implication of his words didn't sink in for a moment.

John and Gene remained silent.

Archer's relief seeped away. "Excuse me?"

"I'm sorry, Pastor," Dwight said. "I know how much you like the girl but there's—"

"Lauren McCaffrey isn't a girl, she's a grown woman of thirty-five, an RN who works in the emergency department at our hospital saving lives. Lauren doesn't have time to spread rumors and as far as I know she hasn't heard this one. I would like to see it stay that way."

John Netz and Gene Thomas looked abashed. Dwight's jaw muscles worked overtime as he clenched and unclenched his teeth.

Archer continued. "Anyone in this church who has taken the trouble to get acquainted with Lauren will realize without any doubt that she is a dedicated Christian above reproach."

Dwight waved that information away like a pesky gnat. "A source at the hospital overheard her admit she's having a child—"

"Which source is that?" Archer kept his voice

as calm as humanly possible when seeing an innocent human being get slammed by a vicious tongue. He looked at Gene. "You work there."

"It wasn't me, Archer. I didn't hear her say it but some of the techs were talking about it a couple of weeks ago. One of them heard her."

"Do you remember a name?"

"I don't know all the hospital workers yet but I know Lauren has been sick lately. She's missed work—"

"Half the people in our church have been sick."

"Pastor, we need you to see reason about this," Dwight said.

"I don't believe you're the one seeing reason," Archer snapped.

"Look at it from my viewpoint," Dwight said more loudly. "I have grandchildren in this church and Lauren McCaffrey is popular with all the kids. If you had children wouldn't you want to make sure their role models were above reproach?"

"We received a letter of recommendation from her church in Knolls when she joined us this year." Archer was suddenly overwhelmed with frustration and sadness. What did they want Lauren to do, submit to a pregnancy test? This was unconscionable.

"You know they never reveal anything bad in those letters," Dwight said.

"Really? If that's the case why do we even bother? You accepted her as a member. You can't go around dismissing her from her volunteer positions over a rumor any more than you can fire a pastor over that same rumor. It's a double standard."

Archer received no reply. He stood up, feeling as if he'd preached a long sermon to an empty auditorium. "I want you to pray about this overnight. We can meet back here Monday morning." He wasn't about to give up his Saturday for them. "Not a word about this to Lauren. Do you understand me?"

The three stooges murmured apologies and awkwardly left the office. No one thought to have prayer.

Grant swept past the ER central desk and placed a chart in the discharge slot, taking mental note of three more slots that had been filled since his last pass through. One down and sixteen to go if he counted the patients in the waiting room still seeking attention. They definitely had an epidemic.

He had paused to study the new charts when the bell rang for the triage nurse to report to her exam room. Make that seventeen.

A glance into the waiting room showed every chair filled with patients and their families and friends. Three children who looked to be under the age of five raced across the floor in a game of tag, stumbling into legs, stomping toes, creating chaos. A young woman pressed her fingers against her forehead and moaned, and a boy who looked like he was about thirteen held an emesis basin beneath his chin.

"What is this, a preschool?" an older man complained loudly to his friend. "Can't these people find baby-sitters? What's taking them so long back there?"

"Probably taking their coffee break," the friend said.

Grant shook his head and stepped away, hoping the rest of the staff didn't hear the complaints. They didn't deserve it. The triage nurse was getting things done. The secretary and tech were two of the most efficient workers in the hospital. The other two nurses on duty were new and inexperienced and were nearly tripping over each other in their nervous awkwardness. They had forgotten orders three times in the past hour. That slowed everything down but they were trying.

Grant stifled his frustration. Two new nurses should never be scheduled to work together but too many staff members were sick.

An angry shout echoed from across the hall. Grant stepped into Trauma One.

According to the report, the patient on the bed strapped to a backboard was a twenty-two-year-old male—the victim of a hit-and-run accident at the edge of town. Tina, one of the new nurses, was struggling to get his vitals as he growled curses and threats at her. Witnesses on the scene had called the ambulance immediately and prevented the victim from moving until the attendants immobilized him. A sprinkling of glass from the impact remained in his hair and his road-stained T-shirt held smudges of bloodstain. He jerked at the straps that restrained him and cursed at Tina again.

"That will be enough, Tina," Grant said softly.

When she turned there were tears in her eyes. "I'm sorry Dr. Sheldon, I couldn't get—"

He reached for her chart. "I'll take care of it." He ignored the blast of renewed swearing that redirected its focus on him as he checked for tenderness in the man's neck. The man's appearance was all too familiar. His stringy hair obviously hadn't been washed in days. His eyes darted from Grant to the nurse to the ceiling. The knuckles of his right hand were abraded and blood encrusted.

An informed guess might convince Grant this guy had probably punched something in a fit of fury—perhaps even the car that hit him. That same informed guess said the young man was tweaking—coming down from a high of several days, maybe even weeks. Methamphetamine? Images of St. Louis flashed through Grant's mind.

"Mr. Smith, are you experiencing pain in a particular spot?" he asked as he palpated the man's pelvis and then slipped his hands along the back-board to palpate his back.

The patient glared at Grant and his whole body seemed to radiate with pent-up fury. "Everywhere!" he growled. "Get these straps off me!" He spat another string of abusive swear words.

Grant turned to the nurse who hovered near the doorway. He ordered a CBC and appropriate x-rays then stepped closer to her and lowered his voice. "Are the police on their way?"

"Police!" shouted Smith. "What're you people up to?"

"They should be here any minute," Tina said.

"Thank you. Let's give him twenty-five of Demerol, slow IV push."

She nodded and turned to leave. He followed her out and caught her in the hallway. "Order a urine drug screen," he said quietly. "That can be done after he returns from Radiology."

"Yes, Dr. Sheldon."

Grant took the time to glance at his watch on his way to the next room with the sick child and discovered, to his surprise, that his shift ended in thirty minutes. At the rate patients were coming in—and at the rate charts were stacking up at his desk—he wouldn't be out of here for another two hours.

He checked the child and decided on a blood test. Now he had to find a nurse.

The good news was that since it was already six-thirty, fresh nurses must have arrived thirty minutes ago. Although Lauren wasn't scheduled to work tonight he could always hope. An experienced emergency room nurse was always worth double her pay.

"Dr. Sheldon." The secretary turned and waved at him before he could enter the second trauma room. "There's an ambulance on its way here with a patient in full cardiac arrest."

"What's the ETA?"

"They're about five minutes out."

"Is Lauren here?"

"No. Muriel and Eugene are. Betsy and Tina are staying over to help out for a while."

"Call another nurse down from the floor and send Tina home. Assign Eugene to the Bob Smith case in Trauma One and send the police there as soon as they arrive." If they had any trouble with Mr. Smith, Eugene could handle it. Tina had looked like she'd had enough for the day.

Lauren drove along the potholed road a little faster than usual. She swerved and missed most of the deepest ruts but right now she didn't care if she fell into one of those holes and never found her way out.

"Why, God?" She swerved around a ridge of rock that jutted at least a foot above the road. "I don't understand. All these years I've remained pure and now I've been humiliated not only in my church but also at work. Why is this happening?"

Besides all that, she was homesick. "Am I doomed to be alone the rest of my life? Will I never have a marriage, a family?" She knew she was working herself into a raging pity party but she went with the mood.

When she had first told her parents that she was moving to Dogwood Springs they'd used every argument in the "Parent's Manual of Guilt Trips" to convince her to stay in Knolls. They'd enlisted the rest of the family for help—not just brothers and sisters but nieces and nephews, aunts and uncles, cousins.

During one moment of weakness, she had actually told Mom she would stay in Knolls with the condition that the whole family would stop trying so hard to marry her off to every man between the ages of twenty-six and sixty who walked into the church without a wedding ring on his finger. Within twenty-four hours of the time Lauren made her offer, Aunt Gertrude had actually set her up on a blind date with the son of one of the new farmers who had moved into their neck of the woods. Without even asking her. Lauren's humiliation had been complete.

Since her childhood her parents and grandparents had taught her that she shouldn't waste her time asking God the whys and hows of life. Those problems were best left for Him to figure out. She was supposed to ask the "what" question. As in, "What do you want me to do for you, Lord?" And the "where" question, as in, "Where do you want me to serve?"

All this time she'd believed she was doing the right thing. She served Him through the church and she served Him at work when she ministered to the ill and prayed with them. When it came to matters of the heart, Lauren knew she'd tended to be a little too eager lately. There had been an embarrassing number of times that she'd wished she'd kept her mouth shut.

If she was one of those people meant to remain separate and single then why did she have this strong longing for a husband and children? Did people in her church and place of work see her as a woman of loose moral character? If not, why would such a rumor spread so quickly?

She turned onto the grassy trail where tires had worn dirt tracks deep into the ground. Oak, hickory, and hedge trees loomed over those tracks to form a deep green tunnel. She parked in the shade of those trees, surprised that she didn't see the ancient brown pickup Mr. Rosewitz and Mr. Mourglia drove out here every Friday afternoon to catch their limit. They should be here any time.

Lauren leaned her forehead against the steering wheel. The loneliness that had occasionally attacked her since moving from Knolls seemed to bite more deeply today and she lacked the strength to tackle it the way she usually did. She felt over-whelmed.

Was this move to Dogwood Springs the wrong thing to do? Should she go back to Knolls where she had so many friends and so much family she could scarcely take a breath?

But even if she did move back there she'd still feel this particular loneliness.

She got out of the truck at last and ducked beneath the heavy overhang of branches, particularly avoiding the thorns of the hedge trees. As she stepped through the gloom of shade and listened to the rush of the waters ahead, she sought the familiar peace she always found when she was alone in the wilderness like this. Today that peace eluded her.

Above the chatter of the racing creek she caught the rumble of another sound and automatically glanced over her shoulder toward the parking area. No one was there. The sound was almost a growl—low and guttural.

When she stopped to listen the growling stopped. She peered through the trees, past shadows and rotting tree trunks and piles of last year's leaves. Nothing moved.

After a final study of the woods she gave a shrug and ducked beneath another low-hanging limb to follow the brushy path toward the creek. She was stepping from the trees into a clearing when the growl reached her again, as if a stalker watched from some hidden spot above her. A pinprick of tension wormed its way across her shoulders and down her spine.

The growl roughened, stopped, deepened then roared. Lauren's stomach tightened into a knot of nausea. She gasped and turned back toward the truck but the sound registered at last. The mechanical grunt and cough metamorphosed in Lauren's mind from a furry flesh-eating creature of the forest to a gas-eating monster of steel. Of course. That company was still excavating the site above Honey Spring.

Somehow it didn't give her any comfort to realize that a monster was not stalking her. It was stalking the future of Honey Creek and the hundreds of people who depended on its source for water, for recreation, even for an occasional fish dinner.

The vague unease in her stomach increased. "Oh no. Not now." She was getting sick again. The force of the nausea hit more swiftly and violently than ever before and the future of Honey Creek fled from her thoughts. As she lost the contents of her stomach, the edges of her vision grew black. Lauren sank to her knees unable to stand and her prayers now deepened into silent desperation.

"Dad?" Beau's voice rang through the line, taut with excitement. "There's something strange about the bright white flecks on the x-ray films in some of these patient charts you gave me to look at."

Grant glanced at a nurse rushing past him, heard the complaints all the way from the waiting room, felt the anxiety that seemed to affect everyone in the ER. "Can this wait? Things are really hopping right now, and—"

"It's important."

Grant suppressed his frustration. "Those flecks on the films are artifacts from the ancient machine they need to replace in Radiology."

"Are you sure?"

"They're just superficial scratches. Film processor defects. I hear the x-ray techs complaining about it all the time."

"This is different."

"I don't have time to argue with you."

"Then listen to this. I checked the addresses of those patients. Almost all of them are located in the same area of town. The same area, Dad. Doesn't that seem weird?"

Grant frowned. "How did you find that out?"

"I used the map Brooke grabbed from City Hall the day we had to drag her out of there."

"Oh yeah."

"Right. Remember the day we went fishing with Lauren and she told us Honey Creek supplied about a third of the town's water? But it was only a certain section."

"Are you talking about some kind of water contamination?"

"Maybe. I need to make some calls and see if it fits but I don't think the waterworks supervisor and the town mayor will listen to a sixteen-year-old kid."

"They will if you tell them you're calling on my behalf. While you're at it would you find out what the mayor knows about a dump site cleanup above Honey Spring? We had a patient in here the other day who'd been working with a crew from Springfield."

"Does that mean you're giving me permission to make those calls?"

"Call whoever you need to and let me know what you find out." He glanced across the bustling ER. "And hurry."

❧ CHAPTER 26 ❧

Archer was still in his office having a heart-to-heart with God when the church secretary knocked at the office door and stepped inside without waiting for an answer.

"Archer?"

He looked up in surprise. "What's wrong?"

"Do you know anything about a werewolf?"

"A what?"

"There's a little child on the telephone asking

376

to speak to Mr. Archer. He says he's calling you about the werewolf."

Archer caught his breath. He'd heard the word the day Levi and Cody were talking to Lauren on the steps of their porch.

He picked up his receiver and punched the button with the blinking light. "Hello? This is Mr. Archer. Levi? Is your mother acting funny?"

"Yes," came the child's frightened voice. "She started shaking and she won't talk to us. She doesn't have any claws or fur yet but her eyes are white."

"Okay. Remember what she told you to do when she started doing that?"

"I'm supposed to call somebody."

"She also told you to go to Mrs. Walker's house. You remember that?"

"But I don't want to leave my mom. What if she runs away again and we can't find her this time?"

"I'll be there as soon as I can and I'll take care of her. You take your brother to Mrs. Walker's house. Do you understand?"

"You'll come now?"

"I'll be there in five minutes." He disconnected, grabbed his car keys from the corner of the desk, and ran out of the office. "Call an ambulance," he told Mrs. Boucher as he raced through the outer reception area. "Give them Gina's address." Maybe the ambulance would beat him there.

• • •

Lauren awakened to find herself face down in a tangle of vines and last year's moldy leaves. When she groaned and pushed herself up a jangle of noise rang in her ears with the force of a train whistle. The forest spun around her like a giant blender filled with leaves. The sound obviously came from inside her head. She blinked toward the sky but it looked as if clouds had drawn a blanket over the trees while she was unconscious. Maybe her vision was dimming.

She was too weak and sick to do battle with the twin forces of fear and confusion. She was alone in this place and no one knew where she had gone. Someone had already died from the effects of an illness with the same symptoms that were attacking her. She couldn't push that memory from her mind.

Now she understood more completely than ever before why the patients who came into the emergency room were so often frightened.

Alone.

"Am I alone?" Her prayer was barely a croak of sound and her arms threatened to give way and plunge her face down into the decomposing leaves once more.

No. He was there. He knew.

But did He want to rescue her from this? Maybe she had complained once too often about her loneliness.

Or maybe this illness was affecting her mind and emotions.

"Lord, help me." Lauren could barely whisper the words but in her heart she shouted them.

The nausea returned with a vengeance. As darkness once again rimmed her vision, she felt her body slump into the cushion of damp leaves. Her last coherent thought was one comforting memory—Mr. Mourglia and Mr. Rosewitz would be here any time. They always came fishing on Friday afternoon, the barber and his elderly buddy, the ones who had first told her about this place. They would be here before sunset, when the fish were hungry and the air was just right . . .

Archer screeched his tires against the curb i front of Gina's house, parked the car, and raced past the over-trimmed hedges. The front door was unlocked and he barely slowed his steps as hc plunged inside. The sobs of a child permeated the air.

"Levi?" Archer called.

A tiny form came racing through the doorway from the kitchen. "Help her Mr. Archer! Help her!" He grabbed Archer's hand and tugged. "Hurry!"

Archer swung the child up into his arms and ran with him to the threshold of the kitchen, where the horrifying sight of Gina in full, arching seizure held Cody wide-eyed and gasping in the far corner of the room. Gina's eyes were rolled back in their sockets, her face grimaced, and her legs and arms flew in wild abandon.

"Take Cody to your neighbor's house." Archer placed the child on his feet. "I'll take care of her now."

"How?"

"I've already called an ambulance and they should be here any minute. Levi, go now."

"But Mama needs us!"

For a few precious moments Gina's movements grew still. Her arms flopped to her sides and her head fell sideways. The only sound was the continued gasping sobs from Cody.

Archer knelt beside Gina and placed a hand on her arm.

She didn't react.

"Gina?"

She didn't move except to breathe. At least she was still breathing.

"Levi," Archer used his most authoritative voice, "your mother wants you and Cody to go to your neighbor's house now."

With great reluctance, Levi walked over to his little brother, who continued to shake with spasms of soundless sobs. Levi took the younger child by the arm and led him from the room. They were stepping through the doorway when Archer felt Gina's arm tense. Her face tightened.

Levi turned and looked back at her.

"Go now," Archer said.

Levi reached up and grasped the doorknob then pulled the door shut behind them. As soon as the latch clicked, Gina's arms jerked with a returning seizure. A hoarse moan spiraled from her throat.

Where was that ambulance? He'd given clear directions for Mrs. Boucher to relay to them. What if they'd misunderstood?

He pivoted in search of a telephone and saw one on the wall beside the kitchen entrance. He jerked up the receiver as Gina's convulsions intensified.

Grant answered an emergency telephone call from the front reception desk while an eager code team assembled in the newly evacuated cardiac room.

"Grant? Archer. Need your help."

A child screamed from one of the exam rooms, joining the chorus of children who continued to play in the waiting room, still bouncing off of legs and chairs and vending machines.

Grant covered his left ear. "What's wrong?"

"I think Gina's having a grand mal seizure."

After long experience working a busy ER in St. Louis, Grant seldom felt overwhelmed here in Dogwood Springs. Right now he wished he could split into three or four different people. "Where is she?"

"At home. I'm with her now. She's had more than one."

"Ambulance?"

"Tried twice but no one's here yet."

"We have a rash of emergencies. The ambulances are probably out on calls. We have one coming in now. How long have the seizures lasted?"

"I'm not sure—a few minutes, maybe. She was in the middle of one when I got here but then there was a break. She didn't regain consciousness. What do I do?" Archer did not sound panicked but the thread of concern intensified in his voice.

"Keep her from hurting herself." Until Grant was sure what was happening he had to consider Gina's seizures to be life threatening.

"I put a pillow under her head."

Grant looked out the window. No ambulance yet.

"Don't I need to put something in her mouth to keep her from biting her tongue?" Archer asked.

"If the seizure has broken and she's unconscious, turn her onto her side so her tongue won't block the air passage when she loses muscle tone. Is there sugar nearby?"

"I don't know. We're in the kitchen though. Let me look—"

"Wait—Archer?" It was countdown time. The ambulance could arrive any second. "I might not be able to hold for you. When you find the sugar try to place a little of it under her tongue. Don't use a spoon because she could bite it and break some teeth. And don't put your fingers in her mouth."

"Why sugar?"

"I'm just taking a chance it could be hypoglycemia. Even if this is a new onset of epilepsy the sugar won't hurt her. It's an educated guess. Hurry."

He heard the slap of the receiver hitting the counter and then the rattle of dishes and the slam of cupboard doors. The sounds from the phone mingled with the sounds in the ER.

Grant turned to the ER secretary. "Where are the first responders in this town?"

"Probably out on calls," she said. "Things are going nuts."

The call reached them and the ambulance came racing around a corner and into the bay, lights flashing.

"Archer?" Grant called. "Hello?"

No answer.

He had to disconnect. As nurses ran out to meet the ambulance attendants Grant hung up the phone and followed. Archer was on his own.

Archer found a canister of white stuff at the far end of the kitchen counter. While the sound of Gina's jerking motions seemed to bounce from the flat planes of counters and doors, he plunged his hand into the canister. It felt like sugar. He brought a handful out and touched his tongue to it. Salt.

He shoved that container aside, dusted his hands, pulled the next container toward him and was removing the lid when he realized the movements had stopped. He pivoted toward Gina. Her head lolled to the side and the spasms in her arms and legs had gentled and grown slower. The tight grimace released and her mouth fell open.

Archer grabbed the receiver from the counter. "Grant, her seizure's—"

The dial tone mocked him. He was on his own.

Well, not quite.

No. Not at all.

"Lord, I don't know what's happening but you do. Give me a double dose of your wisdom and keep me calm." Archer dropped to his knees beside Gina as he prayed.

Her muscles gradually relaxed. He placed his hands on her left side and logrolled her limp body toward him. Her arms flopped uselessly against him; her legs were heavier and less movable than he'd expected. He had to hold her body on its side with one hand while he adjusted her legs with the other.

Once he had her securely on her side, he bent her legs to stabilize her in that position and then leaned forward until his ear was next to her mouth. He heard breath sounds. He rushed to the counter and jerked the lid from the next container then plunged his hand inside and lifted his fingers to his tongue.

Sugar. This would work. He carried the container to the floor beside her and gently pried her mouth open, taking care not to put his fingers near her teeth. Her tongue presented another problem. Grant had instructed him to place the sugar under her tongue.

This could be done. He grabbed a generous three-fingered pinch of sugar and reached for her slackened jaw then sprinkled the sugar along the side of her tongue.

That accomplished with no observable reaction, he reached for another pinch. Before he could get it to her mouth, however, the movements began again. He tried to give her another dose before her face contracted and her mouth clamped shut but all he managed to do was sprinkle sugar across her face and scatter it on the floor. Her body jerked and her elbow hit the container, knocking it over. Sugar scattered everywhere. She kicked him in the leg and rapped him on the arm with her hand. The contortions returned. The invisible monster once more had her in its grasp.

Archer released her and reached an outspread hand to scrape up a fistful of the sweet medicine, praying under his breath that she wouldn't inhale what was already in her mouth and choke, praying that what he had already given her would work its way through her system, praying for divine inter-vention.

"Lord, one breath from you, one thought, is all it would take to heal her."

He waited, feeling inadequate and useless.

Somewhere in the midst of his prayers the

movements stopped. He scrambled to her side, prepared to reposition her when she caught her breath in a sigh. Her eyes fluttered but did not open.

"Gina?"

"Pulseless v-tach." Christy the paramedic pumped her patient's chest in the time-honored dance of desperation as she gave Grant a rushed report. "We got him back for a few seconds but then he went down again."

The EMT handed over the bagging to the respiratory therapist on the code team. The elderly man had monitor leads across his bare chest. His skin nearly matched the bed sheet. An IV had been established in his left forearm.

"How long since your last shock?"

"About two minutes."

"We need to shock again now."

Everyone cleared as the hum of the charge reached maximum. Grant pushed the defibrillator button and the older man's body arched and fell back.

"Nothing," Christy said.

"Continue CPR," Grant told the nurse and gave additional orders.

In the room they switched from the paramedic's defibrillator unit to the hospital's when they transferred him from gurney to bed.

"What happened?" Grant asked.

"He went into respiratory arrest almost as soon as we arrived at his house," Christy said. "His friend Mr. Rosewitz drove by his house to see about him when he didn't show up at their usual rendezvous at City Hall for their fishing date."

"That's where we were supposed to meet." A man probably in his late sixties had followed them inside, his pale face anxious, his hands wringing as if a film of lotion covered them. He must be Mr. Rosewitz. The man stepped to a corner, keeping careful watch.

Grant realized he knew the patient. Ernest Mourglia loved to work the community puzzle at City Hall. He was the mayor's uncle.

"When did you find him like this?" Grant asked Mr. Rosewitz.

"Couldn't have been more than fifteen, maybe twenty minutes ago."

"Has he complained about chest pain before this? Do you know if he's been feeling ill lately?"

"He was kind of sick when I talked with him yesterday." Mr. Rosewitz inched into the room as if afraid to get too close. "He said he'd rather go fishing and be miserable than stay home and be miserable. He wanted to keep his mind off his stomach. If it helps, he told me he had a bad taste in his mouth. He said it tasted like he was sucking on a penny."

Some zephyr of awareness stirred Grant's memory. A metallic taste in the mouth.

They shocked Mr. Mourglia again. The monitor's death march remained unchanged.

Less than a minute later they shocked again. The monitor beeped then began a steady rhythm across the screen. There was a collective sigh of relief.

Grant pressed his fingers against Mourglia's neck. There was a pulse. Yes!

"BP?" he asked.

"It's 85 over 60 and climbing," Eugene replied.

Grant stepped closer to the patient's friend. "Mr. Rosewitz, do you go to City Hall very often?"

"Just to meet Ernest." The man gave his friend a frowning glance. "Is he going to be okay?"

"We need to run some tests and find out how his heart is doing. Do you know if he's had heart problems in the past?"

"I've seen him turn white and grab his chest, but the stubborn cuss says he'd just as soon die as get all trussed up in a hospital. Couldn't ever get him into a doctor's office. If he dies of a heart attack in my barbershop it'll be bad for business." Mr. Rosewitz's voice roughened. He cleared his throat. "Wouldn't want the old fool to die on me."

"You're a barber?"

The man nodded. "Been at it forty years." His voice wobbled.

On a hunch Grant asked, "Where do you and Mr. Mourglia go fishing?"

Words could not have stated the man's confusion more clearly than the tilt of his head and the meeting together of his eyebrows. Muriel turned from the patient's side with a frown on her bulldog face.

Grant wasn't certain where he was headed with his questions. Still, he had a hunch and he needed to follow it further. He hoped Beau would call back with more information soon.

"Please humor me for a moment," Grant said. "It could be important."

"We fish at Honey Creek up close to the source."

Grant's hunch, which had been foggy at best when he'd spoken with Beau, now began to take a more concrete form. "Do you know a young woman by the name of Lauren McCaffrey?"

The man's features lightened a fraction. "Sure do. She's the one who sat down there in my barbershop and pestered me until I finally gave in and told her about my fishing spot. I've seen her at the creek quite a few times since then." His brows lowered a fraction. "We try to beat her there. She gets all the good ones if she gets her line in the water first."

The possibilities frightened Grant. It looked like Beau might be onto something with those x-ray films. Maybe the flecks weren't artifact at all.

Lauren had been sick with a bad taste in her mouth.

"Mr. Rosewitz, have you felt ill in the past few

weeks, suffered nausea, any of the symptoms your friend had?"

"Can't say that I have."

"Do you eat the fish you catch?"

"I don't like fish. I give 'em all to Ernest. He loves 'em and he doesn't have much income."

Frustration surged through Grant. Until today he'd been so sure the illness was a virus or bacteria. Something more ominous could be the cause of those bright white flecks Beau had mentioned.

"He's pinking up nicely," Muriel said. "Looks like he'll make it."

Grant nodded and gave more orders then said, "Let me know immediately if his condition worsens. I'll be in Trauma One for a few minutes and then at my desk." He excused himself and rushed from the room.

He checked on an angry Mr. Smith and declined to release him from the backboard, not because of spinal damage but because the man's continued combativeness not only endangered him, but others. Smith refused to give a urine sample and shouted his frustration at the straps that restrained him. After being assured by Eugene that the police were on their way, Grant left the room.

He didn't go far before Dr. Mitchell Caine came striding through the side door to take over for his shift. The elegant doctor's steel gaze swept the central area of the emergency department with its busy staff and crowded work areas. His features darkened.

Grant gave a quick report on the patients most in need of attention and then left Caine staring after him as he rushed to his office.

As he reached for the phone Grant was reminded of Archer's frantic phone call. Gina was having seizures. His suspicion, after some of the clues he'd received lately, was heavy metal poisoning. But how could that be causing Gina's symptoms, her seizures?

It could be affecting her central nervous system. How widespread was this problem? He dialed home and let the phone ring four times before Beau picked up.

"Beau, what have you—"

"I need a little more time. I'm making calls now."

Grant's hand tightened on the receiver. "Find what you can and call me back ASAP. Also do a Web search for symptoms of mercury poisoning."

Beau caught his breath. "You think that's what these patients have?"

"I don't know, just check."

Grant hung up and jumped back into the patient race. He had a lot of faith in his son's deductive reasoning but what if they were already too late to save these people?

CHAPTER 27

After placing another generous pinch of sugar at the edge of Gina's tongue, Archer repositioned the pillow behind her head and gently straightened her arms and legs. While he watched her face, her lids fluttered once again. They didn't open. She obviously didn't have the strength to open her eyes.

"Gina, you're not alone. I'm right here and I'm not going to leave you until the ambulance comes."

She winced. Her shoulders moved slowly as if she was fighting her way out of a subterranean pit in her mind.

"Who's there?"

A gush of relief escaped his lips. "Archer. Lie still for a few minutes. I know the floor is hard but we don't want to set off more seizures."

"Seizures?" She winced again and lifted her arm a few inches from her stomach, though she still didn't open her eyes.

"You've been having some seizures. How do you feel right now?"

Her soft breathing deepened. "Head hurts bad."

"I'm sorry. I wish—"

"My boys?" Her eyes came open then, slowly, with effort. "Levi? Cody?"

"They went to your neighbor's after I got here."

In slow motion she reached up and grasped Archer's arm. "What happened? Did I hurt—"

"You didn't hurt anyone. Levi called me. When I got here they were frightened but safe. As soon as the ambulance gets here I'll go to the Walker's house and reassure them before I follow you to the hospital."

At this promise, she released him. Tears filmed her eyes. "I've messed up everything."

"How can you blame yourself for an illness you didn't create?"

"I thought I could control the attacks."

"This is something you would never have been able to control and I believe it's physical, not psychiatric."

There was a slight nod of her head. "Lauren . . . she'll keep my children. If anything . . . happens to me."

"What's going to happen is you're going to the hospital."

"Will you call her?"

"Of course."

The color in her face deepened to a healthier shade of pink. "I have to give it up. I can't go on like this."

"Gina, you can't—"

"Shh. Listen." Her voice grew stronger though still soft. "Lauren told me to give it up."

Archer waited. Gina was certainly not talking

about the obvious, because Lauren would never tell anyone to give up her children or her hope for a future.

"I tried to control my life for too long." She stopped and swallowed, and her tongue worked across her lips in a grimace. "Sugar?"

"Doctor's orders. I called the hospital for advice and Grant told me to try sugar under your tongue in case your seizures were a reaction to hypo-glycemia."

Gina's eyelids drooped, her lips parted, and some of the firmness left her expression. Archer waited.

"Second opinion," she said a few seconds later.

He frowned at her. "Gina?"

"I need a second opinion like Lauren said." Her voice had an ethereal quality, half whisper, half rasp, but there was an assurance in it that hadn't been there before. "I asked Him for one. Do you think I'll get it?"

"Yes." He remembered now. That was the phrase Lauren used the day they visited Gina's house. "God is the Great Physician."

"I give up on myself because I can't do it. He needs to take over for me. He'll help me."

"Yes Gina, He will. He made you; He loves you. Turn it all over to Him."

"I need a new father."

"Trust Him to take over for you. He always does."

"Why would He want to?"

"You know how much you love your children? Multiply that by a billion and He loves you more."

She was silent for a long moment then she said, "You sound like Lauren."

"She's right."

Another long thoughtful silence then, "Yes." She said no more but something changed in her face. Her expression went blank.

"Gina?"

With a violent thrust the dreaded grimace returned to her face and she jerked. At the same moment Archer heard the sweet welcome sound of an ambulance siren.

"Please Lord, take care of her."

Grant was racing through the ER proper when Eugene intercepted him.

"Dr. Sheldon, Bob Smith's gone! I stepped out to help Muriel lift a patient. When I went back into the room I found the backboard empty. One of the straps was broken."

"What's going on here, Sheldon?" The chill of Dr. Mitchell Caine's voice came from behind Grant. "Are we now releasing dangerous criminals before the police can reach them?"

Grant turned to find Caine bearing down on him trailed by two black-uniformed police officers looking less than happy. "No one released him."

One of the police officers stepped forward. "Dr. Sheldon, according to reports we received from the witnesses on the scene, that patient matched the description of a man we've been after for weeks. He uses the street name Peregrine."

Eugene groaned aloud. "The pusher? Dr. Sheldon, I'm sorry. I was only gone for a minute. Muriel needed me and I couldn't—"

"You're not employed as a security officer." Grant cast a cool glance at Caine. "If that man was strong enough to break one of the straps on that spine board and escape, I don't want to think what he might have done if Eugene had tried to stop him. Dr. Caine, there are plenty of patients to be seen and you're the physician on duty now. I suggest you get to work. I'll take care of this." He gestured for the police to follow him into his office.

Before Grant could reach the door the night secretary turned and motioned to him. "Your son's on line two, Dr. Sheldon. He says it's—"

"Important. Thanks, Becky." Grant rushed nto his office and grabbed the phone without checking caller ID with the officers still trailing behind him. "What have you found?"

"I made those calls." There was an edge of excitement in Beau's voice tonight that Grant hadn't heard in many months.

"Hold it a moment. I have police officers with me. I'm putting the phone on the speaker so they can hear this." He pushed the button. "Go ahead."

"I called the mayor." Beau's voice was clear and steady. "Honey Spring is the water source for the patients named in the charts you gave me. Honey Creek just happens to supply the water for a mostly middle-class neighborhood and that's why this mystery flu appeared to limit itself to the middle class."

"Good job." Grant glanced at the police to see if they were listening. They were, with rapt attention.

"What about the excavation at the dump site above the spring?"

"That's when the mayor got really interested. She said she's going to check it all out but she was preoccupied with a family emergency. She said you saw her uncle in the ER tonight."

Ernest Mourglia, who was now on his way to Springfield. "That's right. Jade Myers might be a little overwhelmed for a while."

"I offered to help. She gave me the number for the ditching service out of Springfield and I called them. Get this, Dad, they started work on that project six weeks ago. They ran into all kinds of snags—had some complaints from the locals and then they dug up a bunch of crushed plastic containers that weren't part of the bargain. Some of their guys got sick."

"Containers of what?"

"He said there were all kinds of them but he was upset because he'd been told it was harmless construction material. He wouldn't admit his own earthmovers might have been the ones to crush the containers but he did admit some of his guys got sick for no reason. Dad, I think you're right. That stuff's poison."

"Did he describe the sickness?"

"Like the flu."

That was probably good. The vomiting and diarrhea were the body's natural defense against a poison in the system. As long as that poison was ejected from the body it would be less likely to cause lasting effects.

"I did that Web search you wanted," Beau said. "The symptoms in most of these patient charts match the symptoms of mercury salt poisoning. What made you think about that?"

"That dump site above Honey Springs wasn't on private land. Anyone could have dumped waste there. Archer has warned me several times that methamphetamine production is a big problem in this part of the state. One of the by-products of meth production is mercury salt."

"Meth?" Beau said in a hushed whisper. "You think it could be that bad here in Dogwood Springs?"

Grant thought about their recent escapee. "Oh yes."

"So we're talking about a ground and water contamination of mercury," Beau said. "The x-rays, Dad, maybe those flecks on the film weren't artifact. If mercury was in the water these people drank—"

"I know." Grant tried not to think of the long-range implications right now. He just needed to concentrate on his next step. "I don't want to jump to conclusions but looking at all this evidence I think a heavy metal such as mercury would show up just that way on an x-ray."

"So far the symptoms haven't been so bad," Beau said. "The only thing that worries me is that things can get worse. When mercury gets into the groundwater it can undergo a chemical reaction and convert to methyl mercury. That can affect the central nervous system. But it doesn't look like that's happened yet."

"Yet." Grant knew the facts but he let his son talk and looked up to make sure the officers were paying attention. They were.

"Methyl mercury can cause all kinds of nasty permanent damage," Beau continued. "Especially if it's been in someone's system for a few weeks. Do you know that it only takes a small amount of mercury to poison a whole lake?"

"Excellent work." Grant wanted to grab his family and take them as far away from this poisoned town as he could but he'd already done that. This was supposed to be a safe town. "Have you called anyone besides the mayor and the excavators?"

"No. Jade Myers was going to try to get a

HAZMAT team down here from Springfield. She said she'll need to talk to you."

"Sounds like I'm in for a busy night." Grant couldn't stifle the fear that the mercury salt might be converting to methyl mercury.

"What are you going to do now?" Beau asked.

"I'll call our administrator and he can call County Health." Grant glanced again at the officers who hovered beside the desk, their expressions grim. They were definitely on full alert.

Peregrine's evil had spread.

Grant remembered his most recent visit from Brisco and Scroggs. "We had a farmer in here the other day who was attacked in his own barn in the middle of the afternoon. Want to take a guess what the intruder was stealing?"

"Farm supplies?" Beau asked.

"Liquid fertilizer."

"That's used to make meth."

"And they're getting bold enough to try to steal it in the middle of the day."

One of the officers nodded at his partner.

"You'd better start praying," Beau said.

"I already have been. I just hope He's listening."

There was a silence filled with surprise then, "You're back on speaking terms with God?" In spite of the situation, there was a trace of joy in Beau's voice that filled Grant with bittersweet memories.

"As I said, He might not listen to me."

"He will. He's answering my prayers right now. Keep praying." Beau disconnected.

Something stirred deep inside Grant—a pain he'd ignored for so long that it seemed to be a part of him now. But mixed with the pain was a sense of relief and quiet hope engendered by his son's excitement. The pain was uppermost. How much had he hurt his children by his damaged relationship with God over Annette's death?

Those thoughts remained with Grant as he spoke with the police, gave them all the information he could, and explained his fears about the mercury poisoning.

They called the station from his office.

"Dr. Sheldon?"

He looked up to find the secretary standing at the doorway. "You wanted me to let you know when the ambulance made a call with the next patient. They'll be here in about five minutes."

"I'll be there." He followed her out the door. He wanted to be the one to take care of Gina. Caine had his hands full. "Becky, I need a copy of Gina Drake's medical records with any previous x-rays."

"How soon?"

"Now."

She returned to her station while Grant dialed Mr. Butler's home number. A recorder intercepted his call after the second ring. Grant left a message. No help there. He had the authority and the information. He definitely had a state of emergency, so there was no need to wait on the administrator to take action. The police were already on it.

He dialed Lauren's number and spoke to yet another machine. "Lauren, this is Grant. Please call me when you get in no matter the time. I'll be at the hospital for at least another hour, maybe longer." Maybe a lot longer. "Whatever you do, don't drink any more of your spring water and don't eat any more fish. It could be poisoned. Just call me."

Dissatisfied with the results of his efforts so far, he hung up. As he walked toward the front of the ER, he remembered eight-year-old Stacie Kimble who had suffered the effects of diabetic coma after an apparent virus that had affected other family members.

Hindsight was so much more accurate than medical instinct. Her family lived in the affected section of town and the onset of diabetes would have caused a lot of thirst. The increased water intake would have exacerbated Stacie's condition as the poison entered her system, just as the severity of the gastrointestinal illness could have affected Mr. Mourglia's heart if it was already weak.

How many other mystery cases would this discovery reveal to him? And how many might have been helped if he'd known sooner?

The siren echoed through the office. He needed to stop wallowing in what-ifs. Right now he had a patient who needed help and he needed to contact Poison Control. The situation was out of hand and he wasn't going to stop it alone. No human could do that.

He found himself silently seeking the guidance of the only One who could give him the wisdom he needed.

Grant picked up the telephone at the reception desk as the ambulance pulled into the bay. Methyl mercury poisoning was rare but it could very likely cause the symptoms Gina had been experiencing. Would Poison Control even know how to treat it?

"Mr. Archer!" Levi came running toward him at full speed from across the Walkers' large family room.

At the sound of his older brother's voice, Cody turned from his television cartoons. His face brightened. He leaped from the sofa and raced after Levi.

Both children ran past Archer and Mrs. Walker and rushed to the door. They stopped and looked back at Archer. "Where's Mama?" Cody asked.

"She's on her way to the hospital where they'll take good care of her."

Levi pulled open the door and stepped to the screen to peer outside. Cody stepped up beside him. They stared at the empty porch and the empty sidewalk then looked back at Archer.

"Why was she kicking the kitchen floor?"

"What happened to her eyes?"

"Will she be okay?"

"Can we see her?"

Their voices competed with each other, getting louder with each word until Mr. Walker came rushing into the room from the kitchen, dish towel in one hand and spatula in the other, to join his wife.

He placed a hand on Archer's shoulder to get his attention. "Pastor, is she going to be okay? I was just baking some cookies with the children to keep them occupied but they can't stop worrying about their mother."

"I don't know anything yet." Archer knelt and reached out to the children. They hesitated, as if sensing by his actions and the lack of an answer that news about their mother was not forthcoming. Levi stepped into the invitation of his arms and Cody imitated his brother. Both fell silent, eyes wide, obviously haunted by the things they had seen and the fear that had attacked them far too often these past few weeks.

"Did you see the ambulance when it came a few minutes ago?" he asked them.

Mr. Walker gestured to Archer and shook his head. "We had the television turned up. We were afraid the sirens would scare them."

"Your mama's on her way to the hospital to see Dr. Sheldon. You remember him from last time don't you?"

Levi nodded.

"He's going to take good care of her but he might want her to spend the night at the hospital to make sure she doesn't get sick."

"Can we go see her?" Levi asked.

"We want to see Mama." Cody's voice was hushed, still fearful.

Archer swallowed. "Your mama wants you to stay here and help Mr. Walker bake cookies and then when she starts to feel better you can visit her." He could promise no more than that. He wanted to tell them their mother would be home first thing in the morning as good as new but he would not lie to them.

He hugged the children and kissed their soft cheeks and said another prayer for their mother and for them. When he released them, Levi took his little brother by the arm.

"Mom wants us to be good, Cody. We have to sit down and eat cookies and do what Mr. and Mrs. Walker tell us to."

"You know what?" Mr. Walker rested a hand on the top of Levi's head, "I think our first batch is almost ready to come out of the oven. Why don't you help me do the taste test." He led the way and the children followed while he explained that the cookies couldn't pass the taste test unless they'd been washed down with milk, so they had a lot of work to do.

Archer silently thanked God for answering one of his prayers. The children were in good hands with loving people.

He made arrangements with the Walkers to take care of the children overnight. Mrs. Walker had a key to Gina's house and would go over later to collect some of the children's clothing and toys.

"Mrs. Walker, thank you for helping Gina."

"Of course." She smiled up at him. "But you'll have to start calling me Agnes. Gina has taught Levi and Cody to call me Miss Agnes." Her smile radiated across her face. "They're special children. Levi wouldn't let us go over to the house to check on Gina. He insisted that the preacher was taking care of her and nobody else should be there. Cody was in tears, so we obeyed orders and stayed with the boys."

After he left the house he pulled out his cell phone and hit Lauren's number. He knew he should call Natalie but Gina would want to see Lauren first. As he listened to the telephone ring, he prayed that Gina would be alive to see Lauren when she arrived—and to see her children again.

Voicemail picked up and he heard Lauren's voice, light and clear and filled with her typical vitality as she left precise instructions for the caller.

He left a message and started to worry about her as he punched speed dial for Natalie.

CHAPTER 28

Sharp pain streaked across Lauren's forehead. She opened her eyes but couldn't lift her head from the forest floor. The pain grew worse. She recognized the familiar thrust of a sinus headache and almost welcomed the reminder that she was still alive. She vaguely recalled the continuous nausea broken by vomiting and then blackness that had attacked her for what seemed like endless hours.

How long had she been unconscious this time? The haze in her mind cleared enough for her to think coherently but she didn't have her watch on and she'd left her cell phone in the truck. Had she been here for an hour? Longer? Twilight surrounded and confused her as she opened her eyes once more. Could she have slept all night?

Where were Mr. Mourglia and Mr. Rosewitz? Was it possible they had come and gone without seeing her?

She braced herself, anticipating another sharp stab of pain that didn't come. She managed to raise her head from the pillow of leaves and looked up into the sky, where the vivid pink of a Missouri sunset shone past the grasping fingers of two leafless sycamore branches, ghostly white in their deadness. Why were they dead at this time of year? And why hadn't she noticed them sooner? At least she hadn't been here as long as she'd feared.

Some strength returned to her arms and she sat up. The forest spun around her but more of the fuzz cleared from her mind. She gradually grew aware of the sounds around her, the peep of frogs, the rustle of some nearby nocturnal rodent. Most important, she heard the muted splash of water in Honey Creek.

Water.

Though she was not thirsty and didn't know if she could keep fluid down, she had to try. She was alone. Her fishing buddies apparently had not come and there was no one to help her.

Alone.

Lord, have I been abandoned? Are you even there?

Still taking controlled breaths in through her nose and out through her mouth, Lauren pushed herself to her knees. A little more strength permeated her body, almost as if in answer to her one-line prayer.

After a moment of rest, she tried to rise to her feet but stumbled back to her knees. Her hand came into contact with a fallen branch covered with leaves and stems.

"Help me." The faint rattle of her voice alarmed her. She squeezed the limb with all the strength she could muster. There wasn't much.

Her body needed fluids.

Alone.

But she was never completely alone.

She wasn't was she?

It took great effort to stand upright even with the support of the branch. Twilight hovered ever nearer, hiding the trail from view, yet somehow Lauren avoided tripping over brush or stumbling into briars. The untrimmed branch gave her enough support to keep her on her feet. She followed the wet chatter of the creek until she saw the glimmer of dancing water as it reflected the bare glow from the sky.

She sank to her knees in the rough gravel of the creek bed and laid the branch next to her as she reached toward the water. The icy sharpness cleared her head and slapped away the clinging remnants of nausea. She would drink slowly, cautiously, and replenish some of the fluids she had lost. She would use the water to wash away some of the filth that clung to her. Then she would try to get home.

Grant met the attendants as they wheeled Gina from the ambulance.

She wasn't seizing but the whiteness of her face concerned him. Her eyes were slightly open but glazed. It looked as if it was only the sheer force of her will that kept them open at all. Her paper-white skin strobed red and blue from the lights across the roof of the ambulance. The paramedic had established an IV and attached a monitor.

"She was seizing when we reached her, Dr. Sheldon," Christy said. "The seizures began at least twenty minutes ago, probably longer."

"Archer called me from her house."

"Status *epilepticus*," Christy said. "Dangerous."

"We've already called for an airlift." He gave orders for an anticonvulsant drug. There was a high incidence of mortality related to seizures of the magnitude Gina had experienced and they could have been brought on by a number of things.

"Her blood sugar was 31 when we were finally able to get a finger stick," Christy said.

Grant felt a surge of excitement over the low number but he controlled it just as swiftly. Hypoglycemia often did a sneak attack then disappeared before tests could pinpoint the source of the problem but the low sugar count could also be a symptom of a more malevolent opponent. He couldn't pin his hopes to a simple answer this quickly, especially not in light of the normal blood sugar test results she'd received previously.

Christy finished giving report. Grant thanked her and turned to Eugene, who hovered nearby. "I want a stat CT of the abdomen and a c-peptide level." He turned to the secretary. "Becky, did you alert the hospital to my concern about Mr. Mourglia's mercury poisoning?"

"They have an antidote on hand."

"Good. Call them back and tell them we'll be sending them another patient, though she might not have the same thing."

Muriel Stark looked up from her charting at the other end of the work counter. "You don't think Gina's been poisoned?"

"I'm taking no chances. They need to check for everything."

Mercury had shown up on x-rays of other patients, so he guessed if Gina had any mercury in her system they would find it. Even if it didn't prove conclusive he wanted treatment available immediately. He could only pray that if there was poisoning involved, the mercury had not yet undergone an ionic conversion to methyl mercury. There was no effective treatment for much of the damage that could be caused by that kind of poisoning but there was a good chance they could eventually control the outcome for all the patients involved—as long as they caught it in time.

This was the first time in Grant's life he had actually hoped to find a benign tumor in a patient; the alternative for Gina could be much more destructive.

He led the way into the exam room they'd cleared and helped Christy transfer Gina to the bed.

"Archer Pierce told us he tried to put some sugar under her tongue," Christy said. "I don't know how much he gave her but he sure did scatter it across the floor. I slipped on it and nearly fell when we were loading her."

"Did he say if it helped?"

"He thought it did."

Gina gasped and her facial muscles tightened. "Muriel."

"Getting the drug on board now."

"Also get a repeat fingerstick glucose," he said. "She'll seize again if her sugar is still low."

The older nurse nodded, using spare quick movements to complete her task.

Gina's face relaxed again and her breath came like a sigh. She moistened her lips with her tongue, swallowed, opened her eyes, then winced and closed them again. "My boys?"

"The pastor has them, Gina." Christy disconnected the ambulance monitor from the leads on her patient's chest and replaced it with the hospital monitor.

Gina frowned. "Did I hear someone say mercury?" Her eyes came open again and she studied the faces around her until she found Grant.

"There may be some contamination in the area," he said.

"What area?"

Grant didn't want to alarm her and take a chance on another seizure. "Part of the town's water supply. I want to run some tests on you." He checked to make sure Muriel added the anticonvulsant through the IV tubing. "Try to relax until I can get some tests taken."

"But my children."

"We'll test them as soon as possible." He took her hand and checked for a pulse. Good and strong. A little fast. He needed to reassure her. "Don't you live near the school?"

"Yes."

"That's good. You're nowhere near the affected area." He pulled a penlight out of his pocket and shined it into her eyes. Her pupils were equal, briskly reactive, wide open with concern.

"Do you ever eat fish that has been caught locally?" he asked. "Maybe Lauren has given you some of hers in the past few weeks."

"My boys don't like fish and I don't take the time to fix it just for myself."

"Where does your babysitter live?"

"A block from the school."

This was getting better. "I'll have someone call your sitter but it sounds less likely that your children are affected. Have you or either of your boys felt any nausea recently?"

"No."

"Do you ever get bad headaches?"

"Some." She was beginning to sound drowsy again. "Not as bad now."

Grant relaxed a little more. "Just a few more questions and then I'll let you rest for a few minutes okay?"

She nodded.

As he continued his neurological assessment, he prayed silently. The comfort of that fresh connection with God gave him a peace he had been missing since the wreck. Two years of grief and spiritual starvation had done their damage but God had the power to restore everything. All Grant prayed for now was Gina's life.

Darkness had begun its attack on the sky and the chilly air bit into Lauren's skin. She'd made the mistake of trying to wash some of the evidence of sickness from her shirt and arms. Now the cold combined with a heavy lethargy to seep past her wet clothes and skin to set up camp around her bones. She should have known better.

If she didn't get up and move she could quickly develop hypothermia, especially in her weakened condition. Her old fishing jacket and a blanket were in the truck. She had to get back to the truck.

Using the branch once again for support, she pulled herself to her feet and caught her toe on a stray stem from the branch. She lost her grip and pitched forward into the gravel. She fell hard on her shoulder and cried out with pain.

The sound of the water overwhelmed her, pressing her down as the gravel dug into her exposed flesh. It was impossible to ignore the specter of death as it loomed in the deepening gray around her. There was no way to fight it. Not alone. Depression and fear attacked without mercy. For countless moments she lay in the gravel overwhelmed by weakness.

Somehow she retained her consciousness this time. Perhaps it was the pain and cold. Never had she felt so far from human contact and yet in so much need of it. Even living alone she had never been far from the sound of a human voice.

Until now she had never been truly alone. Shame followed this realization. So many times in the past couple of years she had complained to God—and to anyone else who would listen—that she was lonely. She wanted a life mate, someone with whom she could connect, someone with whom she could share everything.

How must her complaints have sounded to God? As if He wasn't enough for her?

"Lord, forgive me," she whispered. Earlier she'd been praying for God to send someone to help her. Mourglia and Rosewitz would have been nice. But where was her faith?

"If I truly believe in you then all I really need is you. And if I don't believe that then my life has been a lie. Your will be done."

She waited for another moment then tested her strength. She would move forward until she could no longer move at all. And she would trust God with every step.

She reached for the branch. As she shivered, she felt along the sides of the limb and used all her strength to tug the excess leaves and stems from the base of the stick. She wouldn't trip again.

Activity in the emergency room had dwindled from frantic to merely hectic as Dr. Caine gave orders and handled patients like a drill sergeant. Grant left him to it and stepped back into Gina's room to find her smiling weakly at her children, whom Archer and the Walkers had brought in moments ago.

Some pink had returned to her cheeks and though she was still weak from the seizures she was obviously putting forth all her energy to spend these few minutes with her children while she had them.

Grant checked her most recent vitals on the chart and noted that her sugar level was up to normal. It was looking more likely that blood sugar was the only culprit in this case. After the harrowing seizures and the mercury scare that was now swarming across the town, however, he wasn't taking any chances. She was on her way to Springfield as soon as her flight arrived.

While Levi and Cody kept their mother occupied, Grant stepped out of the room and found Archer in the waiting room.

"How's she doing?" the pastor asked.

"Good. You did the right thing with the sugar. I was concerned about mercury poisoning but that's looking less likely."

"Mercury poisoning?"

"We suspect that's our epidemic. Beau figured it out and now the police are on it. We stumbled onto it while you were occupied with Gina."

"Who is it affecting?"

"Whoever gets water from the Honey Spring water supply."

"What about the fish?"

"That too."

The sounds of an approaching helicopter interrupted them. Gina would be on her way shortly.

Lauren felt her way through the shadowy woods. At some point she noticed she'd stopped shivering and peaceful warmth permeated her body. Though the nausea hovered, it did not attack.

Somewhere in the midst of her prayers she thought she understood the word picture God had given her when she first picked up the branch that helped support her. She'd pruned it so it wouldn't trip her again. Perhaps she was being pruned.

Her passion for a family of her own had driven her to humiliation more than once in the past year. She released it. She prayed for the willingness to remain single the rest of her life if God so desired. And she prayed that God would help her find joy in that condition.

And if her life lasted for only a few more hours, or even a few more minutes, that too, was in God's hands.

She wasn't alone.

With another step Lauren felt the soft crush of leaves beneath her feet. She peered ahead of her and thought she saw the outline of the truck in the shadow of the trees. When she reached it she touched the cool metal of the front fender then leaned on it for support as she stumbled alongside the cab. She opened the back door, leaned against the long bench seat, and used the freshly pruned branch to heft herself inside. Just sliding into her own truck felt like a homecoming. She grabbed the blanket from the floorboard and wrapped herself in it, then stretched out on the backseat. No way could she drive home tonight. She would spend the night here and leave the future in God's hands. She hadn't felt this much peace in a long time.

"Thank you," she whispered as she drifted off to sleep.

❧ CHAPTER 29 ❧

Grant's conversations with God had resumed tonight as suddenly as they had exited his life after the crash of metal two years ago but there was no time to pause and relish the joy right now. Dogwood Springs needed His healing touch tonight and for the first time Grant realized God might have him in mind to help administer that touch.

For the second time in five minutes, Grant returned to exam room three, where Gina was being prepped for airlift to Springfield.

She gave him a sleepy smile.

"I've asked the Walkers to keep a close watch on the boys for any unusual signs that might alert us to mercury poisoning but that's purely precautionary."

"Thank you." Her voice was still weak. "My blood sugar really was low this time, wasn't it?"

"Very."

"Why did you do the abdominal CT?"

"I was looking for a tumor. I didn't find anything obvious but I haven't heard back from the radiologist. I saw no scatter artifact on the film—which would have shown up if you had mercury in your abdomen."

There was no change in her expression. Her eyes focused on his with perfect trust. "You think I have a tumor?"

"An insulinoma is a possibility. I don't want to alarm you but you know enough about medicine to understand."

"I'm not alarmed, Dr. Sheldon. Those are usually benign?"

"Ninety percent of the time."

"Just a tumor of the pancreas."

He had never had a patient receive this kind of news with such equanimity. "I don't want to dismiss this lightly, Gina. The low blood sugar that results from an insulinoma is a serious concern. It could be the cause of what you've been thinking were panic attacks."

She raised her head from the pillow. "A tumor explains everything; I wouldn't lose my kids."

"But there are still risks involved and we aren't even sure that's what it is. I don't want to trust my own judgment for something this serious, which is why I'm sending you to a specialist for a second opinion."

She blinked up at him and her smile widened. "A second opinion?"

"Yes. Have you heard of Dr. Manfred in Springfield? He's an endocrinologist, and he's handled many insulinoma cases. I'd like him to see you."

"A second opinion." She repeated the common term as if she'd just made a new and exciting discovery. "Someone wiser and more knowledge-able who can take control," she said. "Yes. Exactly."

Grant checked the monitor. Nothing had changed. "Gina? Are you feeling okay?"

"I'm feeling better every minute. God doesn't waste any time, does He?"

"God?"

"Lauren tried to tell me all along that I needed to turn it all over to Him—not just this illness but my whole life. She said it's like getting a second opinion from the Great Physician and then letting Him take over the case."

Grant had never heard salvation put that way before. Trust Lauren to word things in her own unique way. "She was right."

"He does know what He's doing."

"Yes." Grant had no doubt about that now. He'd never had any doubt about God's ability, only about His love and patience. Those doubts had been brought on by shock and grief. Serving God didn't mean sunny skies, it simply meant God would see one through storms as well as sunshine.

Some of the excitement faded from Gina's expression. "Dr. Sheldon, you asked me about eating fish. Lauren eats it all the time. She's been sick."

"I know." She also carried the water home to drink. "I tried calling her earlier and I left a voice mail."

"She's probably not home."

"How do you know?"

"She tried to hide it but she was pretty upset when she left here. She said she needed some time to think."

"When was she here?"

"Just before I got off work tonight."

"She wasn't sick then?"

"No, but she was upset."

There was a knock at the door and Becky stepped in. "Dr. Sheldon, I've got an urgent call for you from the mayor. Can you take it?"

Grant looked at his watch. "I'll be right there."

"Thank you." He turned back to his patient. "Gina, I'll try to be back before they take off with you."

Lauren somehow knew she was dreaming but she couldn't control the sensation that she was falling headlong into an abyss. She awoke with a gasp and bumped her head against something hard and unyielding. This wasn't her bedroom.

Her head pounded with pain and acid burned her stomach.

She reached out blindly and her hand sank into something soft.

Upholstered cushion.

Her memory returned and fear burst past the wall of courage she had built through prayer earlier tonight.

"Please help me." Her throat was raw. The darkness once more overtook her.

"Dr. Sheldon, I need your help." Jade Myers sounded tired. "I've spoken with Mr. Butler and he's making arrangements for us to use the hospital's outpatient clinic for the weekend. Now we need to staff it."

"Staff it? For what?"

"I want to offer screening, testing, and treatment for victims of mercury poisoning."

"This weekend? We don't even have the agents to treat it."

"I know. I've called our local pharmacists and they're going to see what they can do. Meanwhile we can at least get the screening started and that's where our local docs get involved. Since the test results will take too long to get back from thelab, we need people with professional clinical skills to help us sort out the symptoms and begin treatment before the results get back. This thing with Uncle Ernest has made a believer out of me."

"Have you heard from County Health?" Grant asked.

"They called the state. Someone is on his way down to test the water but it could take three weeks to get the results back. I know the state wants to be sure of their results before they make any announcements and have a panic on their hands but we can't wait that long. I've already arranged for a public service announcement to be made over the Springfield TV stations as well as the local radio stations. I'm not waiting around for more people to get sick."

"How did you manage to get so much done in such a short time?"

"Delegation. I practice it daily."

"What about the water supply?" Grant asked.

"We shut off the reservoir fed by Honey Creek," she said. "We have nearly a thousand residences without running water and you should hear the complaints. I've taken some of them myself. Do you know that some of the people are demanding that we prove there's a problem before we shut off their supply? Uncle Ernest is proof enough for me. Have you heard how he's doing?"

"He arrived safely in Springfield. We're waiting to hear the blood test results but it'll be several hours. Mercury is not something routinely tested."

"And that's another thing. Do you know a urine test for mercury takes twenty-four hours? I wanted blood tests but those have to go to a lab at the Mayo Clinic then they fax the reports."

Grant shook his head in amazement. "You found all this out already?"

"You just need to be connected to the right people. Our city employees are moving quickly and more help is on the way."

Obviously, when Jade Myers decided to do something it got done.

"So will you help me?" she asked. "I need a medical advisor."

"I'm not an expert on mercury poisoning."

"I've come to the conclusion that nobody in Dogwood Springs is. Do you know how many people I've called in an effort to find someone who could help me? Your son is on the Internet as we speak, printing as much information as he can find on the subject. He's a smart kid. You've got a regular father-son medical team going there. He'll make a great doc someday."

"Thank you."

"I wish I'd listened to you the day you tried to convince me our community puzzle might be a hazard."

"But it wasn't the problem," Grant said.

"We might have put our heads together and come up with the solution before so many people got sick. I've called an emergency meeting. The city will have to pick up the tab for the public testing and treatment, then wait for the insurance to reimburse us. I don't think I'll have any trouble getting that approved but to prevent any controversy will you attend the meeting? You can explain the situation so much better than I could."

"When will you meet?"

"In about forty-five minutes in conference room B at the hospital."

"Tonight?"

"It's an emergency."

Grant thought of all the things he needed to get done before that. Still, how could he refuse? "You don't waste time, Mayor."

"I'll call you Grant if you'll call me Jade."

"What about state assistance?"

"The state should help us pay for some of it later but I'm not waiting around on the big boys to come storming in here and take charge. Who knows when they'll get here? We're making some money with our community projects and we have plenty on hand. Everyone in this town is going to be affected in some way and I don't want any more deaths from this thing."

Grant heard the flight crew preparing Gina for transfer.

He wished he knew where Lauren was and how she was feeling. "I'll be there."

"I'll see you then."

He hung up and tried to call Lauren again. No answer. The recorder did its spiel. He didn't even bother to leave another message.

He rushed into Gina's exam room before she could be wheeled out. "Didn't you tell me Lauren wasn't sick when you saw her earlier tonight?"

"That's right, just upset."

"How upset?" Grant asked. "How was she behaving? Did she act confused?"

"Not confused." Gina was wearing down quickly. "Hurt by some rumors. Went out of town."

"Did she say where?"

Gina shook her head. "Couldn't be far. She works tomorrow. Please call Natalie? She'll be worried about me."

Grant smiled down at her. Things were definitely changing for this young lady. "I'll have Becky call her but you do realize that if she knows she'll probably be at the landing pad to greet you at the hospital."

"She means well."

The team wheeled Gina out the doors. Moments later she was in flight.

• • •

Archer made one more attempt to call Lauren when he got home but she still didn't answer. She would want to be notified about the town emergency.

He left another message and hung up.

Barely five seconds later the phone rang. He answered without looking at caller ID.

"Archer, we've got ourselves a problem." It was the gravelly bass tones of John Netz.

Archer slumped. Not this again. "What kind of a problem?"

"Where've you been? I tried calling you three or four times."

Archer bit back a sharp retort. "Did you leave a voicemail?"

"Nope. Hate those things," John grumbled. "Anyway, I've got you now. Some guy from the police department got in touch with Dwight about an hour ago. They're contacting all the churches in town for help. We've got some kind of crisis on our hands. You hear anything about Honey Creek getting poisoned?"

Word got out in a hurry. "Dr. Sheldon mentioned it to me at the hospital this evening."

"The mayor's having a fit. She says we've got a problem and she's not waiting around for the state guys to come down. I think that new ER doctor has her all upset. These newcomers like to stir up trouble."

"If Grant thinks there's a problem then there is. What's the mayor doing about it?"

"She and Mr. Butler from the hospital have gotten their heads together and they want to set up relief areas at the churches. Since our church is the biggest of the bunch, and it's centrally located, we'll probably get the brunt of the incoming."

"Incoming?"

"Refugees. And they need some volunteers to gather up cots and such and to spread the word about the poisoning."

"Refugees?"

"Or evacuees or something like that," John sounded as if he was getting a little irritated with the questions. "The wife and I are heading out right now. You might want to meet us down at the church."

"Why? It seems you and your deacons have this thing well in hand, though I see no reason for people to leave their homes just because their water's been turned off. All they need is uncontaminated water."

"We're having deliveries of clean water brought here, too. Besides, you know how people panic if they think they're being poisoned. They'll need some reassurance. If the poison's been in their homes, as the mayor said, they might want to know for sure it won't affect them before they return. When can we expect you here?"

Archer was not in the mood to rub shoulders with the troublemaking deacons tonight.

"You know," John's voice took on that familiar tone of chiding that he'd used when Archer was a teenager, "you could stand to get a little more involved in things. Chaos is breaking loose in this town. Where's your father when we need him?"

"You have his phone number. If you want him you can call him." Archer hung up. It felt good. Too good. With a sigh he grabbed his car keys. Against his wishes, he would be at the church despite the order from a self-important trouble-maker; part of his calling was to offer solace to those who were frightened and seeking answers.

Grant got voicemail when he tried to call home. He needed to talk to Beau. He also needed to touch base with Mr. Butler before the meeting. And he intended to find Lauren.

He looked at his watch. There was time to drive to her house and back before the meeting. He pulled his car keys from his desk drawer and headed out. The least he could do was leave a note of warning on her door. Then if for some reason she didn't listen to her messages tonight she would still see the note and call him.

Was he blowing all this out of proportion?

Probably. He preferred that possibility to the alternative.

This was going to be a long night.

❧ CHAPTER 30 ❧

Every branch that does bear fruit he prunes so that it will be even more fruitful . . . every branch . . . more fruitful . . .

Lauren heard her mother's voice quoting the familiar Bible passage through the darkness past the pain and she awakened for a moment. She opened her eyes but all remained black, as it had been when she had last closed them.

"Mom?" She couldn't speak past a whisper.

All she heard was the continual chatter of the creek.

How long had she been out this time? Mom's voice hadn't only sounded real, it had felt real, her presence familiar. Comforting.

Mom had helped her memorize that verse from the book of John years ago. Maybe that was why it had come to Lauren's mind so easily.

It was a passage she'd heard a lot when she or one of her siblings was hurt or struggling through their teen years and early adulthood. Until now the words had always felt oppressive. Nobody wanted to be pruned. Nobody wanted to suffer loss and heartache in order to mature spiritually.

But this time the abiding comfort of the words found root in her heart. They reminded her that God had not forgotten about her. Even better than that, He considered her worthy to bear more fruit. That might even mean she was going to live through this. Otherwise, how would she be able to bear fruit?

Right now she would be glad to see another sunrise.

Sometime after midnight on Saturday morning, Archer awakened on his cot in the church basement to the fragrance of freshly perking coffee. He heard soft voices echoing from the far side of the cavernous room and the crackle of sizzling bacon—or was that sausage? It smelled like heaven. The cooks had promised to keep breakfast cooking for the volunteers who took shifts during the night, traveling from door to door to warn citizens about the mercury scare. Everyone needed to be warned about it, not just those in the affected area; too many people ate the fish that came from Honey Spring.

Archer held his watch close to his eyes and peered at the lighted numbers. One o'clock. He'd had a good thirty minutes of sleep. Now to get to work. The good folks of Dogwood Springs would just have to endure his wrinkled jeans and T-shirt.

The door at the top of the basement steps opened and allowed light from the upstairs hallway to glow down onto the sleeping volunteers and others scattered across the far end of the room on borrowed cots. The newcomer made a silent, cautious descent, obviously unwilling to awaken anyone.

Archer couldn't help wondering about the fresh arrival. Ordinarily, everyone knew to enter the basement through the side of the building where the double doors opened onto a level paved playground and additional parking area. Right now there was a huge, hastily painted sign in the middle of that playground offering water, food, and even a place to sleep.

The experts said that the homes were safe but it seemed a few people didn't trust the experts. Some families had come for the night after hearing the first of the public service announcements. If the mercury had crept into their water supply then how could they be sure it hadn't contaminated other areas of their homes?

People were frightened. Archer couldn't blame them. This whole thing was a frightening experience.

With one Dogwood Springs reservoir disconnected due to possible contamination, the city was hard-pressed to supply enough water for the whole town. Jade Myers had vowed not to rest until alternate sources would be available.

That was apparently being taken care of as most of the town slept. The community would weather this storm as it had many others over the years. Dr. Grant Sheldon and his son were already local heroes because Jade had "leaked" to the local television and radio stations that the Sheldon family had tracked the deadly poison to its source.

Now there would be an interesting situation. Archer knew Jade because she'd only been a year ahead of him in school and she'd been a member of Dogwood Springs Baptist for the past seven years. She was definitely attracted to heroes and she was single again after a quiet divorce a year ago from a man who had decided to become someone else's hero. Grant and Jade might make an interesting couple.

The newcomer, still in the shadows, reached the bottom of the stairs and quietly stepped past cots and sleeping bags toward the designated kitchen area. There was something familiar about those movements. Archer folded his blanket and laid it on his cot then made his way toward the smell of coffee.

He was halfway there when he heard the melodious sound of a warm voice joining the soft chatter of the others.

"You're still singing for our Fourth of July celebration, aren't you?" Mrs. Netz asked.

"I wouldn't miss it."

It was Jess. Archer rushed to greet her.

"Jessica," he said quietly.

She turned and her sudden smile warmed him. "I thought you might want some help."

He entered the circle of light as he beheld the vision so breathtaking that all the cobwebs and dreams of the night deserted him. "How did you know?"

"Dogwood Springs has made the news. I heard it before I went to bed and I couldn't sleep for thinking about you, so here I am." She wore a pair of old sweat pants and a T-shirt that said, in faded letters "The Promise," the scruffy hem of which hung to the middle of her thighs. Her tangle of wavy brown hair was held away from her face with one of those claw-like clips that could be used as weapons if wielded with the proper aim.

Archer accepted two cups of extremely weak coffee from Mrs. Netz, who manned the huge percolator at the end of the long kitchen counter. He thanked her then gave one of the cups to Jessica and took her arm.

"How about a short stroll?" he whispered.

"Good," she whispered back. "You can walk me to my car. I brought some supplies for breakfast."

He smiled. Spoken like a true pastor's wife. And that was what he wanted to discuss with her. He needed to talk to her before they were caught up in the night's chaos and separated for however long it took to clear things up and set everything right in the town. According to the guys he'd talked to a couple of hours ago, setting things right could take days or even weeks.

He held the door for her and she stepped out. As soon as it closed behind them he asked her, "Don't you have to sing tomorrow—I mean tonight?"

"Yes, but I'm free till then."

"The last time we spoke I got the distinct impression that you didn't want anything to do with this church."

Jessica stopped walking and turned to him. "Archer Pierce, after all this time I would expect you to know me better than that."

"Better than what?"

"Than for you to listen to me when I'm mad and blowing off steam."

He couldn't let her get away with that. "Excuse me, but you were not just blowing off steam when you told me you could not marry Dogwood Springs Baptist Church."

"I told you I was confused. You reminded me in so many words that the subject was moot because you hadn't asked me to marry you lately." He could see her face in the dim light. She didn't look angry. She looked like she was enjoying herself.

"Do you remember what you said?" he asked.

"Not as well as what you said." There were definite signs of a smile in her eyes as she continued to remind him of his words, as if she wanted to relish them for a second time. "There are three things about which you have no doubts."

He returned the smile. "I don't doubt that God is in control. I don't doubt that I was called to this church. I don't—"

"And you said you didn't doubt that you loved me. Has any of that changed?"

"No."

"Good."

"But Jessica, that also means that there are no plans in the works for me to leave my position of pastor at this church. They might still take a vote and throw me out but right now that's what it'll take."

"I know."

"I've prayed about it and thought about it and prayed some more. I'm not finished here."

Her expression didn't change. "No, but something keeps drawing me here. To you. Maybe even to this church. I miss you too much for this to be over between us."

It occurred to him that the exhilaration of being in love with Jessica could be compared to a wild roller-coaster ride. Or maybe surfing the highest waves in the world. Or skiing down Mount Everest. What would marriage to her be like?

He cleared his throat. "You understand that?"

"Yes."

He took a deep breath. He'd taken the ring out of its case several times recently to look at it and wonder about its future. It was a beautiful ring and it had looked beautiful on Jessica's left hand. He wished he had it now.

Ask her.

"Jessica—"

The church door opened. "Archer?" It was Mrs. Netz.

Archer groaned softly. "I'll be there in a few moments," he called over his shoulder then returned his attention to the most beautiful woman in his life. "Jessica, would you—"

"Archer, I hate to interrupt," Mrs. Netz said. "This is important."

This was not a good time. "I'm sorry Jessica but it looks as if things are going to get crazy. Before it does, I need to—"

The door squeaked open further. "Archer?" This time the voice didn't belong to Mrs. Netz. It was Grant Sheldon.

Archer sighed and turned. "Grant? What's wrong?"

"Do you know where Lauren is?"

There was a feminine groan of frustration behind him. "Lauren again," Jessica muttered.

"Can it wait a few minutes?" Archer asked.

"I don't think so. I'm worried about her."

"Why?"

"I've tried several times to call her tonight but she hasn't answered. I left a note on her door instructing her to call me but she hasn't."

"Maybe she heard about Gina and drove to Springfield."

"I tried the hospital. Natalie was with Gina and she hasn't seen or heard from Lauren." The concern was evident in Grant's voice. "She has an ER shift in the morning and she obviously isn't home yet—or she's too sick to answer her calls. I thought she might be with her parents but Beau called them for me earlier and she wasn't there."

Okay, maybe there was reason to worry. "She wouldn't be in Knolls because she just came back from there. She brought flowers back from her mother's garden to decorate the church for Sunday service."

"Then where is she?" Grant asked with increased emphasis.

With a sigh of resignation, Jessica laid a hand on Archer's shoulder. "I think you need to go find Lauren. I'll be here when you get back." She reached into her pocket and pulled out a cell phone. "Yours is probably low on juice as usual. Take this with you in case you need it."

Grant retraced the route to Lauren's house, with Archer riding silently in the passenger seat. Grant's note was fluttering at the door when they arrived.

"She could still be inside," Grant insisted.

"It's possible." Archer got out of the car and disappeared into the darkness at the back of the house. He returned holding up a key. "Old McCaffrey family habit. Hide a spare behind a drainpipe. I don't know why Lauren even bothers to lock her doors." He led the way to her front porch and unlocked it. The two of them charged inside turning on lights and calling her name.

While Archer disappeared into the kitchen,

Grant checked the bathroom and bedrooms. The place was deserted. They met back at the front door.

"What now?" Grant asked.

"There's one other place I can think of that she might have gone."

"Her fishing spot?"

Archer nodded.

"In the middle of the night?"

"I know it's unlikely but if she got sick there and couldn't get home. . . ." He shrugged.

"Can you navigate? I've never been there at night. I might miss the turn."

"Of course. Let's go."

❧ CHAPTER 31 ❧

A muffled thump in the darkness and the echo of a man's voice helped Lauren fight her way back to consciousness but she couldn't tell if they were products of her dream state or of reality.

She opened her eyes to the same darkness that had surrounded her for hours but a brief reflection of light flashed through the truck, barely there before it was gone again. She blinked and tried to raise her head.

Was she hallucinating?

She closed her eyes.

Another voice reached her, another thump like

the closing of a door. A car door? She had to see. If there were people out there she had to get their attention.

With great effort she raised her right arm and placed her hand against the side window. She rested for a moment and listened then doubted her sanity once again. Auditory hallucinations. She thought about Gina.

Voices again. Male. She heard a rustle of brush, the crunch of footsteps on gravel.

"Hello?" she whispered. "Please help me."

More footsteps. Another thump. She concentrated all her strength into her right arm and raised it from the window then slapped it back down as hard as she could.

She took a deep breath and forced the air from her lungs. "H-h-help me." Her voice was barely a rasp of sound that couldn't have made it past the door.

Had to get out of the truck.

She willed her hand to slide down to the handle and she pulled. Hard. It unlatched and opened with the weight of her shoulders against it. The interior light came on and blinded her.

"Help me!" This time her voice was stronger.

There was a female squeal somewhere in the darkness. A car door slammed and an engine started.

"No, please!" She reached for the armrest and the door swung out, taking her with it. Her body plunged headlong from the truck and she landed hard in the dirt.

Blackness once again smothered her as tires spun in the dirt and rocks, followed by the fading sound of an automobile speeding away, leaving her alone again.

No . . . never alone. He had promised she would never be alone. But she was so cold.

Grant's grip on the steering wheel was so tight the tips of his fingers felt numb. He loosened them slightly and tried to see past the perimeter of road revealed by his headlights while he struggled to keep his imagination from taking him to unknown regions. Prayers whipped fast and furious through his mind, almost as fast as his car was speeding down the road.

"Uh, Grant, there's a curve up ahead that you can't take at eighty-five miles an hour." Archer's voice sounded forcibly relaxed as if he were trying to calm a frightened dangerous animal.

Grant looked at the speedometer and eased up on the accelerator. "Sorry. How much farther to the turnoff?"

"Not far. About a mile and a half. At this rate we'll make it in about sixty seconds."

Grant took the heavy hint and pressed the brake. "You say she wasn't sick this afternoon when you saw her?"

"I don't think she'd have bothered with altar

flowers if she wasn't feeling well. She's probably out with the other volunteers knocking on doors, especially warning people with whom she'd shared her fish. That could be a lot of people."

"But she would have called someone to let us know where she is."

"Grant, she's single and lives alone. Who would she call? How was she supposed to know you'd go tearing off after her like some half-crazed maniac?"

Grant took his eyes from the road for a half second to frown at Archer. "I notice you came out too."

"Somebody had to slow you down."

They'd just reached the curve when a flash of headlights glared around it like horizontal lightning zagging out of control. Grant swung the wheel sharply toward the shoulder of the road and slammed the brakes as the oncoming car squealed its tires and roared on down the road and out of sight.

A moment of shocked silence held them in place for a moment.

"Good job." Archer released his death hold on the armrest.

Grant steered back onto the blacktop at a more cautious speed.

"I guess I didn't mention that this is a party road, did I?"

"I should have listened to your cautions. Lauren

said something about it the day we came fishing out here."

"Look Grant, I know she's special to you, that's obvious. Just admit it and get it over with."

"You think I'm overreacting."

"If it were Jessica I'd be reacting the same way. You obviously care a lot for Lauren."

"It's that apparent?"

"I would say so. You might try prayer."

"I'm relying on it." Grant felt Archer's surprised attention focusing on him.

"Really?"

"I am. In fact, I can't help wondering if my revitalized spiritual connection has served as an alarm system. Ordinarily, I don't think I would be so concerned about a grown woman who knows how to take care of herself. But the poison could have taken her by surprise. All she had to do was drink some water after you saw her this afternoon. In fact, she wouldn't even have had to do that. It could hit her at any time. That's the effect this stuff has on people, and she's been struggling with it off and on since the second night I worked with her."

Archer pointed to a sign that reflected in the glow from their headlights. "Turn up there."

Grant turned onto the rough dirt road.

"See the cloud they raised?" Archer pointed to the dust that hovered around them. "They obviously just came from here."

Grant's hands tightened once more on the steering wheel and his thoughts returned to his most immediate fear. "If they did, wouldn't they have seen Lauren's truck?"

Archer didn't reply. Grant gave the shocks of his car a good workout. From the corner of his eye, he saw Archer lean forward in his seat and plant his hands on the dashboard.

Grant's prayers seemed to hit the windshield and bounce back at him. Archer didn't have to tell him when the road turned again. He remembered this drive now even in the darkness. He remem-bered the potholes and the broken-down fence and the tree branches that reached down and threatened to slap him in the face but brushed over the top of the car at the last minute. He'd never been here in the dark but he remembered the gravel. It meant they were close.

And then he saw the familiar reflection of a bumper and red reflector and the glow of an interior light. He caught his breath.

"It's hers!" Archer shouted in horror. "It's Lauren's."

Grant was out of the car before the motor died, with Archer on his heels. He ran to the open door and nearly stumbled over Lauren's still form, which was lying face down in the dirt beside her truck.

He fell to her side and reached for her shoulders as Archer knelt beside him. She was warm.

He felt for a pulse at her throat. "I have a heart-beat." Her clothes were damp, and a familiar smell lingered in the still night air. "She's been sick." He leaned close. "A lot." She was still breathing regularly.

"Lauren!" He rubbed her face. "Lauren, can you hear me?"

In the glow from the interior light he could see her lips move but no sound came out.

"Archer, didn't Jessica give you her cell phone?"

Archer was on his feet before Grant said another word. "I'll call an ambulance, but we don't get good coverage out here."

"Keep trying until you do." Grant lifted Lauren into his arms. "Tell them to make it an ALS ambulance. It's critical for life support. Tell them to drive in this direction and watch for our flashing lights. We'll meet them on the road."

She wasn't alone. In the distant darkness she heard voices again but this time they sounded vaguely familiar. She would be okay.

Her prayers were being answered. She felt herself being lifted by strong arms, heard a kind voice, words of assurance. If God was taking her home now that would be okay but this didn't feel like the arms of an angel ushering her into heaven.

Would an angel hold her this tightly? Would an angel sound frightened? Wouldn't angels be singing songs of joy instead of shouting in urgent, clipped voices?

And heaven didn't have blaring sirens and uncomfortably bright lights that flashed against her eyelids and threatened to drag her from her slumber.

The murmuring of a deep voice punctured her consciousness more forcefully. "Lauren! Can you hear me?" Gentle but insistent hands nudged her and she tried to reach up and push them away.

"I hear you." The words were a whisper but she heard a shout of triumph in response.

Her thoughts continued to sharpen.

"She's dehydrated. I want an IV . . ."

She felt a pain in her arm but didn't have the strength to protest.

She definitely wasn't on her way to heaven. There was no pain like this in heaven. Still, everything was going to be all right. God was in control.

❧ CHAPTER 32 ❧

By noon on Saturday the flurry of activity had settled into a comfortable routine at Dogwood Springs Baptist Church. Frightened families had been reassured that their homes were safe as long as they didn't drink water from the contaminated reservoir, and they had returned home. The cots had been folded and put away except for one.

At seven in the morning while the noise had been at its peak, Archer had allowed himself a few minutes of rest in the far corner of the room. Sleep had immediately reached up and jerked him down like a helpless victim for five hours of unconsciousness.

Now as he shook his head and tried to revive, a few volunteer workers trickled in for lunch. The aroma of grilled hamburgers brought him upright in the cot just in time to see Jessica walking toward him with a tray that held two plates with hamburgers and fries and two cups of coffee. She wore the same clothes she'd been wearing last night, only they were a little more wrinkled. With a face scrubbed free of makeup and puffy red eyes, somehow her familiar beauty took him by surprise again. Would she always have this effect on him?

"Did you get any sleep?" He stood and took the tray from her.

"Eight hours exactly. I just conked out in one of the pews upstairs and nobody bothered me." She sat down on one end of the cot and patted the space beside her for him to join her. "As soon as I eat I have to drive to Branson and get ready for a show." She cradled her cup of coffee so the steam would rise into her face and she inhaled with obvious appreciation.

"Speaking of show, you handled the reporters beautifully," Archer said.

"Thank you."

At three o'clock that morning a news team from Springfield's Channel 33 had arrived to assess the damage. Jessica had unwittingly become the spokesperson for Dogwood Springs when someone recognized her as a Branson celebrity. The footage would be aired on the evening news.

Jessica leaned over and placed her cup on the floor then straightened and looked at Archer. "Before I leave I need to ask you something."

"Name it, Jess. After all you did last night I don't know how I'll ever repay you. How many different ways are there to say thank you?" Not only had she charmed the people from Channel 33 but she had helped with the cooking and spent nearly thirty minutes making her peace with John Netz and his two buddies on the personnel committee. By the time she finished with them, they had apologized to Archer for the recent problems and promised that Lauren McCaffrey would hear nothing about their questions and accusations. Jessica Lane definitely had a way of getting what she wanted.

"Archer. Will you marry me?"

He nearly dropped his coffee cup. "What?"

"I said, will you—"

"Yes!"

Jessica chuckled. "Whew. For a minute I thought you were going to turn me down."

"Never. You just took me by surprise. I was planning to drive up to Branson tonight between shows. I wanted to at least have my teeth brushed and my hair combed. I'd thought about buying you some flowers, and—"

She took his coffee from him and set it next to hers, then drew him forward and kissed him. "Can we swing by your house and pick up my ring? I don't want to wait until this afternoon. There's no telling what other calamity might befall this church before you can drive to Branson."

He cupped his hands around her face and returned her kiss. "I love you, Jessica. I always will."

Lauren was in no mood for company but did that mean anything to her family? No. They were having a McCaffrey reunion in the waiting area just down the hall from her private room. At this moment, the word *private* was a joke. Two nurses had already warned the guys to keep their laughter to a minimum and not to bother the patient. Even so, her brothers and two of her cousins had managed to use the McCaffrey charm to keep from being evicted.

If she'd been the nurse on duty they'd have been out of there.

She continued to remind herself that it was wonderful to be a part of such a loving family and that this gathering was a precious opportunity not to be avoided. It was also an easy way to spread the word that they needed to dispose of the fish she'd been sharing with everyone within a fifty-mile radius of Dogwood Springs.

How much better she felt today compared to last night. She'd expected to be dead by morning. Wonderful what a little rehydration could do, along with her first dose of the chelating agent that would clear her system of the mercury. Eventually.

Grant had told her that she shouldn't have any lasting damage. Judging by the type of complaints from other victims of the poisoning, the heavy metal had not converted to methyl mercury in the water. By God's grace, the town had avoided a major catastrophe that would have produced deadly effects for years to come. Lauren and the other patients would recover. Mr. Mourglia was doing well this morning and Gina would undergo surgery Monday for the insulinoma they had discovered with the MRI.

As for Mrs. Henson who died last week, the poison had been too much for her system to handle. According to the experts with whom Grant had consulted, she might have had a reaction to the poison that triggered the lethal cardiac arrhythmia.

"Guess what?" came a familiar female voice from the doorway. Lauren looked to see Brooke and Beau Sheldon entering her room. They had been in her room off and on since early this morning, mingling with Lauren's family, trading jokes and soaking up old stories about Lauren's childhood. Brooke now had enough ammunition to use against Lauren for the next three years.

The twins had charmed Mom and Dad within the first ten minutes of meeting them.

"What?" Lauren could not infuse much excitement into her voice.

Brooke held up a shopping bag from Bass Pro. "We got you a present."

"It's a fishing game," Beau announced as he grabbed the bag from Brooke and removed the contents.

"Oh stop it, Mr. Popularity," Brooke tried to retrieve the bag. Beau held it away from her. "Hey, it was my idea in the first place!"

Beau gave his sister the empty bag and handed Lauren the game before Brooke could stop him. "It's a little computer, see? It simulates fishing and it even vibrates when you catch something."

"Yes," Brooke added, "and it has a little screen to show you what kind of fish you caught and you can choose your bait and everything. That way you don't have to gore innocent little worms to death for a little excitement."

"She doesn't fish for excitement, Brooke,"

Beau informed her, "she fishes for food and to relax and to get away from . . ."

Lauren smiled and closed her eyes as the brother and sister continued to chatter. What ever made her think she was lonely?

"You two, it's time to give her a break." It was the voice of the angel from last night.

Lauren opened her eyes and watched Grant enter the room.

"But Dad, we just got back," Brooke complained. "I haven't even had a chance to tease her about the time she got sick chewing tobacco out in the barn with—"

"There'll be time for that later. Out. Lauren needs her rest."

"Okay fine, but Dad, you could at least take advantage of her weakened condition and ask her out. After all, you did save her life last night."

"Out!"

Brooke gave Lauren a smile full of mischief and preceded her brother out the door. Beau turned and looked back at Lauren as if to assess her for himself, then he waved and left.

Lauren laughed. "You're a strong man, Grant Sheldon."

He had a beautiful smile full of kindness. And yes, a little hint of Brooke's mischief. "Not as strong as I'd like to be sometimes."

Gina was right, he did look a little like a young Antonio Banderas. "Did you ever have a ponytail?"

Grant's smile broadened. "Twenty years ago. What made you ask that?"

"Just a guess."

"I'm sorry about Brooke's big mouth. Don't let her coerce you into anything. But if you ever want a fishing buddy or even somebody to help with those teenagers at your church you might give me a call."

"Really? You mean it? You'd help with the kids at church?"

"Do you know anyone more qualified to help with rowdy teenagers than the father of Brooke Sheldon? Besides, she and Beau will be part of that church. And so will I."

She caught her breath. "You will?"

He straightened the blanket around her shoulders. He looked into her eyes and held her gaze. He was serious. "Yes. I will."

"Why the change of heart?"

He checked her IV, glanced at the chart at the end of her bed then nodded and returned to her side as if deciding how best to put his thoughts into words. "Because I realized last night that God hadn't given up on me. I'd just given up on myself."

"I'm glad."

"That doesn't mean I won't still have some questions."

"I had plenty of questions last night."

"Did any of them get answered?"

"They did," she said.

"How?"

Lauren reached up and touched his arm. "You found me. It wasn't my night to die. God is in control of me and my future. Whatever happens is up to Him. It takes the pressure off."

Grant took Lauren's hand in both of his and smiled down at her. "I know what you mean."

❦ About the Author ❦

Hannah Alexander is the pen name of a husband-wife writing team, and is the author of more than 30 industry published inspirational novels, novellas and short stories of romance, women's fiction, suspense and medical drama with a dose of subtle humor. All are set in homey small towns.

Hannah Alexander has won The Christy Award, Reader's Choice Awards, has a book named as Library Journal's top five picks in Christian Fiction, and has won three Holt Medallions. Thank you so much for taking time to read this novel. If you enjoyed it, Hannah Alexander would very much appreciate a review from you on the site where you purchased it, Goodreads, or other book review sites you enjoy.

Center Point Large Print
600 Brooks Road / PO Box 1
Thorndike, ME 04986-0001 USA

(207) 568-3717

US & Canada:
1 800 929-9108
www.centerpointlargeprint.com